Made In Japan

S. J. Parks

S.J. Parks, a literature graduate, has lived and worked in Japan. Parks has a writing MA from the University of London and now resides in England with her family. *Made in Japan* is her first novel.

MADE IN JAPAN

S. J. Parks

HARPER

Harper
An imprint of HarperCollins*Publishers*
1 London Bridge Street
London SE1 9GF

www.harpercollins.co.uk

Published by HarperCollins*Publishers* 2017
1

A catalogue record for this book
is available from the British Library

ISBN: 978-0-00-820101-2

This novel is entirely a work of fiction.
The names, characters and incidents portrayed in it are the work of the author's imagination.
Any resemblance to actual persons, living or dead, events or localities, is entirely coincidental.

'The truth is always something that is told, not something that is known. If there were no speaking or writing, there would be no truth about anything. There would only be what is'

–Susan Sontag

Prologue

The irony is that I am the one left to explain. I should commit it to paper, but I am no good with words. No one talks of shame any more, but when I walk out with this newborn, that is what I will feel. This child will want to know it all, and to understand it, and I doubt I will ever be able to bring myself to tell the truth.

It is evening, and in the thin dusk I am trying to gather and collect my thoughts. The senbei cracker fragments lie across the desk beneath the light that the evening has lent me. The blown rice will not be marshalled easily into my cupped hand. I do know now that he will not come. I know that he will not visit me again. The hot chocolate from the vending machine is too sweet and enough time has elapsed that the excuses are brittle and dried. A small sesame seed on my tongue brings a sudden burst of taste. 'Etahin,' so he had said.

The temple bell across the grounds sounds gently.

I should be the one to explain.

Naomi
The teahouse, Japan, 1989

Chapter 1

'Architects spend an entire life with this unreasonable idea that you can fight against gravity'
–Renzo Piano

Heathrow Airport, July 2012

Wednesday 18.45. Hana Ardent clipped into her seat belt early, as if to secure misgivings she held over travelling on her own. Two men fed the locker above her head as the other passengers politely squeezed past them in the aisle. She eyed them with the interest of one settling in for the long haul – in this case, flight BA4600 to Tokyo. Eleven hours and forty minutes, enough time to accommodate her entire week's lectures. That's if she were to attend them all.

If she could choose her companion for the journey it would not be the business traveller but the man in the maroon woollen. It was holey and not entirely clean and it held for her some comfort, as if he might live on the same edge of domestic chaos that she inhabited. He was a little older than her, possibly late twenties, and some part of his life must have necessitated this apparent neglect. By the time they touched down in Haneda International she would surely have discovered the answer. That Hana could have no say in the matter of her fellow travellers, even though she had paid a fortune for her economy ticket, riled her. She should make it into a game. Then again, perhaps not.

currency to exchange whatsoever. She opened the cover of her own book but had no inclination to read it and closed it again.

'So your first trip?' He seemed no longer able to concentrate on the merger documents.

She narrowed her almond eyes and nodded. She had never had the opportunity to go back.

'Family?'

So simple a question but not so easy to answer. There was no family, no relatives, in fact; no one to visit. There never had been; how easily small openings in conversation could hit a nerve. A stewardess of an over-painted age stopped to offer drinks and Ed leaned in to pass her one as he asked how long she would be away.

Knowing that after the flight they would leave as strangers, she recognized an open opportunity to tell him anything she liked – a gift. What truths you could tell a stranger when a friend might pass judgment. A license to download. And so, without editing or exaggerating, she could talk to him more freely.

'Six weeks or so. I'll be teaching primary in the autumn,' she began, applying the free lip balm generously.

Ed's firm had sent him out to live in Tokyo the year before and he would probably stay another couple. So she might know someone on arrival – someone who would speak the language who she could call on if she had a problem. She weighed up whether he would offer to take her round. It was more likely they would leave the flight as they had begun, as strangers.

'There was lot of work after the Oshika Peninsular incident.'

The reference sailed passed her until he explained.

'Tohoku. The Great Eastern Earthquake.' He hammered it home: 'Last year the earth shifted almost a foot.'

She was wide-eyed. Her lips parted.

A foot – virtually the space she took up in her seat. It shocked her.

He drew attention to her book, changing the subject.

Chapter 1

'Architects spend an entire life with this unreasonable idea that you can fight against gravity'
–Renzo Piano

Heathrow Airport, July 2012

Wednesday 18.45. Hana Ardent clipped into her seat belt early, as if to secure misgivings she held over travelling on her own. Two men fed the locker above her head as the other passengers politely squeezed past them in the aisle. She eyed them with the interest of one settling in for the long haul – in this case, flight BA4600 to Tokyo. Eleven hours and forty minutes, enough time to accommodate her entire week's lectures. That's if she were to attend them all.

If she could choose her companion for the journey it would not be the business traveller but the man in the maroon woollen. It was holey and not entirely clean and it held for her some comfort, as if he might live on the same edge of domestic chaos that she inhabited. He was a little older than her, possibly late twenties, and some part of his life must have necessitated this apparent neglect. By the time they touched down in Haneda International she would surely have discovered the answer. That Hana could have no say in the matter of her fellow travellers, even though she had paid a fortune for her economy ticket, riled her. She should make it into a game. Then again, perhaps not.

Against the window seat, following the indecisive summer light skittering across the tarmac, she traced the line of the ailerons at the edge of the wing. A cloud shift darkened the metal span, making it appear suddenly less resilient. Just like her determination to go. It was not as if she had ever been forbidden to make the journey, but she knew it was against *her* wishes, against her last wishes, though of course it had not been put in to so many words.

Ed introduced himself as he toyed with a loose thread on what must have been a favourite jumper. He explained he lived in Tokyo, was relatively new to his company and made so many trips he had to fly economy. There was, he said wearily, nothing special for him in an international flight. As he leaned back in his seat and focused his pale-grey eyes, shot with what might have been premature cynicism, he did nothing to calm her nerves. She checked her seatbelt. The line of flesh folded over the thin fabric at her waist was a little testament to her need for comfort food. Hana had dressed for the flight and might appear perhaps as a girl trying to stave off the onset of woman. Her thin tribal shirt complemented the scarf tied, Frida Kahlo-style, around her head, swaddling those of her thoughts that had a propensity to wander off. She was defenceless in the face of all things creative and still trying on a persona for size but hadn't finally decided. Once he had settled, there was nothing between them but his wool and her thin sleeve of batik cotton.

It was her first trip to Japan she told him and she shared her excitement as the plane circled London and she drew him into a search for identifiable landmarks around her home in Dalston. But there was no sign of the Georgian terraces with tall, confident windows, built to see and be seen, and brick, that unmistakable colour of London rain. As the plane rounded the city sprawl, she didn't notice his stolen glances for the playing fields of his West London Grammar.

'So Hana means flower.'

He would have guessed she must be half Japanese. She knew she had chatted too much even before the engines drowned her out as they fought against gravity. Ungenerously, he shifted a scuffed leather document case to his knees decisively. But she carried on, telling him that her mother had lived in Tokyo in 1989.

'A lot went on that year.' He seemed obliged to tell her and rewarded her blank look with a catalogue. 'Tiananmen. The fall of the Berlin wall. Aung San Suu Kyi under house arrest.'

Hana laughed at his mock gravity and continued the game, adding a great earthquake to the list, which he claimed not to remember. He seemed tired of their first steps of acquaintance as he slipped the sheaf of documents from his case. She shouldn't have talked so much.

He was returning from a business trip, he apologized.

Hana was left to survey the mood-board of Southern England – earth tones, fading to the shadows of a Sandra Blow sketch – and she busied herself with the intricacies of weaving a plait. She could see he was well-defended in a carapace of media; pads and pods and luxury headphones, which, she supposed, kept him reassuringly locked in some sort of solipsism. She liked his choice of his music. Easy Classical. She listened until the strains that came secondhand were too much effort to hear and she drifted back to Japan where she hoped she could paint over the outline sketch of her own past. In a matter of a few hours she would brace herself and prepare for a new perspective and then touch down on what would be another side of her.

When her hands left her hair she felt his eyes across her shoulder. The soft hair braid lay like a gift of intimacy between them. It was quite contrary to her intentions.

She read the open page. Clause 5. iv. Pursuant to any change in market conditions the vendor shall . . .

A lawyer? She wouldn't have guessed. They would have no

currency to exchange whatsoever. She opened the cover of her own book but had no inclination to read it and closed it again.

'So your first trip?' He seemed no longer able to concentrate on the merger documents.

She narrowed her almond eyes and nodded. She had never had the opportunity to go back.

'Family?'

So simple a question but not so easy to answer. There was no family, no relatives, in fact; no one to visit. There never had been; how easily small openings in conversation could hit a nerve. A stewardess of an over-painted age stopped to offer drinks and Ed leaned in to pass her one as he asked how long she would be away.

Knowing that after the flight they would leave as strangers, she recognized an open opportunity to tell him anything she liked – a gift. What truths you could tell a stranger when a friend might pass judgment. A license to download. And so, without editing or exaggerating, she could talk to him more freely.

'Six weeks or so. I'll be teaching primary in the autumn,' she began, applying the free lip balm generously.

Ed's firm had sent him out to live in Tokyo the year before and he would probably stay another couple. So she might know someone on arrival – someone who would speak the language who she could call on if she had a problem. She weighed up whether he would offer to take her round. It was more likely they would leave the flight as they had begun, as strangers.

'There was lot of work after the Oshika Peninsular incident.'

The reference sailed passed her until he explained.

'Tohoku. The Great Eastern Earthquake.' He hammered it home: 'Last year the earth shifted almost a foot.'

She was wide-eyed. Her lips parted.

A foot – virtually the space she took up in her seat. It shocked her.

He drew attention to her book, changing the subject.

'*The Pillow Book?*' The spine was pristine.

For some reason, she did not want to mention that this love story was a departing gift from Tom. She and Tom had been together since school and lately she had wanted to ask him what she really meant to him but had never managed to bring it up. She thought she loved him but she had not yet learned to love herself. They were kind of cut adrift together. She had left him behind to finish his dissertation and house-sit the flat that was now hers.

'From a friend.' She tapped the cover casually.

Ed tried again – 'Visiting friends here?'

She shook her head. But hoped for a place to stay, where her welcome would be whispered over rustling kimono silk, where a bamboo waterspout played over samisen music and delicacies on celadon-turquoise porcelain perfectly fitted her hand.

In reality she was travelling towards a void where she would know no one. And because she was part Japanese she felt foolish, as if she had been left standing waiting too long on a street corner. Hers was a history of carelessness. How reassuring it would be to say she was headed somewhere familiar.

'And so your parents . . .?' he asked.

She stopped him with a look.

She had lost her mother quite recently, and the words would still not come.

At her response he looked away and mouthed his apologies.

'I've arranged a kind of homestay, sort of hostel.'

Ed was well trained in the art of disguising when he was unimpressed but the edge of his mouth curled down; Hana ignored it.

Four hours in and green tea was offered. Ed passed across the plastic cup.

'Sen no Rikyū would be upset. The Zen Master of simplicity.'

Hana's eyebrows quizzed him.

'Founder of the tea ceremony would have banished plastic.'

'You've been to one?'

'The whole ritual is played out very slowly. At half tempo.'

After a pause she interrupted him 'My mother lived in Shimokitazawa.'

'Nice area. You must have great photos.'

Of course there were photos. Photos of boots slipping from her tiny feet, on yellow-wellington days, bright enough to scare the wildlife halfway across the South Downs, where they spent rented weekends. But she had never seen a single photo from her mother's time in Japan. Not a photo, not a face, found among her possessions to suggest she had ever lived there. Hana shook her head.

'What did she do in Tokyo?'

She hadn't told her very much. 'Well. . . she did work on a . . . a teahouse.'

The seat-belt sign bleeped – turbulence – and as the plane bucked, half his green tea escaped across her jeans. As his apologies tumbled out he pushed his napkin softly against her thigh until they both looked up suddenly as if as each of them had been called from opposite ends of the plane. She liked his reserve. She trivialized the accident and holding his napkin to her jeans and continued.

'I'm not a great traveller.'

He touched her sleeve with genuine concern.

Aware that she responded to his attention, they fell into an abrupt silence.

She watched him contemplate the ceiling vents. They were a good way into the journey and the air was stale.

'You've done some miles then.'

'Yes. A lunar mission only takes three days,' he complained. 'That's half a million kilometres.' She could tell he was the sort to be making constant calculations.

'We'd be about a third of the way right now,' he offered.

'To the moon?'

'Yes. You'll find Japan as familiar – and you might as well be travelling through time too.'

It was effectively what she wanted to do: travel through time; find a piece of her mother; find a piece of her own history. She had always accepted the thin yarn of a story her mother had offered, and over the years she had darned and patched it until it fitted her needs. This was how they had always lived together, patching and making do.

Hana woke on the descent over the daytime Pacific to find her head lay on Ed's shoulder. She smiled sleepily at the intimacies of the flight; his stomach filled with her untouched dinner, which he had tidied away. The honesty of their conversation.

She was not embarrassed until Ed opened his eyes and she shifted quickly to a safer distance.

'You 've got the address for the homestay – right? I'm really sorry – I would offer . . . but I'm going in the opposite direction.'

She was disappointed. She had imagined she would have a guide – at least to the centre of town.

'But we should hang . . . definitely,' he added.

It was such a little offer – she wouldn't press him on it.

The plane dipped sharply sending her body temperature up until she felt a little sick. Below were the rice paddy fields and from this height it seemed there was little change in what she had left behind.

'You okay?'

'I'm fine.'

He was, she thought, genuinely concerned. She slumped forwards, fighting what might have been too embarrassing.

When they disembarked she was met in the terminal by a bank of chilled air laced with the smell of fast food. In the café, large, red, paper lanterns radiated a warm light. It was the red of the morning sun that rose early in the east. Her mother had talked about Amaterasu, the Goddess of the morning sun who created night and day and painted the Japanese landscape. It was part of their personal folklore and her mother had said she was her goddess: strong, creative and forgiving. And now on arrival, though she wasn't a tourist as such she didn't feel any immediate sense of belonging; this was a new world to her.

In the queue they said a simple goodbye. She opened her British passport at the photograph where her own almond eyes were lost to the stamps and seals that ward off counterfeiters. Her name, with its distinct spelling, somehow promised she would finally learn the truth about her own identity.

As he left beyond the visa line, she waved, touching the pocket where she had put his meishi business card. And so he left her between the no man's land of duty-free and the threshold of Japan to find her way into the centre.

She marched blindly, past the bilingual signs of welcome and the helpful English guidance into town, to find the taxi ranks. It was too much for her to work out even in her own language. Luggage in tow she ignored the helpfully positioned tourist information desk and, in an ill-judged move, got into a yellow cab.

As the cab drove off, Ed's card lay behind in the plane, forgotten amongst the collected crumbs beneath the armrest that had divided them.

Chapter 2

'Entreat me not to leave thee or to return from following after thee;
For whither thou goest, I will go; and where thou lodgest, I will
lodge; your people shall be my people'
–Ruth, to Naomi (Ruth 1:16-18, King James Bible)

Hana's cab hurtled to join the writhing snake of traffic on the
elevated section of the Tokyo expressway. It followed the
contours of the Sumida River into downtown Tokyo where it
split into so many tributaries, running off to Ginza, Chiyoda
Ku and Tsukiji.

It hurt as she watched the taxi-meter move faster than the
city as they drove across it. Beneath the highway they ventured
into back streets, where the air was already thick with the smell
of yakitori, so strong it might be an impediment to the karaoke
drifting through alleys, eventually getting lost and petering out.
Once they reached Shimokitazawa the noise of the traffic gave
way to the random calls from the pachinko parlour as the car
slowed to the pace of the footfall.

The end of the afternoon was still hot when she clambered
out on the unfinished road at the top of a inauspicious residential cul de sac. As she counted the yen notes into the driver's
stark white gloves he must have read her surprise at the fare
because he dropped his head in an apologetic bow. The empty
street was pockmarked with the shadows of air-con units and
laced with scrambled utility wires that looked as if they had
been restrung in haste.

She stuffed the change into her pocket. Her jeans had crusted from the spilt tea and felt as pleasant as if someone else had worn them before her. Her mind went back to Tom, alone in her flat. Would Sadie keep him company? Sadie had borrowed her jacket and had only just returned it in time before she left and she could never quite be relied on. What was she doing here in Tokyo and where the hell was she? It was it was a long way from home.

The taxi left and as the dust settled at her feet, a regret that she should have come at all gently settled. Shimokitazawa: a quiet residential suburb that the guidebook promised as a 'suburb of film café's, low-key nightlife' with 'hundreds of reasonable restaurant choices'. Not that she had any money left after her cab ride. She consoled herself that at least the budget homestay rates had been agreed in advance; she had chosen the homestay program to save on costs but also for a chance to live with a Japanese family.

As she wheeled her case past the misaligned wall at the entrance of number 65, she realized that she had got what she paid for. It was nearing 6 p.m. as she rang the bell.

Chapter 3

The front door opened before her hand left the chanting, electronic bell. Perhaps the woman always watched for visitors. She was slight, a good head shorter than Hana and as agitated as a bird that does not own the pavement. Her greeting seemed lost in the effort of removing her housecoat.

Hana ignored the temptation to step back and call after the taxi but steeled herself to walk into this stranger's house. It smelt savoury but was not unpleasant. The hall was spacious with a large central staircase of thin matchstick bannisters, empty but for a stainless-steel clock in a plastic mahogany case and from the curling rug at the doorstep, it was shabby. But she managed to hide her disappointment; find a smile and make appreciative noises as she surveyed the gallery landing, the empty walls and tired decor. Her own home was such a contrast to this, decorated with bolts of indigo and woodblock prints, brush-stroked scrolls, thumb-printed pottery and hand-painted china; a densely rich homage to Japan.

There was an unease behind the woman's welcome. Maybe her appearance or the stain across her jeans was to blame? Her middle-aged Japanese host was tiny, and had pulled her thin hair across her scalp into a bun.

With forklift arms the woman communicated Hana should leave her case in the hall.

She was concerned that the lined and tired older woman should not lift it for her and it troubled her that she did not know how to say as much.

'Noru *desu*.' I am Noru. The aged woman slapped her bony breastbone and traced a legible greeting across the warm evening air. The enormity of the language barrier added to her jet lag. She would have so many questions – and she felt so ill-equipped to ask.

The house was silent but for a TV down the corridor as Noru took off on a tour of the lodgings. Hana trailed behind like a dependent child rather than a paying guest.

As they peered into the bathroom, Noru jabbed at the wood-lined bath, then at the shower head, positioned a foot from the floor, and she paused, lending some significance to a pair of plastic sandals by the door.

Hana had no idea. Should she wear slippers in the shower? From the back of the house came a short dry cough. As if attached by an invisible line, Hana followed on to the foot of the stairs where it was made clear that she should remove her shoes before she took to the first step. Was she was just another clueless foreign guest?

Her hot feet left damp prints on the first step and she was covered in embarrassment. As they reached the utilitarian beige of the upper floor, the smell of sour grass became overpowering. What was to be her room was off the open landing. Behind a thin door, with a quick yank of a grimy light cord, Noru showed her two single beds that were suddenly illuminated in all their plainness and just as quickly returned to gloom. It seemed clean enough.

A twin room. Assuming no one else arrived to use the other single, it would suit her fine. She thanked Noru, knowing she could not ask about the twin beds and the distance between them grew larger than just the language barrier.

Outside on the galleried landing, Hana took a seat on the tan leatherette sofa. She watched Noru drawing green tea from a giant floral flask on an old linen chest and accepted it though she had drunk plenty on the flight. It was easier to acquiesce.

'Gohan.' We eat. Noru tapped at her watch and then turned for the private section of the house, heading in the direction of the coughing below.

Alone, contemplating a pair of prints on the opposite wall, Hana was too tired of sitting and too weary to stand. Mount Fuji and a giant wave. She had finally arrived and all expectation was turned on its head. The volcanic cone of Fuji sloped smoothly towards a deep dusk-blue where a small fishing boat charted the choppy waters of the lake below.

Well, she rallied, she had brought her walking boots with her and could hike the Fuji trail to the top if she chose. If Tom could have come too she'd have felt more adventurous, but maybe scaring herself a little was a good thing.

The bitter tea, just the colour of the matting, felt acidic on her empty stomach and she regretted giving away her airline meal. And as a hollow emptiness descended on her, she tried to dismiss it as jet lag.

She could phone home. No, she should not phone home. Not now, not yet. All those years before, her mother, at pretty much the same age, had arrived in Tokyo, knowing no one either. And if she was honest she did know one person – the guy from the plane and with Noru that made two.

Her head fell back on the sofa and she bit into the rough side of her cheek. Her mother must once have loved Japan but it had obviously been a complicated affair as there were such huge blanks in the story. They had never come when her mother was alive: they had never had the resources; it had never been practical.

Now that her mother had gone, questions had begun to

appear. Long-buried questions. Now she felt a fool for not asking, but then again she had been forced into accepting this and it had only now begun to irritate her.

Chapter 4

'The events of human life, whether public or private, are so intimately linked to architecture that most observers can reconstruct nations or individuals in all the truth of their habits from the remains of their monuments or from their domestic relics'
–Honoré de Balzac

Hana sipped at the bitter tea. You really had to *know* how to ask the right questions. Her mother had hidden behind a memory that she would never share. She had cradled it like a burn to the hand and Hana had learned early on not to bring it up. Consequently it had proved a very successful way of avoiding the truth – which left Hana up against it now, up against that generational amnesia that protected the past and, at worst, buried it.

She really must find the teahouse. As her mother had described it, it lay etched on her mind, sitting in temple gardens, over an ornamental lake in one of the most tranquil places on earth. Working on that building and helping with the construction design, had been for her mother an exquisite project. On the rare occasions she had mentioned it she looked wistful, lost, and, when pressed, she would clam up, or ramble on about the way it was built.

This Zen teahouse had become a kind of monument to her and so Hana had brought from home the dog-eared Japanese map, folded into inconvenient ribbons and covered in nothing but kanji characters. The task of finding a major tourist site would be an achievement let alone an insignificant retreat in the middle of nowhere but the guy from the flight, Ed, might help.

With thoughts of freshening up she reached the hall, where Noru materialized, flapping her apron and motioning towards the bathroom at the back of the house. Once the door bolt was secured, she finally stepped out of her jeans. Peeling away the clothes she had first put on in London began the transition. You hadn't arrived, she thought, until that moment when you remove the flight-worn souvenirs from the start of the journey. The deep wooden bath was already full of water and, ignoring the short shower hose, the slippers and the ashtray, she got in and sank into the hottest water she had ever braved. Soaping away the collected hours of arm's-length intimacy and the Tokyo dust, she suspected she was breaking another house rule but who knew what it was.

Replacing the medicinal soap, she sank back for a blissful moment and remembered the London Fields Lido where she had first learnt to swim. She must have been about ten. This place prompted memories she hadn't raised for years, as if, as Ed had said, she was travelling back in time. Her mother, with careful consideration, amid the shouts of pleasure or was it terror around them, had removed the floats from her skinny arms and let her go. Shoulder deep she had felt herself sinking, but her mother, beside her then, had watched her struggle to the edge, to safety. It was never going to be easy, but she had clung to that mantra, and as they walked home hers was strawberry-ice success and they shared the sweet melt line running all the way to her elbow.

The steaming bath threatened to overwhelm her and, having added more from the cold tap, she sank below the water line. She held her breath until it was not quite comfortable, then, expelling bubbles in punishing, controlled bursts, she finally let it all go, turning the water into a rolling boil above her head. It was the first time, she realized, that she was angry. She missed her mother and she was angry with herself for losing her. Now she was actually here she knew she should have asked more questions, demanded answers. She had so little go on.

Radiating more heat than a power plant, she stepped out, and realized her fresh clothes were in her bag. She tried to pull on her jeans but her clammy skin made it impossible and so she threw on a cotton robe she found on the back of the door. It smelt distinctly male and, ignoring a slight revulsion, she threw it on in favour of running to her room in a tiny towel.

As discreetly as she could she lugged her bag across the floor, battling to keep the loose yukata robe closed, intent on getting past unseen. She wasn't sure but it was as if she had displaced someone from beyond the bathroom window vent.

She lay on the bed gazing beyond the weight of her exhausted eyelids, until suddenly energized she searched though her hand luggage for Ed's card. And she searched again, only to find it missing, and, with vigorous frustration she realized she had probably already lost it.

On her way down she could hear more coughing. As if on cue Noru appeared as Hana descended the stairs. She ushered her into the dining room, waved a tea towel in the direction of a chair and hit the play button on some plinkety-plonkety Japanese folk music, then left.

There were five places laid at the table. It was difficult to judge the size of the house. As she waited for the other guests, her eyes ranged over the few effects in the room. A small CD collection included ten copies of the same album from a cute girl band and beside the potted cactus was a range of English football mugs. She supposed they belonged to a teenage boy, but this impression was quickly dispelled when an approaching shuffle announced the laboured arrival of a really old man. Could it be Noru's father? Anticipating the difficulty he would have seating himself, she got up to help him to his chair and, with the arrogance both accrued in old age and naturally excused by it, he sat down at the head of the table and ignored her. Saucepans clattered in the kitchen.

'It is my first trip to Tokyo.' He ignored her, and she chose to turn up the volume. It didn't matter that he wouldn't speak English 'My mother lived in Shimoktazawa in the eighties. For over a year.' He could be deaf. 'My mother, Naomi,' she said again, for her own benefit.

He turned his head slowly as if to do otherwise would startle him and snorted down his nose, shaking his head his up and down in what could have been recognition.

'Ukai,' he said, introducing himself by tapping a bony finger to his chest. He had the tanned, desiccated face of a smoker. His wheezy laugh was lost in a fit of coughing that immediately brought Noru back into the room.

Hana recognized the look on her face, that look of spent patience, which must remain unvented and often accorded to the very old, the infirm, or the long-term ill.

Noru fell on him, rubbing and thumping the base of his back and drawing vigorous circles over his chest.

'So da ne.' She comforted him as you would a young child. No wonder she looked exhausted, this nurse and housekeeper.

'Can I help?' Hana was unsure at first whether she had made herself understood. But her offer was turned down graciously and she turned to look at the becalmed old man as Noru left him as she attended to the cooking. His rheumy eyes shone with his exertions and he looked at Hana directly.

'Na-o-mi,' he said. She could swear he said it, under thin breath. Just a copycat word? She could not ask another question for fear of bringing on another bout of asthma and so they sat in an uncomfortable silence animated only by his laboured breathing and the ticking of a cuckoo clock. The displaced German clock, like her, seemed to have lost its cultural way and migrated east. Did she have any better reason for being here? Contemplating the wizened figure at the head of the table, age itself looking like a wrong turn, she dropped her head with the thought that at least her mother had been spared this.

Chapter 5

Waiting for the evening meal took her back to the goodbye supper with friends. Tom had given a Japanese Kanpai toast and they had shared a bottle of sake Sadie had brought. They had found some shakuhachi flute music and talked of geishas, She had promised them all armfuls of manga comics.

Now she was here it was a sour joke. Moist amethyst and livid yellow pickles sat curling beside some dried fish. Noru fussed about serving them but eventually joined them at the table. At least the dinner was offered in small portions and she would manage the rice out of politeness.

Slipping the paper chopsticks from their sheath she broke them apart, whittling at the loose splinters before she began to eat. This prompted an exaggerated reaction from Noru, who exhaled in voiced panic.

'No. No,' Noru burst out shaking her head like an old turkey bird. Looking to the old man for his reaction to her careless-ness. Noru could not begin to tell her what custom she had offended. Self-consciously Hana picked at the sticky rice and the air-conditioning unit cooling the back of her neck joined forces with her jet lag to bring her close to tears. They didn't intend to make her feel so unwelcome, she knew that, and she forced a smile.

There were still two empty places laid at the table and she longed for a diversion. Just then doorbell went and Noru got up. Hana heard an American voice in the lobby, apologizing.

'Yeah. Sorry it's late. No, I won't eat. Just going straight to sleep, thanks.'

Piles of dark unruly hair and a girl with olive skin appeared in the door and Hana noticed the energy in the house had changed. After an exchange of smiles, the girl said, 'I'm Jess. Dead tired so I'll see you later. I'm gonna head up.'

'Bikyhikibiri!' a man's voice boomed from the back of the house.

As the diatribe continued Ukai turned his milky eyes towards Hana, followed by Noru and then Jess until she was the focal point of everyone's stare.

'You washed with soap in the bath?' Jess whispered.

Hana nodded.

'They never do this here.' She was matter of fact; she was obviously not new to the house. 'We share the water.' It was not good news.

Hiding in the shadow of the doorway clutching a towel, a bare-chested man in his thirties appeared, rattling on in complaint until Noru's response sent him into retreat.

Hana remembered the bathrobe and winced. Moments later he returned wearing a fresh cotton yukata gown over his heavy frame. He was newly shaven and his damp skin shone.

'Kombanwa,' he said to the room, acknowledging the girls before he sat down heavily beside old Ukai, and began again a low, gravelling rant.

'Night,' the American said. 'See you tomorrow.'

She seemed very much at home and very content to leave Hana with the growling man who must, she assumed, be Noru's son.

Noru deferentially placed sticks of startling luminous fish and sticky rice in front of the young man and it had a beneficial effect.

He turned to look at Hana as if she reminded him of someone.

'So, welcome to Tokyo. I am Tako. You met my mother and grandfather?' He had once got lucky with a gap year student.

His dark hair was wet and he looked like an overgrown

22

cuckoo. It was no surprise that Noru was stretched, cooking for two generations and guests.

'Hana, right? Japanese for flower.' He smiled benignly like a prince appeased. 'Ukai can write your name in kanji alphabet sometime.' He jabbed his chopsticks at the old man enthusiastically, revealing his bare chest beneath the yukata and a lurking breastplate tattoo.

'Thanks.' Who would refuse such an offer?

'You know Chelsea?' he asked, pointing at the line of football mugs.

'Yes.' It was drawn out and unconvincing. The Chelsea she knew was a place where her grandparents had lived until she'd gone to senior at the City of London School for Girls. They would take her to St Luke's playground off Sydney Street, and then, later, on those Sunday-lunch visits she and her mother were obliged to make, they would go to the Physic Garden. When she was older she would meet friends at the Goat pub, before trekking home to East London. Chelsea did not mean a football club to her and he could see that.

'So, you are gonna see the sights, right?'

'And lots of temples. When I find them.'

This sent him ricocheting to be of assistance. He retrieved a map and laid a hand on it ceremoniously as if it might be a passport to friendship. Opening it at his end of the table he strategically identified the areas marked and then promptly dashed it away, clearly having an Einstein moment.

'I myself can show you.'

Too fatigued to give him anything but a lukewarm response she hesitated. 'Thank you.' Should she say it? 'Very much.'

'You are British. British and –' he paused '– British Asian?'

This caught her off-guard, for while she was used to people turning over guessing stones – the game had long since ceased to irritate – but she had assumed foolishly, that possibly they might get it right here in Japan.

'Japanese.'

'So. I see,' he said, more winded than intrigued.

Had she expected to walk off the plane and fit in? Outside there was just enough light to see the old wooden house opposite through the heavy dirt on the insect netting. Could she belong here? Idly, she prodded the pink seafood round the bowl with her chopsticks.

'Chelsea is my club,' he continued beaming indulgently and she tried hard to reciprocate the smile. For some reason nothing fitted. Perhaps she might be happier in a different homestay? She wouldn't jump to a rash decision, but tomorrow she could look at different places to stay; maybe the American could suggest one.

She made her excuses and was sorry for not managing to eat what they had presented. She could sense their disappointment but, at the noise of her chair, as she pushed her seat back under the table, they broke from their disenchantment and wished her goodnight.

'Oyasuminasai,' Noru chimed with her son.

Upstairs in the twin room the American girl, despite the humidity, was hidden under a floral sheet. Hana's room was now their room. She had, considerately, left the light on but the air-con was off and there was no remote control. The solution hung pendulously over her bed. She climbed gingerly on to the bed base and reached for the switch until the girl stirred.

'Hospital soap,' she mumbled sleepily.

She would leave it tonight.

As Hana closed her eyes thoughts of home drifted in. Tom would be at lunch now. It was only yesterday he had seen her off from the platform in Paddington and brought her case all the way, in an unusually generous gesture for him. He had given her *The Pillow Book* as she stepped onto the train. It was only as he receded with the station that the realization she was leaving him behind had hit. She had hoped for larger assurances that he would miss her; she wanted him to say it would hurt and preferably badly. She wanted him to work on what she meant to him until her return. But he was not demonstrative; he could be needy and that display of affection was entirely different, veering as it did towards his own requirements, not hers. Did she trust Sadie with him? How could she begin to taunt herself and so soon when she felt so very off-centre already? She would be away for nearly two months and to begin counting the days was a poor start. A poor start. A poor start.

She fell asleep with unexpected ease.

Chapter 6

Population of Tokyo : 37.8 million

The next morning, bending over with the curvature of the earth, time prodded at her ribs, calling for a start to the day that was much too early. But she was used to broken sleep. For a while, when her mother had been ill, her own sleep patterns had been affected and she had wandered around the house at odd hours, drying the last of the cups on the draining board or aligning cookery books. Since she had gone, Tom could wake to find her tidying or cleaning as if she had a responsibility to keep her mother's flat more pristine than it had ever been, as if she might walk in unexpectedly and find Hana was coping okay; that it was all under control.

Her damp bedclothes clung and on waking in the half-light her mouth felt dry – could she safely drink the water here? In the single bed beside her, Jess, the American girl, was still asleep. Hana could hear birdsong, loud birdsong, in the heart of the city. Wide awake but unable to move from the bandage of sheets, she willed her roommate to surface but she was no more compliant than she had been the night before. So Hana lay a little longer, planning her day. She would find the teahouse at the temple. She had read of the wooden structures and the Buddhist temple Asakusa Jinja, and the Shinto shrine at the Meiji Jingu. She would head at some stage for Kyoto, which, though high on her list, would be a push to afford.

Finally Jess stirred and pulled herself up to sit against the wall, crowned in a bird's nest of hair. She looked across at Hana with dark circles under her eyes.

'Coffee!' Her arms stretched as she broke away from the deep sleep of her first night. 'It's good to be back.'

Back from where? Hana wondered but didn't yet say it.

Jess stretched some more.

'This is the best place in Tokyo,' she continued, as if to someone else.

Hana blinked back at her as if a strange creature had joined the room. The best? This was hardly believable and she couldn't bring herself to agree even out of politeness.

'Bit of shouting last night,' Hana contended

Jess nodded.

'Bikyhikibiri. Bikyhikibiri.'

'Which—' Jess looked over a virtual set of glasses professorially '—translates as pubic hair. Don't leave it in the bath.' She waved any concern away and giggled.

Hana's lips soured.

Jess was laconic but friendly and gave Hana the facts quickly: she had been working up north on an aid project and had come back down to Tokyo for a few weeks before returning to Seattle. Though younger than Hana she was a seasoned traveller, happy living out of a rucksack for months. It was the second year she had come to the homestay and the formula worked well for her.

Jess put her arm round her in a welcome squeeze. 'I'm back in Tokyo to make some good money. And you? Why are you here?'

Hana began a vague meandering on the cultural attractions of Tokyo but Jess cut her short.

'You're part Japanese, right? And you chose my favourite homestay?'

Hana nodded and then broached what was uppermost in her mind. She lowered her voice confidentially. 'I am going to have to change homestay.'

'Great, then I get the room to myself.' Jess was deadpan and Hana wondered whether she should take her seriously. 'No, you'll like it here. The family goes out of their way to help. Why leave when you just got here?'

The fact that it felt as cloying as a home for the elderly was too difficult to put into words, too ungenerous, and so she just said, 'Well . . . money.'

'Money? This is cheap. I start my bar work this week. Great money and it'll see me through a whole semester. You should think about it. They always need people.'

Younger but so aware, Hana thought. Jess urged her to come and see the club with her that morning. A club? Hana had worked in a bar but a club? It was a hostess bar. And it didn't appeal. Charity Aid and club hostess. Jess was interesting.

'Emiko will give you a job. And then I could show you round Tokyo. ' It sounded like a bribe.

'No. No, thanks.' Objections that she was here only for a short time were irrelevant. There was no doubt she could do with the money. 'This morning I plan to find the local temple.'

'Local temple? I can show you better temples.'

'Well, you see . . . when she lived here, my mother worked on a project at the teahouse, somewhere in the grounds of one of the temples.'

Jess nodded encouragingly, while at the same time mentally counting the number of small temples that littered each small district of Tokyo. It seemed a little futile to her.

'Did she give you the address?

'No. Well, no.' It was too long to explain.

'You know which one?' she added to make sure.

'Not yet.' Assured that six or so weeks was ample time to discover it.

'So that shouldn't be too difficult to find.'

'Exactly,' Hana replied, misreading the cynicism.

'What's the hurry? The temple will be there tomorrow. Be there the next day. Been there a while,' Jess urged. 'You work nights with me, go sightseeing during the day go home with more money than you transferred. Including the flight.'

She could see Hana warming.

'I need to get a black dress for the job. Will you come? We'll go meet Emiko.'

'Okay, I'll think about it.' She would have to hold her own with this one.

Chapter 7

Seismological measurement of Fukushima earthquake magnitude 9 on the Richter scale

Birdsong came from the same deck that the folk music had the night before. Breakfast was laid out as self-service, and Hana and Jess ate rice and then wedges of sliced white bread, twice the size of a paperback and half as nutritious, that they covered in sugared orange jam. Between mouthfuls they discussed their plans for the day and then headed out.

Before they reached the station Jess pointed out the dormant neon nightclub sign.

'Try it? There's no commitment.'

Hana could see she was never going to take no for an answer.

Jess ran down to the basement, leaving her at the sign.

She quickly returned.

'Emiko – the manager – can see you at the end of the week.' She couldn't have been more pleased with herself.

Hana didn't want to be ungrateful, 'I'll see,' was all she said.

Jess drew her towards the rail tracks.

'Come to Ziggy's to meet my good friend Miho.'

And they headed up the main street with its tiny stores; pottery spilling towards the fresh noodle makers calling beside loud carousels of 'anime' covers for any accessory.

Hana waited patiently in a din of local music as Jess fingered lollipop pens and fake-fur key rings with ears. All this from the home of Zen, she thought, as she waited too long under the awning of sound. She considered her new companion a little critically but in the assault of the unfamiliar she was already attached to her.

'Have you chosen yet?' Hana was surprisingly irritable given they had met so recently.

Jess emerged manga-eyed with a cartoon bag of irresistibles and she was back on message. 'It'll be fun and it's the only temp job a foreigner will get in Tokyo.'

She was as short as a haiku poem but without the poetry.

'And the clients?' hana was worried about dodgy clubs.

'It is tame. It's safe,' she reassured.

Hana's nose wrinkled. She was far from convinced.

'Remember I worked here all last summer.'

'How did you find it?' Hana twisted at her woven bracelet.

'The homestay. Ukai, the old man, once had a share in the business that owned a chain of clubs across the city. Apparently did very well property dealing in the eighties. That was until a big deal in Guam nearly ruined him. It's why Noru takes in foreigners. The house is their only remaining asset and the old man isn't as well connected as he was.'

'So they were an important family?'

Jess surprised Hana by laughing, as if the idea were ludicrous. 'Well, let's say influential. They're *Etahin*.'

'*Etahin*?' Hana hadn't a clue.

'Low class,' Jess said confidentially. Hana threaded her cotton art bag over her shoulder, engaged. Jess knew Noru and the family quite well. So they had hit hard times and Noru was whittled away by the workload and the responsibility. This all seemed to mitigate against an early move from the homestay; they would probably be relying on the income?

'And the old man's health has taken a dive since last year,' Jess added unsentimentally, as if she could hear Hana weighing up her decision. And that swayed it. Hana saw she shouldn't really contemplate moving homestay now, leaving them so early on.

On the way to the café Jess explained that she had worked with the same volunteer group as last year.

'Yes, straight down from Fukushima.'

'Same charity programme?' Hana asked.

'Same programme with the same volunteer group' Jess conceded proudly.

Hana turned in admiration. And a memory suddenly flew to mind. One weekend last month she and Tom had walked along Regent's Canal, and, after getting drenched in an English monsoon, once home Hana had used old newspaper to stuff Tom's wet boots as they dried. Later, when making supper she had unfurled the paper to catch the vegetable parings, smoothing the corners until she was disturbed by a photograph under a headline. It was of a large merchant ship, a cargo vessel, resting incongruously on a landscape of debris: afloat on shards of wood, sections of wall, severed concrete platforms and flimsy girders. A sea of detritus. The bric-a-brac of a town destroyed. The vernissage of a ship – resting on kindling, once houses and stores, garden fences and schools – that had now been washed clean and was drying in the sun. The caption read Tō hoku – After the tidal wave. Across the hulk was a great expansive sky of hopeful blue on a cloudless, unthreatening day; well after the force of nature had taken its random hit on the Japanese coastline. There were no harrowing details. It was majestic; a great feat of engineering resting on the fragments of a community. It presented like a life raft to a culture, the ship ashore resting easily back on the land where it had first been constructed. A huge piece of flotsam cut it loose from its securing lines by the nihilistic force of a tidal wave. It seemed to be a monument to the survival of something grander than destruction and, like a sorrow, rested heavily on the obliterated scene of what once was. In some way she did not understand, it belonged to her. She felt a kinship then with Japan that she had never before felt with such intensity. She too was a survivor of her own family tragedy.

'That was in Fukushima,' Jess reconfirmed.

Hana snapped out of her reverie and was immediately honest with her. 'I couldn't do it. You've seen so much.'

'We get to see the wastelands.' Jess conceded. 'But you rebuild.'

Jess bordered on glib and Hana gave way to a creeping skepticism. She eyed her petite figure. Jess would be particularly ineffective in rebuilding the havoc she had seen.

'You. You are rebuilding?' Hana offered tentatively.

'I don't have a truck license,' Jess drawled amusingly. 'We counsel. We don't get close to the affected communities or their grief, but we counsel the counsellors. To be more accurate, we organize their entertainment: films, music nights. As they are the ones who work with the families, day in day out and they need a programme of events to take their minds off what they have seen and heard. They need to be fresh to counsel the survivors. Many have nothing left to hold on to but the promise of that counselling.'

It was a serious choice for a summer programme. Jess held on to Hana's admiration.

'Last year I was also teaching at Berlitz Language School.' She let this slip casually, as if looking for more approbation.

And it struck Hana that the promised bottom line – the huge amounts of money Jess earned out here – was the result of more hours than she had explained.

Chapter 8

They reached the door of Ziggy's café. Jess hammered on the glass, but no one heard, or else she had deafened them in her efforts to be heard.

'Miho's asleep.'

'So Miho's a friend?'

'It's her café. She's great. Opens early and adores Americans. Some days she'll let me eat without paying. So I wanted to tell her we'll be two for breakfast after the bar shift.'

'But I haven't decided.'

'Come on. I need some company down there. You'll thank me.' The prospect of the basement bar had grown no more attractive than at first. Jess needed her company and chance had thrown her no other allies.

They gave up on any response at Ziggy's café and as they left Jess had to draw Hana from the path of a noodle delivery scooter strafing them at speed. She seemed surprised that she didn't know to watch for them.

'And you are a bit Japanese, right? So you are coming home,' Jess continued, essentially thick-skinned but perhaps she needed to be.

'Not really.' Hana's response was quiet.

Last night, getting out of the taxi, any expectation that she might be coming home had evaporated.

The noodle biker waved an apology and drove on with his ramen soups swinging behind him.

Hana waved back. 'I have never been to Japan before.' She couldn't see why further justification was needed.

'So the trip's about you?' What Jess lacked in subtlety she made up for in perseverance.

Hana could do without the analysis. But she smiled. Would anyone go travelling and leave themselves behind at baggage carousel? Was it an omission, not to have checked the occupancy rates, thus landing Jess as a roommate? But she was warm and kind of vital. And Jess did have local knowledge. Drawing her back to this, she asked, 'So where will I find the local temple?'

Jess had never been and saw no urgency to go on Hana's first day. She stopped at a blinking vending machine; she would need coffee before they took another step.

Hana refused either the chemically warmed or the ice-chilled can. And as if she sensed she was weighing her up, Jess bent over posturing like a sage and rolled the cold can across her forehead for comic effect. 'Wait a minute,' Jess said to the ground. She had found a small kitten cowering with the wind-blown trash under the vending machine. She picked it up and nestled it against her ear, walking on.

'Wait. Won't it belong to someone?'

'It'll take a holiday just for a day or so.'

'And Noru won't mind?'

'Who would tell?'

Hana smiled at her new friend's independence.

'Where exactly did Naomi live?' The cat was tucked under Jess's arm.

'I don't know but she would have known this main street.' Hana wondered how much would it have changed; the racket of piped music, the disarray of wares halfway across the street, signs so numerous they had become wallpaper hopelessly competing for attention.

'You look like her?' Jess asked.

Idly Hana imagined there might be someone on this very

street that might just remember her mother and recognize some similarity, some feature or in the way she walked.

'A bit. Not really. We enjoyed the same things. We were similar in that way.'

'You *were?*'

Hana nodded and pursed her lips, and for once Jess caught the subtlety that she had lost her and said she was sorry.

Hana went on quickly. 'She lived here when she worked on the teahouse. Around eighty-nine.'

'So . . .' Jess registered with the strike of a can hitting the pocket of the vending machine.

'So the teahouse is important.'

'But you are looking for your father?' Jess tugged at the ring pull on the can.

The suggestion winded Hana. The faceless man that was her father had been a completely unacknowledged presence for so long that she had edited him out of her existence in the way that he had surely done for her. How could this stranger not realize that she shouldn't ask? There was a time when she believed her mother had not known who her father was. A faceless one-night stand in Tokyo? But she knew Naomi too well to really believe it.

At first she didn't respond and then replied, 'No,' to Jess's open skepticism.

'Miho's coffee is better than this,' Jess concluded resignedly.

Chapter 9

After supper, Tako skipped in, wearing a clean, pressed T-shirt.

'Ladies, ladies.' He chose to pronounce it as if it were a disease for dogs. He started regaling them with earthquake facts which had become a recurring theme with him, and he clearly enjoyed the response.

'A thirty-nine metre wave.' If he intended to frighten Hana he often succeeded.

Unexpectedly he produced a bottle of Blossom soap and presented it as a gift. Had he heard them complaining?

Noru scowled at her son as she cleared the table. Her house-keeping didn't run to gifts for guests.

'When do I show you round?' Ever generous. He leafed though a guidebook as he held it under Hana's nose. What could she tell him? He was the last person she would choose.

Her smile was noncommittal.

'Okay, so when is best?' he persisted.

There was something about him she didn't trust. She searched Jess, who bailed her out very casually

'We have a few trips planned. Thanks though.' And she grabbed the soap before marching out.

It was Jess's turn for the bathroom first and so Hana took out her battered city plan, tracing her finger across the legend of flags and dots and icons. She had scanned the whole of Shimokitazawa and found nothing.

*

Jess returned in a towel-wrapped turban . . .

'Sweet to give us soap.'

'Sweet?' Hana hoped he was harmless.

As she scratched at the back of her neck Hana remembered the cat had slept in Jess's bed for two days. It was sure to have fleas. Resignedly, she held her feet in her hands and rocked back and forth, eventually coming to settle on the uncomfortable homestay bed, intending to broach the subject of the cat with Jess soon.

On their way up the main street the next morning, Hana passed gift-wrapped melons in the window of the supermarket. They were the price of a European flight at home.

'It is what it is.' Jess was clearly resigned to the cost of living because she knew the short cuts. 'I never eat melon,' she said as if possessed of great wisdom.

Hana would not buy this as evidence of an economic sage but she did realize then, even without giving way to her taste for melon, that she would go to the interview at the end of the week or answer to her roommate, repeatedly. And so, before they reached the rail tracks, she had decided, since she planned to be in Tokyo for at least six weeks or more, she would join Jess at the club. Why not?

Her first quake began halfway to the station with what she thought was a train rumbling. She didn't see anything particularly odd but she could hear the creaking of wooden buildings bracing against the tremor as if shaken by the vibrations of an ancient engine. It lasted for no more than ten seconds.

'We should be inside,' Jess advised and pointed to the pachinko parlour.

'You okay?'

Once inside she was a little shaken but the vibration stopped as suddenly as it had arrived.

'An earthquake virgin.' Jess tried to make light of it to put her at ease. 'We have loads of these little tremors. And the pressure release is a positive thing.' She smiled with a bright idea. 'Let's play.'

Hana reminded Jess they were headed for Nakajima no Ochaya to drink tea but she was caught by the novelty.

The doors opened to a cacophony that drowned the shouts of welcome; chrome ball bearings in Brownian motion, like so many metallic castanets. Lights flashed in purple, red and emerald green in line upon line, and on the small screen of each pinball display an ancient geisha played out a love story or cartoon boy hero dazzled a conquering light sabre.

There were plenty of empty seats peppered with random regulars, most of whom slumped as if permanently attached to the furniture, spent cigarettes between their lips,

Jess whooped like a cowgirl to straddle a chair. She turned. 'Are we feeling lucky?'

Hana was happy to observe and took up a position behind her. Winning balls from another machine clattered. She was far from the tranquility of the teahouse.

Jess took the joystick, jabbing at a console worn smooth as washed pebbles. Bearings collided and bounced through a maze of obstacles and at every winning gate more balls fed her play. It was a while before she was conscious of another person standing behind her. Hana turned to find Tako had appeared like a screen genii. He had a habit of turning up like an irritating pop-up ad. Had he followed them? He wore his shiny athletic jacket and bright white T shirt.

He couldn't stay, but since he knew the game so well he would show them how it was done. Could he show them? Jess made way for him and he flashed his skills until three jackpot winners appeared on screen and a deafening number of balls fell in payout.

He indicated with a generosity as large as the sum was small that it was all theirs.

'Yeeha!' Jess called.

Tako rose for Hana to take a turn.

She declined, not wanting to risk the winnings, and thankfully, in the void of any encouragement, he left them.

'I will add to the money,' Jess announced, 'and we'll go for a big lunch.'

The restaurant was the size of a corridor. A thatch protected an old water wheel and a large, plastic raccoon bear stood to attention.

'Mickey Mouse? But a bit tanned.'

Jess shot Hana a look. 'This is Tanuki. He brings good fortune, especially in financial matters. And sex,' she added in a helpful afterthought.

'Funny there's so much superstition. Mickey Mouse doesn't mean anything,' Hana said. Here it seemed important to hang on to the significance of things.

'He has big balls too,' Jess stated the obvious mischievously. She had an appetite and chose quickly from the menu. They ate and talked of Seattle and London sushi and that thing guys do when they start a row about something trivial when they need to bring up a different injury.

As they left neither could decide who best resembled the potbellied bear raccoon.

'Go lucky,' Jess burped solemnly.

'And you,' Hana wondered for a moment whether she would ever need anything more than good company and so, ditching the teahouse idea for the day, she fell in with Jess.

Jess wanted Hana to see the city before they got stuck into work, so the next day they crossed the whole of Shibuya, took the metro to Aoyama and walked the hill to Omotesandō. There they peered beyond concave glass so unreflective it seemed they could reach in for the Yamamoto and Gucci bags, too expensive to touch.

To vary the homestay offering of rice, pickles and dried or

jellied fish, they chose to eat at the end of the metro line on the pavement terrace of a student café screened off with sculptured tea bushes. They were the only foreigners in the place but drank their way to the point where it didn't matter.

After plenty of warm sake, they returned to the house where Ukai, oblivious to the hour and to their greeting, was still painting in poor light at the dining room table. He often worked at his SUMI-E, and in the cool of the late afternoons he would trim the kiwi vine that ran over the door. The brushwork was some sort of farewell poem in calligraphy; a tradition, Jess had said. Great big black strokes of angry ineptitude.

Jess cast an eye over progress as they passed. 'Not bad for a yakuza.'

Now used to her humour, Hana found branding the old man a gangster amusing.

She was sure he had said 'Naomi' on that first night. If she could just make herself understood enough to talk to him . . .

They took the stairs unsteadily.

'Are these mosquito bites?' Hana inspected her arms before scaling the stairs.

Jess ignored her and returning to a pet subject said, 'I think I saw one of the guys I met at the club in that restaurant, If I don't pull soon . . .'

She laughed like a hyena as Hana held the banister unsteadily.

'Tako?' she suggested weighing both in each hand for comic effect and risking a fall.

She stabilized for a moment. 'Now, the lawyer from the plane . . .' Hana began, holding her forehead in exasperation at losing contact. 'Fluent. And he was great company too.'

'Careless at best,' Jess slurred, and in her optimistic way rambled, 'confidentially, you know, my Japanese isn't bad either.' There was nothing confidential about it and she was, as usual, endearingly keen to come top in the competition for great company.

As Hana jabbed at the air-con remote, Jess promised to search for English law firms in Tokyo and slumped on her bed. Hana found that, on returning to the room this time, it had strangely begun to feel like a haven in the city.

Neither of them saw Tako emerge from the lobby door to listen from the bottom of the stairs.

Chapter 10

On Thursday afternoon they walked to the metro.

'Trust me, we want to take the Ginza line beyond Asakusa temple.'

Though Hana had wanted to head for Meiji Jingu temple in Harajuku, she went along with it.

The approach to the painted wooden structure at Asakusa was lined with kiosks selling souvenir biscuits, miniature samurai swords and polyester silks, and, under the canopied bronze incense burner, people stood washing in the curling smoke. Cupped hands drew the incense silently over their faces and hands. It was, Hana supposed, as effective as any purification for the soul, and she wanted to try it, wafting trails of incense across the air, following the contours of her upper body. Jess could not be persuaded to join in and they left the main complex to skirt the site for the teahouse.

Their hands traced the brushwood fence tied with origami prayers and tagged wind chimes sang as they passed. Before they reached the teahouse, they came across a forest of little statues lining the path, no more than a foot high, constructed from stones, each wearing startling scraps of red cloth, tied as bibs. Hana called to Jess for an explanation.

'Those—' Jess threw out as she marched on '—they're Jizo.'

Hana waited for more.

'For the God of little ones. Any who died in childhood or were Unborn.'

It was unsettling. Futile rags on petrified stones. And they walked on.

Finally Jess stopped. Opening her arms to a building rising up in front of them: a red pagoda with storied eaves like the exposed ribs of a musical instrument. As if the chimes they had heard along the way emanated from this enormous child's rattle.

'*Chashitsu*. The teahouse,' Jess said with a flourish, making the pronouncement as if she had guided Hana to the very heart of her pilgrimage. She watched Hana carefully for her reaction but her rapt face changed suddenly.

'Well, this isn't it,' Hana was obliged to point out. 'A world-famous temple?' she added crossly.

'Yes, but the style . . .' Jess's confidence faded. It was a reference and weren't they out looking for references? Wasn't this why they had come to the garish, red, Buddhist temple in the first place?

Hana walked around the wooden pagoda. For Jess it was no big deal. She would never get the architectural subtleties. The simplicity of Zen. It was stunning but it was all wrong and far from the simple structure she was looking for. As they left they passed the Jizo stones, draped with fading rags, and coldly chilling.

Chapter 11

'Tan-tan-tanuki no kintama wa,
Kaze mo nai no ni,
Bura bu-ra'

'Tan-tan-tanuki's balls ring,
Though there is no wind,
They swing-swing-swing'
– schoolyard song in Japan

The basement smelt of disinfectant. Emiko, the manager, was at the bar, facing away from her, stock-checking her screen; the light was flat, barely sufficient. Someone hollered from the back and she answered him meekly in Japanese. He began testing a UV light and it picked up the white T-shirt she wore over tight jeans. Behind her the light pulsed across an enormous woodblock print, exposing an octopus that filled the entire wall. They might as well be under water.

She pulled up a bar-stool and greeted Hana quietly, with scant energy for someone desperate for staff. The opening conversation was short; like the atmosphere in the room, she seemed a little stale, and as she perched on the stool, Hana knew she was out of place.

Emiko closed her screen; she had a tiny scar above her upper lip, where a kiss might have been planted in a near miss; a fine line between love and hate perhaps. Hana watched her. But for a gentle tick at the corner of her lip, her face was immobile.

At the back of the room men were playing a day's game of cards. Hana had could see pretty quickly that she was not what Emiko had expected. She scratched at her neck. It was infuriatingly itchy and too late she realized it was off-putting.

As Emiko asked another routine question, they were interrupted by rapid footsteps on the stairs. Jess breezed in.

Emiko met Jess's excitement only to dampen it.

'Your friend is here only for a short time,' she said apologetically and with impeccable grace excused herself to respond to one of the card players. Hana looked at Jess apologetically. She had been turned down when they had bet on a certainty. To her surprise she was disappointed. They went back to the street as if they needed air.

Jess began an athletic rant.

'Emiko actually said that?' As Hana relayed their conversation.

It was never easy to be rejected, even when she hadn't staked a whole lot on the idea and she appreciated Jess's indignation.

'So, let's try something else,' Jess continued energetically and flipped quickly to reassurance, tapping Hana's hand to comfort her. As they walked away Jess waved familiarly to a woman standing behind a tsunami of pottery, spilling into the street as if she knew everyone here. As if she belonged.

They ambled over the tracks and the humid air clung to them like disappointment. 'We'll get something to eat?' Jess said.

They would head for Ziggy's. For a moment Hana thought she had a waitressing job in mind for her? It might be in Tokyo but she didn't want to spend her time in a café. At least the bar was different – nothing like it in London.

'I told you about Miho's Pastries,' Jess cajoled, explaining Ziggy's was her regular; it was so reasonable it had become her dining room.

Knocking gently at the window, pressing against the plate

glass, Jess rubbed her empty stomach and reached for Hana to do the same. As Hana peered into the small café she could see shelves of well-travelled coffees and Kilner jars of mulberries and cinnamon lining the walls.

Miho waved from the back of the store. Taking out her earphones she came over to usher them in. The cool of the air-con was as welcome as the brewed coffee and croissant she offered them. Dressed in bleached linen, an indigo band around her bobbed salt-and-pepper hair, she wore huge wedge platforms as if in homage to a style now out of place on a woman of her age. A tried, failed, but not entirely vanquished, style. She was old enough to be their mother.

Hana drank her coffee, her stomach rumbling for pastries that had yet to arrive.

'My best customers today.' Miho smiled and offered more coffee. Hana felt at home immediately.

'Just like a diner. I give you refills.' She was warm and she was generous.

'Here comes noodle legs.'

A pastry delivery arrived from the French bakery, Miho explained, on the other side of the tracks. She approached a large stack of plastic trays on legs cautiously and carefully relieved the boy of the top layer. The café was suddenly infused with the delicate aroma of cinnamon.

'So you are from London?' Miho placed two pastries directly onto the table.

In the background some Eighties track was playing lightly.

Jess's mouth was dusted with icing sugar.

'Could you maybe talk to Emiko? Hana wants a job.'

Miho nodded, eying Hana.'

'Sure.' Her accent was American.

'She spent time in the States,' Jess explained.

'Do you plan to go back?' Hana asked.

A strain came over Miho's face. It was youthful, though crossed with inevitable age.

'I have no plans right now. You know my kid is with his dad. He's just fine. It is about time I get to see him again. I may go back next fall.'

'How old is he now?'

'You want to see a picture of him?'

Miho reached into her back pocket and produced her screen saver. A shot of an old photograph. She was younger slimmer but recognisable, standing beside a man in hiking boots carrying a child in a frame backpack: a rotund toddler with a crop of unmanaged black hair.

'Long time back. Before we broke up,' she concluded.

Jess cooed, 'Cute baby.'

'You don't need glasses.' Miho smiled fondly. 'He's left college now.'

'Good-looking, I bet,' Hana offered.

'And did you get to go to his graduation?'

'I haven't seen him so much. Hardly since this photo was taken. Pretty much.' Miho was unemotional.Resigned.

Hana looked down in silence and Miho noticed her distraction.

'Okay, Hana?'

Hana smiled and traced circles in the sugar dust.

Miho pulled up the skirts of her apron and joined them at the pine table.

'I left him in the States when I couldn't support him. It was best for him. I've been back a long time.'

'Really?' Hana responded. She didn't understand. It seemed like a little tragedy.

'I am not an American citizen,' Miho explained. She caught at a pastry flake on the table and blew it, along with her reminiscences, out of her hand, as if they were really of no importance to her. 'Too many coffees to make an airfare.' She grinned.

'He'll visit Tokyo,' Jess said. 'Hana is back. She had family here.'

Miho nodded as if she guessed she might. People arrived and she had to serve them.

Fleas or no fleas Hana decided it was time to get back to their room.

Jess swigged the last of her coffee and called back to remind Miho to speak to Emiko.

'Okay,' Miho promised. As they left her she was busy with pancakes.

Hana scratched the side of her neck. 'The cat has to go.'

To her surprise Jess agreed.

Chapter 12

> 'A clump of summer grass,
> Is all that is left,
> Of the hopes and ambitions,
> Of ancient warriors'
> –Matsuo Bashō, *The Narrow Road to the Deep North*

Tokyo

Heat trailed Hana all the way from the shade of the cherry trees beside the concrete-covered river and over the level crossing to where the warning bell sounded.

Hana had established the site of a number of teahouses across the city. Some were not attached to a temple and she could discount these and many temples had no teahouse, which narrowed it down a bit. The one over the lake at Hamarikyu Gardens was enormous, and so trodden by tourists as to be disappointing. She felt she couldn't possibly afford the tea ceremony they offered, and she didn't trust the cafés advertising the experience. That afternoon she promised herself she would find the local temple and walk around the grounds, but first she would head back to the homestay to change.

Ukai sat as he often did just under the porch that ran the length of the old wooden house. He was bare to the waist and his frail arms stuck out like undernourished chicken wings. As she stopped to greet him, she saw he was labouring to breath.

Very suddenly Tako emerged from the screen and, standing behind the old man, began shaking him violently. He could not have seen her coming up the track. Was it a manoeuver to help him catch his breath? To stop him choking? It was so hard it looked as though it would finish him. Leaving Ukai motionless Tako left as quickly as she had arrived. Ukai's head hung across his shoulder. She took a step towards him. On his upper arm was a small tattoo. A black bird. He was stock-still. And she was unable to approach him and unable to pass. Was he dead? She had no voice to reach for and she turned for the house, knowing he should not face the end alone. That she was his only witness scared her but she was unable call out. Suddenly the seizure passed and she could see him return to shallow breathing. And as soon as he moved she was reassured . . . released.

Once upstairs, Hana pushed on the lever of the hot water flask that sat on the chest beneath the Fuji prints. Cradling her cup of green tea, she slumped onto the sofa. What had she seen? It was rough treatment. Had she seen some vital essence leaving the man? Jess would be back from her teaching session in a few minutes and she needed to talk to her. The circular fluorescent light was ticking in no particular sequence and it felt like the fragile order that had been established since her arrival had just slipped.

She sipped at the green tea like a bird. That first night, she had felt sure Ukai had recognized Naomi's repeated name. Unable to face going back past the old man, she dug the folding map from her luggage. The corners were worn at the folds and parts of the city were rubbed away. She opened it distractedly and, without focus, looked for the symbols for temple. Perhaps all these years later the teahouse had been replaced and she would never find it.

The door slammed marking Jess's return. Would she have seen him? Was he still alive? Hana finished her tea quickly and braced as Jess's bag of grammar books hit the sofa.

'Ukai?' Hana asked in a low reverential whisper. 'And did you see Tako? What was Tako doing?'

'Ukai was on the porch,' Jess said dismissively, 'sunning himself.' Then she added, 'He waved. They waved.'

Hana couldn't quite work out what she'd seen and didn't want to understand it. Had she got it all wrong? Should she feel so uneasy with these people who Jess had stayed with last summer and had felt comfortable enough to come back to.

'Guess what?' Jess smiled with some degree of self-satisfaction. 'Success.' She lifted an up-turned teacup and raised a toast to more sencha.

Hana, ignoring her, peered through the banisters down to the lobby where the landlady scuttled to tend to her aged father. A silent agitation travelled across the house; Hana seemed to feel the metronomic beat that precedes a tragedy. Noru darted out from the front door leaving the sun to cauterize the hall floor.

Jess could hear nothing special in the silence.

'You got it,' she blurted. 'You got the job!'

Hana was too preoccupied to listen.

A bicycle bell sounded from the road below and then, with the inevitability of a score, a muffled involuntary shriek rose from deep inside house.

Hana dragged Jess by the sleeve to their room.

Jess listened briefly, then carried on. 'Just seen Miho. Emiko can probably take you.'

Hana nodded, unable to answer as she moved to take a vantage point by the window. The insect screen rendered the scene in sepia: across the road beneath the bleached porch , the old man's chair was vacant. Jess came up behind her to witness the family cameo darting around the body and tending to their tragedy. Tako and Noru and a lifeless Ukai.

Jess pressed her hand on the small of Hana's back. It hit Hana in that moment that she not been touched this way since she left London. Heavy with loss she rested her forehead lightly on Jess's shoulder, as if she might share the weight. Below, Tako crossed the porch, head in hands, and it appeared he was weeping. The two young women drew back in silence. She had misinterpreted what she had seen?

Hana sat at the end of Jess's bed, with the satchel of grammar books locked in her arms for support like a favourite pet. And Jess listened sympathetically, as Hana struggled to balance her fixation over the moment she saw Tako by the old man. 'What do you think of Tako?' she asked slowly.

'He's sweet. Organized a birthday present for me last year. Keen but harmless.'

Hana considered this for a moment before returning to the subject of Ukia. 'I tell you, it was as if he had already gone.'

'Already left his body?' Jess was struggling to help.

The question released in Hana the lidded grief that had been working loose. Buried regret welled uncontrollably down her cheeks.

'I know. I know. It *is* hard. And while we don't know him any better really than . . .' Jess's voice trailed as if she realized this wouldn't do for consolation. This man was, to them, no more than a passerby, but she could not say it. It would sound too disrespectful. And Hana's displaced grief needed only the warmth of her arms for support.

Two days later, in the thick light of early evening, the wooden house across the street had been transformed for the wake. The screen doors opened onto candle lit offerings. It had become a Buddhist shrine: a pavilion where gold-leafed balls of rice and oranges ran like a large beaded necklace between the waxy heads of chrysanthemum flowers and carved stands of paulownia wood.

A bare-chested figure swung a heavy chain of burning incense over the offerings, building on the close, dusty air and scenting the house. He chanted a mantra that called upon the absent body. The fragrant smell at the open window of her room drew Hana involuntarily. It was a sumptuous farewell for the old man with a birdlike tattoo, and she fought not to think back to the umbrellas and shiny pavements of the East London funeral. She had had only one question to ask him.

The following day, Tako walked into breakfast and Hana found that there was to be yet another ceremony. In a black kimono, he stood constructing a jam sandwich from the buoyancy-aid bread. And while demonstrating his ineptitude at preparing food for himself, he invited them to attend a memorial ceremony to be held at the local temple – a larger temple not so far from here. The invitation was extended to them both.

'I have –' he said suddenly, remembering, and digging into his pocket '– something for you.' He placed a boxed tube of topical insect cream on the table.

Jess and Hana exchanged glances. It was just what they needed. They watched him leave, sandwich in hand and jam glistening on the wide black sleeves he was so unused to wearing.

Later that day Hana filled the mosquito plug with another tab and Jess sat cross-legged on her bed, a language primer balanced on her knees which she ignored in favour of a sheet of paper listing English law firms in the city. 'I don't suppose that we can get out of the service tomorrow?'

'No. Definitely not,' Hana said. They had to go whether they really fitted in or not.

'Another temple . . .' Jess had seen enough of them lately.

'But you knew the old man.'

'Okay, we'll go,' Jess said quickly.

'I couldn't go on my own and you said you would come. You knew him best.

Jess nodded.

'What do you suppose we wear?'

Jess readily offered to lend her something and Hana picked through a mound of black jersey from her rucksack and found a long wrap skirt.

'This okay?'

'Anything you like,' Jess responded, without looking up.

It occurred to Hana that Jess might have no intention of turning up.

'Please come. I don't know but I might find it difficult. If we went together . . .' she trailed off, 'it would be easier.'

In Jess's reply Hana couldn't tell whether she merely sympathized or was offering a concrete assurance.

Chapter 13

On Sunday afternoon they browsed the Meiji Shrine flea market, strewn with old kimonos and bric-a-brac. It looked as though thieves had emptied every drawer in the neighbourhood and laid them across the vacant car lot.

Hana found a waxed paper stencil, similar to one they had at home in London. Had it come from the very same market years ago? On the lower slopes of the hill in Harajuku, they stopped at a booth to have their photos taken, the template distorting their faces with huge dish-shaped eyes. They laughed as a sheet of portrait squares hit the slot. They had become cartoon Anime, like the cute army; girls disguised as kawai manga dolls, marching past in short white socks and and bows.

They set off downhill, arms linked, and as they reached Omotesandō subway Hana caught Jess's arm for attention. Ed, from the plane was coming towards them.

He was coming up from the subway, taking the stairs two at a time till they faced one another.

Hana smiled. 'Hi'

He needed no prompting to remember her as they damned the flow of subway passengers at the entrance.

'I lost your card.' She grimaced in apology for not making contact.

'Don't worry about it. I've been at my desk since I got here.'

He was clearly keen to make her feel easy. After he had said 'Hi' to Jess, he apologized and said he couldn't stop, but as he turned to leave he said, 'I'm going to Tsukiji fish market early in the morning with a friend. Want to come?'

Hana's heart sank. 'I'm sorry, we have go to a memorial service.'

'Great idea,' Jess yelled after him as he left, still apologizing because he was late.

Jess had often complained, Hana reminded her accusatively, that she had 'done' the fish auctions as a tourist attraction, countless times.

Nevertheless Jess flailed after him till she caught him up, and eventually returning, arm raised as if she had secured European peace, with his mobile number.

Hana looked at Jess as if she had appropriated a friend. 'We can't go tomorrow. It's the memorial.'

Jess nodded unconvincingly, and as they dropped into the metro a bank of warm air lifted their thin cotton skirts, as light as the friendship.

Chapter 14

700,000 *tonnes of seafood processed through Tsukiji Market every year*

That morning Jess woke at 4 a.m. to leave for the fish market, creeping quietly from their room as Hana slept.

Hana slept deeply. She dreamt she was among the crowds on a busy market day in Hackney, though the crowds were from Omotesandō. A monk in saffron robes passed, cycling a rickshaw, and, as he retreated, the sleeping passenger, curled in fetal position across the back, was her mother. As she woke her dream world splintered. She looked across at the empty bed beside her with immediate annoyance. Jess, she assumed, had gone alone to Tsukiji fish market. Raving American. It was very unlikely she would get back in time to get to the memorial which was disrespectful to the family and she would be fawning over Ed. As she prepared to go to the service alone, Hana dressed resentfully in the clothes Jess had been so ready to lend her.

Jess's trip to Tsukiji was unedifying. She had assumed Ed was going with friends travelling through, but it turned out he was taken up with colleagues visiting from the Hong Kong branch and she had barely had a chance to speak with them on the guided tour she had taken several times before. She made her excuses, something about a memorial, and left them early. Once she got back to Shimokitazawa Jess headed straight for Ziggy's and found Miho serving a couple of two-toed builders from the bamboo-scaffold site opposite.

'Is it latte, Jess?'

Jess nodded as she helped herself to a kilner jar of cinnamon sticks.

Miho perched on the corner of the table, pulling a stray hair from her sharp fringe.

'You didn't work last night, so you are in early?'

'I went to Tsukiji market.'

Miho's raised her brows; Jess had been so often before and complained she had seen enough.

'I guess you took the new girl?'

'Well, no,' Jess demurred, 'I left her to sleep. She's busy with other stuff.' She drank from the too-hot latte.

'How is the club? Okay?'

Jess nodded, nursing her scalded lip.

'Is she at language school?'

'Too busy looking for the teahouse her mother Naomi worked on.'

Miho started. 'Naomi's teahouse?'

It was as if she also had her own scald to contend with. It was too late for her to disguise the charged reaction and she looked away.

'So you knew Naomi? You met her?'

Saved by a call for more genmai tea from the builders, Miho left quickly, to serve them. Jess grew curious until Miho finally returned to sit down with her.

'So . . .' Jess leaned in confidentially, aware that she had stumbled on something.

'So tell me.'

Miho shook her head.

Her face was grave as if it was a subject she could not bring up now. 'That woman—' She couldn't look her in the eye, as it all came flooding back '—that woman was responsible . . . for . . .'

'For what?'

Miho wrung her hands as the memory took hold and she looked pained.

'You can tell me,' Jess encouraged, coaxing her with a pat to her hand.

Miho hesitated searching the wall shelves, as if struggling to line up her thoughts. 'She was responsible for the . . .' She held her breath until, barely audible, in a whisper she exhaled, '. . . the death of a good friend.'

'You can't mean that? Is this true?'

'I don't want to talk about it, Jess.' Her voice hardened. 'Not to you, not to your English friend.'

Jess was silenced. She sat back as the unexpected blast from Miho continued – Miho who was usually so mild, whose age had taken the edge off life's disappointments: 'And you are not to encourage her in this, and you are not to tell her.'

Jess was shocked.

Miho's animated breathing counted the beats of the silence between them. 'It is for the best,' she said, more kindly. 'Trust me. The truth would hurt.' She was calmer now. 'So you won't tell?'

Jess searched the line of a knot in the pine table, finally nodding her head and pursing her lips.

'I'm closing early. I have to go.' Miho got up. 'Aren't you coming to the memorial?'

Jess pushed on the heavy handle of the glass door. 'I may not get there,' she said, and chose not to mention she might see Hana there.

Chapter 15

Tako had given Hana the directions for the temple where the memorial service was to be held. He had not, thankfully, offered to take them. She knew that waiting for Jess to return was pointless and she left the homestay in good time to take a short train ride, planning to walk beyond the residential area before it started.

By the time she found the site on a wooded hill, the black jersey wrap skirt she had borrowed from Jess was clinging to her legs. The air had changed. In silence the grey, tiled rooves of the temple swept up towards birds of prey circling in deep thermals of blue. Under mottled pine shade she walked towards the red torii gate, and it felt as if, since leaving the homestay, she had travelled to another country, in the tranquility of the gardens.

She would not have chosen this day as a first visit to the temple. It must, she guessed, be where the local teahouse was sited and, though it was an inauspicious day to do so, she would take time to find the small wooden building, after the ceremony. She walked beneath the torii to fall behind the guests.

Beyond the torii gates was a couple, old enough to be walking towards their own goodbyes, They were among the few individuals left from Ukai's life-scape for whom his passing wrote off their indebtedness or those who celebrated his death as marking an end to his potential to intimidate. Some had profited from his insistence on minimum disclosures and creative accounting and some were merely of such advanced years that they had forgotten who he really was but they had been garnered to attend through custom to pay their respects. It was a small turnout for the man who once owned real estate worth the city of Shanghai and Beijing put together.

Hana made her way to the main building, until the heavy scent of incense bore down on the clear air.

The body lay in an elevated cask in front of the altar, and on either side sat Ukai's immediate family, Noru and her son Tako, flanked by a sparse number of elderly guests. Hana found them a rough lot, more than one bore a facial scar. It was not high society and it certainly put Tako into context.

Beyond the body in the depths of the shadowy interior, gold leaf flickered across the offerings like fish scales, the light coming to rest for a moment on the cheeks of the serene Buddha. Out on the airless terrace, Hana chose to kneel in empty space on one of a pair of zabuton cushions, beside an elderly lady with dyed black hair. The powdered woman wore a light, summer, gauze kimono, coloured like raspberry fool.

In the heavy heat all Hana's discomfort focused on her dislike for this misshapen jacket deforming the elderly woman. She watched as a trickle of sweat released a dark line of temporary hair dye from her temple. A triangle of white handkerchief trimmed with lace arrested the falling beads at the pressure of her lined hands. The woman interrupted her gaze and introduced herself,

'Saito-san.'

Hana bowed her head in return.

Hana was thankful she could not see the body of the old man. Trails of curling smoke from incense sticks below the casket, and the waxy blooms of lime green chrysanthemums, began to add to her nausea. As the monk began chanting mantras, Noru and the other guests added their voices.

Saito-san rose uneasily to add another quill of incense to the ashes in the copper bowl and returned to her cushion. Hana became nervous that she too would be expected to take part and that she too should make some offering. The sweat ran behind her knees and, during the quiet hypnotic drone of the priest, she followed the rigorous curve of the mighty dragon across the beam beneath the eaves, like the reputation of the master builder who had raised it, fading in strength with the peeling paint.

Jess still had not appeared and Hana worried that the square void of cushion beside her yawned like an insult. But, as she'd said, who was Ukai to them? They hardly knew him and the ceremony was so unfamiliar it belonged to another world. As the monk rang the bell it sounded like a human voice. A feeling akin to heat exhaustion took hold and she forgot how she found herself sitting in the small gathering amid the haze of stifled and conflicting emotions around her. After more prayers had been said the mourners began to rise individually, like random seeds on the air, as the incense was left to drift over and purify the body.

A man's shoes, black, pointed and highly polished, passed closely, as she knelt. Iwata paced over to speak with the priest, who addressed him,

'Iwata-san.'

Iwata-san bowed 'Kare wa konakatta?'

'Arimasen,' the priest replied.

Hana listened to them but couldn't make out much. He's not here?

She understood very little – they had expected another guest? She watched Saito-san get up with difficulty and peck, in two-toed wooden geta, towards the priest and the shiny-shoed man with matching hair oil.

'Kare wa doko ni imasu ka?' she asked.

Hana heard – 'And where is he?'

Saito-san bowed reverentially over her heavy obi.

'Mochizuki wa Arimasen.' Who ? Hana wondered was Mochizuki?

The small party was led to the back of the traditional buildings by the priest who paused and smiled at her.

'Welcome. I am Hakuin, abbot here. '

She might have taken his prolonged look as recognition,

since he hesitated as though he had a great deal more to say. But he was distracted and his eyes left her to follow a tall woman in the clean-cut Shimada jacket in the distance. Was it Miho? Hana couldn't be sure as her silvered bob was hidden behind a veil. She had become a totem for the other guests who greeted and circled her as if they participated in a Japanese folk dance, and so Hana kept her distance.

Joining the trail of wry strangers retiring to the tatami room, she began to feel faint. They were a small, ageing crowd and many, clinging to the past in traditional dress, cooing over the tall, elegant woman. Hana couldn't make out any of their exchange. Who were these strangers to her?

Iwata San acknowledged Saito, in the manner of one well-known to the other but fallen recent strangers.

They all asked after the Mochizuki, as if his absence would fill a vacuum.

A tentative woman in black approached Miho, her veil adding another layer of separation between them. Her caution was well chosen, as her reception remained cold and barely acknowledged. It was easy to read their lack of warmth for each another and the strange absence of connection among any of them.

She thought for a moment that the woman she took to be Miho had seen her. Falling in with the milling group, drifting with as much purpose as the eddying incense, she would eventually reach her beside the door. But the woman appeared to be skirting the line to find an alternative entrance.

Wordlessly ushered in by Tako, the guests filed inside, laying crisp white envelopes, tied with elaborate black knots, on a dish in the hall; money shrouded in elegance. With nothing to give, Hana clutched her wrist and bowed gently when it fell to her, excusing her own breach of etiquette. As the waves of nausea overcame her, she left the assembly to stand under the trees in the lifeless air.

The teahouse might just lie beside cool waters further into the grounds, and in the wilting heat she decided she should leave the strangers and try to find it.

Just as she was going, Noru approached her, asking if she would come to eat with them.

She felt obliged to follow and there was the consolation that she might find Miho to talk to, but when she joined the mourners the woman in the veil had gone.

Chapter 16

'I am so sorry,' Jess exclaimed, blowing into their room at the end of the day. 'They kept me late for another class. You okay?'

'You went to Tsukiji market?'

Jess raised a flat hand for her to wait, for her to stop right there. It looked as though it was a rehearsed denial.

The hand pushed further as Jess read her skepticism.

'You didn't go?' Hana jumped to the conclusion she preferred.

'I . . .' Jess lingered. Nobody could easily challenge a silence.

Hana toyed with her hair, weaving the braids of a plait, waiting. She was sick of listening to silent replies. She should be told. But Jess had only to walk the length of their short room for her resolve to challenge her to dissolve. But a niggling disappointment that Jess could possibly be unreliable left her feeling insecure. She was strong, she was creative, and she was forgiving. Amaterasu. 'Are you telling the truth, Jess?' It was so little to ask.

Jess turned emphatically and looked at her wide-eyed and innocent.

Hana was as ready to swallow this as a pill. She bound the plait and said they missed her at the memorial.

Jess vehemently kicked aside an obstruction on the floor and mumbled about school as if she were offended to have been challenged.

Why was it, Hana wondered, with a sense of injustice, that Jess singled out her walking boots for attack? 'I won't ask why you couldn't get them to assign someone else to class today and come with me.'

She left it open for Jess to convince her that she had had no choice in the matter and the effort she made to persuade her was payment enough. Hana did, however, have difficulty in imagining that Jess lacked the ability to coerce them into a timetable change for a memorial service.

In the small room, the clutter, lately an object for her own complaints, made the space smaller still.

'I don't know why they asked us to the ceremony,' Jess said finally 'Still, it's not everyday you go to a reincarnation. How was it? '

'Very complicated and involves forceps.'

'Forceps?'

'For the rebirth.'

'I didn't know.' Jess shifted uncomfortably.

'And rubber gloves.'

Jess finally got it and laughed hard and loud. When the laughter trailed off, Hana opened up.

'I had the feeling—' She paused, not sure if she should broach it. 'I had the feeling that the priest recognized me.'

Jess snorted. 'You think he knew your mother? Some random Englishwoman from decades back?' Hana closed the subject down, though she was on the back foot that afternoon.

She regretted mentioning it.

'It can't be that easy,' Jess continued. 'How old was this priest?'

'He was old,' Hana replied.

'How old? I know you want to believe it but the chances of him knowing her are miniscule.'

Hana was hurt. It was, of course, unlikely and she dismissed the idea. She slumped resignedly and stuffed the neon laces inside her boots.

Jess felt obliged to be more encouraging. She was reluctant to raise the other option but she went ahead anyway.

'Or maybe you look like him?'

Hana knit her brows.

'I mean your own father.' Jess's tone was softer now. 'How did he die, if you don't mind me asking?'

Hana had never known a father and so could not mind.

'I never said he died.'

Chapter 17

'Un bel di, vedremo'
—Puccini, Madama Butterfly

Imperial Palace Hotel, Tokyo, 1989

Naomi was getting used to the heavy thread count of the cotton sheets on her bare skin. Changed daily, they barely bore a trace of his heavy sleep. At first, the starched arrival of room service, bringing so many scratched and buffeted chaffing dishes, had delighted them, though it had never been possible to eat it all. They had tired of the cloying delights of the international hotel and Josh now preferred to eat breakfast elsewhere, partly because he wanted the company bill to bear scrutiny, and because they had lived in the hotel for so much longer than expected.

Naomi was charged with finding a rental apartment and so far they had failed to agree on anything suitable. This morning they were again going to meet the agent who would find their rental in the city. Though Tokyo housed thirty eight million people there should be a good deal of choice out there for their budget; it was just that she didn't speak the language and she had no idea where the signs might direct her.

Her morning start had become increasingly languid when the rest of her day stretched to a distant vanishing point.

Today, as he slipped the last limb into his blue suit, Josh warned, 'It'll be busy so do leave early.'

And, like a skimming stone, he threw the glossy city plan

entitled 'The Detailed Map of Tokyo for Business Man and Tourist' onto the bed beside her.

'I am neither.' She reached to catch it and was genuinely daunted by the question of what lay between the two but Josh had no time for her existential meanderings this morning and was keen she first found them a place to live.

'I'll meet you there.' He dropped a kiss on the crown of her head and left her alone with her question. He was generally more comfortable with imperatives and they would talk over breakfast.

In the three weeks since their arrival she recognized her rootless existence had begun to strain the relationship that she had cherished so much as to drop everything and follow him to nurture it. The heavy closure of the fire-retardant door reduced her to the privileged isolation of an inmate of a luxury Wandsworth prison. And this brought back thoughts of her home in Clapham. Annoyed at her own distortion of the privileges she enjoyed, it brought her once again to ask why she had made the rash decision to leave her course at the Architect's Institute in London and follow him to Tokyo.

If she did not leave the room soon she would suffocate. She threw the map aside and leapt out of bed. She left the lobby in summer whites, prompting the hotel staff to whisper about the ghost on the 47th floor who kept time like no other guest among the business clients in the hotel.

At Shibuya Station she was caught in the spring tide of dark heads, where a crowd the size of a billing at the Hammersmith Palais negotiated six or more optional exits. She was carried across the eddying tide of people to a pillar where the current divided as if at the foot of a bridge spanning a river in spate. She retrieved the city plan wedged in her bag; Josh would be waiting for her. A master in origami had ingeniously folded the map and once opened it clung unhelpfully to her body as a set of streamers escaped on a strong downdraft. She gave up trying to scan the oscillating paper as it flapped aggressively at her face and tore as she tried to restrain it. He had given her a couple of landmarks to head for; first was the Hachikō Statue on the south-west side of the station. Below her a grid of crossings led like an Escher print to every point on the compass in a Kafkaesque joke. From one of the branches she should take the hill up to where they were to meet. She checked her watch and it was nearing 9.30 a.m. She was lost for a lead and he would be exasperated again. She closed her eyes.

Though now used to the city's disregard for personal space, she became aware of an individual standing beside her.

'You lost? Want some help?'

The girl was about her age, unusually tall and her hair was styled in a short bob. Naomi began folding the map, very roughly.

'I'm trying to find the Hachikō exit.'

Her short, close-fitting cotton dress was covered in old roses. And she led her towards the exit.

'You know about Hachikō?'

All it took was a shake of the head and she started on a story as if she were a complementary city guide.

'Every day an old professor left his dog outside the station for the day when he commuted.'

Her English was good. She probably made a habit of picking up lost souls for language practice. A dog story. Naomi looked at her watch.

The girl upped her pace and continued her explanation.

'He was old and—' They scuttled down a flight of stairs on a second wave of commuters '—one time he didn't return and the dog waited for his master for days.'

They emerged from the station at street level, to an obscured sun. Beneath animated screen-clad buildings the massing crowds were cowed in the electronic din of commercialism. Where would Josh be waiting? It was the most kinetic urban space she had ever seen and she drew her attention back to the girl, glad for a moment to have a guide.

Her voice rose against the half-truths of advertisement jingles. 'The professor had suffered a seizure and he died and never returned.'

They came to a halt in front of a statue of a dog.

'Here is Hachikō. This is your Hachiko exit.'

Naomi stopped out of politeness but had an eye on the next waymark as a pedestrian claxon sounded on the massive crossing. She hoped to make the lights but she could see the crowd thinning and the last stragglers beginning to run to beat the change. She would miss it anyway.

'The emperor heard about this act of loyalty so admired in the Japanese character and he agreed to this statue.'

The girl followed her eyes towards the sea of people.

'Where do you go from here?' The girl doll tugged at the line of her sharp fringe.

The lights changed. Naomi's mounting anxiety dissipated as she surrendered to being very late.

'It's near PARCO, Udagawacho,' she said, reading the biro on the back of her hand.

'I know the store. I'll go that way with you.

She might be difficult to shake off, Naomi thought.

'Is it out of your way?'

'I guess not.'

Waiting for the sea of people to move from the edge of the road. Languid little questions followed as they made their way through the crowd.

'Yes, almost a month. An amazing city. '

The Japanese girl was time-easy and very laid back. It was late; it would rile him but there was little she could do about it. Her responses were short.

'An architect but not qualified. And you?'

'PR. My friend is an architect. You should meet him.'

She might be the type who knew everyone. Over the sea of heads a digitized figure cartwheeled across the face of five buildings as the accumulation of bodies waiting to cross deepened.

The girl beside her bridged the alien space between her and the crowd, somehow emphasizing it. The otherness of the place was daunting. Had she really committed to living here? They crossed to walk up the hill together. At the Seibu Store a six-foot seed pod filled a window and shook like a silent maraca; the first sign, in the urban landscape, that was organic. She wished the seed would grow to a pantomime vine and she could climb it and escape.

'PARCO,' the girl announced.

'Thanks.' Naomi hoped it wouldn't be too difficult to shake free of her politely.

'I'll leave you here.' The girl began backing off easily, waving as she left.

'Thanks. Thanks so much,' Naomi yelled back.

And then, on a second thought, the girl turned again, taking a paper from her clutch.

'I'm Miho. Give me a call sometime.'

Chapter 18

A B-52 bomber wingspan formed the lintel entrance to the café. A self-conscious witticism from an international designer. Josh was sitting beside a half-drunk cup of coffee at a table just inside and she met him with an emollient kiss. With a copy of the *Economist* to hand and his leg crossed high, he had the distant ease of man of privilege. He finally smiled.

'Half my waking life waiting for you, then a little more time waiting for the apology.'

'I am sorry,' she said, throwing the map on the table and sitting down.

He cut her no slack at all.

'I nearly drowned in the crowd.'

He glanced approvingly at the close-fitting knee length skirt she had chosen. She had good legs.

'You're a good swimmer, Naomi.'

She thought of the girl in the cotton dress, cum lifeguard.

'Nice choice.' She surveyed the apocalyptic interior of the café, ready to acknowledge that there were some good reasons for coming to Japan; if only to see at first-hand the architectural experiments.

'You want to order coffee? You're too late for a bite.'

Josh proceeded to pick up the map and painstakingly refold it along the original lines, the fissures in his complexion lost in his flexing jaw.

'You been having a picnic with this?'

Often he left the hotel room early to get to the office because he was keen and he finished his working day late as London woke and Sydney was a sparkling hour ahead. Some days he tried to cover it all. Because she hadn't yet found them an apartment he had been obliged to take control.

'The apartment we saw yesterday was great and I just don't get why you don't like it. Great views, central . . .'

'It was just so soulless. We could be anywhere in the world.'

'With Tokyo Tower on the skyline?'

'It's a warren. A ghetto exclusively for Westerners. We should live like locals while we are here.'

'Is international so bad? With a gym and pool, and when else do we get to live in a condominium?'

Josh looked out over the expansive pavement. A smell of sweet soy baking drifted on the air. He had persuaded her to uproot and he supposed he should give her a say in where they lived.

The sun was still struggling to break through the heat haze and, just as she ordered ice tea, the diminutive figure of Mr Kami, the rental agent, left his motorbike and came towards them, swinging his helmet from its retro leather strap.

He laid it on the table wearily as he surveyed them. Slight as a jockey, his simian face ridiculously wizened.

Naomi shook his hand, entranced as he rolled a matchstick between his yellowing teeth.

'I show you a Japanese traditional style without fear or favour,' he said proudly, retrieving his helmet. The girl was certainly opinionated and had wrong-footed him yesterday over the luxury apartment he had felt sure he would secure for them. They were so young yet sky-high real estate values that made his eyes water were within their budget because a company allowance would cover it. Quite why she carried so much weight in the decision when the guy had liked it was a conundrum. His own choice was limited to the pigeon coop he called home.

Josh gave Naomi a knowing look. The man was a walking set of idioms and 'without fear or favour' was his catchphrase.

'Excellent,' she emphasized as Josh recovered his *Economist*.

Mr Kami opened his arms expansively and swung them, helmet and all, in the direction he intended to take them. He would bring them to their senses. They, or more precisely she, had asked for a property with character. Well, he would show them a rental with character. Given his wealth of experience, this was just one step in a well-worn process. The property he had in mind was one they would be unable to settle on but fitted her revised brief and he knew it would send them straight back to the Tower of Babel and the cloying luxury that people mistook for privilege in Hiroo. The detour this morning would ultimately save him more effort in the end. That said, she was wasting everyone's time, including her own. What she was looking for did not exist. She was a romantic, impractical girl, looking for a Japan lost some time back with the shogunate.

The house was indeed traditional. Just a short walk from the prime real estate of Shibuya, set in gardens of a quarter of an acre that some family feud or canny speculator playing the long game had retained. She hung back with Josh as Mr Kami spoke with the occupant in high whispers of disagreement.

Josh lost patience. 'What are we doing here? I should be at work.'

She wasn't going to let him have it both ways. 'Why *are* you here? I could go round on my own. You didn't have to come.'

Josh looked at her from the full height of his education.

'Look, my Bohemian princess, we could end up with a very shaky decision if left up to you. This place looks condemned.'

'You would have me live in a box on the forty-third floor? Did I leave London for the penal colony of apartments in Hiroo Garden Hills?

'Correction: it wasn't a box, it was bigger than, this wooden . . . this . . .' he paused, attempting to retain some tact '. . . this garden shack.'

She had to agree it looked as though it would be over-ventilated in the winter and the towering real estate around it left it in permanent shade.

As Mr Kami beckoned them from the porch, she saw him watching mischievously for her response. She would uphold a pretense with him.

'What a contrast.' She smiled benignly.

'We Japanese are about contrasts,' he said sagely, scratching his bald head.

It was open-plan, dingy and ill-lit. In the entrance hall stood an oxblood chest with an intricate black, metal phoenix over the lock. Unable to resist, she ran a finger along the top. A line in the dust came to a halt at the photograph of an elderly couple beside an incense stick, alight and trailing coils of spent ash on a strip of brocade. The face of the elderly woman in a kimono carried a demure smile as if she too were in on a joke. A figure passed across a curtained doorway ahead of them.

'Very nice.' Naomi said vaguely, searching Josh for what would be a charged reaction but finding he would not return her glance. His arms were folded across his blue summer suit to contain his patience.

'And which room is that?' she asked, pointing in the direction of a figure passing in the distance.

'That is the other half of house, belonging to the owners,' Kami announced.

'So a mere curtain divides the two dwellings?' she asked incredulously.

'There is a possibility to make an adaptation,' he said almost genuinely.

She couldn't help herself but burst out laughing. A large generous English laugh that was full and deep had the effect of throwing her head back and making her pale hair resonate with the sound. She finally came to realize that she was laughing alone and had angered the two men for different reasons. That she was the object of their astonished attention was for a moment a greater cause for amusement. She held her slim arms and pursed her lips in an effort to rein in the uncontained mirth.

'I don't . . . I don't think I should take any more of your time here.'

Mr Kami was surprised that such strength could come from her slim figure. He looked nervously over the shoulder of his check jacket. The landlord had undoubtedly heard the outburst.

How could she possibly live here and how could she remain marooned in the hotel?

'I have a call to make and must get back.' Josh took her by the elbow across the garden as if carefully leading an unexploded device that might go off at any time.

'We have just been shown the ex-granny annex,' she said, by way of excuse, and then turned towards the agent as he returned to join them.

'How quaint. When was the house built, Mr Kami?'

'I believe,' he said, as threaded the leather strap of his helmet between his hands, 'not long before the nineteen sixties. Nineteen twenty-three was the last big earthquake and the Great Fires, and not much survived that levelling. We are due an earthquake every fifty years.' He tapped her hand in a kind of 'nota bene' consideration. Yes, she could work it out.

'Today, in eighty-nine, we are a full sixteen years overdue a large-scale tectonic eruption, according to our best Japanese estimates.' He seemed pleased to be imparting such usefully intimidating information.

The basis of this calculation lay with authorities ranging from folkloric to seismic analysts. His use of the first-person plural for a catch-all of one hundred and twenty million people had began to grate.

'So, you like Hiroo Garden hills better now?' He smiled victoriously.

'I thought you had one more property to show us?' she parried, as Josh's perfunctory farewell kiss landed on her cheek from nowhere, in the way that his decisions often did. He could see she was well able to manage Mr Kami on her own.

'I am going to have to go, Mr Kami. Naomi can take a look

and then we can discuss whether she thinks it is a contender?' Josh rattled the sabre that was his rolled-up *Economist* for emphasis. He nodded towards her. 'See you later.'

As he left, almost as an afterthought, he called back his thanks in the agent's direction.

Naomi turned to give Mr Kami her full radiant attention.

'I hope the next property might be some way between the two styles? Is it somewhere between the two?' She fanned herself with the city plan imperiously.

Mr Kami looked at her from under his barber-trimmed brows. 'You are the student of architecture, Miss Naomi. You will tell me how is the style.' He looked at her less-than-practical sandals and contemplated whether he should make them walk to the next viewing. She was so young, but with the controlling vote over such a large budget, he dismissed the thought and hailed a taxi.

That night, she wore her loose Indian cotton trousers; Josh took her arm as they walked as they often did under the railway arches in Ginza. They followed a noisy line of ten-seater restaurants as if the street itself were a menu card; shelves of moulded plastic meals; levitating chopsticks above glutinous dishes of cascading noodles, tonkatsu and ebi rice; the air warm from the charcoal braziers and the heat of the summer city. And she did not miss the electric blue of home skies at dusk.

'I think you'll like it.'

'Well, after the shack you led us to this afternoon, I am going to have to take a look at it myself.' He would never leave her to make a decision.

'You don't have time to see it,' Naomi protested. She wished he would trust her judgment.

'The presentations to the Aussies finish at the end of the week. And after the G7 summit it'll go quiet.'

'You'll have to trust me, because it'll have gone by then.'

'What?'

And his complaint was lost as she drew him inside a ramen bar, sure that he would be easier to persuade once he had food inside him. They ate a simple dinner of yakitori and soba broth. But even so she could not get him to commit to the property.

Last thing that night, back in the chill of the air-conditioned room, clutching starched fresh sheets to her chin, she watched as he strode in his boxers to open the chilled drinks fridge.

'Water?'

The head of an iceberg lettuce rolled out over his bare foot across the floor.

'What is this?' he moaned. The water was barely accessible.

She had stuffed a picnic lunch above the cans of Asahi beer and miniature whiskies and between the fresh tomatoes she had crammed wrapped slices of ham and a cucumber.

'I can't afford to eat out every meal and, besides, what happened to home cooking? Sometimes for lunch . . . I . . . look – we have to find a house soon, Josh.'

Josh had overlooked the fact that she might feel a need for money when he had so much. But in his defense he felt all she had to do was to ask him.

The cold, blue light of the mini fridge did not illuminate his response.

He finally answered as his head hit the pillow.

'Okay, the architect gets to make the decision on the house. Go and see it again tomorrow and you decide.'

Chapter 19

Shimokitazawa, 2012

As she poured a mixer into the second Whisky Mac, the diamante on Hana's short evening dress caught the bar spotlight like a cheap promise. She could carry as many drinks on the small, silvered tray as a Chinese acrobat now. While watching the effervescence Hana mentally measured her progress since leaving London: she had charted the temples in six districts of Tokyo and had to acknowledge what she could only describe as a personal insolvency. Living in Japan, with all its eccentricities, seemed an occupation in itself and she felt she was trapped sleeping or spending hours in the persistent half-light of the basement club.

The blinking neon arrow to the basement attracted mostly benign regulars. They were now on smiling terms with Hajime, who needed no encouragement to show off his broken tooth. The undernourished doorman had a prominent kanji character tattooed on his chin and she wondered what communication he had chosen to make ever so visible. He was paid to filter newcomers and the clients she had seen were fine. It was a relief that Tako had never once appeared. The job was just as it had been advertised: easy job; easy money.

Two months before she arrived, a hostess was abducted north of the city but she had stopped worrying that the same fate would befall every bar worker in Japan. She had Jess, and, besides, Wednesday night – their night off, when the transvestite danced – was as lively as it got.

Tom had rung, last night, and said he had issues with her

working in a hostess bar. It was hard enough that eight hours behind, they didn't speak often enough, but to have a disagreement too. His criticism was easier to bear than news that he was seeing a lot of Sadie. He had suggested the lawyer Ed should find some documentation: something with her name, or Naomi's name. . . or his name. But there was nothing positive in the Helvetica Neue font that returned her text messages. Ed was out of the country. He was tied up.

Jess was over at the other end of the bar, picking her nails with a toothpick with great concentration. Backlit with amber light from the wall of whisky, she looked like someone Hana didn't know. The bottles were tagged with personal labels for individual clients – Tanaka, Saito, Nakamura, Watanabe – warding off the impersonal among so many people. Jess slipped off her chair, pulling at her Lycra dress, to come and sit beside her.

'Day off tomorrow. We'll get a bento picnic from the 7-Eleven and take it to temple six hundred and fifty three?' Jess' enthusiasm was flagging.

Emiko, dressed as usual as a geisha hostess in her red kimono, brought them a tray of newly washed tumblers.

'Polish those smiles.' Her tone was pleasant.

The air was smoke-filled as Hana took up the lint cloth, behind her an enlarged print of an old woodblock, 'The Diver': an erotic dream of a geisha, lying in folds of generous kimono silk coupled with a giant octopus. Every tentacle, as she carried its weight, searched out an orifice. Emiko had explained that the kanji hieroglyphics floating like bubbles over the geisha, were moans of pleasure.

Emiko followed her disapproving gaze.

'It's okay, the artist got a month's jail sentence for his efforts.'

Emiko motioned Jess to move causing her pretty hair ornaments to backchat in her heavily sprayed hair.

Aiming her toothpick at the ashtray Jess intended to offend.

'Club rules. You girls can't sit together.' Emiko shuffled off in her two-toed socks and wedged geta.

Hana guessed the need for quiet respect among the shaky reality of lucky, nodding cats, of piped birdsong, of posters of tiger-maned genii gulping energy drinks, or large-eyed manga characters endorsing air-con systems. She had to invest in them herself and yet the references were still cold. She could not see how Naomi could possibly have belonged here.

'Smile and play beautiful,' Emiko called from the kitchenette, reminding them again to move apart.

'We are starting to look like corpses,' Jess complained of their nocturnal hours.

Her lips glossed a vampire-red made Hana giggle.

Emiko's silken arm interrupted them to retrieve an ashtray from between them, her departure stiff, the ornamental cherry blossom in her hair shook indignantly. Hana gently pushed Jess until she slipped off her stool obediently.

'I'm done here,' Jess whispered vehemently out of the blue.

New clients arrived and the room became ionized with expectancy. Yoshi was a regular and his party tonight was Australian.

As Emiko had taught her to, Hana called out his regular beer order before Yoshi reached her: 'Asahi, Sapporo, Sapporo.' The longer the memory, the larger the tip. Was this the kind of man who might have known her father? The missing man who hadn't even registered his name on her birth certificate? She had begun to toy with an identikit for him, which she revised and reconstructed at whim: the cosmopolitan business man lost to tragedy; the composer of international standing; the trading-company shogun.

Jess was to host another group of Australians from a shipping company as Hana wiped the condensation off the cold drinks. Deferentially she offered each man a glass as if it were jewel-encrusted. It was uncomfortable for her as she somehow found it sexually charged. Jess fell on the English speakers, as if she was dehydrated and they could quench her thirst.

The karaoke wailed.

Hana wanted to know what Hajime, the doorman, had stamped on his chin. At first Emiko left her to guess.

'Mum. He is not so rough as he looks.' She laughed.

She had to serve shabu-shabu stew, and as she stepped up to the tatami matting, across the smoke-filled room, waving from the exit, about to leave with one of the Australians, she spotted Jess,. Hana knelt to pour the hot sake. Why had she ignored their pact not to go off alone? It was about 2 a.m. and she hadn't finished her shift. She couldn't follow her.

She watched Emiko pick her way through raw scallions and carrots cut as blossom, to adjust the flame. In her concentration Emiko's red-pressed lips might have been made of plastic. She ceremoniously brought a lacquer bowl to Hana's ear, pausing for her to appreciate a skittering noise, eliciting Hana's soft revulsion. This had become a ritual performance and, as the crustacean slipped into the boiling stock, Hana's foreigner scruples made it a regular party trick.

Emiko confirmed that Jess had indeed left the club. Would her anger or concern win?

Emiko's patience with Jess had finally run out.

'Don't worry.' Her ornaments trembled in frustration 'She does this.'

Hana left, emerging from the basement with her eyes closed against the sharp morning light.

When she opened them she saw a lone policeman, on the first shift at the Koban, stretching his arms. In the silence of the early morning, an apprentice monk stood across the road, his Buddhist habit and white leggings shaded under a straw-brimmed hat. He wouldn't see many people at this hour. so the alms bowl he cradled seemed useless. The futility of it all. All she could do was wait at the homestay for Jess. As she left, club music drifted up from the depths, reminding her of home.

No one, she realized, could accompany her on this journey if she never made a move herself.

But where was Jess?

Chapter 20

Hana headed towards the homestay, passing over the level crossing and down the deserted main street laced with its waste of utility wires. Stray branches of plastic cherry blossom punctuated the street at intervals, and were greying with dust. A pink promise stuck in the wrong season.

In the empty twin room she was surprised that she could drift towards sleep.

She woke involuntarily a couple of hours later and Jess still had not returned. Emiko, she reassured herself, had said this was typical.

Ignoring the cheap club dress, she grabbed her smock and ran to Miho's hoping to find her.

Ziggy's was full with post-school-run mothers. No Jess.

She joined a table just finishing their coffees.

Miho greeted her with her customary politeness while she cleared lipsticked cups and quietly drew the crumbs away from Hana's side of the table. It was an act of servitude: the wrong moment to interrupt. Miho left to raise the mothers' bill.

'Itterasshai.' Miho followed the women to the door lingering after they had gone.

Hana had to stop her as she passed.

'Have you seen Jess?'

Miho seemed to read her face, as if she were searching to see what she understood. It was unnerving and she waited too long for a response.

'Yes.' Miho folded her arms and Hana's tension release was instant and prompted her further. 'Today, no.'

Hana's concern racked back up a notch. 'She left the club with some Australians. In working hours.'

'Jess missing again?' Miho's response was unexpectedly flat. So this happens with Jess.

Hana was still concerned for her missing friend and Miho reassured her.'She does this,' Miho told her. Emiko would only tolerate this behaviour from a *gaijin*, and would never let non-foreigners get away with it. 'More than once she has been in trouble on this. She'll be walking in here before lunch, is my guess.' Miho shoved her hands conclusively in the wide apron pocket that fell below her thickened waist. Perhaps Miho had been as careless herself once. It didn't seem to trouble her. She had once told Jess that at her age it took time to work out which kite, among a bright sky of flying ribbon tails, to follow; it took time to grow in consideration and master the strings.

'So, what is it to be?' Miho said peremptorily.

Hana found that today Miho was rather impatient to serve other people. Her obvious lack of concern was some comfort, however, and Hana relaxed and ordered a green tea.

'*Sencha*.' Miho repeated, as if to no one in particular, as if thinking out loud to better tether her thoughts.

When Miho returned with her tea, Hana still felt like she was delaying her from another purpose. She would catch her quickly.

'I wanted to ask . . .' Hana began.

Miho turned back towards her slowly as if she were about to ask her something she could not countenance.

'I came to Shimokitazawa because my mother lived here.'

Miho's faced dropped to what might have been mistaken as an unfriendly jowl.

Hana persisted.

'If I wanted . . .'

Whatever it was she wanted to raise, Miho didn't want the half of it, her reticence to hear her out was palpable. Hana stopped short of giving more detail.

'If I was looking . . . to find the records of someone living here . . .' Hana took it slowly.

Miho waited, caught in the thin skein of Hana's need.

'. . . where would you start?' My mother lived in Shimo in the late eighties?'

Hana thought Miho looked wounded; it might be concern.

'That's a long time ago. If you are looking for family you should go to the Municipal Record Offices. I have a relative there. I'll give you his name.' And she hurried off, calling '*chotto matte*' to an unidentified customer at the back of the café, but glancing back at Hana as if in afterthought she said, 'You want me to give you an address? It's in Shinjuku ku.'

Hana did not want to delay her further.

'I'll find it. Thanks. And who should I ask for?'

Miho looked as though she were plucking a name from a long roster of relatives who worked at the Municipal offices. 'Tachi. Ask for Tachi.'

Hana drank a little tea and bit into the shaped biscuit. It was starched and tasteless. She would go now, rather than wait for Jess. And it felt at that moment as though, for the first time, she had a map. A map home.

Chapter 21

Chinese zodiac: Year of the Dragon; heavenly branch of the astrological element water

Hana was at the bottom of a broad flight of steps in Shinjuku. She remembered a childhood afternoon one autumn, out roller-blading with friends in Victoria Park, where at the scrolled iron gates, out of breath, she had whispered in the guise of sharing a secret with them that her father had died before she was born.

The arms of sympathy and the assurances of the safety of her secret had bonded them. The confessional had been worth the lie as it had won her a lasting set of loyalties. They had sped round the park afterwards and this time in the warm intimacy of linked hands they formed a strong chain against anyone coming close, dividing and joining again as the obstacles approached. Though secure in her friendships, what she could never tell them was the truth: that she had no idea how it was that she had come about. Only since Naomi had passed away and the opportunity was lost had she felt the need to ask about the man Naomi had hidden . . . stolen . . . lost. And if Hana felt lost then Naomi was responsible. How could it have been so difficult to tell her story?

Today it would change. She paused at the top of the stairs, imagining that, when she walked back out of the building, she might discover something. She carried her passport with her in the hope that behind the grey, concrete façade, data running decades back had been kept with a precision for which the Japanese have always had a reputation.

In her search for the man who had chosen to remain a stranger, she was reticent. This was balanced with the chance of disturbing some terrible secret that should remain unspoken. Why her existence was of so little value to him could not pain her any more than his neglect had already done.

The empty pavement suggested a city backwater and on the whole it didn't look too promising. She rallied. All she would need to do was give her name, date of birth and as easily as opening the drawer on a metal filing cabinet, she would discover who she was. They may hold a photograph.

But this man had never made any effort to get in contact and this, along with her mother's fierce resistance in the past to questions, worked like a conspiracy on her determination to go ahead, unzipping her so that she began to empty from the inside. To be unwanted and of little worth was a state that Naomi had done so well to counterbalance.

A wheelie bucket lay in her path and a janitor passed a ragged mop head in an arc of water across the shiny grey floor. It reminded her of the arched brush strokes of Ukai's calligraphy. Jess had told her that this was a tradition and Ukai had been writing his own farewell.

An aberrant wheel squeaked as she skirted the attendant, heading for the windowless lobby, deserted but for two men, in identical uniforms, who staffed the desks behind the ill-lit reception. The fish tank on the counter emitted a faint singed smell where a rough section of cardboard was in contact with a bulb and, as she waited, four pale fish tracked back and forth across the tank. A man in a grey shirt approached. In Japanese she stumbled to make herself understood, falling quickly back on her English though they spoke none. As he consulted the other man his ID badge caught precariously on a thread, she could barely tell the two individuals apart .

'Registration . . .? He looked blankly at her. 'Koseki . . .?' Hana thought this meant 'family registration' but he understood her no better than his colleague.

'Tachi?' she persisted. 'Can I speak to Tachi?' This was met with no recognition whatsoever. Taking her British passport from her bag she opened it at her name: Hana Ardent; place of birth, Tokyo.

Both clerks retreated to an empty desk to consult a small book. Shoulder-to-shoulder, as they leaved through the pages, a lively conversation ensued.

Hana, meanwhile, tapped at the fish tank trying without success to startle the fish off course. A word emerged from their drifting conversation that she did recognize. 'Korean'. She knew she was not Korean. Naomi, in the slim volume of collected facts that she paid out over time, left her certain that she was half Japanese.

As she leaned on the desk for support,the second clerk returned and spoke slowly, 'Here we are for Japanese Nationals. Try British embassy.'

He returned the little red passport.

It was uncomfortable to be going backwards and it was uncomfortable to find she was nobody in this country. And it was not singed pride or frustration that made her eyes start to well.

Chapter 22

A bare leg emerged from Naomi's loose cotton kimono and hung over the arm of the black chair she had sourced from a subterranean store in Shinjuku. Josh would be due back from work soon. For many days she had spent her enthusiasm on furnishing the house they had finally rented. Josh had relented and let her choose the one in Shimokitazawa. Her stumbling Japanese had improved as she had trawled for items for the house and she had picked up some fluency, but she found visual structure easier than the conceptual bricks of language.

She had found them a two-storied house rather than an apartment, and, while disappointing from the exterior, the space was bright and open. Josh complained that they could have lived in a stylish apartment but he had settled in quickly enough. The house had hidden surprises like a vast American top-loader washing machine. It troubled her that when Josh came home he had raised billions of paper yen at a signature, while she had come to value a domestic machine.

French windows lead out onto a slip of a terrace with views out over persimmon trees onto a strip of land owned by the TEPCO corporation; attractive if you could edit out the rather ominous rusting sign stuck in the centre of the vacant plot. It was their first house together and therein lay much of its charm. She had framed woodblock prints from an Oriental bazaar on Aoyama Dori, and sheets of handmade washi paper patterned the walls. She and Josh would go to the Meiji Shrine flea markets on Sundays, where she had fallen with delight on old fabric stencils, and she had found bands of old obi silk, which she had thrown over as window dressings above the blinds. But her interest in these things had stalled and that afternoon, when she had taken out her sketchpad to draw the old persimmon tree in the TEPCO garden, the sight of the English brand of Windsor and Newton paints had made her cry. She couldn't say what prompted it but after about twenty minutes into the sketch she felt better.

Beside her on the floor lay the day's copy of *The Japan Times*, folded open at the classified ads. The headline articles ranged from a dry roll call of recent Japanese finance ministers between Takeshita and Murayama to bathetic editorials on how best to clean a frying pan. She had thrown the paper aside in exasperation. The employment section was unusually small today and beneath advertisements for real estate were a few classified ads for English teachers and bar hostesses. An insurance company sought applicants 'with some knowledge of English. Typing skills essential.' She could rule out most of the column inches devoted to bilingual candidates as she had established early on that any architectural practices she could make contact with would not take her on as she hadn't completed her training and was not fluent in Japanese. She had begun to feel pinioned.

She heard the heavy, wooden, front door signalling Josh's return. For a few days now she had begun to tense when he returned until his enquiries about the job hunt were over. That morning he had left her with a request to find a local drycleaner, and she was in no mood to explain that odyssey either.

When Josh returned he would usually find her contentedly starching some hand-woven indigo textile, which she would tell him, with some conviction, was a work of art and fit for the V&A. And while he might care very little, he did not seem about to dampen her passion. As far as he was concerned, her insatiable appetite for this newly adopted country and its curious ways left her happy. But perhaps she was tiring of her own company.

She watched him walk in and strip himself of the lightweight summer jacket, bringing in the heat and the clammy air. The espadrille caught on her toes swung like a metronome counting her boredom.

'Aha,' she said as she flung her arms wide to greet him without getting up.

He bent to kiss her hello, touching her pale hair, which took on a stronger curl in the humidity

'You look as though you have been sitting here all day?'

She could not tell him she hadn't moved for hours – that she was an alien here and felt secure only in the rickety little house with its American top loader.

'I thought the plan was to produce another glossy publication of photos: *My Month in Tokyo? The Japanese lantern? English across the Tokyo T-shirt Revealed?*'

'I have started sketching today and now you are back I would like to sketch you,' she said, playing the coquette.

'What, now? When I am hungry and will look gaunt and lean and malnourished?'

Her smile was equivocal, more wan than amused.

'You could maybe do something after we've eaten,' he suggested. 'With me reading?'

'The light will have gone. We'll do it another day.'

He left her to go upstairs, eager to change into his own yukata gown. As he switched on the air-con over their bed, he found a postcard she had been writing home on her bedside table. A postcard home. To her mother in Clapham. It began with fulgent news of her last exploration to the shrine at Asakusa but remained unfinished. A half-written postcard. What can have been so distracting? The air-con rattled over the bed with the lungs of a smoker; she would have to get it seen to, he thought.

Once changed he went downstairs, and hung at the door as she prepared dinner.

Very casually, he began, 'You could teach English, perhaps? The pay isn't an issue and the hours are flexible so you could carry on with the arty projects at the same time?'

Her reaction surprised him in its vehemence.

'Teach? Teach English? I can't teach. Do you even know me? I read extremely slowly and can barely spell. What are you thinking of? I would have a class empty of students in under a week and all my spare time would be spent reading up for the next lesson. Not that I would mind the time. What are you thinking of? It would be humiliating.'

'Something else will turn up.'

'Yes. Yes, there are lots of jobs for hostesses in the classifieds. Over your dead body.'

'Well, they're only glorified drinks waitresses paid to talk to clients.'

'You are suggesting I take a job as a hostess? Great career move.'

'No . . . I am just correcting you. And as I say, you don't need the money.'

'Josh, I am useless here. And I should never have come. I am nobody here.'

He turned in exasperation and then came full circle to wrap his arms around her. She found them consolatory but without passion and she felt sure he had begun to find her a burden.

'I need you here with me,' he cajoled. 'And you don't want for anything.'

Money had never intrinsically interested her but she wanted to tell him how uncomfortable she felt that she was in his keep. Silently she worked the wooden spoon around the wok pan. The shiitake mushrooms were soft and brown in chilli-flavoured sesame oil. She tossed colourful vegetables onto a pile of buckwheat noodles and topped them with scented herbs.

'Did you call the Miho girl?' he asked, 'She could be good company.'

'Not yet. Tomorrow. I need to . . .'

He waited expectantly.

'It's July and so I'm going to make strawberry jam.'

Strawberries weren't impossible to source though they cost a fortune and he might think she had set herself an underwhelming task; he would be baffled at her choice in this displacement activity. She knew he sometimes found her skittish but it was something she needed to do.

He inhaled patiently. He might be perplexed, He might find it endearing.

'Is jam-making the English equivalent of Zen?'

And she smiled at his broad understanding and believed she had his sympathies though at times she recognized they survived only on misunderstandings.

Two days ago he had returned claiming he had come for his newspaper to find her dozing under the thin sheet of their kingsize bed, and she knew he had turned back to check on her. While she could view his concern as positive they had both begun pretending to one another.

'You're not pregnant, are you?' he had asked with more distress in his voice, closer in tone to panic than she would have expected. His face was suddenly ugly. She thought not but lately she had found her body so greedy for a sleep that it demanded compound interest and she wondered where would she find energy for a job.

A few days later, Josh had already left that morning when Naomi woke to the sound of an air con that had developed Tourette's. And it was with annoyance that Mr Kami, the rental agent, entered her first waking thoughts before the realization that today she had an interview in Aoyama Dori. It was to be at eleven. And she would have to call Kami to get it fixed before then.

The silence in the kitchen was so unlike home – no music,

no acerbic comment on the latest erosion in the political grit of welfare, no early-morning collisions or casualty counts, nor the white noise of racing results or the interminable predictions of unpredictable English weather. The hum of the downtown expressway was barely audible. She was not a morning person; dawning intentions came round slowly and she began the day as a sleepwalker. Their experiments with rice and seaweed for breakfast were now over and she would boil an egg and cut toast in an act of self-cosseting that might stoke her and bring her a bit of luck. Why had she gambled with life to live the experiment where her only constant was Josh.

She had found the job, lost among the listings for English teachers, for a publishing firm. They produced world classics in translation, and, although she was totally unsuited for the role, she could not stand that her options seemed to narrow daily. She had applied. Josh was so unacceptably pleased she had secured an interview it was hard to take: hard because she might fail and if she failed she had next to no money to buy a ticket home and while she didn't want to leave him she could not stay on much longer and hold onto any self-respect.

As she bit into the finger of toast the thought of disappointing Josh stirred a terror that they might ask her to proofread, a task for which she was unqualified in any language on the planet.

Chapter 23

On a dusty side of town she walked the streets towards her interview and, though the pavements were busy, they were as good as empty to her. Not belonging had become a chronic problem. She was an outsider and with each face she passed it became more obvious to her that she was other. While they could see her, no one recognized her and no one cared. Walking towards the construction hoardings, she started at the noise of an unseen machine and she stopped a little beyond the site to calm herself, annoyed that the mundane should make her so jumpy.

With the help of the biro asterisk beside the newspaper ad and the trusted friend, 'The Detailed Map of Tokyo for Business Man and Tourist', she arrived at the publishers with twenty minutes to spare. She looked up at Kobayashi Press, at the new curving façade, four-storeys high, above a line of fast-food chains.

She scanned the windows expectantly – perhaps for guidance. She didn't know what she was searching for. An enlightenment? An augur of birds flying in formation? Stuck on the inside of the first-floor window was a simple poster advertising the latest publication. A possible conversational opening? But she had never read Ibsen; it would be no help. In arriving so early she had given herself longer to contend with the wheedling little suggestion that she should not go in at all.

Drifting into the nearest fast-food chain she ordered an American filter coffee; though foul in appearance and foul to the taste it did offer the guarantee of a kick and this just might displace her nerves and bring some clarity.

A boy came over and she watched him coax a grimy rag across the Formica; again she had to recognize she was not where she wanted to be. Her lips buckled at the first sip and she felt for another paper finger of sugar from a plastic white cat holder. Her lucky cats were black. The stimulants took her heart several notches above resting pulse.

She envisaged a world of unfamiliar horror titles; masterpieces by unpronounceable authors and a lexicon of knowledge in which she held no currency. If she knew how to communicate it was in the language of the shapes and lines of her drawings, and what if they did ask her to proofread? She was only halfway through the acrid coffee when she decided she would not go into the interview. Failing to turn up when she had committed was not a habit with her. Would she be letting herself down? Josh would be disappointed. Disappointed for her? She was so tired. She began digging around in her bag for coins. Holding an imaginary phone to her ear, she motioned the greasy boy in the bellboy cap for the phone. It was inevitably, hard to make herself understood, and he did not register at first. Eventually she found a pink payphone at the back of the café.

She dialled the number on the neat white card, given to her by the girl from Shibuya Station.

'Hi, yes, Miho. It's Naomi.'

'Yes, yes, I know. You too. We had so much to do settling in. How about that coffee?'

'No. Not today, Okay. No. Well . . .'

The flex was coiled the around her hand in a full bandage by the time she heard Miho say she would meet her for lunch.

'See you there.' And she left her future with the classics publisher before she had begun.

As Naomi waited outside the station, by the statue of the dog Hachikō, the girl came loping towards her. Was it Miho? Large crepe soles suggested a teenage boy. She wore pale citrus-yellow, slashed at the neck and belted in what looked like handcuffs. She couldn't be sure it was her until she was close enough for her smile in recognition to trigger her own.

They walked the labyrinth of zebra crossings where Miho had first guided her and took an escalator down to the basement of a department store to a subterranean market, where, amid the hawkers, they chose from a bar of freshly prepared fish and fried tempura. Miho listened patiently as Naomi explained she'd blown out of an interview.

In the silence that followed the confession Miho laughed that she should find it so grave.

'Okay, if you don't wanna teach, then take Japanese classes.'

The girl had an edgy ease, Naomi thought. She feared it would be awkward if Miho wanted a language exchange and she was keen to see off any such generous offer before it was made. Since she had given up her course in London, a guilt had settled on her that she had to silence and pay off. Earning her keep meant she was determined not to join another class.

'I can't be a student again,' she said conclusively.

She had picked up some words in Japanese, trawling for items for the house, but her world was not made up of conceptual bricks. She carried only small change in the currency of getting around but it was enough for her to manage right now. She lifted the bamboo handle of the teapot. 'Where are you living?' she asked Miho and poured more for them both.

Miho told her that she lived in a photographic dark room. 'I went out with my boss a while back,' she continued, 'but nobody right now. He let me stay and I still sleep in the studio where we work.'

Naomi looked sceptical .

'It's great. At weekends he's in the country and I get the run of the whole place. My wardrobe is the stationary cupboard on the floor below. Deal is I don't bring friends back.'

Piped music played over their conversation and every time a customer arrived a competing welcome of *irrashaimase* went up. They sat beside the chipped ice and bunches of pale radish, spinach and unfamiliar species of seafood. Surely inedible, Naomi felt. They ate sushi and miso soup, and talked of Miho's lovers.

Naomi felt she could trust Miho with her confidence and though she felt uncomfortable, she blurted, 'Miho, do you know where I can get a pregnancy test?'

'It's not so easy to get the pill here, huh.'

Chapter 24

'O mio babbino caro'
–Puccini, *Madama Butterfly*

Miho smiled warmly. A pregnancy test; her new friend was in a place she had been many times before. Contraceptive pills weren't that easy to come by.

'Sure, like a test pack? You want me to help you with that?' She left her basket on her chair and called to the waiter, telling him they would be back.

'Come.'

'I told him to hold our table,' she told Naomi. 'It won't take a minute'

They found a pharmacy at the station end of the store, bought the test, then Miho marched them up to the ladies.

'Go,' she commanded. 'Hand it to me and I will tell you the truth. You want no or yes?'

'No. I need to hear NO.'

Miho knew how she felt. This was a big issue. She bounced around, teasingly shrieking yes and no outside the cubicle and, when Naomi finally handed it to her, she walked off as if to hide the truth and tease her further. After a few moments she read the results.

'Okay, okay. You want to hear it?' Miho read the colour code. 'Yes . . .'

Naomi lost a beat and Miho responded only just in time before she panicked.

'Yes, you got what you wanted.' Miho held Naomi's shoulders. 'Not pregnant.'

'Don't tell me yes!' Naomi chastised, and laughed with relief. It was as if she had been given a new lease of life – a life of her own – and she would do something with it.

They returned to their table. The set-menu pudding arrived and Miho pushed hers aside.

'You want that? I can't eat that. Worst thing for cystitis.' Miho dismissed the sugary fruit jelly. Naomi found she had few conversational filters but balanced this by hiding her private side in a dress sense intended to ward people off. Naomi accepted the vibrant the orange jelly. She needed the sugar just now.

'You save me from an attack. You ate seaweed jelly before?'

Naomi's eyebrows floated. 'Sometimes I just don't know what I'm getting here.'

'Good for the hair,' Miho offered consolation to her new thin-haired friend.

Naomi liked her already . She pictured her in an enormous photographer's studio, wandering across curls of giant backdrop paper. 'You have family in Tokyo?'

'I am an outsider,' Miho said proudly, as if not belonging was a badge of identity. 'From a village outside Osaka,'

Naomi thought her forebears might have been from such a place but she was not from a village outside Osaka. She looked so urban and cosmopolitan and, as she toyed with a soft packet of American cigarettes, her open face led Naomi to feel there were no conversational lines unguarded. Knowing there was nothing like a convert to the city, and aware of her own tendency to cynicism, Naomi reserved judgment. On this side of the world the signifiers were as unhelpful as ethnic window dressing.

'I am *Etahin*,' Miho added.

Naomi supposed it was a rural district but then again it might have some connection with Japanese puppetry. The blank that it elicited prompted Miho to continue.

'I am from a low caste. *Hisabetsu Buraku*.'

Naomi's concept of living in twentieth-century Japan did not include a caste system, and she assumed Miho's vocabulary had dried up before the chapter in the primer on social anthropology.

'Like an Indian caste?'

Miho shrugged. 'I guess. It means I am an outsider.'

'Well, me too.' Naomi patted her city map. 'And this is my best friend.' Naomi guessed she would remember her as they first met, shrouded in billowing paper.

'Now me.' Miho smiled. 'Me and your useless map.'

Chapter 25

When Hana returned to the homestay from the Municipal Registration Office it was past lunchtime and Noru was trimming the overgrown kiwi-fruit vine that, without Ukai, had run riot and crept inside the ground-floor windows. Hana inclined her head in silent greeting with respect for Noru's period of mourning.

Hana ran up to the room to find Jess sitting on her bed, casually eating a bento box from the convenience store; a small, compartmentalized lunch, but irresistible to an empty stomach.

It was such a relief to see her but as Hana came over Jess dug her chopsticks into a slick morsel of chicken. Her mouthful necessitated a convenient lull that Hana was obliged to break first.

'We agreed we wouldn't do that.'

Through the mouthful it sounded like, 'So what?', and then Jess swallowed.

'You went without me this morning.' Hana became grand with indignation though hated arguing as a rule. 'Really . . . reprehensible.'

'What's this olde English?' Jess complained. 'I went without you? You weren't here.'

The relief at seeing Jess worked in confusion with the injustice Hana felt, until her relief won and she backed down.

'So tell me about it.'

Jess was clearly hungry. 'Later,' she said, pulling at a wing, redeeming what little meat there was. 'Nice guy,' she mumbled, and flashed a cheeky look then smiled.

It was all very well. It had worked out okay but Hana had to exact a promise from her never to break their code again.

'Let's picnic.' Jess rifled through her carrier bag; she had bought her a peace offering. A lunch box.

Hana sat on the faded pink bedcover as Jess unwrapped the cellophane from its lid and released the chopsticks. Taking a cherry-blossom morsel from its compartment, she brought it towards Hana's hairline as if to tuck it above her ear as a gift. Teased as she drew back from the chicken-greased flower, Hana lightened up as she popped it into her mouth.

'Sorry,' finally came.

Jess was not ready to talk about her evening so Hana began on the grey men from the municipal office who would win no awards for keeping fish.

'I give up,' she concluded. It was closer to frustration than a statement of intent.

'What? When you English are so keen on your heritage?'

'Yes, Jessica Junior the third. I give up.' She flounced.

'Well, thank God.'

It was so outrageous in its lack of sympathy that Hana took it to be nothing more that the usual flippancy. 'Thank you.' She was no heavyweight support anyhow.

Jess frowned. 'You don't give up now.' She popped an edamame bean from its pod and ate the single bean carefully as she thought through. 'So Miho sent you there and gave you a name?' She was in earnest.

'She had some relative called Tachi who was sure to help. There were only two guys and they both looked like the same person and neither had a clue. I'm wasting my time.'

'I've never heard of Tachi.' Jess focused on her hands, chewing hard. It was as if delaying any more revelations.

And she watched a curious expression creeping over Jess's face. Did Jess regard her as ungrateful towards Miho?

'I know she meant well but it was useless.'

'Interesting,' Jess concluded as if they were now on different teams. 'I'll maybe talk to Miho.'

Hana climbed down. 'I guess she was just keen to suggest something, anything at all that might have given me a lead.'

'Let's just call it Tachi's day off,' Jess said sanguinely, and they laughed as they had not done for a while. Jess grabbed Hana's hand as if she had just remembered. 'I have to tell you. Coming home I saw Tako.'

Tiresome though this might be it was not news. Hana waited for the punchline.

'He was at the back of the house, standing on a beer crate, peeking through the air vent in the bathroom like a peeping Tom.'

Hana grimaced. Some time back her instincts had told her to move.

'Oh God.'

'Let's have a day out?'

Hana, as if she were exhausted by it all, nodded.

'You want we walk round mount Fuji on Wednesday?' Jess suggested. 'There's a swan-shaped ferry.' Hana was unmoved and she persevered. 'Or we'll ride the pedalos; they're shaped like little cygnets.' It was all too much and Hana longed for home.

Chapter 26

Ed finally made contact, in his chosen Helvetica font. He and his colleagues had a trip planned to the club. He would see her there on Wednesday. Hana longed to talk of Broadway Market, Columbia Road, of Sunday lunch in suburbia, of all the coded references of home with someone who had seen what she had seen.

'Let's see.' Jess potted the nail varnish brush and stretched for the phone, back to the old routine since she's started back at the club. 'Wednesday? We don't work Wednesday,' she observed unhelpfully.

Later, when they asked Emiko if they could swap their night, she was difficult about it but did agree to an extra shift, late on Wednesday of the following week.

'We have a singer Wednesday night,' Emiko reminded them as they left.

The crowd was different that night, fewer regulars among business trippers. The music was languid and the lights dimmer. Jess saw him first.

She leant across to Hana conspiratorially. 'Eyes left.' Jess was a game-hunter since the Australians she had been seeing had left town.

Hana followed her sight line across the club. He was in a thin, grey, summer suit lending him years that he had yet to struggle through.

Diluted with sake, and on the way to becoming too liquid

to stand alone, Hana remembered that feeling of drowning in drink. It was the loneliest place on earth. Poor guy. She shifted the strap on her black evening dress before making her way over. She passed him unnoticed. Since the flight her dress code had changed.

It was early but his sentences already failed to find firm ground. Would he recognize her or remember her ? He was surrounded by a group of Japanese men . She had watched these business-bonding sessions, where they became anesthetized in drink with the intention of floating a raft across the cultural gulf between them. They paddled ineptly across inhibitions that still lay submerged, as if silent terracotta warriors in a dam.

He was probably out with his Japanese clients and colleagues from his law firm. He'd told her his Japanese was shakier than it should have been, because he had missed the firm's language induction course So that would leave him floundering in a sound system that didn't include him. Tonight he appeared to be subject to the excesses of an initiation ceremony. The older man, was it his boss, who swung a flask in front his eyes like a toddler yet to learn the requisite distance for attracting attention?

Hana returned from her flypast to confer with Jess.

'Can't be him, in that state?' She knew it was.

'Yup. Ed. The diluted version?' Jess suggested. 'They don't hold their drink well here. An ancient preference for green tea over beer. But what's his excuse?'

'So he's gone native?' Hana couldn't give him many marks out of ten.

She could see him being persuaded to have another glass. Ed's ears were pink and his assent at this stage looked irrelevant.

Though it looked hopeless – what the hell – she would go over anyway. Sooner the better. He was at least still upright.

As Emiko was tetchy that night she waited till she was busy directing the barman moving the microphone for the act.

Jess made for the banquette with her new arrivals and winked.

She walked over towards him but the act, Peach Blossom Nikki, on high heels and muscular legs had so caught his attention that she rerouted before she got there.

He seemed so engrossed in the petite singer as she tested the mic that she went back to leaning on the bar to watch him watching the act. The toned and coquettish body of Peach Blossom Nikki began to sing, wrapping a leg around the stand, falling to her knees provocatively, her happi coat falling open to reveal a dash of red underwear.

Jess sidled up to Hana. 'Very convincing, girl.' Jess toyed innocently with Hana's diamante strap and focused less innocently on Ed.

'Enormous feet.'

'It's a different place tonight.' Hana scanned the people and felt suddenly out of her depth and here was her American roommate, younger and completely relaxed.

Once the act had finished all she wanted was to say hello but she reached Ed at the same time as Peach Blossom Nikki, who was now more demurely dressed in a thin silken kimono. Encouraged by his boss, Peach Blossom Nikki took the stool beside Ed leaving her, awkwardly, to clear away the glasses. Hana pushed the empties around and hung about.

'Hi,' Hana overheard him begin.

Her enhanced breasts lifted on a breathless lilt and it was clear she did not speak English. Ridiculously Ed offered a handshake and a wavering smile; so manners were his first line of defense when feeling awkward? Alcohol hadn't cured him of self-consciousness then; Hana could see his colleagues were laughing at him behind their beers.

'Bonjour,' Nikki trilled and chatted to him in French.

Hana's schoolgirl French was poor and didn't pick up the

Marseilles dockside accent. She saw him lean precariously towards Peach Blossom Nikki, who was urging him to take a closer look at the tattoo on her ankle: a hummingbird dipping its long beak into an exotic flower. He wiped his mouth with the back of his hand.

Hana was firmly against interrupting them but couldn't draw away.

'It's a hibiscus,' he said. Hana grabbed an ashtray.

'Non,' Nikki said with conviction.

'It is a hibiscus.' Ed, as if searching for someone to give confirmation, looked up. She was at his elbow, with a tray of sticky glasses and a blossoming ashtray of stubs.

'You. It's you?' It seemed that finding her in evening dress was a pleasant surprise. He started to get up but obviously had second thoughts.

'A hibiscus?' Nikki lisped for his attention.

He sought Hana's expert opinion.

So she peered at the smooth ankle emerging from the sparkling shoes,

'It is,' Hana confirmed.

Peach Blossom Nikki crossed her legs with exaggerated delicacy, turning the full blast of her captivated attention on Ed, clearly the wisest man in the world.

Keen not to compete for his attentions, mumbling that it was good to see him. Hana left them.

It was a shame; she would have liked to talk to him, but he was far gone.

'Hey, don't go,' she heard him call after her weakly.

He would have no recollection of his text message by now and she doubted that he knew her as the girl from the flight. She left him studying Nikki's ankle and, through the sake, heard him say, 'Peach blossom, pretty.'

Hana knew then he had no idea he was talking to a transvestite.

Halfway across the room, she glanced back to see him head

to head with the giggling performer, his mouth so close he was touching her hair. His colleague interrupted him.

Ed slipped from his stool and headed off in the direction of the gents.

Pretty quickly his colleagues, Nobu-san, Kato and Watanabe-san, joined him.

'You like Peach Blossom Nikki, Ed-san?' Nobu asked him, as Ed unzipped his fly.

'Cute woman. Spent a lot of time in Europe. Been to Berlin, Frankfurt, Paris. All the major cities. Very competent French. I happen to have studied it.'

Nobu-san looked at him squarely. 'Peach Blossom Nikki speaks many languages, Ed-san.' He narrowed his eyes. 'Also English.'

Ed's eyebrows rose on a wave of gullible disbelief.

'And,' Nobu-san said with barely contained mirth, 'not so very much woman.'

His colleagues began to titter and hold their shaking foreheads, and Ed began to feel the butt of something between a sick joke and a schoolboy prank.

He felt like a man who had bought a car only to drive it away as the suspension gave in. His judgment had dissolved in a large volume of alcohol that he didn't particularly like. He nursed a newly developed – but what would turn out to be a lifelong – dislike for sake. And through a thick fog in his understanding he knew that he had missed the chance to connect with Hana. Suddenly sobered he walked back into the stale air of the bar and took no interest in the new singer crooning at the mic.

Hana was helping Emiko fill some small Imari dishes with rice crackers, while the next act performed.

'Quite a dancer,' Hana observed.

'The pole dancer Nikki? She started out a merchant seaman,'

Emiko explained. 'She was making the plastic shoes in Kobe but left her hometown in 95 after the Kobe earthquake. Used to sing on the cruise ships. Etahin. You know? Village people?' Hana roughly understood. She could ask for an explanation later.

Getting ready to leave at the end of the shift she combed the bar one last time for empties. She found Jess beside the karaoke, with a glass in each hand, swigging whisky dregs, after a night of too many complimentary cocktails.

'Nightcap?' She raised a toast.

'You coming?' Hana was keen to go and nudged Jess towards the exit, leaving her Thai silk clutch on the bar.

Now early dawn, the neon arrow flashed intermittent pink across the stairwell. Jess slowed up and burst out laughing.

'Bit of a lack of judgment from the lawyer.'

Hana pushed her. He had been too far gone to feel embarrassed. But if he made contact again, what would be the point? Her legs were heavy as she climbed. And she wondered how much longer she could keep this up.

'He was set up,' she defended him.

'Bit of a hopeless case.'

But she rallied. 'I still have his number. He's got to sober up sometime.'

As the girls' voices charted the basement steps, Emiko found Hana's blue purse and called after her from the exit. It had been a long night. Their voices drifted off and she slipped the purse into the lapel of her kimono for safety.

Chapter 27

Josh was pacing the line of the garden doors. Behind him, in the overgrown, almost tropical, boundary line, loomed the rusty letters on the Tokyo Electric Power Company sign.

'You didn't go to the interview?'

Naomi wasn't sure she could explain.

'Why not?' he persisted.

'I just couldn't go.' She would never be able to tell him that it would have taken her another step along a plank towards becoming deeply immersed in a life that did not belong to her. Towards someone she was not. And she dare not tell him she was already halfway over the threatened drop. He wouldn't understand. He didn't seem to suffer from any moments of self-doubt or from the inability to take control of himself and do what he knew he ought to but could not. On the other hand, when he did lose control, it was apocalyptic and they would party until she found the hedonism almost more difficult to take. It seemed then that his will was something even he had to endure.

She watched as his blood pressure rose. And this was his secret weapon. Self-control that was so strong it extended its grip over her.

'That's a shame.' His voice was hollow.

'I know you're disappointed. You don't have to tell me you are.'

It was okay for him, she thought; he had a title role, he had colleagues, he had respect and he was needed. He had something to do which he valued.

'I have no reason to be here. I have no reason to be,' she said finally.

He must have read the desperation in her voice and so put aside any exasperation. When he approached her it was not caution but gentleness, and he held her for a long time with quiet tenderness.

'I understand.' He held her still.

She wanted, then, to believe that he might really understand, though they both knew that he would not.

Days later Naomi decided she would catalogue, on rolls of Fuji film, the Harajuku dancers and the ankle-socked girls dressed as cartoon characters parading around Yoyogi. At the weekends she and Josh would stroll across the kinetic city braving the digital assaults on their attention from the electronic hawkers. Together they traded the sights as if they shared one pair of eyes, and when she took the photos it was as a record for them both.

Now settled in the house, Naomi devoted some time to organizing their evenings of Japanese culture, of traditional theatre and dance. The list of couples they could call on was short and often began with the Sawdays, a couple from Josh's office. Evie had given Naomi a contact for an English voiceover commercial and she would occasionally spend a whole afternoon travelling to a studio for four second's output. It paid very little and was so infrequent it amounted to nothing. Older than Naomi, Evie was expecting her first baby and had become obsessed with parts of the body that Naomi had never heard of.

On nights out during the performance interval, Evie would feed them information on the latest pregnancy development, despite strong evidence that two out of the four of them found it as informative as Japanese Kabuki without subtitles.

'They induce with seaweed. Great bunches of it placed . . . inside.' Evie would run on about the critical benefits of Vitamin E and the use of Chinese herbs. She would pass round a small black-and-white Polaroid of an alien growth, leaving Naomi thankful that the limitations of photography did not extend to technicolor scans. Statistics on the changing circumference of the baby's head accompanied the show and tell.

Evie, as an expat, was a member of the American club and had picked up all sorts of advice. 'I can tell you –' she touched Naomi's hand and continued in loud confidence '– where to buy a quality bassinet.' She nodded to imply 'when the time comes', as Naomi identified a lifestyle she was particularly keen to avoid.

Mike Sawday had, since an early age, spent more time conversing with numbers than talking to people and any social jitters he had he hid behind a long, lank, fringe of hair. Evie's long-held faith was, that, over time, she could affect a change in him and on this basis she had readily taken him on as a husband. With the pregnancy, a satisfaction had becalmed Mike; behind glasses that covered half his face, he resembled the kid who, at the opening of school speech day, knew that all the major prizes would be for him.

Evie had organized all aspects of Mike's life where he was least capable, thereby seamlessly taking over from his mother. She held him in traces that gave her license to steer their lives where she chose and left him to focus on his numerate strengths, which were quite special, as Evie, a little too often, reminded them.

Naomi's appetite for theatre and numerous recommendations fitted Evie's desire to build on Mike's cultural education and so she was happy that Naomi chose their programme of events. It surprised her that Josh had patience for these strange dramatic offerings.

One night Naomi had persuaded them to see the Bunraku puppet masters. In the womb-like darkness of the second act,

Naomi had not been able to take her eyes off the boxy brocade silks of the life-sized dolls, so stiff that they could stand on their own, as their puppet masters moved nimble-limbed across the stage in their black two-toed socks. It was both dance and mime, accompanied by the shrieking calls of an ancient ritual and mesmerizing shakuhachi flutes. The shadowy masters of the life-sized jointed figures crept beside their anima and dictated the fates of every character.

'Why are we doing this?' Josh asked her that evening as they left the small Noh festival theatre.

'The more we get to see, we can work out where it is we are living.'

It was as relevant to him as seaweed advice for pregnant men.

'And that time we went to the Kabuki theatre,' Josh moaned. 'A full four hours of tortured screaming is hard to nominate a cultural classic.'

'You left before the end,' she reminded him, although even she had to admit it hadn't been easy.

When Evie said she was finding it difficult to remain sitting for a long time in the later weeks of her pregnancy, the intervals between their evenings out together grew, and without anything else in common they lost the habit of seeing one another.

Josh's enthusiasm for Naomi's role as arts ambassador swung quickly from high culture to the more familiar concerts. And when bands from home were visiting they would go to Yoyogi with Sam, an American who Josh had met on a banking transaction, and whoever Sam's latest girl happened to be. And then she brought Miho along and it was even better.

One morning Josh was at the ironing board, toast in hand.

'I can't walk into the office with these creases,' he protested.

These exchanges began with small but well-fingered grievances, thrown like polished beads of gravel that they had carried in their pockets for some time. They came to regard these sessions as a form of pressure release, preferable to the seismic eruption that would follow if they allowed them to build up without being given vent.

'We need some help in the house.' He was keen too that, without a job, Naomi did not feel that her life was limited to housekeeper. While the sentiment weighed in her favour, his proposal was clumsy and made her feel worse.

One morning Naomi was addressing an envelope to a postcode where her parents had downsized. Her father had been ill for a few years and her mother had been reduced to caring, to games of bridge and to dog-breeding, in no special order of importance. She knew, sadly, that, as a result, they were never likely to visit. They had never been in support of her move to Tokyo, had tried to dissuade her from giving up her architectural course and they had never warmed to Josh. And so Naomi's letters often inflated the positives of Tokyo in order to reassure her mother, without wanting to add to her worries.

On paper, her life was close to perfect. Turning over the ready-gummed airmail, signal stripes marching importantly round the flimsy edge, she put down the ink pen, once one of her father's, to listen for the breathless wheeze of a vacuum cleaner that had been grazing two bedrooms on the first floor since the start of Maybelline's – her Thai help's – arrival some hours before. She took the stairs slowly, following the sound of the machine, to the tiled bathroom floor where Maybelline was lying, apparently asleep. She called her name firmly, to be sure she hadn't died in service, but it was only when the hoover was silenced and Naomi had given her a gentle shake that she stirred. The guilty party smiled and opened her eyes.

'So you are really tired?'

'Yes, ma'am.'

Naomi was still unused to the title. 'You have too many jobs?' she suggested sympathetically.

Still half asleep, Maybelline attempted to sit up.

'Do you work long hours?

She nodded.

'At night?'

'In a hostess bar, ma'am.' The girl looked shattered.

Naomi's sympathy evaporated and she left her to come round. These bars had come to represent the blind hedonism she found so vacant in Josh.

Josh told her the hostesses were not what she assumed, but waitresses, assigned to a given party for the evening. On his nights out she had a tendency to default to the idea that Josh was hanging out with prostitutes as she lay alone under the taunting of the dance of city lights; by midnight she had him languishing in an opium den. She really resented the office-bonding sessions in hostess clubs, when so many of his hours seemed to belong to the company anyway. One night she drifted asleep and woke and dozed and woke and dozed as she expected him back. When, finally, the sweet perfume of alcohol arrived like a third person in their room, she turned away to register her objection. She listened as he lost the contest with his clothes and dropped beside her fully dressed. They lay in silence. A single word was enough to trigger recriminations and he had been drawn before. Eventually, she had to speak first.

'Was it a hostess bar?'

She turned towards his inert body, looking for signs of life, hoping to bring him to the first step on a podium where he would stand crowned the cruellest man on earth, at which point she could dissolve in restorative tears. He made no attempt to hide the slur in his voice, as if conversation with him would seem useless to her, though the strategy risked an exaggerated assessment of the ruinous amount of alcohol he had consumed. To her frustration he fell asleep before he could even comfort her with the promise of a discussion. This pattern in their lives became more frequent.

*

Sam had invited Josh to join what he called Poet's Corner, as if his single membership to the gym – imaginatively named 'Do Sports' – were to an Ivy League club befitting the Rhodes scholar he was. Sam had saved himself a month's fees for signing a friend but had readily owned up to the incentive, though his pay in dollars meant he never counted the cost of money.

'Only reason for asking you along,' Sam had pointed out. 'Nothing to do with good company.' He'd smiled.

So Josh had invested in a pair of running shoes, which had involved a trip to Ikebukero, where he and Naomi had spent a good part of Saturday morning finding a pair large enough.

Josh pulled his gym towel out of his briefcase and hung it round his neck in an unconscious copycat of Sam. The men chose adjacent running machines and set them in motion with a jogging pace. Sam winked.

'So good to feel the plastic under your feet again like that green grass of home.'

'And that reconditioned city air in your lungs.'

Josh had an eye on Sam's monitor but couldn't quite see the display. When Sam upped his speed, Josh jabbed at the pace of his own tread, to keep time. They talked deals within the confines of their confidentiality agreements and mostly exaggerated their contact with those higher up the food chain who they regarded as heavies; dusting themselves by association, with the power and influence of the personalities from their respective global banks. Sam's height gave him an advantage on the running machine but Josh had a shorter but determined stride. Sweat built up on the complimentary T-shirt Josh had received on joining.

'You'll come to my party?' Sam asked, after giving him the date. 'A close group'll be there.'

'And every woman you ever slept with?'

'Is that apart from Naomi?' Sam taunted.

'You dare,' Josh threw at him confidently.

Sam flashed his white teeth.

'How long is it with Miho now? A three-week record?'

Outside the locker room Sam handed Josh an isotonic drink branded Pocari Sweat as they headed for the shower.

'How is she doing?' Sam yelled over the cubicle, referring to Naomi.

'She's okay. So-so.'

'Tell her she can design my cabin in Montana any time.'

'Not her specialism. She doesn't have a portfolio in Yankee Red Wood. But we have to find her a job before we both go insane.'

They rejoined one another, skirted in towels, hair wet like a couple of skunks.

'Okay, so we have to find her a job.'

'We most definitely do.'

'I'll invite the architect on Saturday. But he's a big deal and may take some persuading.'

Chapter 28

Shimokitazawa, 2012

Hana and Jess ambled past the tattered apprentice monk at the station, begging in the quiet of early morning. So futile; so sixth century. At the vending machine, Hana managed to persuade Jess not to get him a can of beer, which was her idea of a joke. Lately Jess had begun to talk of leaving. Perhaps she had made enough money, or had caught her own fever of introspection. But Jess was one of those people who needed to be in perpetual motion and wore novelty like a new coat. Hana had come to depend on her and could never see herself working at the club without her. But since the night Jess went missing, they had been more distant with one another. The extra night that week had tired them both.

Jess turned from the monk suddenly. 'I'm gonna leave the bar. We've pissed off Emiko.'

'We? *We* have?'

'Okay, so she prefers you because . . . you kinda look Japanese.'

Hana was unimpressed. She wanted to earn appreciation. And she did not regard herself as particularly favoured right now. She was too tired to protest.

They sat over an American coffee at Ziggy's. Jess chose from a line of sugar in Kilner jars. What was it, Jess wondered, that Hana's mother had done? They drank in silence.

Miho seemed worn, her linen apron crumpled, as she collected their cups. Today she looked her age.

Hana leaned towards her. 'No joy at the Municipal offices, Miho.'

Miho stacked busily and Jess was in a hurry to help her.

Tachi's day off was how Jess referred to Hana's visit that day. She could trivialize it because it didn't mean anything to her. It didn't mean anything to Miho.

'You never met my mother here? Some time back? Naomi?' she asked, with an urgency she had not intended. Jess gulped her coffee her elbows planted firmly and watched Hana watching Miho.

'People come. People go. I didn't always run a café.' Miho was tired and wistful and today her defenses were down. Finally she sat down with them like she used to at the beginning.

Hana drew from Miho's strong, guarded reaction, expectantly. 'Naomi. She was called Naomi,' she persisted.

She caught Jess and Miho exchanging glances.

Miho looked down, weighing a damp cloth in her hand, scanning her face, her almond eyes. What was it she was weighing up?

She locked eyes for a moment until Miho broke it.

'No,' Miho said eventually. 'I don't think I remember.'

Miho's reaction was inexplicably strained.

'You're like my son: a half-and-half westerner,' Miho deflected quietly.

Hana felt half of something and half of nothing and pulled at her low-cut evening dress, her nervous little habit.

'Did you find the teahouse yet?' Miho asked, getting up to wipe the tables down.

Hana shook her head. It was early morning; she had been up a long time and she was feeling entirely misaligned. She was even ready for the thin mattresses at the lodgings.

She rose, about to pay, then suddenly remembered, 'My purse. I left my purse.'

Her cash and credit cards were at the bar. Miho waved away her concern.

'Go. Go on back. You can settle with me later.'

As the girls left the morning heat was beginning to pulse as the day tuned up.

'See you,' Miho's thin voice followed them.

At Shimo's the wet floors glistened in the daylight of the open delivery hatches. Under such exposure the wry geisha print of the fisherman's wife was shabby. Hana saw where, for luck or virility, many hands had touched the most searching of the imposing sea creature's tentacles and the paper had rubbed away. A shout from a delivery guy alerted them and Hana and Jess were pinned back against the sea creature to make way for the hurtling beer-crate trolley. No one was around and they combed the bar and dining areas before searching near the mic and karaoke screen for the missing purse. Hana scanned the bar one last time before she made her way to the office to find the surly punch-permed man in grey overalls. Before he left he dropped the delivery note on the desk and, without acknowledging them, hurried away to the next errand.

The desk lay in the collected clutter of redundant coffee makers, shelved laptops, and reams of antiquated carbon paper and beneath old film posters for *Spirited Away*, *Jameso Bondo* in hiragana script, and *Norwegian Wood*. An ancient fridge blinked. Jess scanned a row of old plastic files and Hana shuffled through a dusty stack of music CDs beside a broken stereo system. Eventually, bookending the shelf above the desk, Jess found the blue, silk purse.

Emiko walked in wearing ripped jeans, and carrying a cup of instant soup. She was alarmed to find anyone in her space and confronted them in a tone sharper than they thought she was capable of using. 'What are you doing in my office?' Emiko looked at Hana. 'Leave my office. You don't go in the office.'

Hana explained they had only come for her mislaid purse, which she brandished in proof. 'I got it. Thanks.'

Emiko's long, white nails fingered the desk papers as if she were cataloguing these along with her recall of events.

Jess broke across her stony calculations. 'Thanks for finding it.'

Emiko glared at Hana and she left with her purse and the strongest sense she has lost face with Emiko.

They left quickly. 'We'll see you later,' Jess called back, catching her arm through Hana's.

Outside the homestay a line of ill-regarded potted plants suffered in the heat. Back in the room Hana was unable to sleep. She worked out that GMT London would have Tom out with their friends, probably at the Rio watching a movie. She missed those evenings when she would cook for them and she had built a hard-earned reputation for amazing food, spending hours on culinary efforts, which they ate through in less than half the time it had taken her to prepare it.

She sent him an open message: 'Thinking of you.'

It really meant: Are you thinking of me? Remember me; it's me.

It was still early, early morning and her eyes were heavy, but she plugged into her music and leafed through the *Japanese Language and People Course Book* at her bedside.

'You can't study now,' Jess threw out unhelpfully. 'Your father must definitely be Japanese. Conscientious student.'

'What?' Hana took out her earphone and threw aside her book.

Jess sat in a cross-legged pose. She had recently taken up yoga and was erratically working through moves she followed on screen, often at the most inappropriate times of day. Her chosen branch of yoga seemed not to demand silence as an important key to concentration. She was determined to find a subject sure to distract Hana. She was in her talking mood.

Miho's warning not to reveal stuff about Naomi had carried some weight with Jess, and she'd said nothing.

'So how do you plan to find him?' It was with such little caution that Jess trod on her dreams.

'This is as good as it is going to get in terms of my search for any heritage. Cultural immersion.'

And if he hadn't died . . . Jess took her pose up to an ill-based shoulder stand, which, buckling under the slim support of the bed base, added to the feet marks on the wall that registered her earlier attempts.

'Is that what you call the nightclub? Cultural immersion? Don't you want to know the truth?'

The phrase that Tom had been so taken with came back to Hana: 'The truth is always something that is told, not something that is known. If there were no speaking or writing, there would be no truth about anything. There would only be what is.'

'There's no one to ask,' Hana said. 'So I suppose I will never know.'

Miho had sworn her to secrecy for a reason, Jess told herself. Should she tell regardless? On reflection, Miho in kindness had fed Jess without payment plenty of times. If she thought it best to stay quiet, maybe it *was* best. Another conversation with Miho first perhaps? But the man Miho had mentioned? Taking a circuitous route to the solution, Jess pushed Hana further.

'You are so in denial about this and yet here we are living in the same area as Naomi did. It is almost as if you can't bear to admit you would like to find him, when in fact you are here to find him.'

Hana stopped the music without responding.

'So you quit that easily?'

'You have to help me, Jess.'

'So we DNA-check millions of people in the absence of any other information? We advertise for an old man who shagged a girl one night over twenty years ago.'

'Jess! It's not . . . Don't. How nice are you?'

Jess's cynicism was so very strong that at times it felt as though there were three people in the friendship. And the third person was often an unwelcome addition.

'You know Naomi would have been so disappointed with me. Working in a hostess club with some shmucky American.'

'Me?'

'You.'

'How do you know that she would've disapproved?'

The grubby octopus crossed Hana's mind, a tentacle in every orifice.

'She was very straightforward. Uncomplicated. She would never have found herself in this position. Simple pleasures, simple interests, and she was really very self-sufficient in an uncompromised way.'

Jess wanted to know more. Miho's words revisited her. Whose life was it that this careful Englishwoman was responsible for?

'Did she go with guys?'

'Yes, but she never married.'

Jess bowed to the inevitable. 'You have to ask Miho . . .' she enunciated; her look gave her away.

So Miho knew more; Hana had thought as much.

With the caution of one only recently released, Jess continued slowly. 'You have to ask her . . . about the . . . you have to ask Miho about—' Jess changed her mind midsentence '—the . . . teahouse.'

Hana was underwhelmed. 'I did.'

'Ask her again. Ask her where it is and we will go together. I think she knows.' And to Hana's dissolving skepticism she added, 'I'm not going to work tomorrow. We could go then.'

Eventually Hana slept and across her dreams she travelled again to a sultry day in the East End of London. She stood with familiar faces in the crowd, but, this time, Tom was absent. Miho was there, mouthing a voiceless chant. It was a busy Brick Lane market day; a Buddhist monk in saffron robes passed through the parting crowds, cycling a rickshaw. And, again, as he retreated, it was possible to see that the passenger curled up in a fetal position and sleeping soundly on a bench across the back of the rickshaw was Naomi. Hana tried to call after her but could only motion to catch her attention. Emiko stood in her way and scolded her wordlessly. Before she could pursue her the world splintered and she woke with her eyes still firmly closed.

The sun had reached above the low buildings across the road and a bright glare warmed her lids. When she opened her eyes, Jess was sitting very close.

'I'm not going into classes today and I am not going to the club.'

'I think you should.' There was the incident with Emiko to consider.

An acrid smell of burnt toast in the air.

'If you become unreliable Emiko will give me the worst clients. Less money. . . if she takes against—'

'She did already. Let's go rescue the house from Tako's breakfast. He would starve if he had to feed himself.' Hunger won over her reluctance, though the bread remained barely a foodstuff.

'I'll have rice.' Hana kicked the wedge from under their door and they headed downstairs.

Chapter 29

Contact with Tom had been irregular but Hana knew he was working hard towards his deadline. She would send a gift when she had seen something he would really appreciate, like a book on tattoo art: embroidered backs of yakuza painted with fish and water lilies, geisha and bright-eyed dragons. Perhaps their beady eyes could spy on him and send word.

Leaving the house she saw Tako looming large in the doorway, his dangling mourning jacket blocking the last of the sun. She held back, not keen to engage with him. He had limited his clumsy attempts to befriend the girls but was still keen to demonstrate his command of English despite not being given any encouragement. His attention was caught by something very interesting in the kiwi vine running riot over the doorway. He appeared to focus on a wasp dipping, like a humming bird, into the side of a bruised and rotten fruit. It must be sweeter, she thought. The decay was sweeter. He went on and on surveying the wasp until she just had to get past him.

'Konbanwa.' He batted the drunken wasp with a sleeve and started on a particularly warm overture. 'Dance festival tonight?' An alarming smile grew across his face. The Obon festival was in August. The festival to honour the dead. Would she go with him?

Hana was keen to remain polite and not to annoy him. She usually relied on Jess to be the one to deal with him, and she had to find the right words to refuse him.

'I won't come with you.' It was easier than she guessed. 'But thanks for letting me know it's on'

The streets were busy and a group of men, carrying a shrine on broad shoulders, passed by in the street to the beat of taiko drums. She wandered alone through the food vendors' calls and lilting flute music. Across in the square, traditional dancers moved slowly to choreographed fans. She bought the tattoo dragon book and a bamboo leaf of street food, which she ate in the dark beneath cherry trees strung with lights. Under the cover of darkness she knew she could have not been followed and she recognized a new pleasure in being alone in a crowd.

In the following days the strain on Hana and Jess's friendship was kept in check because their lives seemed to run in tandem; small resentments had begun to chaff and Jess had taken a couple of days off from the club while the Australians were in town.

She worked shifts without Jess; Emiko was cold and offhand, and Hana found other girls were singled out for better treatment.

It wasn't until two days later, when Jess reappeared at Shimo's, that Emiko erupted. She called them aside and picking at the rip in her jeans told them that a sum of money had gone missing from the office.

'Both of you were in the club out of hours that day. And I found you in the office. I have been given until the end of the month to return what has been taken.' Emiko spat this news out and it came as a shock that she directed it to Hana.

Hana was appalled at what was being implied; surely Emiko didn't think she could have taken the cash.

'It must be returned,' Emiko urged pointedly.

'The beer delivery boy was in the office just before us,' Jess protested.

Emiko's response was a strangled question. 'Why after so many years of deliveries does this man suddenly turn thief?'

Hana was both wounded and furious.

'It won't come to anything,' Jess assured her when they were alone. 'They can't get the police involved down there.'

Hana readily believed this but the thought of the authorities scared her; Tachi's friend had been weird enough.

'Don't dwell on it,' Jess consoled.

However Hana couldn't help but detect an unsettling flippancy, as if the problem had nothing to do with her.

It was raining so hard a sheet of water clung to the window as the thin roof took a pommelling. A July monsoon had hung about and hit in August.

Hana dressed for work. Jess must still be at class. She sensed that the rhythm they usually shared was about to change. She pulled on the grimy light cord. In the gloom of the small mirror, she painted the surprised little Japanese bows that Emiko wore, then infilled her lips in red. Consoled that while the reflection might be an inconvenient truth, she could at least see to cover up the odd blemish that had appeared in protest of her thin diet. At least Tom wasn't here to see it. They had all gone to the Rio, he'd told her, and she very much hoped that Sadie wasn't stepping into her jeans. He was a bit of a broken bird really, but there were plenty of women who would love to help him mend. She paused, spot stick in hand, and listened to a heavy step on the stairs.

Jess came in drenched, and immediately fell back on the twin bed and groaned.

'Christ, when are we moving to that split-level apartment in Hiroo Garden Hills? A beautiful open space on the thirty-first floor. Panoramic views from here to Sydney? Fields of soft, white sofas and a bathroom the size of Manhattan?'

Best not to offer encouragement, Hana thought, though they might be under the roof of a voyeur.

'When I was in Shinjuku the other day, I took a good walk up and down the capsule hotel. Looked like a giant stacked

Laundromat but there was a communal bathroom and every bubble had a TV. What would you say to a move?' As expected, Jess instantly laughed it off. Her tone changed. 'This man bumped into me. He was all crumpled. A crumpled human really. Smelt of alcohol. He had a battered newspaper; it must have been from the train seat. He kept bowing an apology. A man without no home, no job. Just kept apologizing.'

'My guess is a capsule hotel is our next base. He sounds our type of guy.'

'What if the Australian shag last week turned out to have been the first son of a mobile-phone dynast?'

'Dream on, kitten.'

Feigning trebled exhaustion Jess slunk off to the bathroom, leaving a pool at the door.

'You make a very good impression of someone I really couldn't even like,' Jess let slip as she passed.

'Aren't you coming? We're going to be late.'

Jess's head reappeared. 'You are going to be late.'

Hana looked at her questioningly and for the avoidance of doubt Jess added, 'I'm not going back.'

So she would have to go in alone, to wipe the dew drips from the hot held tumblers and listen again and again to the karaoke wailings. Jess had always made it an easier prospect.

'Emiko will think you took the money if you don't come back,' she threatened.

Chapter 30

Hana was at a table at the back of the café, looking out over the yellow sky and heavy summer rain. She ate at Ziggy's as often as she did at the homestay. The air-con was more efficient, and the meals worked out only a little more expensive. She was picking her way through a large bowl of ramen soup, when Miho, catching Hana as she ate without appetite, teased, 'You don't like my cooking?'

She lifted the lid on an old cake stand and returned with a brownie to console her. 'Complimentary.'

'Jess is leaving sometime soon. I suppose I should be leaving too.' She hadn't told Miho about the theft; it reflected badly on them and Hana valued the respect of her new friend.

'I heard this.'

'She says we should leave Tokyo. I can't go now. But I don't know anyone else here, really'. She was so much more able to cope than she'd felt at the start but it would be tough without Jess.

'How about, you know me. You stay here in Japan or you leave for home and you come back? In a few weeks, or months or years?'

'I guess I have to get back for term time.' Hana had already toyed with extending her stay.

'So you decide to head back to London. Jess travelled without you before.'

'Jess will go, whatever I choose to do.'

'It'll look like she took the money, right?'

Of course Miho knew; she should have confided in her.

The two-toed builder had come down from scaling bamboo scaffolding on the construction site opposite. Still in his helmet, he ordered coffee.

'Kohi, onegaishimasu.'

'Well, Emiko thought I took it.'

Miho knew that Emiko did not believe this. She took a filter jug from the warmer.

'You know Emiko is to lose her job too. Guam-san is not a great guy. I know it's not Jess, not Emiko, and not you.' Miho swung her greying, bobbed hair. 'You know I can't pay anyone else to work here with me right now. I wish I could.'

'I'd be good for washing up but I'd take a few misorders. Thanks, Miho.'

The gingko brownie was good. Hana was pretty much resigned to losing her job and her reputation with it, but it was best she spoke with Emiko soon. Returning her plate to the counter, she promised Miho she would be back.

Hana went straight over to Shimo's where Mr Guam and three other men were playing cards, their deck dusted with hours of cigarette ash. It was a surprise to see Tako sitting among them. In this crowd it seemed he had no pressing need to acknowledge her – recently returned from a spot of sex tourism perhaps? She hung back. From under the table a small shaven- haired boy playing a computer game looked up. He had Emiko's eyes. Guam-san peered over his cards through rimless specs, sitting too tightly on his large shaved head. She nodded at him deferentially and then blurted, 'Do you need us on Tuesday?'

The assembly didn't move. She was to them no more than an object floating in their Kirin beer and then Guam spoke without looking up.

'Later you know.'

Offered nothing more, she left as the group returned to their cards and the task of building smoke rings on the air.

The following day, while painting her toes, Hana paused to read *Natsu Dragneel*, one of Tako's manga back copies placed under her feet. She heard the landlady calling insistently from the lobby. It took her time to realize that it was her own name repeated over and over. She moved carefully, walking on her heels to the top of the flight of stairs.

'A man is here.' She jabbed. 'For you.' Noru wiped her hands on her apron with barely veiled disgust.

Could it be Ed? Hana wondered. Sobered up and following through on his promise.

'A man.' As if he was no mere stranger to Hana.

One of Guam's card players looked up at her between the banisters. He was thin and small and if she had ever met a yakuza, this was as close to the cartoon cliché to be unnerving. Why he came unannounced she couldn't imagine and it made her feel ill at ease. Her discomfort came to rest on the small pieces of tissue that were crammed between each of her bare toes.

'Guam San says you come on Tuesday like usual.' As soon as the broken English was delivered he left.

Hana's relief was tempered by the question of how he knew how to find her. Did Noru know her son was hanging out with the very people she objected to visiting her respectable lodgings? Though Tako had never been to the hostess bar.

Noru lost no time in relaying the house rules. She thundered through the swing doors from her private rooms and circled Hana in a rattling invective, largely self-addressed and in quite unintelligible Japanese. This tirade escorted her all the way back through the door and deep into the uncharted depths of the house. It was as if a small electrical storm had been unleashed. There were times, like this, when a weak hold on the language was an advantage. While Noru crackled in disbelief that Hana knew this sort of man, she would surely come to realize that it was an unelicited visit. He had turned up uninvited. If she lost the room then securing the job was no consolation. Back upstairs she ripped the separators from her toes and, with too little regard for the wet polish, smudged it. She lay on her bed and, once the immediate frustration had subsided, she wondered how comfortable she felt knowing the man knew where to find her. So Tako the mummy's boy knew them all?

Just then Jess walked in from the bathroom wrapped in a towel, rubbing her wet hair and seemingly unaware of the landlady's rantings.

'Your turn. Water's hot.'

'Guam sent a ghoul over to say to turn up on Tuesday as usual.'

'So we have still our jobs?' Jess was nonchalant.

'Well, he didn't say that specifically. But I think that's what it means.'

'What d'you mean?'

'Well, he was talking to me. And I assume he meant us both.' Jess unleashed Medusa from the towel.

'And you couldn't ask about me?'

'You said you weren't going back.'

'The girl formerly known as a friend,' Jess jabbed at her.

'Well, the homestay San . . .'

'I am so not delighted with you.' Jess turned her back, to look out of the ugly high window to the east, where reams of aggressive utility cabling appeared to hold the building opposite in place.

'Noru went into a rage as if I had dragged down her reputation. Like her house was where men turn up off the street to talk to half-dressed women. Delay him? And let her think I wanted anything to do with him.'

After contemplating the windowless building, Jess swung round as quickly as her mood change.

'Okay, friend.' Hana was preparing for a tantrum when Jess started to sing a vampy number and pulled provocatively at her towel threatening to expose herself to the street, suddenly a half-dressed stripper. She flung herself on the bed and the tension was broken.

'You know it's okay. It's fine as we are leaving anyway.' Jess lifted the towel and waved it around her head triumphantly. 'We don't need the job and we won't need the room. We are sitting on a live earthquake zone. How many reasons do we need to pack our bags and wave goodbye? Hello, Narita Airport.'

What would it matter if she cut short her stay and left a little early? Hana could see the paddy fields from the air shrinking as their departing plane climbed and with it the receding chance of everything she had come to find in Japan; she was waving goodbye to a small individual lost in the context of her own history. It would be as if she were leaving a part of herself behind.

For a long time Hana had read Jess's need to leave more clearly than she had understood her own reasons for staying.

'I think you should come back with me to Tohoku and join the volunteers,' Jess told her. 'Look, I think you'll find it very rewarding.'

'I am not coming with you, Jess.' Hana knew she was just not up to it. Tokyo was the start of the journey and she would take it in steps.

At first Jess tried to persuade her. They had lived well together; they would travel well together. 'How about Australia?' she suggested. It was a lightbulb moment and she was not entirely serious.

'I am not coming with you, Jess. I can't.'

'I'm still not buying that.' The mane of her wet hair fell over her damp shoulders.

All Jess was asking for was a time delay and she began to enumerate why it was appropriate for them to leave. The thick humidity of summer could be avoided and a short delay would hinder nothing. They could come back when the rains had gone or get jobs in the mountains of Hokkaido and ski.

'Powder snow. Best in the world.'

'If I go anywhere I have to get back to London.'

Jess tried the guilt trip, telling her she was the best friend she'd ever had.

Hana guessed she might just qualify, as Jess was the kind of traveller who might just be a misfit at home. Still, she did not waiver.

However, shortly after her outburst it looked as though Jess might get her way when Noru made clear that the following week they would have to go and find new accommodation.

Chapter 31

Zodiac Snake: charming, gregarious, introverted and smart

Tokyo Imperial Hotel, 3 June 1989

It was a hot humid Saturday evening in late June. Francis Fukuyama, the American academic, just proclaimed it the end of history, as the cold war between the US and USSR had thawed. Tokyo had become the most expensive place on earth while the economy in Japan grew faster than bamboo. That night the city had lost none of its closeness and the aniline-yellow day had given way to sodium streetlights.

Naomi leant back in the taxi. The lace antimacassar behind Josh's head recalled a dignified Dutch Old Master and, despite his youth, he appeared to be growing into his role as international banker. It was only last March he had waited for her at the college steps, calling from the back of a London black cab. Though they had been an item for the whole of her first year, it was unusual for him to collect her. He had slid towards her on a bend in the road and excitedly explained that the bank was to send him to Tokyo and that he wanted her to come too. She had always found his enthusiasms infectious. He was asking a lot. Postponing her qualification and moving to a country where she knew no one but him. His persuasion carried the force of a man used to getting his own way; perhaps this dominance might relax a little if they settled down together, she had thought then. She didn't need to work out the implications if she turned him down. And then he had surprised her.

'We'll get you into a white kimono for richer for poorer.' It was way too early but flattering nonetheless. He had not mentioned it again in all their time in Tokyo.

The taxi came to a standstill outside the hotel. It stood on the site of what had once been a remarkable Frank Lloyd Wright building. Her door opened automatically in that trick that Tokyo taxis had. She stepped out and pulled at the straight skirt of lilac silk she had chosen for the evening, growing in height with Josh's glance of approval. So far she had found Japan to be a compromise, and where the hotel masterpiece had been an unremarkable tower block now stood.

In the entrance lobby they were greeted by two kimono-clad women like porcelain dolls bowing in heavy embroidered silks. It was the first time that she and Josh had been back to the hotel where they had spent nearly a month when they first arrived. Revisiting it brought back the cloying luxury and those first steps, charting her way across the strangeness of the city. That early shaky independence seemed to have faltered. Across the lobby Josh caught the eye of a colleague and excused himself to catch him at the lifts. Naomi watched him talking as the elevators behind them opened and shut as if in response to the overheard conversation: the strength of the Yen; the legal challenges that might allow a Listing; the last hike on the Nikkei. Every sector had its vocabulary and it was as clear as Japanese to her, so she turned towards the restrooms to kill time.

She knew this face, but strangely enough, it was, at first glance, unfamiliar to her, rather like meeting a friend unexpectedly in the wrong context. And so she did not register its pinched discomfort.

Naomi brushed beneath the short hair at the nape of her neck, which had a tendency to form telltale knots. As she dressed for the evening Josh had come on to her and they had made love and had run late. It seemed the entire female contingent at Sam's party had congregated at the mirror to preen. A chin came to rest on her shoulder and a familiar voice murmured, 'You are beautiful. I hope you enjoy it.'

Miho. The pleasure in seeing her felt as good as a coffee rush. Her gamine haircut and open face suggested someone at ease. Naomi envied her this.

'You feel like tonight?' Naomi was a little flat.

Miho's dark eyes shone. 'We can always go back to my place?' The offer was intended to confuse as Miho had never invited Naomi back to the studio, though they often hung out together. Miho had been seeing Sam for a while since Josh and Naomi had first introduced them. From her clutch bag she took a key ring attached to a flip-lid lighter and waved a set of keys triumphantly in front of Naomi. 'To Sam's apartment.'

'Commitment.'

'Going good. Very good,' she beamed. She would not tempt fate and accepting the present served her better than once the disappointments had.

Miho's contentment was infectious.

Naomi searched for her 'raspberry burst' blusher but Miho pulled it from her hand and pushed her towards the door.

'Come on. Tonight you meet my famous architect.'

She described him as a girl in red craned over towards the ladies' room mirror, rubbing powder from a mother-of-pearl compact across her gums. 'You going to Sam's?'

Hana slipped the blusher back in her bag. Caroline from the bank, she realized. She barely recognized her transformation.

Matching red lipstick followed. 'I'm dying to meet his guest speaker,' Caroline said. 'Sam's been so excited.'

'Do we know who it is yet?'

'Big secret.' Caroline winked.

Naomi held her finger to her lips and, after linking arms with Miho, the two glided out together. She assumed Josh had gone up to the reception with the investment banker. While they waited for the elevator she wondered idly whether one door might reveal the architect, stepping out like the man from a child's humidity clock with a sheltering umbrella in his hand. It was her belief that Miho had oversold her connection with the man and that he would be unlikely to appear that night.

In the lobby, Mochizuki was running late. He drew a thin hand through lightly grizzled hair, which he wore closely cropped, and he flicked the ash from the lapel of his dark, well-cut suit. He was in no mood to be guest speaker that night. And he couldn't work out why, Kazuko, his wife, whom he could usually entrust with his appointments diary, had sent him to a private party, in the Imperial Hotel of all venues. It was possibly, across the entire city, the building he most disliked.

This prejudice was focused on the ugly tower shaft that had replaced a remarkable icon by Frank Lloyd Wright. A beautiful landmark that was, as he remembered it, like discovering a Nirvana-like temple, once you had cut through the dense city to reach views of the emperor's palace across the park. Though it formed part of what was a growing city back then, it had taken him by surprise when he had first seen it as a young man. He had expected exotic birds to wing in, pausing to drink at the lily pond. The treasure had, he readily admitted, fallen into some degree of decay and had not kept pace with the demands of a city whose persistent need was for regeneration that, like his workload, was a constant. What he would give just now to be at home catching up with that burden of undertakings. Kazuko had saved herself the trouble of joining him by making excuses about her own commitments. She, he observed resentfully, would not have to eat her way through plates of complicated French gravies.

Naomi let go her hold of Miho's arm. Her backless halterneck dress fell into folds at the base of her spine and from plain yellow silk it ran into a riot of colour. This, together with

Naomi's lilac sheath, rendered them two birds of paradise that might have walked out of Mochizuki's dreams.

'Dance shoes?' Naomi pointed to Miho's platform shoes.

'For the afterparty. Sam insists. You'll come.' And she drifted off, leaving Naomi to follow or find a familiar.

Voices muffled by trappings of intercontinental opulence drew Naomi along the corridor to the crowded anteroom; she watched as Miho got caught in an eddy of people and they drifted apart. Naomi felt for the small butterfly necklace she had chosen, and could make out Josh through the double doors, standing beneath the pendant chandeliers, the accumulated light playing indiscriminately over the well-dressed guests.

She knew Josh would be irritated at her for having made him wait; they lived together in a dance of reproach and rapprochement. In London when they had friends over, she was used to finding she was left with them when he had gone to bed towards the end of the evening, unannounced. One night she had encouraged everyone to creep through to their bedroom where he lay asleep and they jumped on him, only to wake his ill-temper. It had cost her days of peace.

She took a proffered tall-stemmed glass from one of the waiters and walked in. The air was brackish.

Places were set for a western dinner. A familiar crowd of guests from among the European and American expatriates were milling round a long table offering one another ready cheeks, easily drawn into the vacuum of opulence. She found it cloying.

Sam was hosting. He was tanned, and his thick, well-groomed hair was shot with lights, following his recent trip to Polynesia; a short break from the trading job that paid him more money than he knew how to spend. Tonight was out of character: a venue that was too stuffy for him. He was living on the outer reaches of an existence in which he was inevitably about to make a mistake; he might have been a happier as a person but could foresee it coming.

'Beloved,' he beamed as he opened his arms to catch Naomi in a welcome embrace. He had a personality to die for but he was likely to be the eventual sacrifice.

'Looking gorgeous. How's life?'

'Tell me first; yours has just been reduced by another year. Happy birthday, old man.'

'Harsh. You haven't bought me a gift?' He was hopeful.

'No,' she confirmed. 'No, I haven't.'

'Good.'

'No, not yet, but I don't promise not to. And what do you give the man who *takes* it all? Something alternative? Something effective.'

He found this an anti-climax. 'Don't make it too Bohemian,' he warned.

'I don't want to have to give it back to you for Christmas. The head of Salman Rushdie is on sale for three million. How much have you got?'

She shook her head disapprovingly.

'No Salman?' He paused. He was fiercely intelligent and just too confident of his own abilities to find any real challenge in life, but as a result he was hungry for new experiences and it mattered to him that they were regarded novel by those around him, which was not the same as valuing their judgement.

'Are you asking for a book or an author?'

He leaned in in confidence. 'Perhaps I would prefer a little delicacy along the lines of the sexy reader. Is that closer to what you had in mind?'

Naomi pouted disapprovingly. His taste for women was wide-ranging and her fondness for Miho wouldn't let her go further with it.

'Maybe you can choose your own. We will find you something by the end of the evening,' she promised.

They were interrupted by another guest, hailing him as if they were long-lost.

Usually at the end of the evening Sam would end up in a hostess club, with or without a tolerant girlfriend. They had been with him countless times and, no matter what woman was beside him, they had watched him papering over his loneliness. This time she had hoped it would be different for Miho.

The volume of conversation in the room rose as the need to be heard escalated and the exertion of raising their voices drew them into the spirit of the party. Miho stalked past and blew Sam a kiss; her eyes fixed less on Sam than the girl he might be talking to. She pointed to Naomi with approval and bowed smiling. Miho's esoteric style was not what she expected for Sam who had a catalogue of trophy women behind him. Given Miho's easy, languid manner, it might just work but she would need record-breaking levels of patience.

'Roppongi after dinner?' he called after her.

'I'm on,' Miho responded to what she knew was an invitation to find a club as she strode over to a crowd in the corner.

'You and Josh coming?'

'Count us in.' Naomi hadn't seen Josh in a while and was scanning the room.

'He's over talking to the derivative guys under the portrait.'

Naomi cast around and saw a group she recognised beneath the copy of a Boucher painting. She ignored the small, welling resentment that she had begun to feel at Josh's customary insouciance when they were out. His appetite for a deal was so consuming it swallowed his passion for anything other than work. And now it was swallowing his passion for her.

'So you've decided to stay in Tokyo. What's next?' Sam asked her.

When she had first arrived, Naomi had been very vocal about how her commitment to staying was open to review. She had given herself a couple of months to settle in and was going to take it from there. She'd been with Josh for over a year and she was conscious that her life was synchronized with his but not dictated by his. The discovery that the oppression of liberty was real fired her hunger for greater independence.

'You can put your artistic talents to redesigning my apartment, if you like.'

'Sam, your apartment is beautiful. It doesn't need redesigning.'

His money gave him leave to be generous. The apartment was newly built and lavishly fitted with Italian marble floors and minimalist open fireplaces. It was filled with very large canvasses he had collected from a dealer, in Meguro, specialising in Russian art that was just becoming available from the Eastern bloc. His choice of venue tonight definitely ran counter to what most of the guests would have anticipated.

'I am looking for work.' she threw in, as a tall girl in a blue, low-cut dress caught Sam's eye.

The girl was immediately all over him, pressing close and passing it off as merely flirtatious, which he barely acknowledged. They must have once had something, and she was still hopeful.

'Sam, darling,' the girl cooed, 'we are so looking forward to the guest speaker. You've played your hand close. Someone special. He's definitely coming? Surely now you can tell me who it is. Look, if he's as well-known as you say he is, I want to sit next to him.'

'Got you down.'

'You're sure?' Sam loved to indulge people.

She turned her attentions for the first time, to Naomi. Sam introduced Fiona.

'Yes, I've met Josh, right?' she said, positioning Naomi as his accessory. 'Has Sam told you who this mystery speaker is going to be?' Naomi had no time to answer before the girl asked. 'How are you finding Tokyo? Tough to be here in the rainy months. What are you doing here? Only the desperate are left here in June.'

Naomi had asked herself the same question.

Fiona seemed not to want answers.

'Everyone's out of town, gone home for the summer. The festering month. God, we're all that's left.' She cast round the room dismissively and then looked down over her own high cheekbone. Her dress was cut too low for comfort and too tight on the waist, the chiffon was forced to lie in uncomfortable horizontal folds. Was it a dismissive glance or a safety check on the amount of cleavage presented to the room. The answer came when, as if suddenly finding herself in the wrong company, Fiona hailed a man and set off in his direction like a billiard ball looking for a pocket. Naomi thought she saw him across the room take his napkin and feed it to the garrulous girl, about to pot the red.

'So you'll design my lakeside cabin in Montana?'

His smile was the smile of someone who had never found life that difficult and so could invest generous amounts of goodwill in his friends, which he had found, like money, made money.

She smothered the impossibility of the task in an excuse.

'A redwood log cabin? I don't have any experience with wooden shacks, Sam. Wood. So medieval. We moved on. Steel and glass? Good lakeside view.' But she was a failed student and the responsibility would eat into the reserves of confidence that had been leaching away since she arrived. 'You need an American architect.' She changed the subject. 'Where's the guest speaker?'

'Mochizuki. We're lucky to have him. Works with traditional principles'

'So plagiarism some might say.'

'You should meet him,' Sam said conspiratorially, turning to his right and guiding her as he spoke, only to find themselves colliding with the elegant Japanese man standing behind.

'You know my new friend Mochizuki?' Sam asked Naomi.

Miho had described him earlier. He was thinner, almost lanky and less self-assured than she had expected. She guessed more artist than engineer. Sam shook his hand and took his arm warmly.

'We last met at the dinner for the Guam Airport funding.'

And he turned to Naomi, 'His work is renowned. You'll know it.'

He had a generous face and was greying at the temples. He touched the collar of his black polo shirt.

Naomi ran quickly back and forth across the gallery of a virtual library and crashed into a trolley full of candidate books before she discovered she couldn't raise a single piece of his work. Her face gave away not just the blank but the pain of finding nothing.

Had he heard her comment on plagiarism? His jawbone tensed. He looked as though he would rather be elsewhere.

Naomi eyed him up. He was much older but clearly took exercise. And he was marked by a self-containment brought by success and it drew her in the same way that power and money were aphrodisiacs for some. His movements were slow, measured. Attractive. She felt his dark eyes rest on her collar-bone and she watched as he followed a thin black strap from her shoulders to the butterfly on her necklace. It was as if he had had touched her.

'Butterfly.' He bowed.

'Naomi.'

'So, we should build in man-made materials I think you said? I could not disagree more.' He spoke English fluently.

He had overheard her. And she was crestfallen. Under the light as it caught her hair she turned fragile.

'But this vogue is over, no?' He recovered as if he had been too harsh on her.

'Okay, Ciocio-san.'

She was aware he looked at her for too long and he noticed he had been caught.

Sam turned on his heel to face the room and lifted his arms. Like a thespian, he was so weaned on the attentions of others that he could no longer do with out them.

Mochizuki inclined his head toward her; His confidence was a force, but his humility put her at her ease.

'Do you know much of Japanese traditional architecture?' Mochizuki asked her. The keenness with which the architect squeezed this question into the tight interlude between Sam's call for attention and the time lapse between seizing it gave it urgency.

'No, I . . .'

'Okay, okay, okay, everyone,' Sam bawled to gain audience, and then announced that it was time for everyone to take their places and eat.

'That . . .' the architect said as he moved away from her, 'that, is a great shame.'

He hadn't yet smiled and she hoped that the reason might be cultural but feared that he was annoyed with her, as she was in turn with herself, for her comment. Sam began again.

It was best to filter off in a different direction to Mochizuki with the excuse of looking for her seat, only she discovered that she was positioned directly opposite him as they approached one another from different sides of the table. Mochizuki had an air of detachment as if an observer, whose achievement had no need of the obvious calibration that some of Josh's friends relied on. He didn't wear it or hold court to impress.

Josh was positioned two away from him on the same side of the table and he winked at her as they sat down to begin the meal. A large glass centrepiece of trailing white orchids and a spray of greenery screened her view of the architect across the table and she shifted on her chair to hide behind it and began the requisite opening conversations with those beside her with a rare intensity of interest.

The chef at the Imperial had a Michelin star and so they ate well, course after course, and washed it down with Puligny-Montrachet, Pétrus and listed wines on the menu that ran like a primer for French Chateaux. At the end of the meal Sam stood up.

'We are gathered,' he began.

Whoops of appreciation went up and when they had subsided he went on to applaud the French, continuing the theme of his evening, for the wisdom of their saying, 'Show me a man's friends and I will show you his character.'

He played to their vanity and they were then bound to listen appreciatively to anything he had to say. It was easy to see why Josh adored him. Naomi looked round the room and had to wonder how many of the company enjoying his hospitality were more than acquaintances. She and Josh knew Sam well but they had rarely seen any of these friends before. The crowd heckled.

'I want to introduce you . . .'

Excited mumblings ran round the room.

'I want to introduce a man who proves I am not the only celebrated American in Tokyo,' and he began to make his way to the anteroom with the intention of escorting the guest speaker to his table. His much-vaunted speaker arrived in the form of a life-size cardboard cut-out of the ex-president of the United States of America. The laughter went up and somebody leapt up to punch Sam playfully on the shoulder.

'This man gets the Russians to believe they must buy arms that they don't need and to ensure they have a hard time affording them he floods the Middle East with oil so they don't have the cash to pay for them. Let us salute a great man when we see one. No, now look,' Sam apologized, 'I am afraid we have here a bad case of laryngitis.' And he threw the cardboard aside ushering it out with a demand for a round of applause for 'Ronald *Regan*'. And he dispensed with the joke.

'No, I promised you a great man and you have come here to hear one.' He conducted the applause to a diminuendo. 'To be serious, I would like to introduce Mr Mochizuki: a man with numerous international awards to his name for work that crosses continents, gracing the skyline of so many international cities. His illustrious career speaks for itself. We are hugely privileged to have him come here to talk to us tonight.'

As the polite, gentle clapping subsided, the architect stood up .

'Thanks – I'm gonna give you my translator. He's more eloquent.'

He began through the interpreter standing beside him; he spoke slowly as if primarily addressing him rather than the guests in Japanese, leaning in to make his job easier. 'I have worked on many large projects,' his hired vocal cord said, and went on to list a few prestigious buildings in Europe and Asia.

Naomi realized she had seen colour plates of the most recent of these, though would not have attributed them.

'But aside from these commissions, which I have been lucky enough to be asked to design, I have a private passion, very close to my heart.'

He paused to gauge their attention and Naomi's among them, and she assumed they were about to be regaled with his recent scrapes while flying a light aircraft or his scoop on the protection of the otter on the Sanagawa River. She had underestimated that behind his professionalism lay a need to exercise those skills, to the exclusion of just about everything else.

He began again conspiratorially, but setting up this gift of confidence was beyond the wooden delivery of the translator.

'This quiet passion of mine is for a very small, beautifully formed historical building. One of the most important forms of architecture.'

The interpreter stood vacantly waiting to catch the next ball to be thrown, like a dog at play.

'I suggest this is the Japanese teahouse. It offers us a way of living and is more than just a shed.'

Mochizuki started as the interpreter used the word shed. He had specifically not used the word *koya* when he had intended to convey a sense of shelter and protection.

He could not let him go on and somewhat uncomfortably he tapped the interpreter on the forearm and graciously suggested he might take over and have a go at speaking directly in English himself. He spoke it well enough.

'A Japanese teahouse is found within the Japanese garden. This positioning in the landscape is important because before you reach the sanctuary of this building you must take a rough path towards it. A building should always be a sanctuary; if it is merely a shelter for daily activities we reduce our lives to merely this limited toil. We must be aware as we approach our sanctuary that we do so. It must be in full consciousness. The teahouse is a fine example of such mindfulness in architecture.' He nodded. 'Yes, it is important that the approach route is uneven, maybe a difficult path. You must not be sure of your step and so you must concentrate on the way. This is the Buddhist way, *ne*,' he said for confirmation.

'It is constructed according to the old concept of *miegakure*. The path is always crossing back on you so you cannot see where you are going to end up. It doesn't give you any perspective of where you are at that time and you must think only of your own spirit at this time. This mirrors our lives.' He settled his gaze on Naomi.

So Mochizuki the renowned architect was a spiritual man, she thought. The humble subject of the building he had chosen to talk about and the strength of his passion struck her as quaint. So his passions were closer to conservationist than a man ready to indulge in the cheap thrills of speed or the underwhelming narrowness of causes adopted in the absence of anything else, after all. Naomi ate very little of the lamb presented in blackcurrant jus. She was excited by this man, and he had stolen her appetite for anything other than his words.

'Making this journey to the teahouse. You only know to follow the path. It will take you.'

She was drawn to these words and took them to be his personal philosophy. In speaking as he had done, he had endorsed her own directionless wanderings that had begun on leaving London and she found, in his dry delivery, she had a thirst to quench.

He gestured again to his colleague, the redundant interpreter, and then sat down, bowing as he did so, and, as he caught her eye, she smiled uncomfortably as if she were the butterfly that he had pinned on a collector's mat; as if he already knew too much about her. She felt transparent. Her hand went back to the necklace at her throat.

The interpreter dropped his head towards the architect and after conferring was handed the speech to continue reading on his own.

He cited Tadao Ando, Fumihiko Maki, Louis Kahn, Álvaro Siza and the responsibilities that these international architects had carried. These familiar names settled in her mind as a profound reminder of what she had left behind; how much she missed representatives of what had inspired her reading. And now she sat before a globally respected architect who reduced the skills of these men, whose work she admired, to craftsman. He had humbly compared his skill to a potter at a wheel, drawing a fabric between his hands, though he sculpted cities.

At the end of the talk, Sam, in conclusion, rose to announce their appreciation and to thank him for coming.

Once Sam had finished, Naomi saw Miho leave her seat, smiling conspiratorially at her, to go talk to Mochizuki.

Mochizuki noticed Miho's smile for Naomi and gently inclined his head in her direction.

As the pair left the room together Naomi couldn't understand why she was so reluctant to see him leave.

In the brighter lights of the anteroom, Miho took a sip from her glass and tried unsuccessfully to extract an American cigarette from its soft pouch.

He came to her rescue and lit one for each of them.

'Great,' she said. 'Great. I had no idea that was what you were going to cover.'

'No. I changed my mind, which was okay, but it gave the translator a headache.' Mochizuki felt he had humiliated the man and regretted it.

'He was getting it wrong.'

'Right.' Even her exhaled smoke was drawn towards him.

'Even monkeys fall from trees,' he said, excusing the interpreter.

She knew Mochizuki would never use the man's services again, not because he was no good but because he, Mochizuki, would feel embarrassed at having shown him up and would feel bad about it. He was clearly brooding over it. Miho had wanted, on behalf of Naomi, to ask him if they needed any help in the office but he was not in a good place to consider such a request. She needed to divert him from his preoccupation with the interpreter.

'I thought I might just see Kazuko this evening.' Kazuko had, in fact, told her the chances of her turning up were less than slim.

'Well, she's pretty tired after the conference.'

'Say hi to her for me.'

'I will. I will do that.'

Sam came up, placing his hand on Miho's bare back, just above folds of turquoise silk; it was understood to be supportive rather than proprietorial. They flipped to English when Sam offered,

'We are heading out for the afterparty. Will you come with us?' His smile was generous.

Mochizuki was gracious. 'I am going to head back. I have quite a bit of work still to do on Guam Stage Three,' he confessed, knowing Sam understood the timelines on the Guam project.

'That's too bad. Sounds like you need some more lackeys. Maybe you could think of something Naomi might be able to do for you?'

'Yes, there's a consideration,' Mochizuki said weakly, by nature readily obliged to accommodate a request but really less than inclined to do so on this project. 'I will give that some thought,' he said honestly. After saying his goodbyes, he left them to look for the interpreter with whom he had agreed to share a cab.

Miho jabbed Sam in the stomach.

'Good, Sam. Good.'

Mochizuki found the man under interrogation from Caroline but managed to draw him away while stealing a last glance at the opinionated girl he had been asked to consider.

Naomi was talking to Josh as he left.

'So do we take it,' Josh quizzed, when Mochizuki was out of earshot, 'that we will have to cut our way through a concrete jungle of a city where all the roads lead us nowhere and the paths take us in a circuitous route around the building before we can find the lobby door to the office.

Sam caught his riff as he approached. 'Sounds like London planning to me, buddy.' Then he laughed generously.

Chapter 32

On their return to the dining room Caroline rose to give a vote of thanks; she wore the trendy shoulder pads of an American football player as she toasted Sam for another legendary party; an unctuous speech leavened only by the fact that she mentioned herself as often as she did him. The chef bought a cake and cheering marked the close of the celebrations.

The assembly milled around the tables for a while smoking and helping themselves to after-dinner drinks and Hershey's chocolates – a special request from Sam.

Josh turned to Naomi. 'A bunch of Buddhist crap,' he complained, treading with inadvertent carelessness on the inspiration she had received.

Naomi wanted to leave. 'Where's Sam?'

'He hasn't done Roppongi for a while. I'll find a taxi cab.'

As they left the hotel, Sam touched the sleeve of the MC and gave him leave to continue serving the other guests on his account.

Four of them took a waiting cab, with Sam in the front seat.

'Great to see you, Miho,' Josh charmed.

Naomi rested her head on the white, lace antimacassar as Sam pulled a bottle from under his lapels and undid the top buttons on his shirt, turning to offer the bottle.

'God,' she said, 'what is the point of stealing your own booze?'

'It isn't my booze. It isn't my party.'

'Oh, really. Well, whose birthday were we celebrating back there then?'

'It happened to be my birthday on the same night as the party.'

'That was not how the invitation read,' Naomi told him.

'You're right. I invited you to my celebration.'

'So whose booze, whose party?'

'I'm putting the bill for tonight on the company expense account. Berridge is out of town and he's not going to ask to look at the guest list, for Christ's sake. You were all my valued clients this evening. If we hadn't gone over the top, he'd be asking questions. The bill has to be large enough to be plausible. Why else would we eat at the Imperial with an international guest speaker?'

Josh whistled appreciably at the nerve of the man.

'What gives you licence?' Naomi objected.

'Equity warrants,' Sam shot back in veritas.

Sam's company was unknowingly paying for the whole evening and it would be passed off as client entertainment. The evening would be unlikely to be deemed personal as it was of a scale that was too large for anyone to try and pass off. Anyone but Sam. He was high now on euphoria and other things too.

It was after midnight; the streetlights illuminated the yellow haze of the city night. It never got any darker than this. The taxi slowed as a cordon of policemen took random checks; a baton motioned them to stop. The car came to a halt and the driver wound down his window to speak briefly to the slight, uniformed figure. He hung his head inside the car with a cold mask strapped from ear to ear.

'Sanitary wear,' Josh sniggered, hanging over the bottle to hide it.

The policeman took one look at the *gaijin* in the back seat and summarily waved them on. They were held up only momentarily; the assumption that they were Americans was as good as diplomatic plates, giving them licence to be treated differently, as privileged outsiders. Naomi had not done any drugs that night and was lagging behind Josh and Sam. She thought back to the architect; she had found his perspective on life so completely different.

At the stoplights, the sound of a saxophone reached their ears from under the expressway. A repetitive strain swung its way towards them that to her ear was slower and more melancholy than it should have been.

'It's so sad, practising under the arches.'

'The limitations of living in a six-mat tatami room with paper-thin walls,' Josh offered derisively. 'He'd be beaten if his neighbours had to listen to that.'

As they sped past Naomi pictured the lone figure sheltering under the concrete underpass, listening to the echo under the bridge of his own notes, looking for pearls in the mud flats, looking for his soul in the music. Josh was wrong.

'So where are we going, maestro? I vote for the Ink Stick,' Sam said, settling on a favourite haunt.

'Okay. Okay, but not yet. We first have to go to Lennon's tonight,' Josh drawled, as if it was time for a little more European nostalgia.

Sam overruled him.'Lennon's after.'

As they got out of the taxi in Roppongi, the drone of the sleepless expressway thirty feet above their heads stole their voices. A dirty night, of a grey favoured by Zen monks, had settled on the shabby line of buildings marshalled to follow the stanchions of the overhead road. It was interrupted by a narrow pink tiled tower, covered in neon signs pretending intimacy on immediate acquaintance. They made for the underground bar forced into hiding beneath a faceless building, cowering under superstructure of the roadway.

'This elegant building –' Josh gesticulated, as if he were getting off on himself '– this building is worth more than the Empire State.'

'Not true,' Sam countered. 'Only the plot, not the real estate.'

This property bubble—'

Not this time,' Sam said, interrupting Josh. 'This time is different.' And Josh gave up.

Naomi watched the boys drink and dance and shout into one another's faces. She knew then she was not just tired, she was tired of this life.

Miho suggested since it was hours since they had eaten that they stop at small noodle shop that appeared like a weed in the cracks between the high rise.

A planner's requiem, Naomi thought, not just sober but too out of kilter to join them.

Miho, nurturing their friendship, leant close, bringing a piece of gyoza delicately balanced between her chopsticks to Naomi's lips.

She ate without losing too much of the pale, limpid dumpling. As tired as a child, she held Josh's arm.

'Let's go home. Please let's go home,' she whispered, but she knew it was Sam's night and Josh would inevitably follow him. Josh was so in thrall to the American she believed he would pull Sam out of the fallen rubble before her, if made to choose.

The Beatles tribute band was in an old apartment building on the side of a parking lot. An impossibly small elevator took them to the seventh floor.

'What we don't need now . . .' Naomi suggested

'. . . is an earthquake.'

'What a way to go.' Josh hugged her.

'It's been a good night,' Sam objected.

'"It's been a hard day's night and I been working like a dog",' Sam and Josh sang as they emerged, at the top of their voices, in clashing accompaniment with the four Beatle-wannabes, haircuts circa 1960, on official vocals. The singers wore perma-smiles and stroked guitars without strings, to the recorded backing, the whole act older than the port at the Imperial hotel.

'They are all the same slanty-eyed Beatle,' Sam observed with substance-induced originality.

Miho was used to rising above his comments and remained unresponsive. She often treated him with a superior indulgence, ignoring any childish behaviour. One of the reasons they got on was that she had never once questioned anything he did, no matter how objectionable he became. She was his unconditional woman.

Miho and Sam got up and danced themselves into a sweat for a few songs, then drifted back to the table to pull Naomi and Josh on to the dance floor. Naomi went through the motions but their hedonism tasted like the alcohol at this hour: sour. After they had worn themselves out in wild, exaggerated enthusiasm, they took the bench – ranks of labelled bottles of scotch promised a journey she did not want to take.

Josh called for a whisky glass from a psychedelic shirt that was the bartender. Balking at the order the barman eventually offered them a bottle, refusing to sell separate shots by pulling glasses off the shelf and shaking his head. Bottles of Scotch ambered the wall, all tagged with client's names.

Naomi waited it out, expecting a familiar end to the evening. She had near choked on their self-indulgence and couldn't take any more.

'I'm not buying a whole bloody bottle,' Sam remonstrated, throwing a hopeful punch across the bar. He hated being treated like an idiot. His unbridled existence caught and undesirably snagged.

'You are if you want to drink whisky here,' Josh reasoned with him.

'I want a drink. I don't want to take a bottle.'

Miho sat back, coolly downing the last of a long drink, watching the westerner's inhibitions float away on alcohol. Often they give rein to such indiscretions but they seldom got physically abusive – too often defeated by incapacity first. She lit a cigarette, and seemed keen not to involve herself with the hovering bartender who might look to her for support.

'The boys are behaving badly.' Naomi took Miho by the hand. 'Let's dance.'

Miho followed her onto the dance floor.

'He was Korean,' Miho said, referring to the bar man nonchalantly as they danced. 'Like you. Me. We are all aliens.'

'Foreigners,' Naomi corrected her but the word settled on her like a judgement and she wondered how much of the sentence she had to run and how long she would be condemned to this sense of no-man's land.

Sam had become irrational. Miho watched him from the vantage point of her stool.

'It's Jack Kerouac.'

Naomi was blank.

'You're not up on your American idols,' Miho scolded.

They heard Sam shout: 'I'm not going to pay for a full bottle. I won't be back to this shithole to drink my whisky.'

Even Sam turns ugly after booze, Naomi observed to herself.

To appease Sam, Josh bought him the bottle and concluded helpfully, 'He's not coming back to this shithole.'

Sam happily made every effort to drink it, as he and Josh twisted in time, with one another and the bar for support, shouting to the beat.

This was the regular pattern of 'Josh at play', reduced to a small boy and unaware he was lost. Naomi took him by the arm.

'Take me back, Josh,' she said, gentle towards him.

He cupped her cheek in his hand sweetly 'Okay, baby.' He said,

And she loved him all over again.

As they left, he swiped the Scotch bottle he'd bought to take with him, ignoring the misplaced assumption on the part of the barman that it would be labelled and placed back on the shelf.

160

Convention had it that he should be the one bringing her home but so often he was in her care, unsteady from a night of excess, with her doing the leading.

She wondered how long she could keep pace with him chasing his empty desires.

Chapter 33

Shimokitazawa, 2012

Hana left a message with Tom. His calls had become less frequent in the last week or so and he hadn't filled in the gaps. She suspected Sadie had finally conquered him. Earlier on this would have bothered her more but a new independence had settled on her. Everyone was 'system down' on her at once; Jess too had become signal erratic and only hopscotch reliable. Tako had disappeared for a while and they guessed he might now have a girlfriend. She decided to go alone to walk at the temple where Ukai's memorial had been held. Miho, she was sure, knew something of Naomi that she would or could not tell. So she would find the answer herself.

There were only three people in her train carriage, including an elderly woman, bowed to the inevitability of age and the dominance of a writhing grandchild. Hana wondered idly where his mother might be and what his father did. In a short time, paddy fields emerged, only to return as quickly to a rattling continuum of urban sprawl.

After she alighted, she made her way uphill as she had for Ukai's memorial service, to the rarer air of the temple. Beyond the totem of the red torii gate, she bought a ticket at the temple kiosk. The serving acolyte had stepped straight out from a gold-leaf screen, depicting the Tale of Genji, the eleventh-century masterpiece she had seen in the museum at Ueno. Over stippled flecks of gold leaf beneath dream clouds, the heroine Murasaki wept in lover's purple, with cascades of hair to dry her tears. Her ticket checked, Hana followed the unreliable path ranging across the grounds to look for the teahouse. She left the meanderings of the stepping-stone path and headed over a mossy bank of yellow-green. Finding herself blocked by a woven wooden fence she strode over it and almost stepped on a woman huddled on the ground in a cotton scarf, sweeping the bank of dead leaves with a dustpan and brush. Without admonishment, she sent her, with a wave of her brush, back to the path.

The trees stretched above cascading temple roofs, casting a purple shade. And she came across a party of tourists necklaced in serious cameras as they meandered past her at the head of the pond. To avoid them she headed uphill through bamboo caught behind thin woven frames of earlier growth. She failed to find any building fitting the description of the teahouse and beyond the open space of some utility buildings she exhausted her search and made for the red umbrellas of the open-air café selling matcha tea and pastel biscuits. She ordered with resignation and watched as the party of tourists arrived to join her.

'Did you see the lake?' a retired American man asked her; a party of garden enthusiasts from Boston, she guessed from his accent.

Too politely she tried to dissuade him from showing her the shots that he had taken on his image finder.

Too politely she let him share his enthusiasm for the first frame as his damp shirt touched her shoulder when he leaned over to show her. She could see it now in the small square of the digital image. There, by the water's edge, was the round window of a small, terraced building standing over the lake.

'The carp . . .' he began.

Abruptly she left him and she left her tea, and she ran as if fleeing from a swarm of menacing tourists back to the lakeside.

Running her fingers across the rough, rendered surface of the wall, she walked round the sides of the small teahouse. It was the size of a single room; a peaceful place for contemplation alongside the frenetic castings of the world. On the lake beyond the maples the water plumed as a duck landed and she climbed the step to the terrace. She had arrived. It was Naomi's building; she knew it was. A place of quiet contemplation, where she could almost hear the turning of the world, and, just now, possibly a little further than that. On the open platform that stood over the waters of the lake, beside her from a simple bamboo pipe; water fell gently into a small rough-hewn basin and she sat beneath a small, round window and wept.

Once back in Shimokitazawa, Hana left the station and made straight for Ziggy's to find Miho. A rising fury that Miho had lied to her took her marching back to the café. Nothing else could quite account for her unease and now she had to find out why.

Miho was serving walnut coffee cake and greeted her with the assumption that she would take English tea.

'How is Emiko right now?' Miho asked, referring to the issues Jess had had with Emiko.

'Miho, I went up to the temple,' she pronounced. She was not prepared to let Miho off the hook, and would not be diverted from her mission.

'Where Ukai had his memorial? At Guzeiji?'

'Yes. And this time I had to pay to get in.'

'You went to the memorial?' Miho asked.

'I did.'

'Me too. But I didn't see you there.'

Hana's eyes narrowed.

Miho must sense her steely determination, should guess she had some connection with Naomi?

'I saw the teahouse,' Hana said, watching a dam of history welling behind the older woman's eyes.

Miho should know Naomi would have told her about the teahouse and her association with the project years earlier.

'The teahouse. The teahouse by the lake?'

'Is there more than one?' Hana didn't intend to let Miho toy with her.

'No, I suppose not. Not in this case.'

'So you know it?' Hana waited for a response and watched Miho carefully.

Chapter 34

It was past two in the morning and Mochizuki knelt, accustomed to the humidity at a low table, in his yukata cotton robe. Beneath the only pool of light in the darkened room he pored over figures for the third stage of the Guam project. He fumbled for his cigarettes in the sleeve of his yukata. Beneath the desk light the clouds of exhaled smoke threw him into soft focus, and at this hour he looked like the loneliest man on earth. Ukai had been pushing a lot of work his way recently and the volume was getting too much. What concerned him slightly more was that at some stage soon there would be a payback, a time when Ukai would expect him to show his gratitude and he neither knew when it might be nor what form it would take. He did know that it was not necessarily going to be legal.

Across the silence a sleepy voice called him from another room.

'*Kun.*' There was a pause as she listened for his response and then she called him again. '*Kun.*'

He had returned from the Imperial Hotel where Kazuko had booked him to speak to a small crowd of mostly English and Americans. He was piqued that she had made the appointment, and when he returned home after the event she had gone to bed and he had made no special effort keep the noise down or the lights dimmed.

He gave no immediate reply but eventually the slap of the folder on the desk told her that he had finished for the night.

Once in the bedroom he walked over to the window and pulled back the paper screen to circulate more air. The cloudy eastern sky was perma-bright, stale yellow, another nicotine summer night. Behind him the house was silent but for the beat of their retro fan.

In the darkness of the bedroom, he felt his way around their western bed, drawing back the light, silk summer cover. Kazuko lay awake now, propped up on the bed on one elbow.

'You are working too hard. You ought to speak to Ukai,' she told him. The length of their marriage was such that she knew him well enough to speak her mind. She spoke with clarity even now in the middle of the night. 'You've known him how long? This association with Ukai has lasted so many years; you should feel free to express yourself. You should feel free to approach him and tell him enough is enough. Time for him to release you from that old burden of debt.' Her voice was characteristically low and was becoming soporific.

He began to run his hands over his eyes. She was his counsel, his wife and his best friend, and while he knew she was right he was the only one who knew that his debt would never be released.

Chapter 35

Sam jumped out of the Roppongi taxi, handing his wallet to Miho, her silk now crumpled. They were outside the Ink Stick jazz club on the Sendagaya Road and Josh and Naomi had followed, drawn like magnets along a concrete façade to the punched-steel door, where a bouncer, claiming numbers, refused them entry. She had lost the contest to go home and reached in support for Josh's arm as he stood with difficulty.

'Bloody curly-haired yakuza.' His alcohol-fuelled temper was immune to the small courtesies of his adopted country. As Josh started to lose it, the bouncer backed down and let them pass. Beneath a low-metal caged ceiling and clammy walls they joined the moving shadows, smoking and drinking away any absence of purpose.

'Let's go catch breakfast,' Sam suggested after a while. 'Tsukiji Market?' He wanted sushi from the edge of the fish market where stalls sold fresh fish straight off the boat.

In the pale watery light of morning they made for Tsukiji on the Sumida River. At this time the catches of tuna and other fish would have been unloaded for auction at the dockside.

They arrived at Tsukiji subway station, as stale and dry-mouthed as long-distance travellers. Though the road was not entirely deserted they found no evidence of the river, a dock-side, or a bustling market. A large basket flew past on a bicycle, close enough to collide with Josh's meanderings. He shouted at the trader's near miss and when Naomi declared she wanted the basket Josh ran after the man and accosted him. But he failed to be understood. They were flotsam to the trader.

Beside the red shrine stacked with enormous white sake barrels emblazoned in a Japanese script, a man was handing out packets of paper tissues from a box, advertising some new venture.

'Are you sure we've got the right day, here?' Sam turned to Miho.

Naomi was clinging to Josh's arm, now tired and cold, though a warm July day dawned.

'It's okay,' Miho said languidly. 'It's around here someplace.'

'Shall we go home?' Naomi tried Josh again, who responded by throwing his arm over her shoulder for his own need for support as much as hers.

'You have to see the auctions first,' Sam told her intently.

Sleepily Naomi leant her head against Josh as they walked, enjoying the silence after the enervating noise of their gilded crawl.

It was Sam's night, and nobody contradicted him.

Their passage took them through a narrow lane of stores selling cooking utensils, of tiny shacks huddled together and crammed with pans, industrial sized steamers and bamboo mats for maki rolls; sieves and ladles hung like superstitions from the ceiling. In each there was room for the vendor and no one else. The closer they got to the centre of the market, the more alien it became.

They paused for a minute to watch the old bonito seller sitting at his makeshift wooden box, grinding the hard dry fish as the blade on his wheel worked it as if he was turning wood. Fine flakes of blossom pink fish caught on the air and fell gently, settling like a prophecy; the pile of shavings to be sold as garnish that melted in the mouth smelt of sweet wood smoke. The whirring of the blade finally set her teeth on edge and Naomi drew them towards the anemones and shellfish breathing through visceral tubes in livid seaweeds, beside mottled blue sea urchins with purple spines. She yelped for the others to share the horror of a livid green sea cucumber as it made a bid for freedom. The stall was a squirming mass, tickling her disgust. Every pouting shell, every lurid, creeping stick of flesh and every limpid sucker would find its way on to the tables of the Tokyo fish restaurants that day. For a moment she was less hungry than she might have been.

'Is there any fish left in the fucking sea?' Josh wailed.

The ground now was wet under foot as they moved through the market.

They were unaware that the man handing out papers at the subway had followed them and trailed them without urgency. On either side there were busy stalls dividing large carcasses of tuna or dolphin into chunks.

Sam felt it appropriate to share his knowledge. 'Seven hundred and fifty-thousand metric tonnes of albacore, yellow fin, bluefin and western-Pacific skipjack caught in eighty-eight alone. Half the world's entire catch.'

'How much is left in the western Pacific?' Naomi was wide-eyed.

She was interrupted by the acceleration of a cylindrical, one-man vehicle stacked with polystyrene boxes, beeping his way through the ice melt and adding to the din. The market began to resemble a factory. As the next one passed, Josh leapt on the back and feigned kisses to a presidential crowd waving his arms to entertain them, skipping back after a few metres before the driver had time to register his clowning passenger. Josh played chicken as another wave of vehicles passed until Miho pulled him behind a stall.

Naomi watched the razor teeth of a saw turn its way through the frozen carcass of a man-sized headless fish, drowning the shouts of the vendors. Eventually they reached the heart of the market where a crowd gathered at the dockside auctions; Sam and Josh were heads taller than anyone else. Unseen behind them was the slim man in the starched, blue jacket.

The serious business of bidding was in full swing. Traders in grey uniforms raised their hands to the frenzied patter of the auctioneer, their earnest faces hard with concentration. Wooden boxes, like coffins, containing enormous fish encircled them. And headless and tailless carcasses lay unceremoniously on the bare, concrete floor. Josh lay alongside one at the end of a line and he was shorter than the ridged torpedo by a good three feet. Naomi focused on the glistening brine under the bright-yellow unnatural light. Sam kicked him to get up and he rose with the juice of sea fish clinging to the back of his Savile Row dinner jacket .

They stood huddled together on the edge of the bidding crowd. Naomi cast a glance at Sam, who looked more pallid under the fluorescent lights. He was watching the game with genuine interest, quietly following the emerging bids from the traders as they followed the syncopated rhythm of the auction-eers; the catch was now a serious commodity. Josh had half an eye out for Sam as he watched with fascination. When he deemed it appropriate he hung on to Sam's shirt at the elbow, instinctively aware that he was about to make a bid. Josh knew they would be lynched if they interfered with the day's business.

'Don't.' He glared at Sam. 'You'll get us all into trouble.'

Sam was too tired to put up a resistance and turned away, stepping aside from the auction babble.

When their attention flagged, Sam and Josh turned to move on, but they found Naomi and Miho were no longer standing behind them. They craned their necks around the edge of the crowd, looking over the heads of most of them, searching for the girls.

'Where did they go?' Sam entreated.

Chapter 36

Josh and Sam were sobering up. Tsukiji Market seemed less of a playground to them than it had. They had been searching for the missing girls for a while.

'You think they went home?'

They began to work their way back through the market, slowly, criss-crossing the route they had taken, covering their wake in broad bands. They retraced their tracks for a while and then returned to the site of the auction but neither girl was in sight.

Sam seemed less concerned. 'They'll be here somewhere. She's with Miho,' he said, as if the fact that one of them spoke Japanese was a comfort.

Josh pushed away from Sam. 'Let's split and meet back here in ten.'

Josh moved past the crowd of traders to the trucks and trailers beyond, finding his way between the refrigeration and ice-making units. A short distance from the crowd he looked inside the back of a huge articulated, cold storage vehicle. It had doors that would secure a small fortress but for the moment they were unbolted and hung wide open. The cavernous bastion already breached and the stuff- gone. The engine was running and awaiting the fish load; it was about to depart. He peered into the depths of the refrigeration trailer and felt more than just a physical chill, far from reassured at finding nothing. Without a soul around, the whole area was eerily empty after the throbbing activity of the market. Across the street four men, as dark as their clothes, were separating rubbish into containers. Losing sight of indulgent, nocturnal Tokyo, he felt himself waking to the threatening potential of a dockside city, and then heard Sam calling for Naomi. One of the men interrupted his work, raising his head to the foreigners, pendulous entrails dangling from his hands. Josh carefully picked his way over the pools of water and black hoses snaking their way to feed the parked lorries and vans. Back in the centre he was strafed by piles of boxes staggering towards him and the immediacy of small, delivery vehicles. The deep-throated voices of the generators drowned all other noise.

'Shit!' He jumped back, retreating to shelter behind the open door of a trailer, when a small forklift nearly ran him down. Since he had been up all night, a slight paranoia crept over him and he became convinced that the driver had aimed for him. He felt vulnerable and isolated and decided he needed to get back to Sam. He made his way quickly back to the auction where he found him vacantly picking his teeth.

'Seen them?'

Sam shook his head and Josh sagged in an articulated weariness. He had his hands in his pockets when somebody pushed him from behind, his tired body overreacting. He swung round aggressively.

The girls stood smiling beside him. Sam squeezed Miho's buttock with a dawning grin on his face.

Naomi could see Josh's anger flare. But at her innocent smile the shadow began to lift in relief at seeing her as if warmed by the daylight. When Josh had had left off scowling, Naomi presented Sam with a package.

'This,' she said proudly, offering him a paper-wrapped package, 'is your birthday present.'

Josh was further annoyed that Naomi looked so pleased with herself. The spotlight of the night rested solely on Sam.

Sleepily Sam took the present. 'It was yesterday,' he complained.

Naomi began to object to their unenthusiastic reception. 'Do you deserve it?' she tested him. 'Open it when we have breakfast.'

'It smells,' he said second-guessing.

'You know it doesn't smell,' Miho cautioned him patiently.

There was a remarkable absence of the smell of fish. It was all too fresh. Naomi leaned close to Sam's ear and imparted confidentially, in a sing-song Chinese accent, 'Old Chinese saying: fish and the company of friends smell after three days.'

'That's guests,' he countered.

'Today friends,' she laughed.

Josh was watching Naomi closely. 'One day, if it's Sam,' he added, 'and it depends how old the friends are. He just got older.' He laughed as if the pressure of losing the girls was finally released and in the outburst of that release his emotions overcompensated. He laughed too loudly. 'He stinks,' he added finally with tears in his eyes.

'You need food,' Sam observed and suggested they find a sushi bar. Without waiting for an answer he turned heel, his jacket over the shoulder of his crumpled shirt. A curious inverse applied to Sam, where the less tidy he was the more attractive he became. As they moved off, the blue-jacketed man followed, stopping behind them when they stopped. Josh turned, recognizing the familiar figure that had reappeared behind them.

'What does he want?' Josh blurted.

'Good sushi. New sushi,' he garbled, as he pounced on them. He was blocking their path with his body and hemming them in against the wheels of a delivery van parked at the side of the road.

'Good fish. Good sushi,' he continued unappealingly. They were tired; they wanted to eat and did not have the stamina to come up with an alternative when a solution had been thrust upon them. Like many travellers they bought the idea out of weariness, sold because their resistance was low and no contest in the face of a seller who had about him all the energy of desperation. They followed him across the market, clustered, concentric bands of activity, each supporting or supplying the other, laid out like a casebook economic model.

Back on the outskirts, where all the sushi bars and stalls traded, was an alley marked by traders' bunting; the short, split noren curtains, heavy in the stagnant breeze. Low shaku-hachi music played at the entrance as their hawker led them to a covered bar. He leaned against the wall, brushed aside the short indigo cloth, flapping at eye level, and guided them inside.

'Irasshaiemase!' Hoots of welcome met their entrance.

It was all new, with five seats in all; five being a lucky number, but two were already taken by a couple of men from the lorry park enjoying miso soup. Naomi felt awkward, as if someone who didn't have the right had invited them to a party. Conscious of the lack of spaces, the hawker went off, bidding them to wait with pantomime gestures.

'Ocha wa ikaga desu ka?' a woman asked. Then, in English, 'Tea?'

They all nodded and Sam dumped his parcel. It hit the counter with a reassuringly solid thud and he opened it.

'Fish. Fish. Fish. Fish. Fish. Fish.' His voice was loud with exaggeration.

'It isn't any fish, Sam,' Naomi counselled him. 'It's an expensive delicacy.'

'You bet.' He nodded with mock gravity. 'It isn't any fish. None of it is really.'

'Look, it's fugu,' Naomi said.

'You know fugu,' Miho added cajolingly. 'It's a good delicacy.'

'It's fucking poisonous.' The fish was a great delicacy but did carry a health warning.

'It's a great choice,' Miho urged. 'You just have to make sure you cut the liver out.' Sam decisively thrust the package towards the sushi stallholder who was busy cutting through slices of sashimi with the precision of a skilled artist.

'No, no, no. Not here, you can't,' Miho warned.

'Why not here? Now is as good as any time. Let's get the liver cut out. Listen, if the fish is poisonous I say we all eat it for breakfast. That way I'm not going to be the only victim. Anyone for Russian roulette?'

'You got to have a license to cut this fish,' Miho cautioned. He looked at the tiresome present, and then she let him off the hook. 'You know, Sammy, you can't have fugu this time of year. Only in the winter. We couldn't afford Fugu anyway. This is yellowtail.'

He laughed and held her. 'Thanks, Naomi,' he remembered to say, before taking a toothpick from a glass box in front of him and sucking with concentration. 'Marvellous. Sweet, thoughtful gift,' he added and laughed again.

The warm green tea sharpened her senses as Naomi watched the sushi chef embed rice in his palm, shaping it with three fingers, repeating the process with the alacrity of a well-honed skill. With a knife as sharp as his talents he took a live prawn and in two curt strokes removed the head and split it in two, laying the butterflied flesh aside. Taking from each tray he worked methodically and laid the opalescent pink, sticky ochre, and unguent white pieces of fish, across the rice in serried files. The balance of the meal was chosen for its texture as much as its colour.

He decorated the dominoes of sushi with green and purple translucent seaweed and a bowl of soy. The wasabi radish he added was shaped as a miniature Mount Fuji. They took their chopsticks from a glass jar at the end of the counter. It was a democratic eatery and the best food, fresh from the quay, was for the drivers and delivery boys who ate like the emperors of corporate Japan. In a babble of explanation worthy of a west-coast actor/waiter, the chef described his offerings, directing his patter to Miho. Josh slumped over the counter submitting to his fatigue. Naomi surveyed the glistening appetizers and, reading her hunger, took a bite from the innocuous-looking white fish. It was a mistake. The cartilaginous morsel was unappealingly brittle in the mouth and a completely unfamiliar texture. Miho sat with her knees drawn up and her side plate raised to her mouth eating hungrily.

'You'll like cuttlefish,' she inaccurately supposed, through her mouthful.

Naomi's heart sank and her energy began to flag.

'This is exceptional sea urchin,' Miho continued, her bare back hunched over her food. 'The colour is very good.'

Naomi looked at the sticky, mustard mess that still lay in the lacquer bowl. Sam and Josh put down their chopsticks in synchronized protest and, as they turned towards her, she registered their objection. It wasn't as if the idea of sea urchin was new to them; it was just that now, in the early morning light of their extended day, they had reached the limits of their endurance.

Their stools scraped loudly as they rose to pay, confusing the chef with the timing of a settlement at the start of a meal. He was more perplexed when they turned to go, leaving payment behind them and a largely untouched masterpiece in sushi. As they left he tried to offer them some tissues from a cardboard box beneath the counter. Nobody recognized him as the man at the subway. Naomi turned and accepted them, graciously, following after Sam's creased, white shirt, brightening with the creeping strength of daylight as he stepped out from beyond the canopy.

'Where are we headed'? Naomi called after him. His next idea met with unanimous approval since they had all lost the power of free will.

The new capsule hotel rose before them like a giant lorry fender, formed of a bank of cubicles.

'Four in a row,' he said.

Josh climbed a ladder and swung over the chrome step into a freshly made starched futon and cover. He turned and called the others.

Sam followed him with a bottle from the vending machine and threw it to the back of the capsule, and, hanging onto the mouth of what looked like a washing-machine door, he held his hand out for Miho to join him.

'We can't both fit into one capsule!'

He pleaded with her to try, and, despite her initial protestations, they crammed into one. Before they pulled the shutter across, he brandished the bottle at Josh triumphantly.

Josh and Naomi followed them into the adjacent capsule and could hear Miho's mock screams, which eventually reduced to laughter.

Josh turned on the TV in their cramped pod. They were so far into early morning it seemed they had gone through fatigue and had a second wind. He switched it to mute, to play like wallpaper.

He held Naomi tight and she felt a warmth between them that only manifested when he had abandoned the state of readiness he lived under as he moved millions of dollars across a computer screen, mindful not to drop any of the small figures, which, if they fell, crashed into so many shards of financial implications that it equated to the GDP of a small country. Instantly she forgave his flickering tempers and lay breathing in the easy rhythm of his ketone breath.

On the screen an Asian-looking man crossed a square, which was emptying of people. He stood, carrier bag in hand, at the fender of a Chinese military tank in an extraordinarily vulnerable gesture of defiance. The grocery shopper's protest. The TV was mute and she could translate nothing of the NHK broadcast.

'Wonder what that is?' she said, before they surrendered to a sudden sleep they had so long deferred.

*

Naomi woke, she could not tell how much time later, when Sam knocked vehemently on their screen door.

His wide smile placated them.

'You want to go back to the Imperial garden room for a full English breakfast?

'You are so right.'

Josh acquiesced sleepily; so often in awe of his American friend.

Their eyes only had feasted on the fish, which Miho alone had stomach for, and so Naomi picked up the pace of enthusiasm for the idea.

Hands resting on the white tablecloth at the Imperial Hotel, they ordered pots of black coffee. They were back where they had begun.

'Good start to the weekend,' Sam reflected.

They had run through the night for more than a full twelve hours and the thought drained Naomi. Josh's tangled hair fell across his forehead; the lines beneath his eyes were deeper and shadowing neglect. It was this helplessness about him which so often toppled her. She wanted to catch him up and shelter him.

Taking refuge in his safe world of numbers he said to her, 'I've got to go into the office this morning.'

She needed to shield him from himself, but she turned away. Losing him again to work, which left him with so little left to give.

'You've got to be kidding,' she protested, mindful of the plans that they had made for the weekend, and all too conscious that they had not spent a full weekend together since she'd arrived to join him.

Miho broke into the uncomfortable silence that followed. 'You can always come back with us.'

Naomi wanted to go home and sleep.

'Or I can come over later?'

As they split, Miho dug into her bag reaching for the the architect's card and gave it to her.

Sam called after her, 'Call him. He needs some help. Big project on. If you're interested?'

Back home in Shimokitazawa, Naomi walked up the steps to their house and turned the key in the lock. Across the road, the company apartments crowed morning, and festoons of futon mattresses hung over the balconies to air. In her spacious home, it seemed unfair for her to question whether she was in the wrong country with the wrong person. Thumbing the card in her bag she decided to call the architect first thing Monday.

Chapter 37

In the morning, once vertical, Josh was like a fully functioning alcoholic able to make the early subway train, though parts of him were still shut down and not yet open for business, and Naomi watched as he moved across the kitchen like a shadow boxer, mentally preparing himself for the day's contest.

He took toast and coffee in hand as he worked across the room. If he could have cleaned his teeth and swigged coffee at the same time he would have done. A patch of damp ran down the back of his T-shirt, growing dark, minutes after he had put it on. He changed into a clean shirt before he left for work and she wondered why he didn't eat bare-chested over breakfast. He was so well-trained; it was a habit he would never adapt.

Behind Naomi on s-hooks swung the red kitchen colander she had chosen to work with the greys of the rented kitchen. Leafing through the day's headlines, the intrusion of world news was thin. Her bare foot ticked beneath a field of the blue and white dragonflies resting on the hem of her cotton yukata dressing gown. The political associations were still alien among news of Styrofoam waste. The earth tremors never received mention. For a time she had been used to mouthing words as she read but Josh's ridicule had helped cut the habit.

She had learned not to interfere with his finely timed departure. Halfway across the floor he stopped, mug of coffee in hand.

'I can see it now: Apprentice to international architect in her early career, the Pritzker Prize-nominee Naomi Ardent pays tribute to that early influence.'

She didn't look up. 'Don't, Josh.'

'The committee . . .' he continued.

'I said don't, Josh,' she repeated, looking up at him now and raising her voice.

In her eyes he could see beyond the irritation that had prompted her outburst. It could be fear; fear on account of her timidity.

'Well, okay,' he soothed.

'You know you are winding me up and I just can't handle it this morning.'

'You'll be fine. The man's a friend of Sam's.'

'He's not really a friend of Sam's; a business acquaintance maybe. His wife is a friend of Miho's.'

'Well, that's good enough.'

'I just don't want to talk about it.'

And she sailed out of the swing door, the unbelted yukata dragonfly gown billowed open, exposing her naked body. She stood contemplating the large rusting TEPCO sign beside the persimmon tree. Tokyo Electric Power Company, it said in small letters beneath. Somebody should give that sign a lick of paint. She returned to the idea that if she did not get taken on by the architect, she might not stay. It was a relief to come close to acknowledging it but it would be harder of course to settle on a conviction to go; for weeks she had not even admitted to the possibility.

As he left, Josh planted a prerequisite kiss on the top of her head, wishing her luck and when the big, heavy door shut, and she found herself alone, as usual the silence of the house stood before her like a bare-fisted challenge .

Miho's hours were flexible and they met for brunch at the Kanda bookstore, with a café on the upper floor. Miho chose it partly because it was cheap and partly because she wanted to take Naomi round the shelves to trawl for inspiration on Japanese architecture.

'So, do you go to his office in Ikebukuro?'

'No. The other one.' She had agreed to meet at the regional office outside the centre.

'But that's miles away.'

'Yes. Yes, it is.' Naomi broke the seal on a sugar cube she didn't need and wondered whether to tell Miho that she had concluded that the inconvenient back office location meant the meeting was not going to end in a serious proposition.

Miho was camouflaged against a backdrop of books.

'Should I bother to go all the way out there?' She would decide on a whim and, caving in to superstition, felt Miho would be her oracle.

'It's a strange choice, that office. But of course. You should.' Miho climbed the library steps and leaned far to her right, balancing her large platform shoe on the bookshelf.

'Tadao Ando, Taniguchi, Junzo Sakakura,' she called down. 'It's a "No" on traditional.' Abseiling the shelves she looked out-of-her mind anarchic.

Miho's activities drew the attentions of an assistant who finally sourced a large coffee-table book from the discounted section.

'Only this one?'

The assistant was sure.

Miho patted the discounted remainder, an interior of a church on the cover, as the waiter arrived with water and *o-shibori* hand towels to take their order.

'I don't need that and it is still too expensive.' The dated church interior promised to be of little inspiration when she was looking for traditional Japanese architecture, though the name was Japanese. Nakashima. George Nakashima.

Miho left the table with the book, returning a couple of minutes later. 'I bought it for you.'

As they sat down to eat small bowls of rice and pink, gingered fish, Naomi didn't want to be ungrateful and handled the book.

'You have to take a good look at it now.' Miho barely removed her chopsticks from her mouth. It was pretty much the only thing Naomi hadn't quite come to terms with about her.

By the time the waiter brought them coffee, she had only just broken the cellophane wrap on the volume.

'I have to leave,' Miho apologized. 'I read with the children at the nursery. I'm a volunteer every Wednesday, across lunch hour.' She punched Naomi's shoulder to wish her luck. 'Gambatte,' she called back as she left, catapulting Naomi into a recurring set of worries about meeting with the architect.

He had asked her a week ago to come for a chat. 'A chat'. She was sure she could be of use but the cost to her of getting nothing out of meeting made her all the more nervous at seeing him. She threw some coins into a plastic tray beside a curling bill and left to visit the Mingei Kaikan folk-craft museum for the afternoon, which she chose because she had visited just about every other museum in the city within a day's radius.

Chapter 38

The day she was to meet him was the eighth of August, a lucky day in the local calendar. The offices of Mochizuki's architectural practice were a control centre in a state of emergency, set up, in haste, in a shabby domestic building unsuited to the purposes of running a thriving business. His client meetings took place in the borrowed elegance of Tokyo Tower where the walls were lined with colour enlargements of past projects. The grunt work, where the sous chefs to his confections worked, was here, out of town, where the leases were cheap and suited his current business climate, which had recently taken a compromising turn in the form of a heavy favour for Ukai.

Mochizuki was at his desk, contemplating a rhombus of light that fell on the wall in front of him. His long fingers held a cigarette and he smoked with deliberate pleasure. His narrow eyes closed slightly further, in an effort to avoid the wayward coils of smoke, his deep enjoyment reading like some erotic satisfaction. His wavy grey hair was not 'establishment Japan'. A day-old tan remained after his weekend walking the beach with Kazuko. She had suggested that if he could just take a break he would find himself twice as productive and he had listened to her, as he so often did. His movements were studied and calm and fluid.

Madori floor plans covered the walls and lay stacked on tables and desks. Here and there a few models of past concepts now lay gathering the dust of over-familiarity. There were desks for three other people in this, the main room of the house, but for Naomi's arrival Mochizuki had contrived to ensure there was no one else in the office, sending his loyal troop out on errands.

Iwata-san had been dispatched to collect the western girl in the jeep.

Naomi could not believe how far out of the city she had had to travel but it was against the tide of commuters at Shibuya. She had memorized the *kanji* alphabet for the small town to the south west. Chigasaki. The train timetable ran accurate to the second and nearing her destination she slipped her copy of *Anna Karenina* into the lurid, plastic basket that she had found in Harajuku. She recognized the station name in *kanji* letters. She would need two and a half thousand letters to read a newspaper and could devote an entire lifetime to writing them. And though she had at best a dozen letters she felt empowered, travelling out this far. Today the symbols did not wave at her sense of alienation like a reprimand. Looking up she caught a glimpse, through the urban sprawl of pachinko parlours and drive-through food chains, of Mount Fuji.

Despite the absence of postcard blue-majesty, it struck like a talisman. Perhaps her journey might not be wasted.

Naomi blinked, pulsing draughts of hot air circling her legs, as she came out of the station. The light bleached the urban grey of the pale, dusted metalled roads, empty of drivers and as quiet as a one- horse town. A car approached.

Across the road Iwata hunched, gripping the steering wheel, his hands at twelve o'clock, he glanced down at his watch. And then he saw her, the lone gaijin. It wasn't difficult to spot the alien in Chigasaki. As a rule there weren't any. As he crossed the road towards her he began nodding in an obsequious greeting. He moved with an exaggerated, deprecating stoop, like a bird on the run, which, for all practical purposes, slowed him up.

'Mochizuki-san's office, Iwata-san,' he said, introducing himself, courteously ushering her towards the jeep.

Kusottarre, he thought, admonishing himself. What does she think she looks like? A woman from the fields? By degrees he dismantled what she had thought was fashionably poetic and reduced her to a *Etahin.* Mochizuki's really not going to appreciate this one, he decided to himself, and looked forward with relish to his expression when he saw her. He reckoned she'd be a five. The boss should stop experimenting with these foreign imports; they drove the rest of the staff to distraction. Even when they had acclimatized they behaved like loose cannons. They never lasted very long and it was no secret that some of them entertained him outside hours and were a disruption in that.

'Konnichiwa,' she responded. *'Hajimemashite, Naomi desu.'*

Iwata-san was unctuous, small and dark, like an oily starling. He wore a combat T-shirt underneath his regulation office shirt. They travelled the short distance to the offices in virtual silence, past signs on the low walls of suburban gardens proclaiming 'May peace prevail on earth' in English. Naomi found they served as a reminder that, of all the adversities these peoples had had to deal with, some of them had been man-made. Fifty years between earthquakes, she recalled Mr Kami telling her, and, between these, the odd world war. The signs became little scars on the road. Laced with power lines, the mess of utilities belied the Japanese organisational systems. Surface power lines, Kami had said, were easier to reconstruct after a quake.

They stopped at the American-style traffic lights, their generous glare-catchers like eyelids in a manga comic, adding to the sky clutter. And, as they drove on, Naomi ran through her last college project for fluency. A Chelsea riverboat construction inspired by the forms of the Thames barrier.

Beside the front door of the office were two large white cones of powder.

'What's this?'

Iwata told her in broken English that the little mounds were salt and that he had been asked to put them out to cleanse the threshold and ward off evil spirits.

'Not me? You can't mean me.' She laughed.

'For all visitors today,' he said pointedly.

So, she was among other candidates for interview? Before she stepped across the threshold, she released her hairclip and shook out her pale hair, then entered.

Mochizuki rose as she was shown into his office and shook her hand across his desk. When asked if he would see Naomi, he had felt obliged, not least since Sam's bank had holdings in the Guam Venture. He knew enough about this sometime student of architecture that she could never work with him on the airport in Guam. It would be highly unprofessional to take such a risk, and they were already in the third stage of the designs. Quite what she could contribute he was at a loss to imagine. They had not reached the point of 'restroom fittings', and her one strength as an English speaker was lost on the wind when the developers were Japanese and other client with whom he communicated very well was someone he had known since they were at school. Giving his time to speak at the Imperial Hotel, should, he guessed have Sam indebted to him, but conversely he had called for yet another favour.

He gestured she should sit down as he walked away to dispatch a cigarette, waving the last of his exhaled smoke. He returned, finally giving her what might pass as a smile. Naomi snagged her light cotton skirt as, releasing a tight hold on her basket, she placed it on the floor. She brushed down her skirts.

Mochizuki read her nerves and sought to put her at her ease. 'How have you been?'

And she found the casual opening more difficult than intended. She could not respond with, 'well, Josh and I spent the weekend eating brunch and drifting round Tokyo' or 'the city is exciting but I am spending too much time in my own company' or 'I might be about to regret the move here'. A shaft of sunlight was in her eyes. He drummed his fingers and looked at the unusually silent desk phone that he had had to reroute.

After a pause she said, 'Good, thanks. It was good to have the opportunity to hear you the other night.'

Referring to the party reminded him of his first impression, where he overheard her allude to his work as imitating others. Today she seemed deferential and polite. He leaned back, crossing his leg so high on his thigh that his foot was almost on the desk.

He paused, inadvertently stirring the anxiety that had begun in the morning as she snapped at Josh and which had intensified as she found she'd waited on the wrong platform in Shibuya. She recalled they were building a new island to house the airport at Kansai, but couldn't make a conversational start.

His preliminaries drew on the evening they met and after his obligatory enquiries after Sam he asked her where she was from. In answer she managed a tortured lead into the construction projects.

'Since the recent opening of the M25 orbital road, the airports serving London at Stansted and Heathrow are due to expand,' she told him, to a reception so hollow she felt lost in the space.

Mochizuki brought his hands together, tracing a line between his teeth with his forefinger. He found the girl a delicacy, reminiscent of his wife at the same age but a pale version; her eyes were tight when she smiled, not so unlike his own, but her hair made her fade before his eyes as the morning sun created a halo around her temples. She had the appeal of pale, sweet, bean-paste mochi cakes. He would just then have liked to put his hand out to touch her upper arm to assure himself that it would not pass through her.

Naomi was relieved when a woman whom he thanked as 'Saito-san, our accountant', broke the hiatus with two small coffees, delivered on a small floral tray. So the accountant served the coffee. The setup was not what she had expected of the renowned international practice.

'So did you get some of the principles of traditional Japanese architecture I was trying to explain?'

Sam had briefed her on the airport project but not on this.

There was very little in English print that she had found on indigenous wooden structures, though she had made another visit to the ancient temple in Asakusa, focusing on the construction. The temple approach was a concrete walkway wide enough to land a plane, built to accommodate huge crowds, and had no relevance to what he had told them about laying a circuitous route to the entrance of a traditional building. She mentioned her trip to Asakusa anyway.

'One of the few structures to survive the Great Kanto Earthquake of 1923. In the Buddhist style.'

They were headed towards a topic that was already beyond her. She may as well leave for home now. But she clutched at the work in the book Miho had bought for her. Nakashima's furniture reminded her of the dated seventies shapes her parent hung on to.

'I'm interested in the work of George Nakashima,' she gambled. How much longer that interest for her would remain beyond the week wasn't under discussion.

His eyes lit up. 'Such a master.' He was energized. 'An architect I most certainly admire. He worked with wood. A recycling tradition.'

His enthusiasm shifted his whole frame towards her and, as he leant on his elbows across the desk, he described some of his beloved projects and a well of knowledge on the subject broke free.

At the end of their talk he thanked her for coming and though she felt more comfortable it was unclear whether he had a role for her.

After supper that night, Josh poured over travel magazines.

'We have to get away.' He turned another page.

'But you've only just got back from the last business trip. We should take a weekend trip out to the countryside if you need a change of scene.'

'Can't imagine anything worse. I really do need a break. You wait. A couple of months at work and you will too.'

'Josh, please don't. It might not work out. That architectural practice is so shabby it doesn't look as though they could afford more staff. '

'Don't be ridiculous.'

'I was hoping we could talk about it.'

'Well, we are.' He turned another page to reveal the turquoise-blue of the barrier reef. 'How about Australia? If I can get the wind business in the roaring forties off the ground there'll be lots of excuses to visit.'

Her eyes rested on the TEPCO sign for strength. She began to clear the plates, looking to him for a little more interest.

'Are you, in fact, going to even ask, Josh?'

'I did ask. I'm asking. How did it go?'

'He talked about his inspirations mostly.'

'Sounds positive. Nothing committal?'

'No.'

'We should get away before you start.'

'Josh, if I don't find work can you tell me how I am going to afford to stay here?'

Josh had never asked her to contribute and did not see it as an issue. He had made promises to her before they left and yet again another conversation had been drawn round to the same subject. He threw down his magazine, moved over, and, on his knees, buried his head in her lap like a child. He entreated her as he looked up.

'We will get married, hun, when you want.'

She got up abruptly; to become another half she had to feel whole herself. It had become a permanent state though remained unspoken and it left her vulnerable.

'Coffee?'

His head stayed heavy as she rose.

Chapter 39

Kazuko gently moved aside the purple hats of aubergine ends and the lacework of carrot peelings from her chopping board.

She placed her teeth against the ribbed grain of the pouch of seaweed and pulled at the resistant nick at the edge of the packet.

Mochizuki called to her from his cushion on the wooden living room floor.

'Shakira has called in his favour.'

'Yes? The teahouse?' she replied, as she beat the package and cast it aside for recycling.

Her husband's university friend had visited while she was away. He was one of those remarkable students who had lived so hard that by the age of twenty that he had seen it all and given up on the twentieth century and become a Buddhist monk. Given his urbane good sense and marked intelligence he had become, in a fairly short space of time, the abbot at the local temple.

'Yup,' Mochizuki drawled, scratching head as if erasing a folly.

As the kettle boiled she covered the tricolour of dried seaweed to top the floury udon she had bought fresh from the noodle maker that had celebrated it's hundredth year last fall.

'The grant has just come through and it has to happen now. He's trying to coerce me into helping with the rebuild,' he moaned. Everyone wanted a piece of him.

'Are you complaining? When this is all you ever wanted to do. So you don't have the time. You'll make time.'

He came in to watch the progress of supper. The udon noodle maker had supplied them for so long, pulling strands of noodles from the press in the window of his store, like ribbons of time. If only it were that easy.

'I don't have the recipe.'

'A recipe for time.' She laughed.

He went back to his makeshift work base on the floor, absent-mindedly folding a newspaper to form an origami structure, quickly losing concentration as he did when he needed to eat.

'You ready?' Kazuko asked.

After plumping the noodles on to two plates and then draining the pale-pink white and green seaweed, she strode in with the evening meal. She paused and hovered over him.

'The origami bus shelter?' She loved to tease him.

As they tucked in, she suggested getting more help.

'Why not this foreigner? You have hired similar girls in the past? They were always amiable girls.' She looked at him knowingly. She was aware of his habits and she knew when he was restless. He had often had an English speaker in the office to help coordinate with the Americans. Proofreading, taking calls, and more besides.

He helped himself to more soy, drawing lines across his meal.

Udon escaped from between her sharp lacquer chopsticks, and she pinched harder.

'Why not that friend of Miho's?'

'Very cute,' he said provocatively. 'Sam asked. Miho has asked and now you?' He looked at her in mock disbelief.

'No use to me in the office.' He raised his food from the plate and stopped.

'Do I owe Sam?' he objected. 'Do I owe Miho a favour now?'

'No, but she is a good friend of mine.' Though they were closer in age, she was almost as a sister to her. 'She is your sort and she helps me out, at the nursery. I know she'd like to get this girl settled. Sam is a good friend of theirs.'

She, too, was trying to get him to hire this Naomi.

'I don't owe Miho.' He stopped eating as a small red line appeared on the left side of her mouth. 'You got a little snick on your lip.'

He rose to see but she dabbed at it with one of the small paper napkins she always laid out, folded it carefully in four and tucked it into her sleeve.

'Take more salad.' Attending to him with a devotion that might be afforded a child. He helped himself.

'Managing people takes up time. An unskilled assistant is more like a training session. Sometimes more trouble than it's worth.'

'It worked out before with the other foreigners,' she encouraged. 'Would you think of trying it for a short, fixed period? A limited role?' She became gentler when he would not heed her advice, which was barely ever the case. 'You don't make it easy for yourself,' she cooed

'I'll give it some thought.' He slurped at the yuzu citrus juice left in the bowl as he resigned himself to her willful suggestion.

When Mochizuki took Naomi on he had no idea what to do with her. It seemed that everybody but him thought it was a good idea. Sam, Miho and – because of his workload – Kazuko were all keen. This latest commission, though a small project, wouldn't match what little of a skill set she had but he determined that she should serve a purpose if he had to hire her. She could work on the charity side of the business rather than large-scale projects; those projects he recalled he had heard her suggest that he had plagiarized. The nerve. Though it was closer to her experience he could not give her that satisfaction. She would have to prove her worth.

Chapter 40

On Naomi's first day with the practice, Saito-san, the accountant cum coffee maker, introduced her to the players who had been absent during the interview.

'Hajimemashite.' Her head bounced up and down along a short but incredibly formal line of introduction.

When she got to Iwata he was surly and made so small an attempt at a bowed greeting it was a twitch.

In the office there was only one dictator and Iwata was his right-hand man. It was Iwata who took her round, to hang over shoulders and take all it in. Questions were difficult to raise as barely anyone spoke English. Coffee came round at the break and she was served first as if a guest. Now so used to being an outsider, she intended to work on their reticence but hadn't a clue where to start. The superstitious piles of salt she'd seen on her first visit had gone. As she had left that morning, and Josh had wished her luck, she recalled the moment he had met her on the college steps with all his promises. It had all changed. But then it was not in her nature to look back.

During the first week Mochizuki drove her out to the temple. En route he outlined work needed on the teahouse. The car – a large saloon – was an old, brown banger and it smelt of stale cigarettes. His preoccupations, she assumed, focused on his larger project and she had some sense of the difficulty he might have in occupying a tongue-tied westerner in a Japanese-speaking office.

Off the main road, up the hill, they turned onto the uneven track leading up to the temple; the wheels took the corner and stirred up huge clouds of dust in their wake.

Making for a large red torii gate that straddled the road like some giant kanji letter in the Chinese alphabet, Naomi felt an irrational reluctance to pass beneath it. She was miles from anywhere recognizable and they seemed suddenly in the depths of a countryside she didn't know.

'You'll see the teahouse,' he said after a long silence, just as the dust from the track had begun to obscure the window and she had glimpsed the first of the white buildings.

Mochizuki slowed a little before suddenly, just past a turn off, pulling on the handbrake. Cussing, he reached over to the back seat, fumbling for a carefully gift-wrapped package before he got out. The architect traipsed back to the bend, retracing his steps.

She watched him from the car, a lone figure on the road making towards the tree line, and then she saw the monk. He wore the black habit of the mendicant Buddha, his face hidden behind a wide-brimmed coolie hat. The hinge creaked as she stepped out; the dense bamboo canopy was already alive with the sound of cicadas. The novice cupped a begging bowl in his hands, submitting to fate and passing benefactors as his teachings required. He was part of the world and the world would sustain him. In silence he accepted the gift-wrapped parcel of food.

As Mochizuki returned to the car the monk stood quietly, a part of the track and a part of the trees and, as they drove away, he disappeared in a trail of billowing dust.

'He is often there,' he told her. 'The Buddhist says inner purity is in devotion to his everyday duties, to the most basic of tasks; fasting the body to feed the mind or washing vestments with care. He savours every moment in his life, not just a selected few.'

She noted his bony artistic hands had a light hold on the wheel in the ruts.

'There is no part of his existence where he does not seek to find his skin prickling in the knowledge that he is alive. You have to strive to become a part of it. You can't take it for granted.'

She could add nothing and they continued, jolting up the uneven road.

Once they had parked he handed her the rolls of madori plans he had prepared for the meeting with the abbot, laying them carefully in her arms one by one. As he shut the boot the sound occupied the empty grounds announcing their arrival on heavy humid air.

Naomi's senses sharpened. In the pulsating heat they made their way up to the white walls of the monastery, surrounded in green.

The architect wiped the sweat that was already accumulating on his brow and they walked without a word to the tune of cicadas shaking in the trees. At a brushwood-woven fence, a pebbled path cut through a very well-kept monochrome garden of moss and azalea. A shaft of sunlight broke through dense canopy of surrounding trees and fell on three garden rákes hanging from the eaves of one of the whitewashed outbuildings, their shadows stencilled on the wall.

The lines of the grey roof tiles fell carelessly across the halls of worship, living quarters, treasure house and bell tower.

You see –' he followed her eyes '– we only see the parts of the group of buildings at any one time; in the east we don't stand back with a perspective on the whole.' This notion, he explained, predicated the lives of the monks. 'The Rinzai sect have lived in the precincts for seven centuries.' They were begun in 1256 and the construction, he explained, which was predominantly made of timber, had only taken two years to complete. 'Now we will meet an old friend of mine.' Then he leaned towards her confidentially and said with startling mischief, 'I has seen his very arse,' and he looked for her reaction after such serious philosophies.

.

What? He was testing her. She suspected he would be very capable of toying with her.

'We have taken a Japanese bath together.' He looked disappointed that she hadn't risen to the bait.

They left the shade, and beyond the temple buildings they came to an open meadow where the ground fell away quite steeply. Young voices drifted up from tall grasses, heavy with seeds, but they could see no one.

'Catch him, Catch him.'

'Yasuki *Baka-chan*, idiot you missed him.' An adult voice floated up from the ridge below.

Naomi followed him across the meadow, her long skirt spilling the dry seed heads She found herself wishing for a hat.

'Okay, demon tongue, but where are your magical tricks when we want you to make a catch?' they heard the hidden voice say.

Two slim boys of about nine or ten, shining with exertion, came into sight, running through waist-high grass, and disturbing clouds of insects in their path. Had they been scaring birds for a living their fields would lose no seed, displacing everything in their wake with their brown bony knees and sharp laughs.

They found the abbot on a brow below the ridge, a silhouetted figure bent, hands on knees in the manner of a baseball coach, giving encouragement, his bald head bared to the sun and the back of his neck lying in thick folds above the collar of his black habit.

'*Chotto mattete*, Tako-chan, where's your strategy? You're running round like a fool. You couldn't catch your brother at this rate and he's a million times easier to see.'

Naomi had assumed that the two boys were playing catch with one another. They stopped in their tracks at this admonition from the voice beyond the field ridge. The chuckling stopped and the darting and dashing become a game of stealth for a time. It seemed, as they crept and pounced in the grass, that they had regained their lost concentration. The focus did not last and soon gave way to shrieks of excitement as one boy then the other cupped his hands and dived into the grass. Failing to secure a thing, they tired, and their game slowed.

As Mochizuki and Naomi approached, the abbot held his hand aloft to bid their patience as the game concluded.

At last Tako, the taller of the two, whispered, 'Hold it', with a seriousness that matched younger boy's intensity Tako then lunged with the speed of a martial artist and placed his cupped hands on the kid's shirt.

'*Arimasu! Arimasu!*' He scooped up his catch and ran beaming towards the abbot who had been watching them, hands on knees all the while. Tako's run slowed, his legs raised high against the resistance of the sea of grass, the seedheads slowing his progress as they lashed against his shirt.

The abbot smiled benignly at Naomi as he produced from his sleeve and made ready a small two-storey bamboo cricket box. The base was fashioned in the shape of a gourd with tight vertical struts to imprison the insect. As the abbot held the gated box open, Tako held his breath and fed his insect into the jaws of the box.

'But that's not a cricket!' the abbot protested as the boy released a butterfly into the confines of the box.

'Go find me a singing cricket. This butterfly has no voice,' he admonished

Mochizuki waited to hear him out and finally given leave to speak said, 'We find you at play?'

'You must catch one with Yasuku now,' the abbot said, rubbing the second boy's bare head as he relinquished the box.

They let the butterfly go. Naomi could see that its wings were no longer intact and she wondered how long it would last.

Chapter 41

The abbot finally turned to greet his guests.

'Mochizuki, my friend, how are you?' he asked, inclining his head and clapping him on the back warmly.

'Inestimably better for seeing you Shakira.' Mochizuki confessed he had also brought a presentation box of sembei rice crackers as a gift, but had given it away to the novice.

'Hakuin is doing well here with us,' the abbot said, naming the monk.

'I covered him in dust.' Mochizuki laughed as Shakira turned his attention towards Naomi.

'Momotaro-kun. I want you to meet Naomi my new colleague.'

Naomi only understood her name in the exchange.

'Hajimemashite dozo yoroshiku.' She introduced herself in Japanese and bowed her head, which brought the abbot's straw-sandalled feet into view.

Looking at his naked feet she caught an intimate glimpse of his beautifully manicured toes and finished, 'Mr Momotaro-san.'

The abbot laughed and looked to Mochizuki to give an explanation.

'This is his childhood name, his real name is Shakira,' Mochizuki told her.

'We called him "peach boy" because he won every fight in the yard, like in the kid's story. He could lay anyone out. He still looks like that fruit, don't you think so?' Mochizuki framed his hands around the abbot's bald head but she was reluctant to confirm the resemblance.

The man standing before her was a long way from a dirty-kneed schoolboy, she thought.

Shakira adjusted his glasses to look at her and Mochizuki, realising she would not understand their folktale, continued peremptorily, 'An old woman finds a longed-for child embedded in a peach stone. He is supernaturally strong. A real fighter. Just like our abbot here. '

And as he rubbed the crown of the abbot's bald head, Naomi warmed to their boyish intimacy. It was just before noon and she was heating up on the exposed hillside. 'We should take refreshment while we discuss the matters regarding the monastery buildings,' the abbot informed them, as if reading her desire to get out of the sun.

While he was self-determined and poised, untroubled by the heat, another bead of sweat formed between her shoulder blades. She felt its passage across the curved muscle in her back until it rested like a tear to collect in a pool that dampened the cloth around her waistband. As they moved back under the trees the cicadas shook now like rattlesnakes.

They followed him up a pathway of steep and dank steps, some hewn from stone, some earthy and worn by footfalls. A damp, rank smell surfaced intermittently and Mochizuki turned often to check on Naomi's progress. At the crest of the hill the grass was shorn to the width of a black habit and either side the long grass was studded with orange lilies. Through the trees from the monastery below came the muted call of a log beating on the ornately worked bell in the thatched tower.

The abbot stopped

'There. There it is,' he said, pointing out a small building through a cutting beside the lake below them. 'The teahouse.'

It was enchanting. Her first thought was that she wanted to tell Miho about it. Outside the teahouse water was playing from the angled point of a bamboo shaft falling into a small, hewn, stone basin below. The stone was a perfect circle, with a square centre cut to form a basin. Squaring the circle she thought it resembled a sword hilt, and she traced the circumference with her hand, feeling for the roughly inscribed motto. Mochizuki translated it for her: 'I learn only to be contented.'

She gave a vestigial sigh – of arrival.

Mochizuki continued, 'Samurai warriors left their swords to become Buddhist monks and found the hardships of the Rinzai sect to their taste after their fighting days. The discipline was the same.

She watched the abbot wash at the bamboo pipe.

Mochizuki touched her hand gently to follow and bent to cup his hands under the flow, throwing water over his head and drinking. He ran his tanned hands through his silver-flecked hair. When she washed she started at the cold and becoming conscious of his stare, left her hands to cool the back of her neck, glancing to meet his eyes as he looked away.

Across a stone-chequered pathway they followed the monk's lead and, once inside the teahouse, removed their shoes in the dirt entrance hall. In the gentle light she found it a haven. The highly polished step creaked as Shakira stepped up.

Naomi saw the deftness of one much practised in the art; he turned and sank to replace his shoes facing out from the hall in readiness for slipping into them whenever he might leave.

'Wait for me here, my friends, and I will find refreshments,' he said beckoning them to take a seat.

It felt comfortable now to be alone with the architect, she thought.

Two zabuton cushions lay prepared but Mochizuki took another from a pile behind the twisted tree trunk that supported the roof.

It had, he explained, as he slapped the trunk, been selected precisely for its character and suggested freedom of natural expression. 'Like this,' he said, as he pointed to a large hibachi stove chiselled from an old tree root and lined with lead. The root had been varnished to a high amber colour and allowed every knot a prominence which recorded its growth and trials. It was as if he had brought her to the centre of his own internal world and was sharing it with her.

They sat in silence. She was already getting used to his silences and found them easy. Cool air fell from the higher ground through the open sides of the building and they waited. It was as if she were kneeling at an important threshold. But it unsettled her to have allowed the thought to materialize.

After a heavy meeting in Japanese, the abbot left. From the round window, the terrace was edged with maples and weeping cherries, the lake was studded with rocks where terrapins sat basking in the sunlight. Mochizuki ran his hands over the sill and knocked at the eaves to check for rot. It was as if she was witness to a private performance. It seemed a criminal shame to demolish the structure. This perfect sanctuary.

Chapter 42

That night, while preparing supper, Naomi chose a small, hand-tooled, Japanese steel knife. They had been extremely sharp when she first bought the set from a pavement seller outside the fish market but she had found they had a tendency to spoil unless you covered them in vegetable oil after every use, which made cleaning them a chore.

She made a sharp incision and, retaining the roots to hold it in place, she sliced an onion. Josh was leafing through a illustrated hardback book on holiday destinations that Caroline had given them as a house-warming gift.

'Good few days?' Josh asked; he was already on holiday.

'A drift-around-of-a-day really.' Her eyes welled until she could hardly see the onion. 'It was all so, so . . .' and, lost for words, she settled on, 'Zen.'

'Is that good?' he asked, still lingering over Balinese escapes.

He had always had a careless curiosity for how she spent her time; they lived such different working lives. Yesterday her passion for the ukiyo-e woodblock masters of the seventeenth century had consumed her, and now he suspected he could sense Zen taking over from the woodblock prints, as sure as he could smell fried onions drifting in through the louvred door to the kitchen. After a hard day's trading he could find coming home to her enthusiasm tiring. It was like watching someone only ever inhaling. Some days you just had to let it out and relax. What once had amused him he could now find trying. Here was yet another interest and it wasn't the first to arrive this week.

She added mince beef from the international supermarket, to the pan.

'Sam is a good friend, and I'm grateful but I can't add anything. I feel worse than useless and I don't want to be a burden.'

He did not say what he felt like saying: 'Didn't you really want this job?' Instead he turned a page. 'You'll look pretty,' he consoled, keen not to encourage her neediness.

She ruffled his shirt and punched his shoulder. 'The thing is . . .' She wanted to tell him that she had lost herself at the temple. And she wanted to tell him that she had felt, beyond the torii gates, there existed a sense of calm, a separate universe from her or her problems. She'd found herself reduced to such small insignificance and she felt quite comfortable with it.

She peered into the frying pan, where the pink, veined onions had browned and caramelized, before marching through the swing doors ; though buoyed by the day she still had to work out how she fitted in, She laid the table as usual.

He was startled to find her standing before him in an apron, waving a knife at him. 'Don't come on to me with domestic violence please,' he jestered.

She ignored him and, coming back to Mochizuki, pointed the weapon for emphasis.

'The thing is . . . I guess you're right. With his reputation Mochizuki can please himself which projects he wants to work on. And pick and choose. International architect. Can money be an object?' It was as if she were swimming and gasping for air, she spoke so quickly. 'You know, he is, in fact, very philosophical.'

'I think we got a bit of that at the talk.' It was a trial when she stated the obvious. 'So how about we eat?' he said, starving.

'I have had so much time on my hands I am prepared to go "dan dan" . . . go gradually – the Japanese way,' she concluded.

Now she plays philosopher, he thought.

The new element that she found in herself had brought a change in her and she couldn't quite explain it to him.

She appeared to have gone 'Girl Guide' on him and Josh answered in the affirmative, without having a clue what she was talking about.

Chapter 43

Mochizuki and Naomi made several trips to the temple and each time she went he seemed at pains to let her know why it was so important to him; she believed he wanted her to understand how much the tradition, the old ways with wood meant to him .

The abbot had not reappeared but the novice Hakuin was often at the turn-off on the road begging for alms, and Mochizuki always brought something; lately he had asked her to hand it over. The monk was young and thin, and she began to feel in his gratitude that she had role, a bit part at the temple. They continued with their preparations for the rebuild, They spent a good deal of time measuring the original and photographing the component parts and Mochizuki was generous with his time.

'This is nine shaku. That's four and an half tatami mats.'

Brocade borders delineated the rush mats and she could easily see the layout. It was such a small building and yet, because it came with stipulations from the National Treasuries Office who had contributed to the funding, it became more of a responsibility . . . an important task.

'It seems such a shame. There doesn't seem to be anything wrong with it. Why deconstruct it now?'

'No.' He looked at her seriously. 'It is time to start afresh.' His eyes narrowed.

'This is about regeneration. See this.' He went to a large beam of twisted wood spanning the opening to the recess. 'In some buildings this could be rejected for lack of uniformity.

But here it has been absorbed in the design.' He ran his hand along the length respectfully, following the deeply curved under-belly of the gnarled wood, planed of its bark.

'These branches can be stronger,' he said, 'because they have already shifted and moved, and when they are seasoned over time in this shape they can bring stability. They have been tested by the wind and can have greater strength.' He had reached the end of the supporting beam and beckoned her with a nod to come over. 'Look here.'

She stood close enough to his cotton shirt to feel his gener-ated warmth, and she followed his index finger as it traced along a small carving in the wood running into the corner of the building.

'This is the number five,' he pointed.

The character was scored, cut in five straight lines, a lower-case 'h' given ground and a cap.

'And here.' He stretched up to the upright strut that joined the beam where a second character, exactly the same, had been carved above the first. 'They match.'

Could he be flirting with her? she wondered. No, a silly thought.

He smiled as her eyebrows lifted in comprehension. Her eyes widened and he marked the length of her lashes.

'This is the tradition. Where they know well on site which elements have been hewn to fit together.'

'So they are simply labelled like this?'

He traced over the numbers again, brushing against her arm as he did so. 'The matching pair. They have made it easy for us,' he said significantly. And then he added, 'With these matching numbers', retreating from his reference to the pair of them. She stood a moment before she moved.

Chapter 44

Naomi moved with the rhythm of the train out towards Imaichi. Mochizuki was feigning sleep and beside him the master carpenter, his traditional Haori jacket over a modest shirt and tie. The men had worked together on the restoration of the temple bell tower before this.

Quite what the girl was doing with them, the carpenter did not know, but that the architect could be an eccentric, he knew all too well. He recalled when they had first met in Shibuya, where Mochizuki and friends hit the bars and yakitori restaurants. Shibuya, he reminisced, had been a dark tranquil sea of people. Today the crowd had wrapped him in a mantle of age-identifying him as one who didn't belong there.

Under the birdsong on the platform a boy with the leonine-red hair of a kabuki wig had jostled him. Pushed him over almost. He looked and behaved like an ancient god. If you swept away the familiar homogeneity so too went the ability to see the subtle change in differences. Life seemed to have moved on and he had to hold on. Despite being an ally of traditional values, he knew that, as time progressed, it moved inexorably west. The beauty of the old values rested on the premise that familiarity of form freed you to appreciate either departures from that form or the antithesis of the formless. Resting on his mind like a flash Polaroid, the indelible souvenir boy reminded him that he could no longer look for the subtleties between people when a noisy individualism, a call for all things new, was clamouring for attention.

His gaze settled on the girl. Her youth gave her the potential for enthusiasm and energy. But he wanted very much to bring her to the same point of understanding and draw her spirit with his. To kindle a loyalty towards tradition, passing on his passion.

As they slid through the flat plains of new forestry she opened her eyes to his smile. Mochizuki leaned across to take Minamioka's measuring rule from its leather pouch and pointed it at her like an archer's quiver before unfolding it to its full length.

This, he explained was the rod, or *motozue*; one of three rules that they would use in the construction process. Marked out in shaku units, roughly the equivalent to a third of a metre. It had been around as a standard since the earliest timber buildings.

She appreciated his investment in helping her to understand, and, as the carriage climbed the mountain, she was pulled hard against the support of the partition.

On arrival, Mochizuki bought only two bento lunch boxes from the station kiosk and handed them to her to carry. Minamioka, the carpenter, he explained, would eat with the men from the timber yard. Light crystallized the freshened air as they alighted at Imaichi and they were met by the platform announcement as the owner of the sawmill bowed in a greeting now commonplace to her.

The grey truck from the mill was waiting in the station forecourt; its black trade name lay flat and unreflective under fine particles of dust. The sawmill was a family concern within Shinoda Construction.

It was nearing lunchtime and, as if in respect to a favoured client, work had ceased and the plangent whining of the cutters was momentarily quiet, allowing them to accompany Minamioka on his visit to the wood yard, prospecting for lumber, in peace.

He had done some preliminary measurements and wanted to check the available sources this morning and pick out some trophy pieces for the project. Two men carrying a section of large tree trunk passed them in the yard beside the shed on the left the gates. The wood shed had the internal proportions of a temple and large bolsters of hinoki, sugi, keyaki and akamatsu, or red pine, lay seasoning in rows like a wine cave, breathing noiselessly in the hushed moist atmosphere. Shadows of tall trees split the shafts of light that filtered through the high windows. She followed as the men paced round the stock, their voices muffled by the sawdust floor. The mill owner pointed out the different areas for each variety and those naturally seasoned logs, which had been lying for three years or more. Some of the trees were imported from Taiwan and some had been grown locally.

'Two-by-four planks have no place in traditional Japanese architecture. The wood remains an organic form,' Mochizuki told her, pointing then to Minamioka,

'He is looking for strong trunks to use as the structural members. The diameter of these dictates the height of the building.' He ran his hand along the weathered section of wood feeling for knots as he went.

Grey as buckwheat noodles, she thought.

Minamioka conferred with him and Mochizuki translated for her.

'Any movement in the timber later on,' he says, 'will be greatest running perpendicular to the branch. The knots are a weakness and the success of the teahouse rests on his ability to predict how the wood might move and what its structural strengths might be.'

She ran her fingers ran along the cut section of the wood, following the grain, as the master carpenter decisively chalked up the end with a kanji letter to denote that it should be reserved for use as one of the columns.

'It's good, very good,' he concluded in English.

Towards the end of the morning they left the carpenter to his discussions with the mill owner and took a walk up the south-facing slope behind the wood store, working their way up through the trees to where some of the lumber had been cut. On the upper reaches of the hill they stopped where, below, many trees had been felled.

'Why have they cleared this section?' she asked

'This slope is well-drained and not densely planted. The grain grows tightly in the lower moisture levels in this soil and the wood will be slow-growing and hard. The conditions don't hinder the branches. There will be a few more knots on this wood.'

His ranging gaze over the woods came to rest on her. He was pleased that she should ask and suggested they take a seat on a large tree stump and eat lunch. As he leant across to take his bento box from her he kissed her very lightly on the cheek.

She did not respond and she did not object. He had not stolen it. They both looked out across the slope to the plains of paddy fields, content not to take his unvoiced comment on the day any further.

Josh would never see the indelible mark he had made on her that day.

Chapter 45

Tokyo, 2012

It was Sunday morning. Back home in East London Hana would have been walking the length of Columbia Road flower market, lined with heads of peonies, the wrapped promise of rosebuds and the darting colour of fragile anemones. She and Tom would be about to take brunch in the café opposite the quilt shop. She was homesick and it prompted her to call Tom. But as he answered, he sounded strange.

'Hello?' He paused too long, he sounded odd when he finally responded. A hangover?. Had he broken something in the house? Work issues? Was someone there with him?

'You there?'

'Yes, hi, I'm here, is it cutting up?'

'You sound different.' They talked a while until she said.

'I can hear you not listening. What are you doing?'

'Getting ready to go out.'

'Where?' Just then she heard a voice in the background. A girl's voice. 'Who is that?'

'It's Sadie,' he said unapologetically.

She had misgivings then that what was to be a fine morning, might not turn out to be quite so fine.

'What's she doing there?' It left her rumpled. It was too early for Sadie to drop by. But then again she was eccentric.

'We were going to the flower market.' There was an edge in his voice. A determination.

So they were going for breakfast. A group of them? After a

late night? She held back from jumping into a vat of the wrong conclusions.

But his voice had sounded strange. She knew him by now.

'To our café? Tom? Is that what you're telling me?' She didn't want to believe what she already understood. Bloody Sadie, who borrowed her jeans her coats her shoes and now Tom. It would hardly be his fault – she'd have sucked him in.

'Well?' The distance between them became more than just the miles. Everything felt taut and about to snap. 'I wanted . . .' She couldn't bring herself to tell him what she wanted. They knew one another so very well.

'I'm sorry.'

'Fuck you.'

She caught crying in time not to.

Decibels of inevitability blocked her ears for anything else he had to say and she wanted nothing more than to be in London and able to confront him. How could he?

She put the phone down.

Chapter 46

Ed needed to be reminded of home. He would get Hana and the American girl over to his apartment. It was a showstopper of a company flat, he had to admit, and it would make just the right impression on Hana.

Way back in the Eighties, had the grounds of the Imperial Palace been up for sale, they would have been worth more than the State of California. In the intervening lost decades Japanese property values had become sickly under the iron lung of financial easements. Ed's law firm punched above their weight with the real estate agents; now rentals to the international firms had dropped off with the size of the Japanese equity markets. The equity warrant bubble, so huge around the time he was born, had burst, and along with it the property market where the superfluous cash had been invested. History, it seemed, had repeated itself.

Piano lesson over, Ed lay on the floor of his spacious apartment enjoying a post-coital cigarette; a totem of ash threatening to fall and cover him. The girl had left. Now on his back with his legs up over the Western sofa, which Yumi from the office had helped him choose, he surveyed his view. The atmospheric pressure had vacuumed the sky, blown it clear of fluff, and left a rare continuum of blue; across the city he caught a glimpse of Mount Fuji. This celestial housekeeping, clearing the outlook to the volcano, was as unusual as a guest from home or indeed the forthcoming maternal visit. Even on the 41st floor he usually overlooked a city in heat haze or the blanket sea mists stole his views. This weekend he was mindful he could at any time be called back to Tokyo Midtown to prepare the merger documents for the Red Dragon Corp. It had been a bone-crushing week and, had he stayed a moment longer on Friday night, he would have been tempted to call Human Rights Watch on his own behalf. Thinking of Hana brought a rush of embarrassment over that evening at Shimo's. He knew he had behaved badly at the club, though he could recall so little. He was making a mess of his personal life here and he had to sort out this unsatisfactory fling with the piano teacher, the closest thing he had had to a relationship.

Sex with his piano teacher had been inevitable but had a scripted conclusion about it. She was cute and keen but he felt he was taking advantage when his commitment came in the absence of any other. He had not wanted to get into it but it had all become such a habit – why had he given her a key? The cigarette drooped threateningly and finally covered his chest in ash; he rubbed the stubble on his chin in indecision before he swung his legs across and came onto all fours, remembering too late the recurring complaint from his T7 vertebra. He blamed the piano lessons on the need to do something while his sports injury mended; that and sheer loneliness.

His mother would not approve of the piano teacher and he remembered her blousy words now:

'Remember when you are in Tokyo that some things don't travel well. Holiday wines, for example. You'll be drinking sake. And don't forget the reputation those Japanese girls have for man-trapment. They used to be called a fishing fleet. They are absolutely desperate to leave the country and live abroad. They will play any role initially until you marry them. Be warned. When I come over and visit, we might just try a little original sake. They warm it, don't they, like glühwein, which in my opinion doesn't travel well either.'

With this pronouncement she had relaxed, having got it off her ample chest.

With her words ringing in his ears, he picked up the phone.

'Hello. Yes, Hana.'

'I'll have a few friends over.' He began. She warmed to it.

'Yes, yes. I'd really like it if you can come and if you want bring your American friend?' He stretched into his lower back. She agreed easily though chose a difficult day.

'Great.' His back-tinge shortened the conversation. It was a day he'd promised the piano teacher. 'Okay. I'll get you the details.'

A few friends? He'd had so little time to make any out here. He thought of rent-a-crowd from the office. Best keep it small. Yumi, though, would help him. If he got a couple of the young lawyers to come? One of them had a cousin visiting. The piano teacher would have to come too, and Yumi, as thanks for all her help. And so there would be eight of them.

Chapter 47

They were due to go over to the Ed's apartment for dinner. Hana still liked him, despite his poor performance at the club. He must be lonely to have got so trashed and she was sure the invite was his way of making it up to her. They dressed for the occasion from the narrow choice of their rucksacks.

'He's good-looking.' Jess rubbed her stomach hungrily as if she would eat him alive.

Hana wearied at the thought of watching Jess spending the evening like a salesperson on commission. She corrected herself. She didn't want to be unfair; perhaps Jess was a romantic.

Her own influences stemmed from a European culture which had once relied on the poetry of courtly love, predicated on the notion that it was perfectly sane to go war over a woman, albeit one of supernatural beauty; long Hellenistic traditions that had refused to die out entirely. And she guessed the lack of any early male influence in Jess' life had something to do with her outlook. She knew Jess wanted male attention and was so easily satisfied with any immediate gratification. What was Hana's own excuse for a bit distant, aloof? She couldn't tell, and had never thought to question it. It was that she had Tom.

Tom was a big issue. He remained in the flat but had acknowledged that when she got back it would be easier for him to move out. This rat's nest would greet her on arrival and it prompted the fleeting thought that she should extend her visa indefinitely. Deep down she knew they had to move on and somewhere as yet unverified she had come to terms with losing him.

She had, after all, left him when she stepped onto the train at Paddington. If she had been honest it had been a relief that he couldn't come with her on the trip. The London friends they had made together belonged to them both and they would again, in some form. It was unlikely in the erosion of their own relationship that one or other could bag a friend as their own. Though Hana just couldn't feel entirely comfortable about this value attrition; her network was based on the flimsy knots that held a net from unravelling into a mess of tangles.

Jess was pulling her dress over a belt to make it shorter. She turned for approval. 'What do you think?'

Hana gave her a painted smile.

Her lips matched the little red scarf Jess had tied round her head, knotted at the top like Frida Kahlo, just the same way she always wore hers. Jess was festooned with jewellery too, most of which did not belong to her.

'Well, where did you find that? '

Jess touched the headscarf.

'I found it in the store on the other side of the grade crossing.'

'The level crossing,' Hana curtly translated for no one other than her own benefit.

Hana's obsession with Kahlo had not waned since art school. The flavoured patterns, colours and totems were more than homage; they were her defining look now. At one time back then she had really associated with Khalo's admission: 'I used to think I was the strangest person in the world.' When they browsed the Tokyo flea markets or hunted down a new noodle bar, it was as if Frida Kahlo walked with her.

Jess, a muse in mourning, wore black with a regularity that smacked of lack of imagination. Though aware of a paucity of spirit, Hana was irritated by this appropriation of what she saw as her own signature image, and was riled that this evening they were about to set out as the same person in optional skin tones.

'Well, I think the necklace is mine.'

'May I borrow it?' Jess asked innocently.

Hana unwound the large bobble-fringed scarf from around her neck, removed several skeins of coral and turquoise, lifting them over her head and dropped them carelessly in a heap on the end of her bed.

Halfway out of the door she threw out, 'Many as you like.'

After a second's thought she marched back in and grabbed Jess's red lipstick, and, without waiting for the answer before applying it to her own lips, asked, 'May I?'

She felt appropriated. Sometimes, she fumed, you travel through life with people you don't even like. This summary conveniently ignored how fondly attached they really were and how much she needed her.

They left for Ed's and it was anyone's guess who would make headway with him that night.

Chapter 48

'Come, come with me.
Indulge my friendship,
Sleeping butterfly'
Poet Bashō, seventeenth century

Tokyo, 1989

Naomi and Mochizuki had spent the morning sizing up the teahouse at the temple.

'Hungry?' he asked.

Naomi followed him up an incline towards the temple restaurant selling ramen and soba to visitors, a place busy only on festival days and weekends. Perched on the hillside, the ground behind it fell sharply away, covered in a tumbling mass of dense, lush undergrowth and sapling trees. It was nothing more than a rudimentary shack with the bare essentials for cooking and they found they were alone.

Mochizuki had got his feet wet surveying the teahouse, stepping back to assess the elevation overlooking the pond. He took his shoes off and straddled one of several benches covered in red, felt cloth and shaded by a large, red, paper umbrella. She sat at the end of the bench in a demur side-saddle.

'You're looking hot, Naomi-san,' Mochizuki observed with mock formality, languorously stroking sweat from his neck with a firm hand as he looked up towards the brolly. 'You will spend more summers in Japan. You will get used to this,' he said exhaling deeply.

The nonchalance with which he predicted her future and teased her was amusing.

'Well, what are the guarantees?' she toyed.

'You begin to fall in love already,' he continued playfully.

Naomi stopped the game abruptly, finding herself covered in gentle embarrassment.

'It's a wonderful culture.' He looked at her slowly, searching to see if she had or had not misunderstood him.

Finally the old waitress, Mompei ducked under the short noren curtain; it blew in her face and her tray clipped the wall.

'*Dame!*' she swore, making her way over to them. Two complimentary glasses, half full of water, stood in a pool.

She greeted them, wiping her hands on her besmirched apron. She had hefty wrists, all the better for lifting vast batches of buckwheat noodles on holy days. Naomi remained outside their exchange.

'*Irrashaimase.*' She uttered her welcome formulaically with the menu cards 'Going barefoot now, is it , Mochizuki?' she gabbled in Japanese.

'You walking home?' she goaded him. 'Or to the love hotel at the bottom of the Yokohama Road?' He returned an explosive snort; they were familiar and these were the easy terms of their playful banter.

Naomi hadn't a clue what they were saying as they sparred. She did understand love hotel, though the subjects were unclear. Then Mompei nodded towards her.

'If there were teeth left in your head to remove after that suggestion, I'd do it for you,' Mochizuki said, laughing.

In answer to Naomi's quizzical look, he explained, clearing his throat and searching for gravity. 'This woman suggests we build a hotel.'

Naomi knew she had not said this. She had heard love hotel, and Mompei's nod towards her had particularly infuriated him and then made him laugh. What was this ridiculous conversation he was having?

'Is she okay? Can you translate the menu for me?'

He ran down the menu muttering, *'Tsukiji. Kitsune. Oyako. Oyako-donburi.'* His tongue searched his front teeth in anticipation.

'Okay, Moth-eaten, what's it to be?' the waitress asked Mochizuki. 'The parent and child?' She nodded towards Naomi.

Naomi thought he looked for a moment genuinely infuriated.

'Eta. Etahin.' He chose very specifically to call her an untouchable.

The woman placed her fists on her waist defiantly. Naomi couldn't work out the reason for the altercation.

'You couldn't lick your fingers to a good meal. As for cooking one . . .' Mompei drew her mouth into a long point until it resembled the crinkled end of an ill-sharpened pencil.

The damp air was soon heavy with the smell of cooking as they talked over the structural supports for the water-based section of the teahouse. The waitress returned supporting a four-storey pagoda of soups and noodles, and laid them across the red felt bench. Taking up her chopsticks, Mompei caught the wayward strands, teasing them into place. She then produced a canister covered in cherry-blossom washi paper and from it generously scattered ribbons of dried inky seaweed, a few on each meal, for nutritional balance and decoration.

Naomi removed her chopsticks from their paper sleeve, joined at one end like Siamese twins. She broke them apart easily and began rubbing the splintered edges against one another to remove the shards of rough wood.

Mochizuki leapt up like a man possessed, holding her wrists to stop her. He seemed to regain his composure as soon as he had lost it.

'This we never do. It is a bad omen to rub the chopsticks together. You know you must never do this, Naomi-chan,' using her name to soften the rebuke. 'Only at a funeral can we use them this way.'

Naomi apologized but still felt his touch on her wrists.

'There it is.' He pointed to a large, golden egg yolk floating in a pool of broth. 'The reflection of the moon on the water.'

'Quite a poetic lunch.' Naomi chose irony though he didn't respond.

'Not entirely accurate.' He began slurping his noodles hungrily and quite knowingly and mindful of her reaction said, 'You should take more air with the noodles, Naomi-chan,' comfortable now with the diminutive address he used for her.

'Some noise,' she added before attempting to follow his drain-clearing lead. He smiled at her open criticism and broke into laughter over her attempts.

When Mochizuki had finished his noodles he balanced his chopsticks across his bowl. Elbows on his knees, legs wide apart, contemplating the dirt floor, he found an old pine cone, split and dried. He picked it up and threw it hard, aiming at a tree across the track. It shattered against the trunk, casting dry seeds and broken integuments under the tree.

'I have sown the seeds of a new pine tree. I have something I will show you. A little box with an ivory in just the shape of the cone.' He looked at her searchingly. 'I love this place.' And into the silence he added, 'You know the poet Bashō?'

'No, I don't,' she owned.

'He created the first-ever haiku verses. They are like a snap-shot in time and it is here, in this place, that I remember him most.' The colour rose in her cheeks, he noticed, or was it the reflection from the red brolly?

The atmosphere was still and the trees hardly moved in the pulsating heat.

And now he chooses to talk to me of poetry? she thought.

Chapter 49

'A problem for architecture, the truest form of art, which has not been a genuine concern for other artists, lies in where to plant the species in the city garden of structures, and where to plant the specimen that, ipso facto, covers land, where once stood ancient woodlands.'

Naomi had been given the task of reading the translator's proofs for a publication covering a retrospective of Mochizuki's works. It did not come naturally to her. There were compensations in getting to know what he stood for and believed in, and, in reading his words, she came closer to falling under his influence. He had been absent that morning and she asked around after him. That day he had suggested they would have an office picnic on the beach but he had not appeared all morning.

Saito-san was keen to maintain her reputation as the ears of the office and came over with the feigned purpose of borrowing a highlighter to find out what Naomi was asking of the others.

'Is Mochizuki in?' Naomi asked again.

'Probably with Ukai. The only man he answers to,' Saito-san told Naomi flatly, and she scurried off as if she had already said too much. She was keen not to be drawn into further revelations.

Naomi had heard the name but knew nothing of the man.

She turned three more pages of copy before she found, tucked between the loose leaves, a portion of thinly lined file paper and on it a note, hastily written in biro. Someone had drawn lashes round the vacant spaces of the punched holes in the cheap grey paper. The first few lines were in in Japanese kanji and below was presumably a translation; the postscript read: Bashō, seventeenth century.

Come, come with me.
Indulge my friendship,
Sleeping butterfly.

Kobe was engrossed in his comic book, so she ruled him out as the perpetrator of a prank. Nobody, it seemed, was looking for her reaction to the note. So she took it to be an ode to the season from Mochizuki because he had been at pains to introduce her to the poet Bashō.

Iwata was busy making runs in the jeep to deliver the larger items and the chairs to the beach, and had concluded his trips by ten. A delivery van arrived with the food and Saito-san spend a good part of the rest of morning in the kitchenette. Naomi found her with the furoshiki, wrapping cloths that had been bought for the purpose, wrapping the picnic bento boxes with large ties for handles.

'You need a hand?'

Saito-san told her that Mochizuki had rung in and would be late for the picnic but would join everyone later on the beach.

So she would see him today, she thought.

Iwata looked pinched and resentful.

The sea was so far out across the volcanic sands that the line of water could have been a heat haze. Naomi stood on the low sea wall with her back to Mount Fuji looking way out across the volcanic black beach to the Pacific Ocean. It was difficult to believe any tidal force could cover the distance and rise like Hiroshige's blue wave in the woodblock print and threaten the town.

Even here, on the margins of the sea, humidity clung to the beach party – to their clothes and their hair – adding to their heavy expectancy. Mochizuki had still to arrive and it wasn't until he did so that Saito-san would start the picnic. There was a mutual assumption that Naomi would only work in the office for a short time and so their efforts to assimilate her were half-hearted at best. Outside the job of work they opened broken conversations with her but, without a common currency, floundered beyond any subject, other than what the bento boxes would contain.

It seemed to Naomi like a long time before Mochizuki strode over the sea wall towards them and, as with a new breeze, their spirits lifted. Frankly, everyone was relieved to see him, not least since the picnic was his idea.

He marched straight over to Naomi and sat beside her. Saito-san handed the bento boxes round and he ate like a prince among his tribe. No one was in any doubt that Naomi was his sometime-honoured guest. She fell on the plum-blossom carrots. Observing this, Mochizuki loaded his own share onto her plate.

Iwata, she could see, did not approve of the additions to her picnic.

'I was once given a necklace of carrots,' she told Mochizuki. 'Unpeeled with their tops intact. There were nine, laced on blue nylon string, lying in a box wrapped in beautiful paper. A nine-carrot necklace, like the gold.'

He laughed appreciatively.

She felt him touch the loose hair across her back.

Quietly he asked her, 'You get my poem?', his warm breath close to her ear.

She blushed at his intimacy, letting loose the gingered chicken from her chopsticks.

He took a virtual step back, aware that he had frightened her.

'Bashō, our great poet of nature,' he said loudly. 'I like him more than you like bento lunch.'

He got up to leave her, casting a suggestion behind him. 'You'll come and give me a hand at the publishers in Nagoya? I have to travel to Gifu. You'll come?' And before she had a chance to answer he left her to think about it. 'I must attend to my staffs.'

He ran off to retrieve a baseball glove from the basket, calling in Iwata's direction to grab the bat, 'Oi Chinko.' He called him playfully.

'Chinko?' Hana queried, as Saito-san came over to provide more tea. She giggled behind her white lace-trimmed handkerchief. She pointed between her legs and then looked towards Iwata's crotch. She walked off with the flask laughing. Out on the sands the men ran to the bases they had laid out from their low-slung beach stools. Naomi dozed as Mochizuki's infectious laughter crossed the sand.

Chapter 50

Josh had excelled himself and had lit the coals on a Weber BBQ they had bought at the weekend in store, at Tokyu Hands. He stepped in from the terrace with more meat.

'I may have a business trip.' Naomi tried the idea for sound. She was nibbling a crisp. The BBQ was covering the struggling potted tree they had bought, in acrid smoke.

'A business trip?' He treated her job as a joke.

'Yes, middle of next month.'

'But that's exactly when we planned to go out to the country.' They were always planning a tour and it was often postponed in favour of his own business agenda. The timing was inconvenient for him. 'There's no money in it. So when are you giving this in?'

She followed through. 'Yes, Mochizuki has asked if I will review the proofs for the retrospective and the publishers are down in Nagoya. It'll take a couple of days.'

Josh snorted. 'I don't think so.'

'What?'

'I don't think you should go.'

She decided to leave it until she found him in a more amenable mood.

Chapter 51

The crane. A symbol of longevity, immortality youth, and good fortune

Outside the office window the young fruit on the satsuma tree was ripening; weathered blossom still hung in clusters, destined to remain barren, lagging behind their season. All that morning Naomi had been checking the faint outlines of generations of copies against the original draft plans. Mochizuki had widened her brief. Watanabe and Takeshi were silently engrossed in their screens. Watanabe had retreated to one of the angled desks at the back of the room. The phones were silent and the whole office worked to the tune of the air-conditioning units. They could all bear witness to what was an unprecedented row that broke the calm of the morning.

Mochizuki had reappeared after coffee and was sitting at his desk behind his copy of the *Asahi Shimbun* newspaper. The headlines that day called again for the imminent resignation of yet another member of the ruling party caught up in a corruption scandal. Mochizuki's interests, however, lay in the back pages where he checked the latest baseball results. Naomi resumed her tired comparisons of the grey sheets of instructions.

Mochizuki finally swopped the baseball scores for the figures on the Guam project on the desk in front of him. Iwata was heading towards Saito-san's office in the other room and had almost fallen over Takeshita's prominent feet protruding from beneath his desk and he responded by giving them a friendly kick. Mochizuki stopped Iwata on his way past and stipulated quite curtly that he, Mochizuki must see the elevations for the

Guam hotel before they were sent to Shinoda construction. Iwata seemed surprised that he should have to get approval for the documents before sending them and drew the plans from the chest near accountant's office. He threw them on his desk for Mochizuki's approval.

Mochizuki looked briefly and handed them back. He dismissed them summarily and let him know that he wanted Iwata to send the earlier draft. He earnestly stroked the stubble on his chin.

'No, we have a later draft for construction,' Iwata contradicted him.

Mochizuki's casual ease evaporated and he demanded to see both the earlier and the later draft. Iwata agreed, assuming that, with two copies on the table, he could support his case. When he returned he placed the cover sheet for the two sets of plans beside one another.

'Send the earlier one,' Mochizuki confirmed.

'I can't send the old plans for construction,' Iwata countered, 'they are incorrect.' His voice becoming plangent. At this mounting insurrection Mochizuki ran his fingers through his hair to control his agitation, and then yelled at Iwata at point-blank range

'I'm telling you, send them!'

Stunned, Iwata retreated with the conflicting plans. Watanabe and Takeshita exchanged glances, waiting for the next act. Mochizuki rifled round in his pockets for a packet of cigarettes, then clasped one between his teeth; the paper clung to his wet lip while he frisked himself for his matches. Takeshita was quickly out of his seat, fumbling for his lighter till he leant over Mochizuki's desk with a light. A sense of unnatural ease, like the first drag of nicotine, descended over the office.

Later that morning Naomi sought out Saito-san.

'What was that about?'

Saito-san took pleasure in translating a nugget of some importance. 'He will get Iwata to send the construction QS the early version. Not the latest approved and signed,' she said, with eyes as large as the implications. Different Specs. Different costs.

With that gift imparted she turned on her heel importantly and went back to her office.

Towards the end of the morning, having fielded a couple of calls from the aggressive Mr Wang from the IT company, Naomi was composing a fax to send in reply to a query on Italian furniture imports.

Unnoticed until he was standing over her Mochizuki asked, 'You want lunch?'

Josh would be working late that night and the invite made her feel suddenly less of an exile.

'Yes. Five or ten minutes. Okay?'

'You can leave it,' he said. 'My wife is expecting us for lunch.' And the invite became a demand.

And yet again she'd been singled out from the other staff. It was, she thought, quite an honour. She was keen to meet her. His wife would, he had said, be there.

She invariably ate alone; she would stay at her desk, or more often than not she would head to the beach because it gave her a thrill to sit in view of Mt Fuji. Today, finally, she would meet Mrs Mochizuki. Miho had told her a little about her.

They left together, passing the punched-aluminum gates stifled by kiwi vines, and walked three blocks. Only a small dog crossed the hot tarmac, pausing midway to scratch. There was no smell of the sea, just a dry dust on the wind.

'Can I buy you a drink?' he asked, as they passed the vending machines.

As she scanned the beer, fruit and isotonic drinks, he mimed feeding her a 100-yen coin; her eyes warned him not to and he stopped. She asked for iced coffee. A can hit the pocket with an engineered thud, as satisfying as delivering a bowling-ball strike. She let the cold can roll down her neck across her chest until she realized he was watching. She gave another warning glance as his hand hovered over her chest to take it from her. The jeep rounded the corner and Iwata drove up just as Mochizuki appeared to have his hand down her shirt. Iwata wound the window down to ask if he could give them a lift.

With a wave of his hand Mochizuki dismissed him and Iwata sped off, accelerating as if he had many better things to do with his time than chauffeur the girl around.

Mochizuki held out his hand for her ring tab and then threaded it onto his little finger. The bitter coffee was as close to the real thing as she was, now, to Columbia. He contemplated her a moment, and suddenly seemed to change his mind. He turned and insisted she go on without him, directing her the rest of the way.

'I'll catch you up,' he promised.

Chapter 52

'The kimono sash my wife has tied,
Will never by my hands be undone?
Though the sash be cut or severed,
I cannot that knot untie,
Until I see her again.'
–The Man'yōshū (eighth-century anthology of Japanese
poetry)

The Mochizuki house was a few roads back from the beach; a modernist beach house in a line of off-the-peg American builds: a simulacrum of average which no one had thought to finesse before repeating a bad joke so often it became a semiotic nightmare. Their house was saved by the isolation afforded by the garden that shielded it from its neighbours. A mature pine tree had been accommodated in the construction and half of the grey, timber façade was deferentially set back against a different plane to give it room to grow. The patchwork timber door was ajar, expecting her. The blades of a traditional black fan rotated noiselessly as it moved from side to side in the blind surveillance of an abandoned ship.

Mrs Mochizuki's tanned bare feet announced her approach across the bleached wooden floor. She was well-groomed and wore a crisp open-necked white shirt and capri pants; her dark hair closely cropped. She paced towards Naomi and her strong smile made up for the vague western handshake.

'Hajimemashite, Kazuko desu.'

Naomi guessed she must be about thirty-five. Her eyes were bright, but not themselves illuminating. The brighter the light, the stronger the depth of the contrasting shadows. She was definitely staring.

'My husband does not accompany a guest's arrival to the house?'

Naomi was unsure whether this was a question or a statement of fact.

'But we like him even so. He can be forgiven.' She signalled Naomi to go on in ahead.

The open-plan living room was light and spacious without a colour register besides indigo and white. Two large fig-like plants guarded the doors with huge textile hangings, like pieces of modern art, to animate the sparse scheme.

Kazuko explained how she collected these unfathomable blue textiles made by farming communities. Strands of cotton were resist-dyed before they were woven with depictions from folklore: moons, masks, fish sushi.

'You eat chicken?' she asked as forcefully as if it were a statement of fact.

Naomi nodded.

As Kazuko moved to the kitchen, Naomi snatched a glimpse behind her, like a shutter exposure on another world: riotously stacked shelves, colourful cookbooks, tea caddies, angular pots and plants and a pastel-coloured rice cooker besides a shelf of plump white-cat votaries in varying sizes, all holding up a left paw and decorated in red and gold. The door swung shut. There was something strikingly confident in Kazuko's manner and her voice was strong and resonant, unlike some of the other Japanese women she had met.

'Ikat,' she said, referring to the textiles. 'Always have these designs with blurred edges.' She shared her passion easily.

They stood to admire a large indigo hanging of a carp that seemed to swim across the threads with a muscular flick of his animated tail.

'He will bring you good luck,' Kazuko concluded, and turned back to where the open shutters offered a view of the garden, which seemed part of the room itself.

Kazuko offered her a chair, which Naomi noted was in the style of a George Nakashima.

She poured two glasses of iced mint tea. 'Nice to see you.'

She had immaculate English, Naomi thought. 'So kind of you to have me to lunch.'

'Mochizuki tells me your boyfriend's away in Australia and so we thought that was tough. I am away a lot myself. My job.'

'What is it that you do?' Naomi asked.

'I am involved in climate change conferences. Translation.' Naomi nodded appreciatively. 'I was involved in the Copenhagen summit.'

They passed pleasantries until the ice had melted in their drinks, and still Mochizuki had not joined them.

'How long will your boyfriend be away?'

'Only a fortnight, but he is covering Asia-Pacific and in the months we have been here he is at Narita Airport more often than the flights are scheduled.'

'You are not married? '

'No.'

The older woman got up to take Naomi's drink.

'May I show you something?' And she led her upstairs.

Upstairs it was cooler. Kazuko spread a kimono over the corner of the bed, as if she were casting a net, so that the design was flat and easily visible. Immediately she looked round to gauge Naomi's reaction, to see perhaps, whether she too would be entranced by the subtle art of the silk painter as she herself had been. The background was a heavy, apricot silk that had been embroidered to look rippled and watermarked. Naomi scanned the heavy decoration on the sleeves and at the base of the T-shaped kimono.

'See the dragonflies on the sleeve panels?' The upper part of the garment was unembellished but at the hem there was a deep blue of semi-circles. 'Fish scales. Like every kimono it is made of panels of the same size. One size fits all.' Kazuko laughed. She lifted the kimono. 'Will you?' And she held it open for Naomi to wear.

It was so long that it enveloped her. She stretched her arms out and curled her hands upwards.

Kazuko laughed again. 'You look like a kimono stand but not quite so wooden.'

She tried to collect the sleeves that fell to well below her knees.

'This is a kimono for an unmarried woman. The sleeves are long. Short sleeves for a busy married housewife.'

'I guess that would be more practical,' Naomi offered. For some reason she felt uncomfortable discussing marital status in this curiously empty bedroom with Mochizuki's wife. She hoped it was a spare bedroom.

The hem of the cloth was woven in eddying circles. A figurative cherry tree hung over a vestigial pond and, dotting the cloth, stray crimson blossoms fell in a snowstorm scattered on the water.

'It's beautiful. Exquisite.' She felt slightly awkward under Kazuko's searching eyes.

'*Hana fubuki*, we say: cherry-blossom snowstorm.'

Kazuko untied a woven band and slipped it from its hold around another box. Inside, beneath the tissue paper, was another silk kimono.

A crane with feathers of gold thread flew over a large cart from the Edo period that spilled over with embroidered flowers. It was garish and overworked in reds and oranges.

'It is a very traditional design,' Kazuko said, reading Hana's hesitation, 'and I now prefer the folk craft. But I must see you in it. This kimono has sleeves for a married woman. See, they are shorter. I wore this before my own marriage ceremony. If I wear a kimono now it is the short-sleeved.'

Naomi swung the large wings of satin around her. 'Those nineteenth-century habits seem hard to kick. I suppose with housekeeping and carrying children short would be easier.'

Kazuko came up close, so close they might be breathing the same air. She smoothed the fabric slowly and then turned swiftly away.

'Try on the whole outfit?' she suggested. 'As far as possible.'

Naomi had no reason to object and no reason to want to dress in her satins.

Kazuko started to pull out lacquered boxes from the wardrobe and revealed neatly folded satin obis, woven silken ties tasselled in mauve, purple and rusts. None of the colours met with Hana's western understanding of harmony.

'And your shirt?'

'It's fine.' Politeness would demand she would not remove her shirt.

Dressing Naomi in the kimono, Kazuko crossed one side of the kimono over the other and very deliberately smoothed down the silken lapels, ironing out the creases right over left, and then, changing her mind, closed it left over right, carefully across Naomi's breast. Looking her in the eye, she smiled reassuringly, cool in her crisp cotton shirt but for a bead of sweat that rested on the down above her upper lip.

The under belt was tied about Naomi's waist at which point she became a mannequin and gave in as the obi sash followed.

She felt frisked. 'Hello, airport security.' Naomi immediately regretted her flippancy as Kazuko looked at her quizzically. 'It feels as though you're checking me like airport security,' she explained.

Kazuko was lost in her role as dresser. Once finished she stood back to admire the effect and broke into Japanese.

'*Oningyo mitei.*' She laughed, pleased with the transformation of the western girl. 'You look like a doll,' she translated. 'How does it feel?'

Hana was stiff and bound.

Kazuko pointed to her capri pants. 'I am the westerner today. You are the beautiful Japanese woman.'

Naomi obliged her in a catwalk move across the room to the window, the delicious sound of the silk train following her like audible shadow.

Kazuko clapped. 'Bravo, but you must take smaller steps; you are in Japan now.'

Naomi gave herself up to her hostess and it would not have been so easy were she not alone in the room with the other woman and so many miles from home.

She stepped lightly. 'How is this?'

'That's good. *Dan dan*, we say: slow and gradual.'

Naomi felt a kindled interest in Kazuko's gaze, a searching look that seemed beyond the critique of someone merely entertaining her lunch guest.

'I am sure you look very beautiful in these.'

'Oh, I never wear them; they were made for the wedding-ceremony day.'

She would not ask how long it had been since Kazuko married.

'The silk is hand-painted. I keep them in cedar, lined with tin; in the rainy season humidity reaches over ninety.'

'You will have to keep them for your own children, one day.'

'No. We don't have children. We can't.' Her response as rapid as it was blunt.

It was too soon to ask where between a discomfort and personal tragedy this fact chose to nestle in her consciousness. It was too soon to say 'sorry', to ask why, to talk of adoption. She wanted to move on.

'Let me show you a hairpiece too.' Kazuko brought out two lacquered combs set with mother-of-pearl.

'Just beautiful.' Naomi had enough of playing mannequin. 'I am sure it'll take an age to unbind me? I don't want to wear them for long in this heat.'

Both women were distracted by the voice of Mochizuki from downstairs.

'*Tadaima*,' he called.

Kazuko watched Naomi for an interval of time, which prompted Naomi to suggest that they go down and join him. And again she asked whether she could take the kimono off. The knot on the obi was so carefully tied she hesitated to start unravelling it herself but as she fingered it the older woman broke into a smile and urged her to keep it on for lunch.

'It'll take too long, He's back already. Come, come down.'

Chapter 53

Mochizuki arrived to find Naomi walking down the stairs for lunch, coming towards him dressed like the Queen of Sheba. Tentatively holding the banister, she attempted to make her way down in the blanket of cloth. He threw out a manufactured cheer of approval and glanced swiftly at Kazuko but it was too short to question her, dressing the *gaijin* in her own wedding robes. He had fleetingly wondered who it was descending the stairs in the familiar kimono.

Kazuko set down a platter with a rough, uncontrived beauty, styled with a knowing naivety and attributable to one in a line of followers of the fertile union between the potters Shōji Hamada and Bernard Leach.

They were to eat kneeling beside the small charcoal brazier on the terrace, Japanese-style, overlooking the traditional garden. Mochizuki slumped like an etiolated boy in a misshapen baggy shirt.

'I smile to see you in my kimono. You know when I first met him it was at the environmental conference in Kobe. Here was this young architect talking about his great plans for sustainability.'

Mochizuki gave her a look of: don't start.

'Wood as a renewable resource. No steel. No concrete. No manufacturing costs. And you plant in its place. You know, we Japanese we have a long history of building in timber. He was a great speaker.'

He smiled.

'Now he's getting rusty.'

The jibe was lost on him; for it was made in good humour. He responded like a teenager on the edge of some conjured indignation.

She—' as he often called Kazuko in the course of conversation '—is translating at the talks on climate change in Canada next month.'

Kazuko leant forward to balance bamboo sticks of food on the hibachii stove.

'Yes, it is an important step in the negotiations to get governments heavily involved on the issues. The scientists have been pressing for this for years but not until the stratospheric "ozone hole" did anyone take real notice.'

'So now there'll be some action?' Naomi asked. The events of her own life had left this problem way down a priority list with her. Like the Doppler effect – the noise about it had moved on.

'You know, it's like if your relation is suddenly diagnosed with something, only then they finally give up smoking.' She excused herself and added, 'I mean, detecting that tear in the sky was lucky.'

Mochizuki relaxed his languorous hold from the arches of his feet, idly brushing flakes of wayward cigarette ash that had settled on the zabuton

'So now we buy up the suntan-lotion companies,' he quipped.

'I remember when it was in the papers back home; it was as if a meteor had fallen to earth in your own garden and we all felt vulnerable. But after that . . .'

'I would miss my garden,' he said wistfully.

He caught Naomi staring in the direction of the moss-covered stone lantern. Constructed in five sections, it was small and squat and lay hidden in the undergrowth

'The ishidoro. You can see it often at shrines.' He held his hand away to count from the lower little finger, enumerating the levels of the lantern with each digit. 'This, the stand of the lantern, is earth. Then you have water.' His head cocked to one side as he looked out to register the plinth. 'The body of the lantern is fire. Fire contains fire,' he said, beating his chest for their amusement. 'The roof is the symbol of wind, and this ball on the upper section is air. Earth, water, fire, wind, air,' he reiterated. 'Ancient Chinese symbols. This is the harmony.'

She understood his deep-seated affection for the ways of an older culture and its inherent poetry. She felt, and not for the first time in his company, that, through his eyes, she was getting closer to something elemental and to a wholly different way of looking at things. She felt at ease with him, but the heavy kimono had begun to be uncomfortable.

Mochizuki sat cross-legged, pressing his feet together, unaware of the effect he was having.

They watched the glow from the naked fire with a primitive fascination. A faintly acrid smell of charred soy sauce hung in the air.

Kazuko brought different bowls of sticky white rice and they ate without conversation. Kneeling in the kimono and eating over the silks was quite a trial but there was no pressure to trade views and and they relaxed as they listened to the garden.

Kazuko went to bring salty pickles in a tiny pottery saucer. A strong gust blew in, lifting the fine wisps of hair framing Naomi's face.

'Ame,' he predicted, rightly so, as just then the rain started to fall. He smiled at the timing of his prediction, and poured her tea that smelled of wood smoke but tasted clean and refreshing.

Instantly gaining momentum the rain suddenly blew through the sliding doors; they had believed they were beyond its reach.

She was mindful of the silk as they leapt up, objecting loudly as the zabuton cushions were peppered with spots of damp. It touched the skin on her bare arms like an unwelcome overture.

They hastily pulled back and retreated to a safety zone within the room and, with hypnotic fascination, watched through the open windows as the porch changed colour. A rain chain ran from the eaves of the porch; one bronze cup after another pooled and spilled as the water clung to the chain in a kind of physical insecurity and moved like plastic to swell the brimming cup below. They sat water-watching like ancient samurai in repose.

'You have a great garden here,' Naomi said to Mochizuki.

'It's hers. She made it some years back.'

Kazuko, at this point, had decided lunch was over. 'You got a fax from Daichii,' she threw over her shoulder as she walked off. He punctuated the air with a grunt.

On entering the kitchen Kazuko displaced a large white cat who tiptoed over to Mochizuki and began courting his affection, getting as physically close as it possibly could, winding its long tail up his leg entreatingly. The air inside was now perfectly still and slightly suffocating.

'Neighbour's cat,' he said, by way of apology.

Naomi's kimono became heavier and she rose to change. Kazuko followed her upstairs to help and when she untied the innermost sash of the dress Mrs Mochizuki said gently, 'You must look after him while I am away. He has a business trip coming up to Gifu.'

Beneath the silks Naomi's T-shirt was damp and clung to her body.

'You will go too?' Kazuko entreated.

Chapter 54

That night she had her nightly call with Josh who was still in Australia. Naomi lay back against the pillow and attempted to balance the telephone against her chin to free her hands.

'I have never seen him so angry. He is normally so mild-mannered. I barely recognized him. Best to stick with working on the teahouse.'

There was a small time delay before Josh responded. She picked her book from the bedside table and opened the spine to fan herself. *The Red Chrysanthemum* proved more effective than the air-con, which was always playing up. The irritating agent came to mind. She wondered how Josh was doing in the depths of the Aussie winter.

Josh was a few hours ahead, winding down his day. 'He is under pressure,' he said over the phone, picking a travel chess piece from the opposing side as he played himself.

'He is generally very easy with the office. Indulgent almost.'

'Yes.' Josh allowed himself to castle, changing the two fortresses for better defence.

'This issue was clearly important to him,' Naomi continued. 'The horseplay between Iwata and Takeshita couldn't have angered him so much. They're always at it.'

Josh gave some thought to his move. 'Stressed?' His line of thinking had not moved on particularly.

'I guess. What's Sam's thinking on the Guam Hotel?' she asked. A conversation with Sam on this was still pending.

'As you describe them,' Josh said, 'the offices sound scruffy.

Financial trouble? But everyone is making money this year. Japan is a "best bet".'

'But he hates that project. He's sending stuff out for construction that's not signed off or approved.'

'Sounds like it's a scam. It's all about the costs. You know what I think? I think he must be a bloody yakuza.'

'Don't be ridiculous, Josh. I am proofreading his book. A retrospective of his life's work.'

'And when did he last come up with a blockbuster? What date did they dry up?' he countered.

'He reads Bashō.'

'Bashō?'

'Poetry, Josh – you've heard of poetry?'

He tapped the board with a chess piece before his next move.

'What are you doing?' she asked. The sound was unidentifiable down the line.

'It's a white pawn.'

'Chess?' Infuriated that he was playing while on the phone to her she threatened. 'Okay, a board full of chess pieces will welcome you home if I am out,'

He turned back to the board to find a bishop on the other side had taken a white pawn and was annoyed at the unintended casualty. He had not been concentrating.

They ran through the pleasantries they knew by heart and then Josh tried harder.

'Their house? What's it like?'

'It was kind of exquisite, pared down, what you would expect. It was really kind of them, Josh, but slightly strange. Anything in the heat plays more slowly. They have a genuine George Nakashima.' She found it addictive to be in Mochizuki's company.

'What?'

'You know, the guy who wrote *The Soul of a Tree?*'

'For God's sake, don't go too native on me.'

'We can't all crunch numbers for a living.'

'I don't want to be here any longer than I have to but it does feel closer to home. It's been good – we've got the go-ahead to invest in some people who build wind farms.

'Is that a good idea?'

'A bloody good idea; it's the gale force roaring forties down here.'

He rang every night at around ten his time and then went back, like an addict, to his risk predictions; a gambler promised a win if he kept playing compulsively because he knew he was on the side of the casino.

'Come home soon,' she said.

'To Japan?' he scoffed, more at home where he was.

Naomi picked up *The Red Chrysanthemum*. She would, she decided, go on the business trip, and when she called home, if she called home, she might or might not give Josh her attention. She read for a time and then cast the book aside. She thought of Mochizuki, she thought of Josh, and then lay back and pleasured herself before sleep.

Chapter 55

'Oft I go to him
By paths of dream
Never resting my feet
In the real world
And it amounts to not a single glance.'

—

Tokyo, 1989

Water had pooled on the platform that formed the beginnings of the foundation for the teahouse. Reflected in the patches of water, the opaque sky was soiled white and over-washed. Rain was gathering. The clouds pillowed like the weighty breasts of a girl beneath thin cotton. Around the ornamental garden, the leaves dripped in the humidity and it was not clear where the murky, oriental pond ended and the livid moss banks under wet shrubs began. In the middle of this, the construction site looked like an act of vandalism. Beneath the funematsu sail pine, an abandoned cement mixer stood, catching rainwater in its gurning mouth. The white sand beneath the tree had lost its customary moonshine, now an occluded, yellowing, damp crust, as mud from the construction had spread across the virginal blanket. The whole site looked like a desecration.

Uprights, chosen by Minamioka as the structural supports for the building, stood inanely pointing to the sky. The treated wood of the pillars was defaced by the rain, running with long dark stains of neglect like graffiti. Amid the mani-cured green of the washed garden the building site looked more like the lost ruins of an ancient civilization: totems telling of decay, where the pillars stood for dead trees rather than joists, upon which the strength of the whole construc-tion would lie.

Naomi was sitting alone at the gate, an occasional drop getting through her thin summer skirt. As she waited, she pushed on her cuticles, exposing the white half-moon at the base of her nails. Her thoughts trailed back to Tokyo. The Guam project for the passenger lounge was nearing completion and she made a mental note that she would soon have to dispatch the client copies with a set of internal layout drawings. Scrambled subway maps.

She sighed and looked up over towards the teahouse site where play had been postponed. On the side of the cement-mixer drum, in both Kanji and English. were the words 'Ukai' in black stencil. It surprised her to find Ukai Constuction here in the temple gardens on the teahouse project. She ran her hands along the split bamboo seat, absently tracing the pronounced growth ridges like finger joints. Ukai's influence was felt on just about every project that the practice handled. The rain looked threatening, and she regretted that she hadn't made provision for it.

A tall figure walked up from the path down below. She watched him approach, his head visible now and then among the shrubs and bushes. As he got closer she could see he was wearing a light American raincoat with the collar tuned up. His stride was strong and purposeful. He smiled broadly as he came to a standstill in front of her. He had been lunching with the abbot.

'So Iwata brought you?' Mochizuki questioned.

'No, he had something to do so he got me a taxi.'

'My firm's total profit blown on your taxis,' he said, and then he laughed loudly.

She looked away, seeing nothing but verdant green. 'You had said it was okay for me to take it this morning if I needed to.' She was defiant as he loomed over her.

He dropped the subject and looking in the direction of the teahouse site said,

'Come on. Let's go look'. He touched her shoulder encouragingly. 'You didn't dress for the weather.' He touched her again, feeling at the delicacy of the thin blouse.

They moved off to inspect the site and he made her walk on ahead of him, along the narrow path between the short-cropped azalea bushes. He watched the hem of her long skirt dampen and discolour with flecks of mud along the short distance. The moisture made the thin cloth cling to the back of her calves as she walked. The brooding cloud cover thickened and it became gloomier just before the onset of rain. The shrubs around them began to call to one another as the first heavy raindrops fell. Mindful of her flimsy clothes, he lifted up the corner of his raincoat.

'Here,' he said, motioning, offering to share its cover.

She held the corner of the coat high over her shoulder and they walked back down the hill as the rain gathered momentum. It was difficult to walk along the narrow path two abreast. She moved closer towards him so that her hip was nestled in behind him. Her body brushed against him as they walked and he was very aware of her warmth through the thin wet cloth of her shirt. The rain picked up, turning quickly into an aggressive deluge. They took their cue and sped up but they found themselves too late and caught the worst of it. Running together under the raincoat along the narrow path was as successful as a three-legged race. So she broke away from him and ran on ahead to a nearby wooden building, the yoritsuki changing rooms, near the gate to the outer garden. She ran up to the loka terrace and took cover beneath the protective overhang but the angle of the rain drove beneath the canopy. She slid open the shoji doors and ran breathlessly inside.

The acoustics of the deafening rain were muffled inside the wooden changing rooms. He followed briskly after her to find her leaning against the wall for support. She turned to him, beaming and panting with exertion. They were both very wet; his look as good as a challenge. Her cotton shirt clung, on her rising breath, to her breasts. He dropped his case and put his arms around her; beneath his raincoat her hands met him and ran up his back as they kissed. Rainwater still ran down their faces. He stopped and broke away just as their need for one another became more desperate. She sank to the floor and her eyes tempted him to follow her. Mochizuki held his hands up in protest, surrendering not to her but to circumstances that would allow him to go no further.

She ignored his resignation, approaching him on her knees. Gently determined when she undid his flies, finding him hard and waiting for her. Gently exposing him, she ran her hands down his buttocks to draw him closer. She ran her tongue up the stiff shaft and round the helmet-like ridge, closing her mouth over the smooth tip and toying with the small indentation at the top, pulsing her tongue as she held him firmly. His hands rested on her head, his thumbs pivoted against her cheekbones. When she paused he gently pushed back her head so that she had to look up at him. Her lips were parted needily. She lay back, drawing up her wet skirt. This time, his resistance gone, he joined her on the floor. Then, as suddenly as the rain came, the cloud passed. They stopped, at the same time as if exposed in the sunlight. They were partaking of something forbidden in the teahouse complex in the temple grounds; it was the middle of the day and they might get caught.

'We are the outsiders, Naomi-chan. We have to be careful which rules we break.'

Naomi stole home early that afternoon. She stood virtually alone on the station platform. As the train stopped, with nurtured precision the doors opened to a persistent computer-generated alarm. Tinny interjections pulsed in and out of her consciousness, her waning concentration. The rain had passed and it was a warm, hazy evening where the air temperature stole nothing, imposed nothing. In the light, dense, heavy particles, the flotsam of the world, floated like dowdy angels.

She did not feel as she supposed she might. She stepped through the sliding doors, finding sanctuary in the relative calm of the carriage. The shrill of the station's overloud, overbearing and plangent voice muted as the doors closed behind her.

She took a seat, to be carried inexorably home. Insistent advertisements called her: bright betrayals of western models wearing bananas; a million and one Kewpie girls in sugared wedding gowns, not a groom in sight; posters for energy elixirs for tired salary men; comic offers of hemorrhoid remedies; banners that decorated the ceiling in some sort of festival of quotidian Japan. The interconnecting carriage of very few people ran on forever.

Her skirt still carried the mud splashes from the temple but she could find nothing across the afternoon that made her feel besmirched. The act of love would have been a natural conclusion to the understanding between them. Long, velour bench seats offered tens of free seats like a vendor selling nothing anybody wanted. In half an hour they would be going at a premium. Standing-room only. Now she sat alone but carried the afternoon she had spent with Mochizuki for company.

The low-lying tenement buildings crawled in pursuit of the train tracks, their scattered heights intermittently dominating the evening sun, the windows offering half-second glimpses of broken privacy amid untimely neglect. Small groups of people on bicycles held back by the barriers at the crossing, moved off again like clockwork as the train moved on. Josh would return from his trip to Australia that night.

She drifted into reverie again until a curve of sound reached her untending ears and she arched her back and rested her head, aware that she had found a place to inhabit with the architect that felt right, and to be woken from her being and nothingness no longer seemed like a threat.

Chapter 56

Mochizuki's publishers were in Nagoya and Naomi thought they must have gone to the wrong address when they climbed the narrow external staircase to the top floor of an unmodernised scruffy warehouse.

The nervous publisher had stains under the arms of his white shirt. And while Mochizuki's staff jumped to his assistance, the man jumped because he was jumpy.

The publisher presented the prepared layouts on the long trestle, and they walked round the table and circumnavigated Mochizuki's life's history.

'So how old was I when I produced this?'

'Young, Mochizuki-san.'

'Exactly. I don't want to give such prominence to this because it is not honed. It is a very good effort but it isn't truthful,' he said as Naomi leafed through volumes of work that lay on the bench before them. The breadth impressed her; a meandering line of projects, conceived according to his principles rather than the impulse to achieve as an imperative. Page after page showed his conviction and love of wood as a material. Mochizuki's had told her his designs valued space as much as the objects that defined it.

Mochizuki congratulated the publisher on his proofs as he accompanied him round. He was keen to get the retrospective published because he knew that the deal on the Guam Hotel would tarnish his standing and he was preparing for the financial fallout.

Naomi handled the sheets of domestic houses, a subway

station, corporate buildings from his early days, and more recently, a private gallery on the hillside outside Shikamura.

The retrospective volume would feature the best. She could see.

The publisher was delighted at their reception. Halfway round the trestle they came to an abrupt halt.

Mochizuki said nothing and the publisher looked to Naomi. They stared at one another for enlightenment.

'No.' Mochizuki took some nourishment from his cuticles. 'This section must come earlier.'

This request threw the whole flow of the book into confusion.

The publisher sucked his teeth. '*Chotto* . . .' The deadlines were too close to make such a radical alteration.

'And this? This should be photographed again.' Mochizuki demanded. 'This isn't me.' He was almost apologizing. His work meant everything to him and he was defined by it. It was worse than nothing if it went out as the compromised version. He himself felt compromised.

'We'll come back. We'll come back and review this.' They left the overworked man with hours of rejigging.

Naomi couldn't understand what had suddenly sent him ricocheting so off course.

Back in the car she asked, 'What did you mean when you said your work wasn't truthful?'

'At this time. At this time of my life.' He paused. 'Early on, the efforts made to give it individuality robbed it of purpose. By trying so hard to be noticed, my work fell into the category of merely competent. I had not fully understood. The realities of youth are blind to context and the compensations of age are larger if we don't force the design. There is no history without personal experience. I was not telling the truth; I was broadcasting. I am mindful now that there is a pleasure in the juxtaposition of texture, like the fabric of being.'

He was older. She never noticed his age.

Chapter 57

They picked up the loan car from the construction company. It was a large family saloon. It fitted like a bad start, so inappropriate for just the two of them.

The locking bleeped. 'Mochizuki,' he said, bowing exaggeratedly as he opened the door, introducing himself as her chauffeur for the trip.

'Where are the white gloves if you're going to be driving me around? Give me a Tokyo taxi.' A sweet-sour smell of air freshener cocooned her, warning of a claustrophobic journey of some hours ahead. As soon as they hit the road, it began to rain. Heavy summer monsoon rain and he soon pulled off the expressway into a gas station.

'Who loaned this car on empty?' He was annoyed and it was only the start. Naomi pulled a lipstick from her clutch and applied a peach shade as four attendants descended on them straight out of the formula one pits in zipped overalls with chevrons shouting on the arms. One bounced on the balls of his feet at their window as Mochizuki told him to fill it up. 'Mantan.'

The pump attendant offered the tab on a small blue tray. While Mochizuki signed the chit, the boy hung in and stared at Naomi.

Mochizuki pushed the tray back impatiently.

The car kangarooed across the forecourt to the café.

'You seen a girl before?' he threw out in English.

Naomi found it proprietorial.

'Let's get lunch,' he said, before pulling on the handbrake 'He never see a good-looking woman before'?

'You've never driven this model before?'

He punched her softly in protest and they ran the short distance out from under cover.

Cries of *'irasshaimasse'* greeted them as he chose a table by the window, overlooking the car lot, then took out a cigarette.

'Travelling with you I don't get to smoke much,' he complained.

They ordered doria rice dishes from a plump teenager with bad skin, in a two-tone American burger-bar uniform.

'Same from one vast factory supplying the whole country,' he mused, regretting his decision, but he knew that they had to get up to Gifu that evening and all they had time for was fast food.

The Mickey Mouse pad and pencil returned to offer fluorescent sundaes; crème caramels in a perspex holder. 'American coffee or American coffee?' he asked and ordered without waiting for her reply.

'The teahouse garden . . .' he began, his hands moving earnestly in front of him as if he were holding the subject as an entity. 'That garden—' He was momentarily drowned out by a chorus of welcoming waiters and began again. 'That garden has two parts: an inner and outer section.'

'I remember a gate on the path leading up to the pond. With a cedar bark roof,' Naomi conferred.

'So,' he affirmed, reassured that she had understood him, 'that garden has to be a journey' He angled his head for emphasis. 'The teahouse becomes a sanctuary for the tranquil spirit. Like a feeling you get after you climb the mountain. You are refreshed and pleased that you have completed that task.' He paused to inhale deeply. He retrieved the stub of his cigarette from the ashtray.

'In this same way, you are leaving the world behind like a . . . like a . . .'

And here his English faltered as he stumbled for the correct expression.

'Like a religious retreat?' she offered. It was not his point.

He reached for his water and, changing his mind, leaned across the table and took her water glass. He turned the glass around until the stain of her peach lipstick met his lips and he met her eyes with the challenge. He downed the water in one and slapped it to the table defiantly.

It was unequivocal. She felt unthreatened out on the road trip with him and she picked up his glass and drank. And she took a swig without looking at him once. It might be a response. It might not.

'Yes, yes. Okay, like Buddha goes up the mountain to meditate.' He was encouraged to continue. 'You have to let everything from the world outside fall away. You have to travel with the architecture of the garden, along the path. It takes you away on a set journey and you cannot see ahead. Your thoughts cannot wander from the path.'

Was he urging her to make a journey? She drew on his eloquent passion for Zen, which she had already began to share.

The waitress filled the water glasses and he lit another cigarette. Toying with the rim of the glass and watching her closely he said to her, 'We have a room at Gifu.'

'What do you mean, "a room",' she bridled at the assumption suddenly.

'It's nothing.' He looked down. 'It's a Japanese room. Big and long, like everyone sleeps in. You can sleep at one end. I'm gonna sleep at the other end.'

He threw it out as if matter of fact but it was news to her.

'It is high season and, if it is okay for you, it's cheaper for my company.'

'No. Jesus. What sort of company is this?' He shouldn't assume.

'My company got caught up in a lousy deal recently. We have a little financial trouble right now.'

Naomi thought she could trust him. She didn't doubt that much of the declaration was true. She said nothing.

'Liquidity. That's all.'

His honest admission left her open to his vulnerability. He looked at her as though he depended on her. It was true hotel rooms in Japan were sold for multiple occupancy. She hesitated and lowered her guard.

'The company booked it?'

She made an excuse and left him for the restroom.

She was precariously balanced over the porcelain hole in the floor and the cubicle was impossibly small. It all made her feel clumsy and unsettled. She stood aggressively on the low handle to flush it and on her return she found he had left the table. The trail of thanks and *sayonaras* from the waiters echoed in her wake as she left and, though a customary practice, felt they could be mocking her.

He sat at the wheel of the car and looked resigned to not be getting his own way. Her sense of having been cornered evaporated; in the newly broken sunshine drew steam in the air.

They drove out of Nagoya towards Gifu. The arterial road was lined in two-dimensional façades, like a movie set; pachinko parlours; car dealerships, and colourless neon signs like exhausted geisha caught sleeping in the daylight without their make-up.

As they drove, her thoughts turned to Josh. He would have checked into his hotel room in New York by now. He always shaved at night before he slept. This saved him time in the morning. The suitcase would be open at the foot of the bed. Would he be relaxed about the room with Mochizuki? How would she feel if Josh was spending his first night in New York in a room with his female colleagues? It was a small revelation that it did not matter as much as it should to her.

Chapter 58

Mochizuki hung so comfortably over the check-in desk he could have been a regular. The lobby was badly lit and two long-sleeved spinsters in kimonos hovered on the steps, unable to pull on a smile after years of disuse. They mumbled a vacuous greeting. The inter-war architecture was of a register deeply unknown to her, illuminated by two rice-paper lanterns, book-ending a domineering reception counter.

Naomi held back to avoid the watchful eyes of the reception as the sole room was allocated. She had agreed to the arrangements but now, under the scrutiny others, she wished she had not – but here in the lobby it was too late. She could take a look and then decide, but she already knew what would be.

A porter in a happi coat stooped on bandy legs, waiting for their bags. As Mochizuki left to have a cigarette she made a point of not looking at him.

Left in the cavern of the lobby she trailed the porter, following a dank smell of sulphur emanating from the hot spring somewhere in the bowels of the building. They took the elevator to the fifth floor.

In the tatami room the shoji window was ajar, and from below the rock-bed stream sent a breeze that caused the fluorescent light fitting to sway, casting tidal marks that washed the painted *fusuma* wall panels of grey *sumi-e*. She stood in the middle of the room. Gnarled trees in early spring bloom were rendered in thin ink, and, on the opposite wall, the startling eyes of a searching, whiskered dragon. It was as if this long mythical creature had leapt from the top of the bell tower at the temple to join them. She would not give in to notions of being watched. Ancient Chinese dragons had masculine strengths, which might she thought, overwhelm her, but then again, this one carried the potential of a more feminine genii.

Leaving her scrutiny of the ink paintings she made for the basement onsen. By following the tart odour, the spa was easy to find.

She turned the clammy handle to the changing rooms.

Two women chatted as they dressed, one naked but for plastic bathhouse sandals. Her waxy skin glowed a faint jaundiced tinge.

Naomi began to remove her clothes and fold them as the woman drying her underarm released a salvo of words . But she understood nothing. The woman laughed as she rubbed her belly and Naomi left for the onsen.

Palls of steam rose like smoke on a windless day, obscuring the surface of the water. She had the onsen to herself. Lying scattered across the stone floor were empty pieces of pale wooden bath furniture. Gathering up a small stool and coopered bucket, she sat beside a waterspout. Filling the naturally fragrant bucket she threw cold water over her bare shoulders. Her skin recoiled, tensing at the shock. The white curds of soap held to the curve of her naked inner thighs. She could feel the soft touch of her fingertips as if they belonged to somebody else. As she looked up, in the mirror, across the steam-filled bath, she could see she was not alone.

Turning to the distant figure, she found Mochizuki sat on the other side of the second pool.

'What are you doing?' she shouted, incensed, partly that he had been watching and partly that he had the benefit of sitting neck-deep in steam-obscured water.

He did not answer immediately, and then called back, 'This

time is reserved for the male guests. I was going to ask you the same thing.'

You took your time, she thought.

She could either leave or take to the waters. She picked up her bucket to march out but aware how comic this might appear, instead she made for the edge of the onsen bath with all the naked dignity she could muster.

Cautiously, she sat on the edge of the mineral salted water. It was blisteringly hot. In a slow process of acclimatizing one limb after another, she entered until she too was up to her neck in scalding water, sitting on the pebbles at the bottom of the pool. But far on the other side she could see him leaving. Counting down before she could leap out, the acrid smell of sulphur curling her nose . She was a little afraid to stand and a little dizzy So this was how Japanese women famously kept their skin from aging?

The lobby telephone clung to a pillar like a limpet. She lifted the receiver and stress-tested the cord before putting it back down. Should she make the courtesy call to Josh?

'Well, how is it?' he asked. 'Nice hotel?'

'It's a traditional onsen.'

'I thought this was a business trip. You're at a spa?'

'We just saw the publishers in Nagoya.'

'Good room?'

Should she tell him the booking was for one room?

'How is the old man doing?' he asked.

He didn't need to know, she decided. How would he understand?

Chapter 59

The soft wet breath of dusk fell as they took a stroll before dinner, heading for the river. Along the water's edge, the lanterns were lit on the huts lining the banks, selling trips on the famous Nagara River. They were on business, she tried to fool herself as she walked beside him. Japanese folk music issued from flimsy structures so impermanent they might be swept away at the end of the evening like a pack of cards. From a hinged flap a hawker's arching diphthong did its best to catch them as they passed.

'U. . . k a . . . i . . . ikanga desuka?' Shadowy figures came and went to offer a deal one better than the last. Easily rebuffed with the wave of his hand, the hawkers retreated like ghosts shown the daylight. He chose a lantern-dressed boat hut halfway along because nobody had made any overtures. The lights cast on the water only intermittently, like a poor transmission. Heavy with the smell of cheap citrus aftershave, a short rigid man leant against a bike stand outside the hut, and a girl in short skirt and boots clung to the silvered buckle of his belt, the magnet for aspirational wealth. Naomi thought the girl very young. They slipped apart at the arrival of customers.

Mochizuki negotiated the boat hire and Naomi wandered further up the river, beneath the trees, looking out over the dark movement of the tranquil river, absorbing the sounds on the bank. She thought of Miho and Sam. Her musings were displaced by the sound of Mochizuki's voice – 'uso!' – floating up in the midst of a warming conversation.

She knew it to mean 'lies'; the negotiations must be going badly. She wandered back unhurriedly on the soft dirt track through the trees to show some support.

Mochizuki and the ferryman were down by the water's edge looking into a flat-bottomed boat of a kind, she thought, that one should particularly never trust. She looked it over, prejudiced against the project from the start. The water was black and uninviting.

Mochizuki was balking at the cost. 'He's not selling a cruise. We're talking a small boat. A piece of driftwood. On the banks of the Nagara.'

'Is he our boatman?' Naomi doubted his skills and didn't want to spend the evening with his citrus aftershave. It was a pleasure craft rowboat for two.

'We don't need him,' he said. 'I'm going to row.'

'Can you row?'

'You want to row?' he barked, rounding on her short-temperedly.

She was unflustered. 'I,' she said fulsomely, looking down at the splinter of a boat to see whether it had rowlocks, 'would insist.' An ironic, not fully informed decision.

'So, okay. Me first.' The negotiations had made him demanding and it took a while to cast off.

He walked the short length of the rowboat, lowering his centre of gravity for stability as it bobbed. He took up a position on the transom, his back to the river and facing her as she stepped the short distance from the bank. She noted he left her to be handed aboard by the boatman. As they sat opposite one another in the darkness, his frustration amused her and she was indulgent of his bad humour. She watched him as he fiddled with the short oars that had been caught under against the sides of the boat.

Slowly and quietly she announced, 'My feet are getting wet.'

One oar was secured and he was teasing out the second from its snare beside the seat. He didn't notice the pools of water in the bottom of the boat and he managed to free it, becoming absorbed in positioning it in the rowlock. As she watched she became aware that he was falling a little beneath her line of vision. Her cry was plaintive this time and accompanied a very decisive retreat from the sinking vessel.

'It's going down.'

His concentration broken, Mochizuki looked at the pooling water and hurriedly supported her towards the bank, clambering out to join her as water reached his knees. He was very wet.

'You hired the Titanic.' Naomi's words were broken by a peal of spontaneous laughter.

'Dame da yo.' Heavy browed, he strode passed her to have words with the boat-hire, unable to share her sense of amusement.

During discussions, a couple of wiry old men appeared like voles from the bank, and the upshot was they were offered a larger complementary boat with its own boatman. They sat on the upholstered seats, like a pair of economy-class travellers who got lucky on an upgrade In view of the satisfying sight of someone else pulling on the oars she finally sank back to relax, relieved to be with someone who knew the waters.

They travelled down the river in silence, watching the oars move through the water and the boat stir the still air suspended over the river. They sat back, pleased to be out inhabiting the cloud-covered moonless night. Other boats of laughing parties paddled past them, making their way up towards the bridge.

'Everybody has to see this when they come to Gifu,' he offered as a token of his returning good humour. 'I wanted you to see this.'

Just beyond the bridge was the spot where the Ukai fishermen with their cormorant birds congregated.

'Fishermen – we call it ukai – release the tethered birds to catch the fish but rings are so tight round their necks they can never swallow and eat the fish. The catch belongs to the fishermen, who take every fish.'

Naomi sounded in sympathy with the cormorant.

He began to laugh.

'They get what they need. Every employer is a cormorant fisherman. A taker. I have my own master to contend with.'

She remembered he had talked of earning favours once. But he had his own staff. 'You're one too,' she responded.

As they passed beneath the bridge, the oars ceased to slip through the water and they continued in a silent glide between the damp pillars. Out on the other side, in the limpid eddies protected by the arches, the boatman passed a line through a rusted metal ring. The line paid out as the current pulled them downstream until it jolted.

Mochizuki moved in his seat. He watched the dart of light toying with the smooth curves of her cheekbones, damp with the exertion of gentle pleasure, caught in a radiance that skin only shows at night.

Up ahead the bows of the cormorant fishers were lashed together. At the prow of each boat a fire of logs hung in spherical metal braziers swinging over the water through the darkness. Small sparks like fireflies floated on the wood smoke as it drifted across the water. The fishermen stood like mythical figures yoked to a chariot of fire driven by dark birds that took flight in the darkness. He watched Naomi as she turned in her seat to get a better view of the figures. On each boat a man stood upright holding a small flock of inky black birds tethered on leashes, strung out like musical notes on the water line. The fishermen were moving slowly in front of the braziers. The birds – black crochets, silhouetted against the light of the fires – were playing out an ancient ritual like the silent shadow performance of the Wayang Kulit puppeteers of Indonesia. A ring around the neck held each bird as they dived, swooping and splashing in a random staccato rhythm, and in their turn they caught a fish only to be pulled in by the strong arms of shadowy men. Time and time again a bird leapt into the water bringing in a fish, which was then torn from its gullet, like voracious young feeding from a parent.

'These are the *ukai* fisherman,' Mochizuki whispered.

She didn't respond; she was completely absorbed by the fishing and lured, like the sweet ayu fish, by the hypnotic light of the fire in the braziers. He had, for a moment, lost her to the spectacle. He asked the boatman to take them little closer to the cormorant fishers. The rope was loosened and the current brought them downriver towards a group of *ukai*; the boatman's oars played with the current to keep them level with, but not too close to, the fishing boats.

From this vantage point, Naomi watched closely as a cormorant perched on the side of the boat. It dived.

'See. He will catch but he cannot keep,' Mochizuki whispered.

Its catch stuck in its throat with its unvoiced satisfaction. The ugly black birds flapped their bony wings in mild protest as the burnished face of the fisherman beneath his bandana neared to steal the fish from its bulging throat before releasing the bird to fish again. He lifted the neck ring, stroking its constricted gullet as one of the sweet fish, dazzled by the brazier light, emerged from its throat. Let loose to roam the length of its leash the bird went back, following an instinct, as playful as hunger, taking greater pleasure from its expectation than the catch.

'It's wonderful,' she said to the darkness.

They watched until the fishing was over and the birds were bundled into open weave baskets, like lobster pots, to be transported back and fed.

Back on the shore Mochizuki tipped the oarsman who slid away in the darkness as quietly as he had appeared. When they passed the boat hut, Naomi glimpsed the belted boatman and young girl, his face buried in her neck, one leg thrust between hers.

In the lobby Mochizuki left her to go up to the room.

'I'm going to order dinner,' he called back when he was halfway down the corridor, as if it were an afterthought.

In the room Naomi wrote her diary and then changed into a yukata for the night, she opened the shoji screens to the small balcony and the river scene below. Points of light below were lost in the darkness, as the night had fallen. There were no stars. It was, she felt, as if the sky was inverted.

Chapter 60

A low table near the window in their room was set with small, black, lacquered trays and hand-painted dishes. He returned wearing the complimentary yukata, flushed with the heat, his wet grizzled hair standing on end; towel in hand, he rubbed vigorously, drying it upwards from the back of his neck.

'Time for a cigar?'

She didn't bother to answer but drank her beer.

He smiled, 'So you ordered Asahi Super Dry. Good,' he said as he bent to pour himself a glass. 'You want to toast to us?' He raised his glass as he stood.

Still turned away, lifting her glass half-heartedly; she remained contained and private. 'To your retrospective,' she said.

'It's pretty *ne*,' he said, coming closer to join her at the window. 'They have put lights on the castle.' He waved his glass in the direction of the hillside where the illuminated curling eaves of the castle stood against the dark. 'Silver Mountain is behind the castle.'

She smiled, acknowledging its charm.

And then, as if he purposefully wanted to break the charm of the moment offered by the lights and the castle against the hills, he said, 'It's a youth hostel. Made of concrete.' He looked down at her and grinned.

The door to the room slid open, and in stepped a serving woman.

'*Haiiii . . . Gohan wa ikaga desu ka.*'

From a textured, red, lacquer box she served rice with a bamboo paddle. Naomi sat demurely, Japanese-style, her knees folded beneath her, with the yukata crossed tightly over her legs. He sat directly opposite, in a matching robe. And they looked like a pair of Hinamatsuri dolls.

Muttering quietly in a strong dialect, the woman poured warm sake from an earthenware flask.

As Naomi raised the thimble-sized sake cup to her lips, she felt him lay his eyes on her. Her breath stirred the vapour, which rose so that she could anticipate the pleasure before the warm sake hit her tongue. He took up his chopsticks and started to eat. From under his brows his glances were furtive. They were silent until the woman left them.

'*Yama. Umi. Yama. Umi.*' He pointed with his chopsticks to a dish of thinly sliced octopus and shitake mushrooms layered and lying fanned out on heavy dish; the red skin of the octopus as if it were trimmed with coloured lace. He had finished speaking before she had registered what he said.

'What's that'?

'*Yama. Umi. Yama. Umi,*' he repeated.

'It is something from the mountains. Something from the sea.'

'*Kaiseki ryori* . . . Zen-style cooking,' he explained.

'You bring me more poetry?' she purred. 'Delicious.' She picked at a baby-pink stalk of crunchy ginger, pickled in rice vinegar.

A flower floated in her miso soup. 'Too beautiful to eat,' she continued.

He hung on her words.

'So fresh,' she said, as she pushed her chopsticks into the flesh of a small black-and-gold fish, skewered and cooked as if still writhing. He drank in her excitement as it danced its way across the various offerings.

'You don't eat it in the correct order,' he admonished.

'To hell with the order.' She laughed and drank more sake; cooler now and less sweet.

'Shall we get more?' She toyed with her cup.

'We got a drinks chiller in the hall.'

Naomi got up to get him a beer. She came back, brushing past him carelessly.

'How long to get through the contents of the fridge?'

'I have to open it with my teeth?' he jested in complaint.

Obligingly she returned with an open bottle. He poured it from a height and the suds of froth touched his upper lip as he drank. Naomi eyed his enjoyment. He glanced at her along the side of his glass.

Her yukata was large, tied loosely at the waist. It had fallen from her knees and it lay open so that he could see the soft skin on the inside of her thigh and she stared at him purposefully until her legs fell open in invitation. Breathing strongly he rose to move towards her.

'*Haiii* . . .' Out in the hall the waitress announced her arrival. When she entered Mochizuki was standing at the window. The woman put down a tray of sake and began lighting the burners under the raw meat. She prattled on to herself, asking how the meal was going, was it to their liking? As she shut the fusama doors she said she hoped that they enjoyed the meat, enunciating the word flesh.

Mochizuki crossed the tatami in bare feet and pulled at the light. He lay like a shogun on the zabuton, leaning on one elbow. It was dark but for the light of the candle burners and he looked at her with open hunger now.

'You know what there is between you and me,' he said softly. He held his fingers up to demonstrate, his thumb and forefinger a millimetre apart. 'It's not much.' Their heads were close and his voice was low. He bent to kiss her lightly on the side of the neck. Her stretched palm ran up the back of his neck and held him there.

'This much.' He pulled at the lapel of her yukata robe, tugging it away. Slowly his tongue found her nipple and, wet with saliva, teased it hard. She thought fleetingly of protection and the thought passed.

Her fingers closed and she pulled him by his hair down on top of her. His hand caught the weight of her breast and his thumb played with her nipple, pulsing her sensitized flesh.

Her legs were still caught up high and open. His tongue trailed down past her belly button and on to explore her. He felt her with his tongue until she was tense and waiting for him. Her outstretched arms caught him up and pulled him roughly, lifting him until she could reach his thigh and drive her hand down to guide him into her. He moved slowly inside her and the tension for her was emotionally unprotected. Towards the end she was quieter and came first, haltingly, stroking the muscles on his wet back as she waited for him. Their heads lay close. She listened to his breathing.

'Nothing between us,' he breathed.

She laughed. The light in the burners had died out and it was pitch black in the room, the window slightly open. The town was silent, the cormorant fishers gone home, but the sound of the river drifted up to them like white noise.

The next morning she found him with his back to her, standing at the shoji window in the white daylight, looking down on the town. Behind him she pulled at his yukata sleeve with the intention of planting a grateful lover's kiss on the bone of his shoulder. Brushing her lips against his skin and resting her head on his back she was caught in surprise. The blank light of day revealed the tattoo of a bird stamped low on his right shoulder blade. It was as welcome as a cautionary tale. For a moment it seemed she didn't know him but as he turned his face was reassuringly familiar.

'I had it from a long time ago.'

'It looks like a cormorant.'

'It is a cormorant,' was all he said.

Chapter 61

Ed's apartment, 2012

Yumi, the office PA, had arrived at Ed's apartment early, clutching a bag of her own cutlery. He had called her to say he was short. She had dressed early for the occasion and with the help of dyes, paints and depilatories, she held onto some appearance of youth. Though she often imagined otherwise, Ed was destined to be no more significant in her life than the pillow bear sitting guard on her floral duvet. She would do anything for him.

Ed was unstinting in his verbal thanks. Yumi stood in her flat shoes, devotedly polishing the glasses, which were the only items he had in long supply. He crisscrossed the apartment, altering the temperature dial, turning the lighting low and changing his choice of music twice. They had all accepted his invitation, including the visiting younger cousin Roddy and he had had to ask the teacher.

On the door chime, Ed left Yumi opening the wine to greet the piano teacher. His hand went inadvertently to the familiar small of her back as he planted a polite kiss. Inconveniently he recalled her arched naked beneath him and took refuge in the elegance of assumed manners. It was only a few times and it had escalated without him meaning it to. Why had he given her a key? He had no experience in how to reverse out of what he had started. He knew he was, by nature, useless socially. He could justifiably wrap it up. It had been a bit of fun for both of them. She wouldn't mind – they only slept together a few times. It was over, he concluded. As of now, right this minute. At the door chime he broke loose as a few more arrived along with Hana and her American friend.

Hana's mood had lifted as the elevator rose towards the forty-first floor. On the way, by the prospect of the dinner, Jess told her she had booked a flight out. The lift was a good place to shout had they needed to. Jess said she wanted to get back to where she could make a difference, to where she was needed. Was there any genuine evidence of this in Tokyo? she'd said. She tugged at her so often on a wind change she could no longer keep up with her. The big news was almost an anticlimax. Of course she would miss her.

Hana stepped into the apartment where the city lay at her feet, beyond an expanse of glass. It was, at first sight, a paradigm of desire, though slightly intimidating.

'The air is thinner up here?' She smiled and complimented.

She surveyed the furnishings and assumed Ed's borrowed style was a reflection of his wealth; if you happened to like the five-star lobby look, and while she did not, she was not immune to the effect. Ed made every effort to put them at ease, welcoming them with a real go at a charm offensive.

'Good to see you. It's been too long. Shame you couldn't come when Jess came with us to Tsukiji.' Any easiness on his part was assumed.

Jess went to Tsukiji? She looked at Jess for confirmation that she had lied, but got nothing. Jess started pressing Ed about the plans to move the market to the other side of town and so she left her to it; she would cool down for a moment.

Hana found herself alone on the runway sofa as the city lights paintballed the sky. Jess had Ed collared. Roddy ambled over, choosing to sit uncomfortably on the floor, his back against the chair base beside her. Regarding him with no small degree of resignation, because he seemed a little isolated, she leaned over to befriend him. He was here to finish his Oxford dissertation. She felt obliged to begin with a question on his area of study whether she wanted it answered or not.

'It's on the *"Eta"* peoples of Japan.'

Her mind wandered to who it was she'd been living with all this time and whether she knew Jess at all.

'*Eta?*'

'Like Indian low caste. They have been at the bottom of the ladder. Ghettoized for centuries. These village people are stuck as an underclass. Pressed into all the dirty jobs.'

Of course Jess had been at the Tsukiji fish market and missed Ukai's memorial when she had specifically asked her to support her and be there.

Roddy pushed up his ample glasses. 'This immobility has voided the need for an immigration policy.'

She nodded politely.

'The system was perpetuated by municipal records, which, of course, are categorized quite comprehensively.'

Hana would beg to differ but it was easier to drift off and let him ramble on than engage with him.

She liked Ed herself, and Jess had turned it in to some sort of competition.

'The data on family history has been freely available to business corporations.'

'Readily available?' She was drawn into listening to him despite herself.

'Companies have made background checks to ensure they avoided hiring the wrong type of individuals.'

'I have been looking for someone.'

He met her admission with interest.

'I spent a day at the records office looking for someone.'

'And what did you find?'

'Nothing – a completely fruitless task.'

He shuffled nervously in his uncomfortable seat and looked grave.

'That could blow quite a hole in my theories.'

'I asked the consulate. I searched online. I went to the municiple offices,' she explained, finding at last someone who would listen to the catalogue of her searches.

'On the other hand the census of people here in Japan is quite baffling.' Again he pushed his glasses up the reddened bridge of his nose.

A loud laugh. Jess was across the room, elbow on the seat back beside Ed, no distance between them; she had locked him in conversation.

'I was looking for a man,' and for the first time she said it, 'my father. Possibly.'

He laughed undiplomatically at her uncertainty.

She shouldn't mind. He was younger than her, still a student.

'She wasn't married, you see.'

He nodded, serious beyond his years. 'Like *Eta*, unmarried mothers were treated with the same clerical hand of discrimination.'

'Is that true?' She thought of Naomi and the man beyond the records. It seemed tonight she should give up on the labyrinthine data that would tell her nothing very much at all.

'Remember the sarin gas attack in ninety-five?'

She did not.

'Incident on the Tokyo Metro.'

The boy knew so much, she thought.

'It had,' he said, 'been perpetrated by a terrorist group headed up by the self-proclaimed prophet Asahara who was himself a member of these *Eta* people. At the time Asahara had predicted that Armageddon was timetabled for nineteen ninety-seven.'

'Are we still waiting for it? she asked

'You can wait if you want to spend life worrying about the future.' He scrambled up. Another drink?

In fact, she worried more about the past.

'Well,' he drawled on, 'you could say he was years out and then the nuclear power plant in Fukushima province blew.'

Hana saw the vernissage of a tanker on the shards of a civilization.

'That nearly took us all out. Maybe the east are the *pariahs* of the west. We left them to clean up the mess.'

A huge tanker washed back ashore.

'And we are still waiting for the big earthquake; I guess that'll finally do it,' he said confidently.

Hana had become used to suppressing her fear of this and had resorted to ignoring the jolts of pressure release, roughly in fortnightly bursts, she had experienced. She preferred to stick her head in the sand and ignore the huge mammal in any Japanese room, occasionally responsible for knocking pots off the shelves and stamping so violently across the floorboards that the walls would shake and roof tiles would fall at its contained vehemence. Most days it slept and kept its trunk out of the way so that nobody need trip on it and rile it.

Chapter 62

Hana couldn't take in any more and left Roddy with his cousin and found Jess wearing so many necklaces she'd leave a tribe bereft, applying more wine to her evening. Feeling confrontational despite the company she challenged her.

'You went without me but you said you hadn't.'

'Well . . .' Jess was vague.

'We had agreed we would go to that memorial together. Can I trust you at all?'

'You were . . .' she began accusatively. 'That . . .'

Hana rounded on her '. . . was a lie.'

And as she walked away, excuses followed.

'Just leave it, Jess' Hana said dismissively, walking in Ed's direction.

Hana watched him assume a smile that was a little too bright. She scanned for a visual clue to stock her conversational armoury before he reached her. The first to hand was the painting behind him. She did not like the Futurists and the work was a small step from comic book: an explosion of geometrics in primaries. That was all it said to her, broken shards of emulsified colour.

'Your painting . . .' she began, returning his smile.

'I am glad you like it.' He ended her sentence in a rash of nerves as welcome as hives.

'Very machismo,' she conceded. Giving it a moment's hesitation. 'I only like it in context.' And then, for fear of launching into another academic subject that evening, she corrected herself. 'I don't actually find it . . .' And she bottled out before she could tell him she really didn't like it.

'Yumi found it. The sofa, the dining table, the . . .' It was as if he wanted to own up: nothing was his. This wasn't him; he was indebted to others for the sophistication.

He was phrasing another question on art when she asked, 'Ever homesick?'

Ed, as a Londoner, had seen what she had seen, and like a giant, mental, camera obscura, they could each project places in Brixton, in Stockwell, Hackney, and share them like they were walking together in the same conversational landscape. A joint pleasure.

It got late and the evening's energy ebbed around them while they sat together conspiratorially. He was guilty of ignoring the others until her field of vision became the black skirt of the piano teacher, who had up to that point kept her distance. She was about to leave and rejected Ed's weak protest. Yumi might share a taxi? he offered eventually.

She would wait it seemed. As she sank onto the vast sofa, thighs so close to him that they touched Hana wondered what their relationship was . . . Prising himself from the small space between them, he went to arrange a cab. Yumi, a little giggly and inebriated, offered her a dry sembei pretzel, making out it was some sort of consolation.

Chapter 63

The music was low and moody. Hana was still trying to excavate pretzel paste from the furthest reaches of her incisors and concluded she was in the way while Jess seemed to entertain some thought of staying, working with the inebriated tide of a belated overture from Roddy.

Standing in the open-plan kitchen, the city blinking like an unreliable landing strip she picked at the cheese board until the taxi buzzed up to the apartment. Roddy stumbled to meet her goodbye and she drifted off to join the departing Japanese girls. Ed caught the move and stopped her . . .

'Can you stay? I wanted to ask. Could you?'

It triggered Jess's bid to make the taxi.

'Talk to you about it tomorrow,' she called back as she made for the lift.

'I'll come with you?'

'No, no you stay.' Jess was reassuring. 'There's some washing-up here,' she added laconically.

As Ed manned a position at the lift shaft, countering the universal aversion to goodbyes, she found the coffee. While it brewed, she lingered in front of the ugliest piece of art she had ever seen, with a perplexing sense of contentment, wondering how long she should stay.

Chapter 64

They had become lovers. Mochizuki lay across the tatami smoking a cigarette, a flight of ducks animating the expanse of the pond behind him. In the afternoons they would leave the world behind and make love in the teahouse gardens by the lake or in the tatami rooms of the Yoritsuke beside the outer garden. No one disturbed them and they never saw the abbot anymore. In the period of what felt like a deconsecration of the teahouse, they had made it a sanctuary for their love.

As they lay with her head on his chest, he told her of his passions.

'I would like you to see the Minka farmhouse out in the hills. Surrounded by bamboo forest. I love it there and you should see it.'

'We should go.'

'You can get away for a weekend?' he asked.

She longed to go but this, she knew, would be impossible. What excuse could she make to Josh?

On the days when she did go into the offices her colleagues were cold and treated her as a stranger. Though she might understand why, she chose to put it down to the lack of time she spent with them and their inability to communicate.

A week later Josh arrived on an early morning flight. She heard him root around the bedroom softly in an attempt not to wake her before leaving for his Saturday gym session with Sam. After a long flight he always needed to exercise or he left too pent up. She slept late, always content to have the house to herself. She wasn't expecting him back until lunchtime. They had tickets for a concert in Harajuku that night, and they had made plans to drive out to a hot spring on Sunday. It was easier for her when they all went out together because it diluted the burden of untruth. It was as if by not telling any of them it rested on each one of them equally, but when she was alone with Josh his ignorance about it was sharper and more accusatory.

She held her head under the shower and closed her eyes. She would hide the truth for as long as she could. The strength of the deluge of water was a comfort. She felt for a shower gel nearest to hand and rubbed at her naked stomach without shame or guilt but her movements were slow and satisfying and she recalled a shared an erotic pleasure. But the Acqua di Bravo smelt of Josh, and interfered with the memory of Mochizuki.

When the doorbell rang in an electronic sing-song, she remembered Mr Kami, the property manager, who was due to take a look at the air-con.

Hanging on the back of the bathroom door she found Josh's large, white, cotton shirt, and wrapping a towel around her head she flew to the front door, cursing herself for forgetting.

Preparing a flood of apologies she double-jumped the stairs and opened the door with a 'sorry', only to find the architect standing on the porch. He smiled approvingly at what greeted him.

She stood back as if they were strangers, searching for an explanation of why, now, he chose to violate the space she shared with Josh.

Wrong-footed by her reception and her distance, by way of explanation for his unannounced appearance he offered her a package.

'Why did you come?' she asked. Why had he risked a confrontation with Josh?

'I brought you something.'

'Yes, but . . .' Had she encouraged the opportunist in him?

He read the alarm in her eyes. 'I was in Aoyama. I saw Sam; he was headed to the gym with Josh. I wanted to see you, *chocho*,' he said, using his pet name – butterfly – for her.

She could not ask him in.

He handed her a small box wrapped in a furoshiki cloth.

They stood opposite one another on different thresholds of the same house. Her house.

'You gonna open it?'

She stepped back and sat down on the long step that ran the length of the entrance hall. Josh's shirt rode up her tanned knees and the tail of the towel turban fell across her shoulder.

'Shall I stay out here?'

Knowing that Josh was at the gym played like a mantra, reassurance. Mochizuki had walked in to the entrance hall before she made answer.

The wrapped cloth was difficult to untie when a nervous energy demanded her strength and, resting it on her knee, she fumbled at the knot. How long would Josh take at the gym? How could she explain away the visit? She wanted him to leave as much as she wanted him to stay.

He stood over her waiting for a reaction to the gift that might have delighted her at another time or – now, he understood – any another place. Not until she looked him in the eye did he bring himself to sit beside her on the step. If Josh should return to find them sitting there as easy as an idiom, she would find it hard to explain away. The wrapping cloth fell away. It was a black, lacquered inro, the size of a cigarette box, with an ivory netsuke of pine cones tied at its base, decorated with scenes in gold leaf. An expensive gift. Beneath long dream-like Eastern clouds was a small refuge among fields. He took the box from its lining and turned it over.

'See here,' he said excitedly.

In a long boat there was a solitary fisherman and perched on the bow was a bird.

'See,' he said again delightedly.

The cormorant fisher.

'I don't know what to say.'

'And pine cones . . .'

The exquisite gesture was lost in discomfort.

'It's beautiful. Thank you, but I think you should go. Josh will be back soon.'

She rehearsed the two men meeting at the end of the road.

'Leave me a file or something. I could tell him you dropped it off.'

Silenced, he got up to retrieve a folder. His long fingers walked calmly through the case of files until they found an item that he felt comfortable leaving. He dropped a folder on the step.

'Naomi-san—' he bowed exaggeratedly '—as you send me away. I have to go.'

She rose on her toes to take him by the back of the neck and pressed a kiss hard on his mouth.

He turned, shrugged, and on leaving said, 'You give me so little.'

She stood chastised. As if she had not risked enough. Just then, over his shoulder she saw Mr Kami swinging his motor-cycle helmet in his hand, slowing up mid-flight on the wide-hewn steps under the pine tree in her garden. Perhaps he had stopped for the shade.

'You have to go,' she hissed, and pushed him roughly.

What Kami might have seen, and how long he had been studying his approach, were questions that remained as useless as trying to rewind the past. She was cutting herself loose to drift on a small raft that she could barely keep afloat and his attempts to join her here would sink them both. She felt as hopeless as if there were now no alternative.

The men passed one another with a restrained good morning.

She showed the property maintenance man cum agent into the sitting room and apologized that she would have to leave him for a moment. Kami refused a drink and studied the ceiling where one of the offending units hung, humming and clucking irrationally.

When she returned dressed properly, he proposed to check each of the systems around the house and report back to the Chinese landlady: 'Without fear or favour.'

She liked him no better than she had when he first found them the house but tried to communicate otherwise.

He acted as if he had seen nothing

'I tell her,' he said again, referring to the landlady, Mrs Fukamora. 'About . . .' And he paused for effect, to torture her, referring possibly to what he might have seen. Then he said, with over-obvious candour, 'The air-con.'

His nerve was best ignored, she decided, as a reaction would suggest it was important enough to be any of his business. It had taken him so long to turn up she would have to leave him to it. She could not send him away when the system was in such great need of attention.

She sat in the window seat with a Japanese primer laced with black kanji and left Kami to his preliminaries. He was always so keen to save the landlady money that she wondered if he was related to her.

Josh yelled on arrival, as was his redundant habit, though the heavy door always marked his entrance anyway. He dropped his kit and paused momentarily to pick up the file Mochizuki had dropped on the bottom step. The cover page showed nothing but dense Kanji and he lost interest, guessing, since he had seen a familiar motorcycle on the road – he recognized the symbols for air-con – that it was Kami's. He blew in, with the endorphins that a run and a morning on the rowing machine brought, to ionize the room. Crossing to the bay window he ran his hand along her shoulder affectionately and greeted

Kami, who was tinkering with the switching over in the open-plan dining room.

'Mr Kami, your file. You dropped it?'

'No. No, not mine, but the friend of Ms Naomi,' he replied, mischievously

Josh looked at it again and looked for her to shed some light.

'Mochizuki dropped it off,' she blustered casually. One glance enough to see Kami was enjoying his position.

'He dropped it off?' Josh repeated. 'Work?'

'Hmm.'

'Your Japanese is getting good . . . an instruction manual?'

Kami came up to peruse over the file. 'Very good Japanese, but conversation always best way to learn languages, *ne* Naomi-san?' Laced with irony, he sought her agreement.

How far would he take this? She was furious with him and beholden to him at once. She couldn't wait to get the little man out of the house.

'Have you finished? she asked as she rose, getting ready to dismiss him. 'And when? When do we get the system fully functioning?'

Chapter 65

'Architects spend an entire life with this unreasonable idea that you can fight against gravity'
–Renzo Piano

Naomi sat back against the antimacassar on the cracked leather-ette seats of the taxi. They headed home after a meal in Roppongi with Josh's American boss. This part of Tokyo was a tourist playground and an architectural tart; at night the neon signs pulsed with so many demands for attention that they cried wolf and become wallpaper.

'You okay? You were very quiet tonight.'

'I think you made up for that,' she said, her tired objection diluted to the point where he wouldn't have detected her disenchantment.

'I want to meet your boss. We hear so much of the illustrious Mr Architect. When do we get to invite them over for dinner, hon?'

'When are you next in the country?'

He ignored the charged line. 'This weekend. We are here this weekend.'

'That is far too short notice to get the Mochizukis to come over.' The plural made them a set of strangers to her.

The prospect of sitting opposite Mochizuki and eating politely in the company of his wife and Josh, pretending she didn't know what it was like to lie beside him and watch his pulse return to the steady pace that called them to sleep. She could not do it. Josh would talk of raising money, when it was not a commodity Mochizuki chose for conversation. Stopped at the red light Josh's face was caught in the neon lights, which played over his profile, flashing blue and red and turning him into a ghoul.

'No, it won't work. I don't want to offer them some culinary disaster from my short repertoire.'

'Well, we'll take them out.'

'They don't really like to dine out.'

'Well, we can try them, surely? I tell you what. Just ask them to brunch at Spiral in Aoyama.' Spiral was a relatively new piece of award-winning architecture completed just a few years before. Josh was being thoughtful, which only added to her discomfort.

She was torn between resistance, over which he would question her, and a need to avoid the situation at all costs. While this invitation played on her mind it was for him a simple notion of little substance. It was another of the common contests of wills that blew through the house with the predictability of a weather system. She would find herself unaccountably and stubbornly opposed to him, and on the margins of these opposing fronts, the arguments would ensue. She waited for him to loosen his hold on the idea but with Josh it was so often like trying to close an umbrella in the wind and the wind would take it until it was turned inside out. In some instances when he forced an issue she would find herself exposed and left to cry. A light frost would ensue between them; this gradual desiccation had worked away at their foundations and she had begun, now, to find it easier to lie.

Three days later they sat at the dinner table beneath a pendant light illuminating the pale porcelain plates. Her chicken recipe failed to rouse any enthusiasm; a light supper between heavy hearts.

Josh asked her about the teahouse, which had long become the excuse for her to escape in the afternoons with Mochizuki and was coupled in her mind with the illicit affair. It was uncomfortable to hear mention of it, though she knew Josh was merely trying to understand her day.

'Minamioka is the carpenter. Comes from a family who have worked on the temple for generations. Can you believe that? Generations.'

'Yes, you told me,' he said, relinquishing the subject after the first failed attempt at kindling any interest between them. Then, mid-mouthful, he threw his arm to his neck slapping himself in surprise. 'Let's hope the goddam mosquito season is nearly over,' he said aggressively. 'If you get the agent over for this air-con there won't be so many.'

He leapt up to fill the vaporizer, which was plugged to the wall, with another mosquito mat. As he squatted he removed the tablet from its foil. His back towards her, he asked her, 'Have you invited the Mochizukis over for dinner yet?'

After searching for it, Naomi pulled a vaguely disinterested voice from somewhere, thankful she did not have to face him. 'You know, I don't think she's in town.'

Josh walked back to the table and he would have it his way. He often dealt decisively with what he called her fey artistic ways and gave instruction when he judged she was incapable of making a decision herself. He had done as much after he asked her to come to Japan.

'We can go to Spiral.' He was firmly decided. 'Weekend after next.'

A mood like a weather system came over them and looked set for some time.

Chapter 66

Minka farmhouse, mountains outside Kyoto, 1989

Hour upon hour upon hour with two couples in the confines of log-jammed weekend traffic was never going to make their journey easy.

The car finally drew up on the cinder drive. A forest of bamboo covered the gentle sides of the hill, surrounding the tall, thatched Minka farmhouse, protecting it from the wind, casting a pale-green light filtered by lowering skies.

Naomi knew it to be a place that Mochizuki loved and curiously here she was with Josh. Sam and Miho were mercifully also there to distribute the attention loads. She couldn't quite work out how it had happened this way but she took each day at a time right now. It was nearing three in the afternoon and while they hoped to arrive before lunch, after several hours crawling the expressway, they were now starving.

Miho opened the car door for Naomi. 'You feel a little better?'

The nausea had passed but sour breath left her throat like cardboard. She couldn't predict when it would return.

'Motion sickness's tough.' Sam began to unload the car.

She wondered whether it was. She had never had it before. No one else in the car had suffered.

'We were on the road too long. You'll feel better when you eat.' Miho took the French loaves from the parcel shelf and Naomi found the smell of bread was a new assault.

'Come on.' Miho tugged at her sleeve. 'Let's get the food going.' Naomi stayed in car while they unpacked: the inertia of having travelled for so long. She would remain in her seat and drive the same number of hours straight back if it meant she did not have to go through with spending the weekend up here in the very countryside that Josh hated. He would behave badly. For him the absence of anything to do touched him like an insult.

'Porter.' Josh handed Sam a bag.

Mochizuki had wanted her to see the structure. The reeded roof was aged black with curious quiffs to the ridge ends, which hung over the roofline like a porch.

Josh leaned in to the car subserviently. 'Anything else we can do, m'lady?' he asked, turning cockney chauffeur, his hand ready on the cloth bag filled with Naomi's sketchpad and chalks.

She stopped him. 'I'll bring it,' she said quietly.

'We have come all this way to the backside of Japan for you to study the architectural merits of a barn. Weren't there any textbooks on the subject that could have saved us the trouble?' Josh joked.

It hadn't exactly been sold to him as a study trip. It was a generous offer of a weekend from Mochizuki in exceptional countryside. She believed he so wanted her to see the little masterpiece of traditional architecture that was the farmhouse even though he could not take her himself.

'What is that?' Josh called as he passed a large tin drum on a brick platform.

'The bath. We'll collect the kindling and get it going for later.' Miho had been to the isolated spot before. No lights. No stores for miles around. Her progress under the weight of the food bags was slow.

He wrapped his knuckles on the empty drum. 'No hot. No cold. No running. Unbelievable.'

Miho chose not to tell him that all the water would come, bucket by bucket, from the hillside stream.

He walked towards the house mumbling, 'We could have saved the petrol.'

They had accepted Mochizuki's offer to stay at his country Minka before they had worked out how far it was from the city and Josh was already beating himself up for agreeing to it. Mochizuki had been so enthusiastic. He loved the place. It was his retreat, and Naomi, he had said, should make some sketches of the roof trusses. He seemed perfectly content she would be away for the weekend with Josh. It unnerved her that he wasn't jealous. That he had been instrumental in arranging their weekend. She wondered what was he doing just then.

Josh was quick to be riled; overtired and overworked. While it made him less loveable, it didn't stop her from feeling guilty.

He had made it quite clear that a trip to an isolated farmhouse was not his idea of fun, and had only been persuaded because Sam was keen to go, when Miho had sold him the idea. The isolated farmhouse was so tranquil that Mondays didn't exist up there. There would be nothing to do but watch insects watching the bamboo grow. Josh had whimpered and complained it would be a hijacking, but Sam convinced him it was important to get out of the city sometimes. Besides there was a game this weekend they could watch on TV. It began to rain lightly. Nobody had told Sam that there was no furniture save the mattresses and a couple of cushions, and that there wasn't a TV for miles.

Naomi stepped up from the low entrance hall. The roofline was a steep pitch of about 60 degrees to cope with snow in the winter. Ash stood in the hearth of the square fire pit, bordered with zabuton cushions. She filled the kettle from a pipe over the stone sink and hung it on a hook in the mouth of a carved fish, suspended over the unlit fire. She lay winded on the cushions while the boys complained as they walked round the old beamed house; Josh was incensed when he found that the bamboo pipe fed straight from the hillside.

Sam whooped to see a small fridge at the back of the kitchen connected to the only power supply in the house. Though they were without light, or a means to cook other than the empty hearth, the chiller was thoughtfully stocked with Asahi beers.

Miho was at the stone sink unpacking food.

'Josh?' Sam threw a can towards him and he opened it immediately, as if in doing so it could change the whole course of the weekend. The effervescence ran over his hands, covered the tatami matting. He yowled.

'Jerk.' Sam laughed.

'Can I have a hand setting up the fire?' Naomi asked.

'Or we could do without tea? Josh suggested.

She watched Josh downing the cold beer, his head cocked back, and his eyes swung round to rest on her and in his silence she could hear blame. It had all been her idea. She was sure that this was all he knew. It was the wrong weekend with the wrong people and she still felt nauseous.

Naomi and Miho prepared the food they had brought as the boys walked the bamboo woods around the house.

Miho leant against a red pine pillar surveying the lack of furniture, then drew open the large, unpainted, room dividers.

Naomi watched; no blossom and no dragons, as Miho dragged a couple of futons from the cupboard to make a low chair and backrest. She had a sudden urge to tell her – to tell Miho that she was having an affair with the architect. Miho had first introduced him. Instead she tore at a pack of unopened buckwheat noodles. She hesitated. Perhaps the time would never be right. Her instinct counselled silence.

When the men returned from the woods all four of them lay back in a mess of arms and legs on the makeshift futon. She could tell them all and rely on the safety of numbers, but then Josh interrupted her thought.

'Jesus Christ. What were we thinking? Miho, I thought you said it was owned by the one of the heads of a *kabushiki kaisha?*'

'Yes, and Mochizuki has some share in it too.'

They chased a large, black centipede from the thatch heading behind the divide and threatening the bedding, keeping score as they found more and shaking them into empty beer cans until they were convinced it amounted to an infestation.

Despite the slow, light rain, Miho and Sam left to collect wood. Josh swung his arms round her as if turning to the consolations of sex and he drew her slowly over to the futon. They lay together for a heartbeat. The open pore on his cheekbone, a chicken pox scar, once so familiar, had become ugly to her.

'They'll be back in a minute,' she objected.

He let her go as if she were suddenly toxic and the tension strained to breaking point. When it broke it was as if she had been catapulted to the furthest margins of the room, physically thrown aside, though they hadn't even exchanged words.

He took up a newspaper and fell into an ominous silence. As she removed her sketchpad from the rucksack she offered to draw him but he groaned and turned away. So she turned to the beam formation over her head and thought of the other man.

Sam's laughter broke the still air as he and Miho came running back for shelter, stripping off their wet clothes at the threshold, at the onset of heavy rain. They were so happy. How could they be so happy?

Miho stripped to her tiny bra and Sam used his shirt to rub her dark, wet, hair dry. She pulled him by the hand and led him to the back of the house where she could pull the room dividers and screen off and separate the only room in the house.

Josh looked at Naomi accusatively.

That evening, as they ate on the floor around an open fire of kindling, Josh announced that he couldn't stand to spend another day at the farmhouse and was going back to Tokyo. Sam, he suggested, should come because the baseball game had to be a better option than this. The girls could get the train. Naomi's protest was water thin. It would be easier without him. Josh was her familiar stranger now. Though by not telling any of them it rested on each one of them equally, it should be easier to be in Miho's company and a relief from the troubled relationship.

Miho tried but the boys would not change their minds and they left promptly the following morning, excited at returning to the comfort of Sam's apartment. After dutiful goodbyes, Naomi wondered how many days she and Josh had left.

Miho got her to collect bamboo from the slopes around the house. It was physical and Naomi cut her hands more than once on the sharp edges of the dry fallen leaves. The air was fresh and she loved being outside.

'You like working for the architect?' Miho lay a section of hollow trunks across Naomi's arms, long and hollow like the first rolled plans Mochizuki had handed her at first visit to the temple.

'I love the teahouse project.'

'He's so much in demand it's amazing he can find the time to work on that little building.'

When he spent long afternoons with her at the teahouse, Naomi thought, he didn't count time.

Miho looked at her searchingly. 'You find him attractive?'

A confession right now would leave her vulnerable. 'I don't really get past the grey temples.' She hid behind his age. It was a pleasure to recall the image of his silver temples and she smiled. 'I am so grateful you found me the job. He's a great guy, Miho.' Naomi squeezed her arm appreciatively.

'This Friday,' Miho told her, 'when I picked up the key at nursery school where Kazuko and I work. She asked about you . . .'

'Kazuko gave you the key?' Naomi asked. So Kazuko had arranged it all? Miho's friendship with her was probably stronger than she realized. So this idea was not his. Did Kazuko suspect their closeness, she wondered, and hope to send her back towards Josh? This was a contrivance of his wife's. He might be jealous.

Naomi found the wood lay heavy in her arms.

'Where do we drop these?' she asked, cutting short talk of the Mochizukis. She was now wedded to this woman's husband as physically as his wife. There was no telling when the tipping point had been, when the balance had shifted from admiring him and sharing his values. He had been as a *sensei* to her and taught her a great deal. She was now at the point where she felt attached as if part of him, and she could not live without him.

Back through the thin leaved forest, they returned to their large metal bath.

Through the smoke of the bonfire they filled the tub from coopered bamboo buckets, working hard as they fed the fire below, and in between they sketched and dozed, waiting for it to heat. By late that afternoon it was warm and inviting.

'Genuine Japanese bath,' Miho said, gesturing to invite her into the steaming waters.

Miho first washed in the cold stream before taking the wooden steps.

Naomi hid her nakedness behind a small towel as they sat under the open sky.

'You and Josh?'

'I don't know.' Naomi let her words trail away on the steam.

Miho understood. Any one could see she and Josh were in trouble.

'I was in Gifu on business. Saw the cormorant fishermen,' Naomi began.

'Gifu? On business? That dodgy tourist "Soapland"?' Then as if regretting the criticism she continued.

'The fishing is real clever. Many times the fishermen steal the catch and the birds never learn that they are being used. They never learn.' Naomi met her insistence with silence.

'You ate the river fish?' Miho asked.

The thought of Gifu dinner was too strong for Naomi's stomach just now and she started to get out.

'And when does the teahouse complete?'

'Rains have delayed the programme.'

'We have many different words for rain here.' Miho gazed up at the blue, evening sky. 'We have words for driving rain, chilly rain, autumn rain, night rain and many more.'

'We have just one word for rain.'

'No, this can't be the case. There is more than one type of rain. There is more than one type of trouble.'

Naomi was not to be drawn.

'*Tenkyu*,' Miho said after a little while. 'That is rain from a clear sky.'

'Doesn't look likely.'

'You never know.' Miho scanned the sky. 'And you never have monsoons?'

'No.'

Naomi's replies had become too short and she would not be drawn out. 'You and Josh will come good,' she told her.

As Miho got out in search of tea, Naomi very much doubted it.

Chapter 67

Spiral had been completed a few years earlier by Fumihiko Maki and the focal point was the wide cantilevered spiral ramp, rising from the restaurant and suspended in air like the rising fortunes in a game of snakes and ladders. The mid-morning brunch had been put in the diary at Josh's insistence. Eventually the waiter could be spotted descending from the upper floor.

'Chawanmushi,' Kazuko said decisively.

The listed options were difficult for Naomi: fried egg, eel, fried rice. Full English. She felt nauseous just running down the list and couldn't bring herself to eat a thing. She was pregnant, she knew now for certain, and from the dates it was most likely to be the architect's. 'You go ahead.' Naomi bought time to pour over the menu.

Josh, in deference, signalled that Mochizuki should order before him.

He rubbed his hands together in anticipation of a feast. 'Option American,' Mochizuki concluded swiftly.

Kazuko reopened her menu to review his choice.

'No, *Kun*. You don't want the maple pancakes. It comes with that aerosol cream we just don't like.'

Mochizuki looked at Naomi. Another woman was telling him how to live and had influence over him.

'No. I'll take it.'

'*Waa*,' Kazuko complained and, turning to the waiter, told him to bring the pancakes without the cream. 'Come on,' she told Mochizuki point-blank, 'you don't need the cream.'

'Just a second.' He took out a cigarette from the soft camel packet and hung it on his lip in an effort to remain silent. He flicked at his lighter several times as the waiter progressed to Josh who said, 'Full English for me.'

Naomi's biliousness would not pass. It was all an agony.

Mochizuki took the cigarette from his lips and countered his wife with renewed enthusiasm. 'Yes. I'll change. English Breakfast for me also.'

The Mochizukis sat stiffly before her like two chess pieces. She and Josh sat on the other side of the board but only she and Mochizuki knew they were playing.

'Well,' she demurred, 'I really don't think I want anything.'

It was Josh's turn to rile a partner.

'Come on, you have to have something.' He had accused her of being reluctant to arrange the meal with the Mochizuki's and now he would think she was sulking.

'Did you eat already?' Mochizuki asked, attempting to smooth the waters. If she had had breakfast, brunch appeared all too soon. He was kind.

'No. No,' she protested – Josh knew it to be the case.

Keen to step out of the limelight she elected to go for the buffet.

Josh was appeased and ordered a Bloody Mary, and then, in an attempt to lighten the mood, he insisted everyone join him and ordered three more of the same.

The buffet provided a cornucopia of nauseous options. Naomi was overheating but managed to circle the table once before coming away with a small bowl of plain white rice.

Josh clearly disproved of her choice as she rejoined the table. The buffet was a flat fee. Mochizuki again led the diversion with a ranging survey from his seat, taking in the roof of the building, offering a critique on the architect Fumihiko Maki.

'Maki is managing the space pretty good,' he concluded.

'It's new,' Josh offered

'It's been around four years,' Mochizuki corrected.

If he knew, she thought. If only Josh and Mrs Mochizuki

would leave the table and take a stroll up to the gallery and leave them alone, she could ask him how it would end. She could ask him what the game plan would be; where the affair would take them. What should she do? For now, while the secret remained hers alone, the less he knew the smaller the size of the issue. But she wanted to share it with him.

He assessed the structure with an educated eye.

'Maki is professor at Washington right now. He brings eastern and western elements together.'

Me too, she thought grimly, conscious now she could bring only limited energy to the conversation.

'The Metabolism group,' she offered from her college books without further elaboration, raising the free-thinking group Maki had once belonged to.

'Yes, just so,' he said. He understood; the situation was difficult for her, just not how difficult.

Josh looked at her untouched vodka.

'You're not drinking?' He was willful.

'I just don't fancy it.' He looked at her as if she were deliberately contrary.

He signalled to the waiter as she opened a line of conversation, in the hope he would run with it.

'Josh is working on wind-farm investments just now,' she told Kazuko.

'It is good to hear about increased investment in alternative energy. Way back in seventy-nine, the US advised that CO2 would alter the climate and changes could be substantial.'

'Well, the banks are listening,' he said.

'Good,' Kazuko enthused. 'I'm going to the Netherlands in November; they'll discuss stabilizing greenhouse gases.'

Mochizuki hid behind an adopted form and joked, 'Yes, and as my wife is saving the planet, I have to make my own dinner.'

Kazuko glanced swiftly at Naòmi without meeting her eye but with sufficient time to gauge how she had received this hollow lament.

The chawamushi appeared and was placed in front of Kazuko. It remained untouched while she waited politely for the arrival of the other meals.

Naomi overcame her revulsion to reach for the Bloody Mary and took the smallest sip. Why was Mochizuki playing up to his wife, she wondered, making it so difficult for her? Did he hope to throw Josh off the scent? He must already know that Josh didn't suspect them. Naomi thought this was not the moment to excuse herself and willed herself to sit for a moment longer. It was intolerable that Josh had insisted upon them all meeting.

'Next year in Bergen,' Kazuko continued blandly, 'they will talk targets and timetables but we need intergovernmental action.'

Naomi could give little consideration to the slow inexorable degeneration of the planet when her immediate world threatened to implode. The tomato hit her stomach like acid rain.

Kazuko took her slight grimace to be an insufficient interest in a subject close to her heart and concluded she was wasn't polite; the girl owed Kazuko more than she knew. Did she know how much she had control over her husband? The girl might think the whole affair was clandestine. It looked very much as though the boy did not suspect he was *kakkorudo*. A cuckold. Of course not. And the little English girlfriend would return to him and after a while they would return home to London and the *kakkouddo* would be her ticket back. Soon it would be time; she had planned it this way.

The smell of hot savoury meat signalled the arrival of the English breakfasts.

Kazuko was immediately irritated by Mochizuki's choice of the greasy Western cuisine. She picked up her teaspoon and, turning, offered him the small, soft gingko nut that she had found hidden in her egg dish. To her great satisfaction he ate the trophy obediently from her spoon like a child. 'The gingko for longevity,' she pronounced, with a delighted little laugh.

'The Ginko tree,' Mochizuki threw back, 'is very old species. Just like me.'

Kazuko smiled at him indulgently and then observed Naomi, looking at her untouched bowl.

'Every grain of rice you leave will give you a freckle, Naomi-san. You should eat more.'

'Nice people,' Josh said as they walked back to the metro station on Omotesandō. And she struggled to answer.

Chapter 68

That evening the audience filtered out of the early-evening showing at the Picture House at a languid pace. Miho took Naomi's elbow and drew her from colliding with yet another would-be critic, replaying the departure scene, neither in the movie or really outside the cinema about to have a meal.

'Sam is leaving Japan,' Miho said, breaking the news to her.

Josh had warned Naomi this might be on the cards and she had since assumed she would lose her good friend to the States.

'What will you do, Miho?'

'Follow him once he gets settled, but for now I have to stay.'

'You'll miss him.'

'I will follow like you will follow.'

Naomi ignored her. What exactly did she mean?

'Why has he got to go?' Naomi asked.

'He doesn't want to talk about it but he has backed some of the wrong clients,' Miho leaned in and whispered. 'It has to do with Guam. And that yakuza, Ukai, who Mochizuki works for.'

Naomi's secret remained and she had not confided in Miho. Her many reasons counselled against it. This was all she needed to hear. She decided not to rise to the barb, choosing instead to ignore it.

Miho persisted. 'The airport deal in Guam is a big scandal brewing and Sam has got to make himself scarce. I don't know how involved Mochizuki is but he is good friends with the guy Ukai, who is right in the middle of it.'

'Friends with Ukai?' She knew the owner of the construction

company was regarded as shady. Mochizuki had alluded to favours but how much she did know about her architect?

After he left his training session at the gym, Josh went running and on his last leg he slowed to a walking pace to bring his heart rate down. As he passed the pachinko parlour gaming hall in the high street, he regretted that he had to go home that evening to the strain of living like strangers with Naomi.

He walked into the house, still sweating kicked off his running shoes and headed for the shower. He had decided they should go away, take the holiday he had long been promising. He couldn't ask her to marry him right now, but if they took a break, maybe he could turn it around. They could begin again. He would broach it with her now.

When he found that the house was empty, if he were honest he found a part of him was thankful. Maybe he wasn't ready to patch it up; he had too much on at work to think about and his best friend was leaving. It was tough, tough news that Sam was leaving Tokyo. End of an era.

Chapter 69

'Fool at nightfall
Seizes a thorn
Catching fireflies'

–

The Guam flight landed at Narita at 14.50 and a car was waiting to take Mochizuki home. The driver, chewing a stick, briefly presented the side of his face to receive the address, and then the back of his thick neck. Mochizuki had no need to talk to him. He had landed with all the problems on the Guam project still on his mind, only some of which he could leave with Iwata. Now his attentions turned to the small domestic issue demanding his time. Just when he didn't have it.

As they drew up at outside the front door, he was pressed into his seat by the gentle incline. He was almost too tired to get out of the car, but it was not fatigue that made him reluctant to walk up the familiar slope of the hill. It seemed steeper than the climb on Mount Fuji that he and Kazuko had taken about five years ago. They had made the popular volcanic trek together in June. When they stopped at the last vending machine to rehydrate he recalled how it had upset her to see the street furniture so far up the mountain and associated scattered trash. She had tucked both their empty isotonic cans into her rucksack despite his protestations that there were so many it would do no harm to add to the collection, telling her, 'Someday soon someone would come and clear it up.'

'Who is that?' she had objected. 'The public body for

mountain tops? The Etahin men who want to extend their trash collection round from the end of their road in Chigasaki to stretch their legs a little? Perhaps,' she'd said, 'they would come over on their weekend off. But no, pardon me.' She had got heated. 'They don't get weekends.'

He had smiled at her familiar, world-encompassing social conscience.

'You are welcome,' he had said, 'to get your rucksack sticky on my account', and then, to tease her, he had added, 'Or I can add to the trash?'

Of course he had taken the rubbish from her hands to humour her world climate-changing sensibilities. It was only then that she realized he had been teasing her all along. They were good friends. He never forgot this.

He slung his travel bag over his back and watched the car depart as if it meant something to him.

Today he would have to walk into their home and tell his best friend that he had found himself beholden to a tenacious lover. He could barely deal with the thought. He took a slip of paper from his briefcase and with his gifted Montblanc pen scribbled a few lines. Should he mention it at all? Perhaps the girl would change her mind? He didn't know. He might yet persuade her not to have the child. The child was a thought that threatened to run round his mind at inappropriate times of the day in small slippers and a tiny kimono, calling his name. But he stopped those thoughts short, as if refusing to acknowledge the embodiment of a ghost. He felt old and it was complicated.

'Tadaima,' he yelled, as he always did.

'You had a good trip?' Kazuko called, before coming in to sight to greet him, as she always did.

He kicked off his shoes in the genkan, placed his Issey Miyake brief case above the step, and dropped into his house slippers. He bent to pick at a loose seam he noticed on the case until he became aware of Kazuko standing above him in the lobby. She was beaming, welcoming him back.

'The bag's coming apart?' she said, flipping to share his concern.

'No, no,' he said, 'the seam's loose just by this stain.'

'I can take it in and see to that,' she offered, brushing aside his disappointment. 'Give me your jacket. You want to eat?'

He held it close like a reluctant confessional so that it was she who had to make the effort to take it from him.

He did want to eat but he handed her his jacket, surrendering himself to her but feeling he had already given away anything else she might really want.

'What's this?' She unfolded it, then read aloud, *'Gu ni kuraku, ibara otsukamu, hotakaru kana.'* Fool at nightfall seizes a thorn catching fireflies.

She took another look at the haiku and nodded slowly as if comfort were to be found in the inertia of a pendulum. He had brought her haiku before; she was once often used to him doing so. She said nothing. She knew what it meant.

He sloped over to the last patch of light cutting a harsh angle across the floor.

To Kazuko he looked as though he were a dog that had been kicked. The Guam project had been tough on him and it clearly wasn't letting up.

'So did you bring me some souvenir back? Or only poetry?'

He slumped on the Eames chair and closed his eyes to strategize. In the silence Mochizuki felt the need to rally before what he felt was coming in the form of a tsunami of confessions. He began in self-defence and said accusatively, with some justification, 'Nice to come back to the house and find you here.'

'What?' She drew out the vowels in a long indulgent question that relied on a sensible explanation for what seemed to be a barb.

'You are away so often,' he said, wounded. He would hide behind 'the wounded party'. He would begin with this 'justification'.

His eyes were still closed but he could not acknowledge that he was frightened to look at her. He could hear her back was turned and she was mixing him a drink but he was afraid to look at her as if it were against his principles to shoot someone in the back, which is what it would amount to. He did recognize that his voice lay somewhere between a lugubrious whine and his own register, and she met it with indulgent cheer.

'You are tired and I must get you something to eat. Tea first?' She fired this into the back of the cupboard and gave it added volume.

It was his habit to take sencha tea as soon as he got home and though he often made it himself it was something she liked to do for him.

His sense of duty to her overcame him and he sat upright swinging round in the chair to anchor his feet to the ground and called her.

His voice was urgent as if he experienced some stabbing pain of the body.

'Wait wait,' she soothed, coming to rest on her knees in front of him.

He wiped his face as if dripping in the sweat of exertion. 'It hasn't been good,' he said, looking at her steadily, buying time to bottle out.

Patiently she waited for the explanation, which did not come. He could say nothing.

Eventually she gave him the line. All she said was, 'I know.'

He knew it could not mean she knew about the girl. She was adding to the shared understanding on the Guam stuff that she mostly knew, though of course didn't know the whole there either. It was a mere throwaway line but the dislocation of what she actually said and what it meant to him was larger than he wanted to acknowledge. It released him to speak.

Tumbling words competed now to leave his mouth before they scorched it. 'The girl has caught me.'

She sank back on her ankles and exhaled from the light body blow. She understood him immediately.

Kazuko considered the condition might be the result of a liaison with someone else and not his fault. Still rational she had not yet fallen over her own concerns. She knew he had seen a great deal of the girl, more perhaps than she had predicted when she had smoothed the silken kimono, folded right over left, across her ample western chest that day at lunch, condoning an association.

She herself had chosen her. She'd arranged the dalliance when she had booked their hotel room in Gifu, choosing the old out-of-favour spa to reduce the likelihood of their bumping into any acquaintances of the Mochizukis, a crusty old place that would barely recognize the name, let alone the face, of the renowned architect.

She laughed at the thought of love when what they had – she and Mochizuki – was so much longer deeper and richer. In lime-fired clay the glaze takes on a patina from the fire the longer it stays in the kiln; the fire burns at a lower temperature and what emerges in the end is blushed with the caresses of the fire and becomes something of the fire itself, distilled. They each had this effect on one another. The foreigner had the hips of a fisher woman and the eyes of Kewpie Chan: large, round, cartoon discs, more suited to the four-legged, bovine or canine. In the east, where the sun goddess Amaterasu rose first in the world every morning, it was appropriate that their eyes should narrow in the great light that fell in all its brilliance across chosen people marked with the eyes to see it. This girl was no more than a plaything like the last one. He had had affairs before. She had seen her as a toy from the start. These foreigners all went home eventually; once they had been shown a good time they left for where they belonged. She had handed her over to him just as she had with the Portuguese girl they had hired before.

'Oningyo. She is a doll.'

How could he be trapped then by a doll? This was all she was. She was harmless. Dreams remain dreams and he could not be caught by this toy. She must go back to where she came from.

But then he parted with the actual words. 'She said . . . she has told me,' he stuttered, 'that she is expecting a child.'

On hearing the words spoken they became a truth that fleetingly chastised her for believing she understood how the world worked. How their world worked. It threatened to turn their work, in their wider spheres, to a lie.

She needed a task and began to head for the kitchen and then checked herself. After all these years of their tacit arrangement, had he fallen like some lovesick *seifuku*, some child in school uniform, for a foreigner?

But they left to return home; they all left, and equilibrium was restored. He dallied with these women. He did not dally with her, Kazuko, of the climate-change conference circuit, of the calm voice, the professional, lobbying representative, who understood the mode was as important as the message. Controlled Kazuko. If asked to pack she would allow only hand luggage on the last ship out to anywhere. Whose considered response to the whaling crisis took on arguments from both sides before she showed her true colours without plangency. Kazuko, in her utilitarian urban chic. She let out a cutting wail, a keening sound that came straight from a wounded Kabuki-za character from Ginza; a yowl so extended that it ran the long distance from deep inside her and, as it emerged, disabled a part of her.

Hiding behind the girl's reported words he had not laid bare his own emotional position. Her cry became the anger of all wronged women, the injustice of the victims of thieves. And beyond any acknowledgement was the pathos of a single woman who had once had hopes of a child but who had remained childless.

Her pain and confusion distilled into irritation over how he, her temple guardian, could be levelled by a young girl. He could not be. He would not be.

'Is it true?'

Was it true ?

Whatever undertakings he had made, whatever he had said to the girl in their intimate moments ceased to belong to him. He cast off ownership of his past utterances and if asked, were his life to depend on it, what he would vouch for, now above all things, was his allegiance to her. To Kazuko. In his own mind it was without intrigue, malice or weakened resolve. He was overcome with the pure, genuine belief that he owed his life to the woman with whom he had always felt safe. With Kazuko.

'Do you believe this girl?' she repeated. Getting rid of a child was easier than obtaining contraceptive. For now her mind forbade her to get closer to their intimate details and this stopped her going further. But the impulse broke loose again. 'Those girls bring contraceptives with them.' And finally she dismissed the threat with the only conclusion admissible. 'So you will organize to get rid of the child?'

It was posed as a question. His default rested in a place where Kazuko would sort out the intractable problems. She was right, of course; this was the only sensible course. It was as if the hours he had spent dreaming were merely the dreams of an overworked man whose position in the world was set to slide and the slow progress down would be more painful than the slow climb to get somewhere in life. He chastised himself that he had not worked on a truly creative project in years, so bound up instead with guest speeches and the adoration of acolytes who thirsted for his energy.

The closest he had come to fulfillment at work recently was the temple teahouse project and this he had diluted with afternoons with the girl. He derided himself for his weak will and the meanderings that had led him this far from his duties. Let him fall on the sword of his own stupidity but no, he would not go there. He was no Mishima to a cause when Kazuko was there to support him.

The girl had caught him. He had told her he could not commit to her and it was now obvious she had ignored him. What possible conclusion could he draw from the situation other than that she had tried to trip him up? They were not living in the Meiji era. The girl was wilful and with mounting self-justification he rested on the fact that he had been duped.

'You will speak to her about this,' she instructed.

'Of course,' he whispered in a tone of repentance. And he made up his mind to do just that.

'We must eat now.' And she rose from her knees and prepared two plates, bringing first the condiments to the Nakashima table. She paused to finger the raw edge of bark on the side of the highly polished oak. A design referring back to the integrity of the material; to what it used to be. Things change. Things stay the same. They had saved hard to buy this piece of furniture early on in the marriage. She had worked so very hard on his account, as much as her own, and merely touching on the thought that he no longer needed her sacrifices piqued.

She marched to the kitchen and, taking up her own plate, scraped the meal into the trash. Bringing only his plate to the table she sat to watch him eat, sipping tea she poured from the oversized pot with the worn bamboo handle. They sat for a while in silence as he ate slowly. Eventually she allowed him air.

'We must replace this soon.' And she shook the near-broken handle.

Chapter 70

Sakimake: bad luck in the morning, good luck in the afternoon

Saito-san had told her there were lucky days in the Buddhist calendar; days upon which it was auspicious to marry, days to avoid for a product launch, days on which to hold a funeral. She had no idea what it was today but Naomi called on powers whose names she did not know and those in whom she did not believe, to make this a day that was fair to her. She was not asking for more. It did not have to be lucky; just fair. Mochizuki would seal the fate of the child that she was carrying that was undoubtedly his.

They would meet today just before lunch at the original Olympic pool designed by Kenzo Tange where last month they had come to see a Canadian touring production of Puccini. They had flooded the stage with water and she had wept, and he had shown himself not entirely able to deal with it. She suspected he knew less about the art than she did, an inherited taste like fine wine, an opulence one should take up if one could. She stood under the sweeping eaves of the building looking out over the public space. She recalled one morning when they were working on the teahouse; he had explained the bench under the eaves, where the guests should wait.

'*Ko-shi-ka-ke-machi-ais,*' she had enunciated after him, repeating the word to help her memorize it.

'This waiting makes you tranquil,' he had told her. 'It is controlled. Like when you do not rush into something. You wait and then you can do it better. Like how you count in rhythm in music before you play your instrument. This is not the waiting in the queue, which is not tranquil. It is different. You must wait to hear yourself inside and then you can do it better.'

Today she had discovered another type of waiting.

Such an expanse of empty public space and so much drama. In London it would belong to pigeons and some near-destitute would be taking pleasure in feeding them. Here, black corvids, like punctuation marks, bounced across the concrete, fed by no one but fat on pigeon eggs. A sharp cry in the dry air; a small boy running after his ball had fallen, his soft hat rebounding as he cut his chin. She could see the blood from here. His tardy mother met his fall late, inspected his knees. But Naomi could see she was mistaken, for it was his head he hurt but he was off with the ball again as soon as she had touched him. If he would not keep the child she would not keep the child. If he told her they had a future she would be watching for the child's every stumble and she would not caress the wrong wound.

On a wind shift, the smell from the stall selling yakitori chicken drifted over. Was the noren banner over the canopy waving goodbye? She was hungry and the leaden sky sat like a brooding anxiety on her chest.

Beneath the great curtain of eaves on the stadium she recalled Josh's attempts to liken the structure to a Malthusian curve or some other two-dimensional figure on a graph. Josh would be taking katsudon round the corner from his office at around this time. She had not seen Josh for several weeks. Waiting had tired her and risking the cold she slumped like a teenager to sit on her haunches against a wall out of the wind.

A huddle of coats passed. The smell hit: out-of-season hyacinth, favoured by elderly ladies. Visitors from outside the city. Would he find her now through the engulfing passage of falsetto chattering, through this cloud of starlings? They followed their flag-toting leader inside the building and she searched the expanse of the concourse again, in case he had missed her. And then, there at the end of the concourse, was a fleeting shape in the distance. The traffic moved continuously. She picked him out quickly, that familiar gait approaching as if he had time on his hands, his dark shirt stealing the man and turning him to an empty jacket. She found it unnerving. He had on the crumpled linen jacket he wore the day he interviewed her so many months back at his offices in Chigasaki.

It was days since she had seen him. They offered one another the wrong cheeks and his greeting was awkward but she met it with well-disguised disappointment as he flattened the wayward linen on his lapel in a pointless exercise.

As if he were the one in need of support she took his hand almost surreptitiously and he curled his fingers up through hers to touch the web of skin deep between the fingers, the skin that, though so accessible, a stranger never touches. With this intimacy, she gauged the strength and measure of his emotion at seeing her after nearly a week. To hold his hand was a simple delight.

They walked towards Meiji-jingumae and the ornamental gardens near the shrine where, in her first few days in Tokyo, she and Josh had walked beside sharp spears of iris guarding the water's edge. A wild animal could no longer lurk in the once-Rousseauesque undergrowth, now so changed with the seasons, with the metabolic rate of the city itself. She leant closer on Mochizuki's arm as they walked.

He finally chose to speak.

'You like living at the temple?' he asked.

'I don't care where I live. And for now it's a haven.'

'You are an outsider, Naomi.'

She laughed it off. She could not ask him if that was to her advantage. He should not regard her as needy.

'I am an outsider,' he responded.

Not knowing where his train of thought was leading him, she asked, 'So, we are getting closer?'

'We are both outsiders but you are an international outsider, a foreigner, which is different.'

His own credentials as an international were possibly better than her own. He had worked in New York, Toronto, Paris. She was a Londoner.

'But your career is international.'

The tattered career.

He lifted a long finger, as if bidding her pause; a conductor orchestrating music. Though it looked measured, as if he was in control, he was struggling with a couple of sumo wrestlers that had taken hold of his stomach and he knew there would never be an eventual winner. They might never let go and he would forever be locked in a sickening bout of internal wrestling. On the one hand Kazuko had always supported him and without her it would have been impossible to build the career he had enjoyed and, now, with the girl, was the question of the love child they might have created. He had lived with a woman for his married life and he had made promises, he had been guided by her and she was willing him to stay so she could lead him comfortably towards the future that was as predictable as any old age could be, nursed in the universal respect for his achievements, where students would seek an audience. Or he could begin again with a different girl. He ran in pursuit of the resolutions he had made when he moved his lips, shaping them round words of promises he had given to Kazuko. But logic failed him, his memory failed him and as he ran after these thoughts he failed to stop himself falling in with the hand he held there that moment. His spoken allegiance was lost and he turned sides.

He swung round to grab her and wrap her in his feelings, for he had no other means of expression. And he kissed the top of her head and she swelled with need for him. He stooped closer to breathe in the opiate that was her until they were startled by a party of escapees from the offices nearby who had come to enjoy a mittened lunch on the sheltered side of the gardens. While his head ached in the confusion of abandoned plans, she could read none of it. He made one last lunging attempt to say what he had come to say.

'No, I belong to an old traditional country where I am one of the dispossessed.'

She looked at him as if he were talking nonsense but let him finish.

'I am tied by my obligations and you are not. I should buy you an air ticket to England before I have you live in a monastery.'

His words blew through as if a howling wind bringing a sudden drop in temperature, but she rested on all he had done for her and all he had said before now and she read his offer as concern for her self-sacrifice and as a question over whether she was sure that a future with him was one she should choose.

'No,' she said simply. 'No. I begin to belong here.'

On her response came the realisation for him that he was glad to hear it. While he was with her he forgot his tangled heart and the duty and the loyalties he had forged over the years.

'We must eat,' he said, drawing her from the park and back to the mainstream.

Chapter 71

Earth, fire, air and water co-existent; opposing elements in a contest over dominance.

Kazuko heard him replacing his bicycle in the purpose-built shed that he had put together with Iwata one week. He had cut his hand then and had come in to find her so that she could wash it. His own hammer blow had pinched the skin so hard it had bled. She had tied it with a bandage and asked him to hold it aloft for a while, to stop the blood pooling and they had laughed when he identified that she had turned him into a lucky cat, white paw held high. It had been at the start of the Guam project and they had believed that it would bring him the fortune that would match his fame so she had said he was indeed her lucky mascot and the hammer blow was a good omen. Very distinctly she recalled he had said, 'You know best, Kazuko', and his confidence had filled her with pride.

His bike was on the wall fixture, opposite hers. When he had conceived of the store he had planned it would remain a passageway along the edge of their narrow plot, utilising all the available space. It was a principle of his, from domestic to his larger concepts, like the atrium he conceived where the transparent water system for the whole building channelled through four floors of the glass interior. They would soon, he hoped, get that languishing concept approved for construction. A fresh project and a new perspective was on its way.

Kazuko, meanwhile, opened some mochi cakes and lay them

on a tea platter. He would have told the girl today and equilibrium would be restored. The design of life. She smiled as she laid out a third skewer of dusted sweet cakes across the others in an afterthought of generosity.

On his arrival she took his jacket, poured his tea and sat in the pose she readily adopted for earnest conversation: one elbow resting on a crossed knee, chin in hand, supporting her enthusiasm.

She had today, she told him, witnessed a small breakthrough when the world had been persuaded to hold talks on the big environmental issues in Kyoto. Finally after this discussion, like one well versed in handling the needs of conference lobbyists, she came very gently to ask him about the girl.

'Chotto,' he prevaricated, hoping to communicate the difficulty he had in raising the issues. He had vacillated over when he would he break it to her. He believed he had not seen the girl in any timeframe that allowed him to raise any serious subject with her and consequently he certainly had not told the girl to terminate the pregnancy. All this was difficult for him to admit and at the top of the list was not broaching it. Kazuko waited patiently.

'It's difficult,' he repeated what his tone had communicated earlier.

'What is so difficult?'

Sometimes she seemed more like man to him. But he must stand his ground. She could be so unemotional in responses. This, he had always believed, had allowed her to get things done. To achieve.

He looked away from her undivided attention in a gesture of under-confidence.

'I'm no good at these things. I draw. I create. I'm not good with communication. You know what words are to me. I stumble.'

She nodded encouragingly as if understanding deep conflicts as yet unrecognized by the patient but soon to be vented, translated and divided into neat piles. These could then be settled upon at random and dealt with according to the in-tray. She looked grave with disappointment.

A tremor shook his body and he began to weep. He began to weep in front of his woman because she had consented to look away from the dalliance but now he knew he had hurt her.

They shared the torture of silence and Kazuko's noiseless tears joined his voiced regret.

He put a hand out to her blindly and they interlaced fingers, holding the sorrow together. The small wind chime, with its streamer printed with the slogan 'May peace prevail on earth', sounded on the breeze through the open garden door and the tree camouflaged them in shadow.

Finally Kazuko said, 'You want me to give her the message that you cannot give her?' She had expected his extended ramblings would follow, but he simply said, 'Yes.' The strength of his reaction encouraged her.

Later that evening she opened the bathroom door and was presented with his back bowed over in the steam.

'You okay?'

'I need a cigarette.'

She hesitated, tempted to enter and to wash his back as she so often did, but she decided against it.

She returned, taking a mini drag on the cigarette for him. He could take his chances in the damp atmosphere and see if he could keep it alight. He barely moved as she placed it between his lips but grunted his thanks.

Chapter 72

'Manaiota no ue no koi'
(A carp on the cutting board)

Naomi waited beneath the red wings of the torii gate for so long her back had become sore. She knew now that he would not come. Threaded lanterns danced on air, thick with chanting and the smoke from the yakitori chicken seller. The makeshift stage stood empty, hoping for dancers, and the children from the nursery, in turquoise happi coats, ran across the temple ground as if released for one day only from their small obligations.

The festival was at its height and too charged an atmosphere, and she knew she did not belong. These were not her traditions, these were not her people, and so she turned to leave. Eight men in loincloths came into sight carrying the mikoshi and with every beat of the taiko drum it urged them to lift the festival shrine higher on their shoulders. The sweatbands around their heads were stamped with the corporate sponsor Ukai. Bearing the weight of tradition was an onerous task; marching in step they paced back in time. A red, lacquered phallus was strapped around the shortest man's waist and he toyed with it for the crowd and they roared in support as he upheld their ritual to the fertility gods. Behind her lines of white paper, zigzag folded prayers bound to the shrine with hemp rope. What she needed now was a prayer.

Shoeless, Naomi walked into the wooden teahouse for the

last time. The branch of the tree that formed the door lintel was so low that the average man would have to duck to clear it. He was not an average man. In places between the original knots, dark gnarled bark clung to the rough limb because his designs were steeped in Zen awareness. He'd said in twenty-five years they would rebuild the teahouse. This was not futile – the perpetual renovation that accommodated the psyche living on a fault line. If it was understood that a programme of rebuilding was scheduled, then the accident of disaster could not have the same devastating effect. This was birth and this was death, she believed now. This was preparedness, this was resilience. It was what she must find when the tectonics of her life were about to shift so fundamentally that she would be stripped of everything she once relied on. She would rebuild.

She would look to herself for the sake of the child. Her hand drew across the circumference of her belly; the world was a hemisphere for the child as yet unborn. The baby might look like him. If it should live. If she should ever see the newborn face. And where would they live? On this side of the world where she found herself now, or the country where she began? They were now, for her, the same place. A question of where to belong when they would both be outsiders wherever they chose.

In the distance across the temple grounds the baked potato seller called, 'Jagaimo.'

The call took her back to the many evenings she bought steaming, hot, sweet potatoes from his wheeled cart, which was now all she could afford. She had become a twentieth-century pauper.

'Jagaimo,' came his wailing call again, with a lilt of voiced pain that she could almost feel.

She drew the warm fleece overcoat around her and smilingly hoped for a girl. Who was this child? A leg, perhaps an elbow, even now charted the confines of a limited world that they share, and, from deep inside her, drew a fault line across smooth, taut skin. What would she tell of her story?

There would be no stories any more since the narrative of a child's life was to be watched over and overheard; to be retold and to have said to have taken place. A history displaced.

Chapter 73

Mochizuki had last left Naomi in tears and now sat in meditation in the teahouse to clear his mind. He rose and, stooping beneath a rough branch that formed the lintel, stepped into his shoes to gather a bundle of shrubs and flowers that were lying wrapped in old newspaper outside the door.

He returned to sit before a rough pottery vase and took up a pair of rudimentary scissors. These were forged from two pieces of iron and he imagined the man who had made them testing the large irregular handles for size. He cut the rough hemp string that bound the shrubs and began to assess them. Holding each at arm's length, he examined the shaft for knots and twists, and the way the leaves were angled. Silent but for the branches as they touched the paper, he sorted them into two piles, one that fitted his aesthetic principals that he would use and one that he would not.

His breathing was even and regular. At the base of the vase lay heavy, pink, mottled stones covering the spiked iron holder. From the glazed jug beside him he poured just enough water to cover the base. He chose one of the longest branches.

Naomi expected so much of him and his problem was that it was not his to give her. He owed so much to Kazuko he could no more desert her than he could give up Naomi. He cut a sharp angle at the base of the stem, thrusting the branch into the spiked kenzan, wishing he could punish himself. Stripping every single leaf but two from the second branch, he wanted to rid himself of morbid thoughts, angry that his preoccupations ran in torturing circles so often that he had ceased to function properly and his meditations failed to appease them.

A diffused light fell on the paper walls. He had tried to screen off the world outside in an attempt to better know the man he was within and to finalize his decision with the girl. A shadow crept across the mat from a maple tree and he remembered the first day he had brought her to meet Shakira before the old teahouse had been dismantled, before they had worked together to build a new one in its place.

He toyed with the angle on the shorter stem until it assumed a position that could be regarded as an accident of nature. The broken leaves were pungent and sharp, dominating the fragrant grass matting of the room. Finally he took a shorter contorted branch; a bloom on the withered *hikae*, the third and last stem in his arrangement and brought it to his face. He closed his eyes and took in its scent. He positioned it between the *shin* and *soe*, where, protected, nurtured almost by the dark earthy tones of their branches, the sensual flower emerged.

It was a long time since Shakira had taught him something of the principles of Ikebana flower arranging's rigid aesthetic, which had informed his own view of the importance of the space between substance in his architecture. The buds, so translucent they recalled the veins on a hand, balanced on a small ridge in time, cut and even now presaging decay.

He leant back to review his creation and then picking the stray pieces from the tatami, rolled up the newsprint and tied the debris in a parcel. He stopped to read an article on the old yellowing paper of the *Shimbun*; the Japanese had offered 9 million US dollars in aid to the victims of the Armenian earthquake. This at least should have an impact on the size of his own dilemma. It pained him to think it did not. He opened the shoji door and placed his bundle carefully outside on the step. He then closed the screen and drew back to review his arrangement; he looked at it briefly and then kicked it over with a stark and counterpoised aggression, upsetting the vessel and leaving water to pool across the tatami matting in a stain.

Chapter 74

Miho squatted outside the pottery store, browsing upturned rice bowls floating like flotsam across the road. She couldn't raise too much enthusiasm for styling the photographic shoot for the noodle client. That weekend at the Minka farmhouse had begun the rift in her friendship with Naomi when it had lost a certain intimacy. She had tried a few times to coax her into opening up but each time she had been blanked. She hadn't seen her in a long time now. Sam had suspected the architect was the cause.

Miho reached for another blue bowl to add to the stack. She heard it before she felt it; a dull rattle from the pottery inside the store. The dormant quotidian threat for everyone in the street, and they had all become inured to the rumbling pressure releases of regular earthquake tremors. The store lady calmly beckoned her to come towards her. Inside the shop Miho placed the cradled bowl on the counter and then stood at the back of the store side by side with the woman. It was as if they were on the deck of a ship bucking in the waves, waiting it out in silence as the earth kicked. She held the fragile bowl in her sights, watching the self-animated pottery wobble vigorously. Beside her the woman rubbed her hands nervously. The rice bowl hobbled, staggered towards the edge of the glass shelf and threatened a suicide leap to the floor; the absence of sound was drowned by sound.

After a long minute the uneven pattern of their stilted breathing eased.

The woman spoke first.

'*Keishin?*'

Miho agreed that it was likely a Keishin; it felt like a six on the Richter scale and had been of a relatively short duration.

With their backs to the wall they fell into debate over the correct description for the quake from a list in their earthquake lexicon.

'*So da ne.*' (It is.)

'The great catfish will not be caught.' The woman referred to the euphemism for the sea-based tremor.

'It objects strongly,' Miho agreed.

Before they wrested control of the debris that had shattered across the store, they first began to tidy their experience into words. The jolt was to be categorized, brushing aside the effects of the upheaval as they would reorganize some item of housekeeping.

The motion passed and it seemed it was over. They could hear nothing, but the metronomic inertia that rang in their ears had almost become audible, as the unstable bowl on the counter finally reached the edge of safety and came crashing down to the floor. It was long after they had expected it and in their gentle cries of regret they bonded, falling back on an idiomatic consolation, so focused on the cheap pot, as if the rest of the world would look after itself.

'After the blossom has fallen it doesn't return to the branch,' the woman said.

Behind a curtain she sought out a dustpan and brush, and slowly they collected the shards together, bending to pick up the pieces.

'What is life but picking up the pieces,' the older woman continued.

'After disaster, the laundry,' Miho replied, matching her Zen idiom.

Falling back on ancient sayings somehow united them with the people who had coined them, and they shared an experience across an ocean of time.

Miho was on her knees when she saw Kazuko Mochizuki across the road, her bicycle resting against a telegraph pole. Torn between helping the woman pick up the smaller fragments of glass and checking on her elusive friend, Miho made her excuses and ran across the narrow street now littered with shopkeepers surveying the damage.

Miho had not seen Kazuko at the nursery for a while and she suspected that possibly Naomi was standing between them.

'You okay?' Neither of them had sustained as much as a scratch.

Kazuko's reserve gave in to a tired smile. Miho squeezed her arm in a gesture of unspoken sympathy.

'Can you come over to supper tonight?' Kazuko asked almost urgently.

Miho had a launch party she had to attend but suggested another night that week.

'Come, come after the launch. Any time.'

She was so insistent Miho agreed to see her without promising what time she could get over.

Kazuko set off wheeling her bike to chart the messy sign-blown street. What remained unsaid between them was so much larger, like the space between the objects.

Miho returned to the store to purchase the bowls. She had a job to go to.

Chapter 75

Inafu: *comfort woman*

Later that night, after the launch, Miho arrived at the architect's house in the dark and was relieved to find only Kazuko at home. In the intimacy of a fragile moonlight they shared an unseasonal drink of plum tea, beside the lantern in the cool evening air, as if seeking some warmth from it. The shadow of the neighbour's white cat in the garden crossed the paper shoji screen as Kazuko said, 'You saw your friend at the Minka farmhouse?'

Miho thanked her for letting them stay. 'We collected wood and we bathed.'

Kazuko had done this many times herself with the architect. 'And she is well?'

Miho felt searched for information she did not have.

'I guess she's well.'

'Then I guess it falls to me to tell you.'

Miho cupped her lukewarm bowl of tea, and she knew then that Sam had been right.

'It falls to me to tell you,' Kazuko repeated, and waited for glimpse of recognition. 'Your friend is pregnant?'

This news left Miho with a deafening pulse. 'No. She did not tell me.' Miho had had suspicions about an affair and, in her defense, she had barely acknowledged this to herself. She ran though the times she might have been able to talk to Naomi. Kazuko would feel betrayed; she had introduced Naomi to them both and now she could see Kazuko believed she was the catalyst.

'I was prepared to let it – this dalliance – run,' Kazuko said as she held Miho in her gaze to the point of discomfort. 'You knew they were having an affair?'

'I think . . . I think I did. I think we all guessed this maybe was the case. Perhaps I guessed it was just an affair and you didn't mind.' Miho wondered how it was that Kazuko had come to know.

'How can I not mind, Miho? He is my husband.'

Miho heard her own hollow excuses for not warning Kazuko. 'I didn't know.' It would not be Josh's child, she knew; they would have established that. She released her hold on the cup and Kazuko refilled her tea. Kazuko looked as if she were discussing an item on an agenda, preternaturally calm and unsettlingly determined. Miho guessed she had done all her crying already.

'I really haven't talked to Naomi,' Miho continued thinly.

'Miho,' Kazuko continued with an earnestness that carried a warning for her, 'I would like . . .'

Miho waited for her task.

'I would like you to talk to her.'

So there was an agenda.

'Will you speak to her?'

'Of course I must.' Miho found herself a go-between. It was the least she could do.

'I can, perhaps, live with this situation,' Kazuko continued, 'with this affair. But to save her relationship she must consider this: if I am to give up something so must she.'

What exactly did she mean? Miho needed her to say it.

'I want you—' Kazuko beat out in a rhythm. 'I want you to tell her . . .'

Miho drew back.

Kazuko paused. 'Will she listen to you?'

Miho nodded.

'She must terminate the pregnancy.'

Kazuko sat back on the rush frame of the floor chair; the

moon across the stone lantern casting a long shadow, of sky and earth and water and fire and air: five essential, inert, inanimate, yet to be quickened elements.

'You tell her,' Kazuko said firmly.

Many of Miho's friends had had unwanted pregnancies. They ended by way of a termination and a commemorative stone to Jizo, the god of the unborn. The practice was commonplace. What was Naomi doing, allowing herself to be compromised in this way? She must have some reason for not telling her. Had she intended this? It was unlikely she had told Kazuko, and so how had Kazuko found out?

As if she followed her, Kazuko said, 'He doesn't want the child. He can't bring himself to tell her but she must realize that he feels she has caught him in some ancient game of women.'

Miho studied the thin line of green leaf around her cup. Had Naomi lured the architect?

So Mochizuki himself had talked to Kazuko of the affair, Miho realized.

'It is very easy to solve an unwanted pregnancy,' Kazuko persisted.

Miho saw the unchecked hair fall across her brow; Kazuko was unusually dishevelled. She allowed for the possibility that she could not necessarily trust Kazuko's word. Had Mochizuki said as much to Kazuko, or was she now putting her own words into the package of his reported speech, to give weight to the argument with more than one voice? Kazuko could tolerate an affair, she had said. She must have done so before now. What she could not accept was a child; a child born to another union; a bond for that union which Kazuko was never able to secure. This inability was a private agony she must contemplate alone. It was too unfair and Miho felt sick with sympathy. Despite this she could not bring herself to promise anything before she had found out how Naomi's truth would compare with Kazuko's telling.

'Does she expect to catch him this way?' Kazuko persisted.

Miho had no excuses for her friend. She had no idea how where this would lead. And it was upsetting that Kazuko knew before she did, of Naomi's condition . . . Unable to find words of consolation, she found only apologies but these were soon spent, leaving her with nothing more to say. How could she undertake to be her messenger on this? Or reassure her on the outcome? Naomi must love him to play so dangerously and to risk so much.

The moon had shifted. Kazuko's face was in shade as Miho rose to leave. It was past twelve and as she made her way to the door, her good friend followed her, and all Miho could say to her was, by way of excuse, 'It seems she loves him very much. I am sorry, '

On the porch the full moon washed them both to negatives and in the grey light Kazuko looked more than tired.

'Please,' Kazuko repeated calmly. 'Tell her what we have agreed.'

The next morning at the studios Miho was laying out upturned bowls to form a logo and her mind drifted to Kazuko's drained face from the night before. Miho was unsure how she would proceed. She knew she could not go to Mochizuki directly and ask him if he was behind any of what she had been told. She would first find Naomi and draw her confidence. Naomi had been too afraid to raise the issue and, now, with an even greater secret to elicit, how likely was it that she would open up? Did Josh know and how would he handle it?

The camera shutter ran until Yoshi asked her to move the last prop in the line. Tiring of the long session under the warm lights she lost concentration and knocked a bowl to the floor. The name of the noodle bar now fell short of a character.

'Gomenasai,' she apologized and kneeling to pick up the shards, pieced them together to check for a clean break. The scene of a farmhouse suddenly isolated from the path across the mountains was handpainted in blue across the bowl.

'After disaster, the laundry,' Yoshi said, as he handed her a broom, laughing. Then, in the flick of a mood change, the photographer left, throwing over his shoulder like a tantrum that a replacement was to be found immediately.

Miho remembered at the time she had bought them watching the very last one of the batch fall with the inevitability of gravity in the store during the quake.

Chapter 76

Doppler Effect

Naomi's class of infants was wrapped in woollens, their heads bowed over their open primers. Her heart raced in spite of their small chantings. Mochizuki had sought her board and lodging with the abbot in exchange for teaching the children English. It had all been arranged for her. He had not been to see her in too long. The passing of time had distorted her view of the situation; the recurrent thought that she was on her own, and possibly abandoned, keening and passing like the manifestation of the Doppler Effect as if waves of sound. Her own unvoiced wailing. How far had he gone this time and when he might return to her were unanswerable questions. She began to think she could hear the sea and to wonder what she was doing here at all. She lost control of her breathing and as it competed with her it carried her heartbeat with it and threatened to leave her behind.

'You, Yuki,' she said in haste to the cricket-box boy sitting by the door. 'You are in charge. You are to tell Hakuin. He must come to class as I am unwell.' She ran back to her room and lay down, finding a small joist on the ceiling that offered an anchor point until it began to float as if on a wave, making her feel sickly.

She closed her eyes.

Hope, like the limb of a fallen tree, once regenerating and growing straight and tall, had withered and fallen. Her hands rested on her distended belly, the circumference of the child's world. Now she took alms from the novice monk whose bowl she once had filled. She was a fallen woman and if she brought this scrap into the world where would they find space in the world to live?

He had not come when he had said he would. She hadn't seen him for ten days. The suffocating thought made her gasp for breath. She closed her eyes and drifted into an unsound tidal sleep.

On waking she was wrung out with fatigue. If only she could get a word to him. She would write a letter. Taking up her pen she drank from a cup of cold mugicha tea. It was from the day before and a thin oily sheen patterned the surface, but she would not waste it.

Iwata was due on his weekly visit to the temple at around ten that morning and she spent her time periodically watching for him. It began to snow and with it her spirits dampened. She waited so long that in her disappointment she forced herself to prepare another lesson. She could neither read nor write. She put on the heavy cotton coat and walked into the gardens with the letter in her pocket. The funematsu pine Mochizuki had pointed out to her on their first visit stood laden with white snow so deep it would break but for the supports that had been strapped to the trunk. It hung in the landscape like a great white-masted ship in the mists.

She found Iwata outside the Abbot's offices. He was nursing a cold and clearly did not want to be detained too long. She stood on the icy cobbles balancing precariously as she asked him a favour.

'Iwata-san,' she began, knowing he had never liked her. 'I haven't seen him.' And though she knew he was no ally, she thrust the envelope into his hand. 'Could you deliver this letter to Mochizuki?'

Iwata jumped at her question, but he did at least keep hold of the letter without returning it immediately, which encouraged her.

'Please?' She searched him for confirmation. 'Don't leave it on his desk. If you could put it into his hand?' They both knew how untidy he was.

The letter appeared to weigh heavy in Iwata's hand as he debated the response. He then took it deferentially in traditional style with both hands and a very slight bow.

And though he mocked her, she thanked him and made her precarious way back up to her lodgings.

It was nearing lunchtime and Iwata looked in on Hakuin, who he found in the kitchens.

He slapped him on the back roughly; a greeting he often chose.

'Smells good,' Iwata said, inspecting the dumplings.

'A boy from the English girl's class interrupted my meditations and told me that she had run out of class this morning.' Hakuin felt he should tell of his concern.

'Well, she's all right now. Just saw her out walking.' Iwata dismissed the subject. 'So do I get an invite to lunch?' He rubbed his hands in anticipation.

'Not today, I am afraid.'

'I feed you and you don't host me back brother,' Iwata said exasperatedly. 'I'll hit the 7/11 store then,' he said leaving to deal with his taunting hunger and preparing to expectorate on the step but remembering where he was just in time. 'I visit Guam next month. I'll say hello. Shall I bring you a souvenir?'

Hakuin, who had first fallen into trouble there as a teenager, guessed what sort of souvenir he referred to and hung his head as Iwata left.

In the car Iwata turned the ignition, wrapping up as he waited for the engine to warm before he switched on the arctic blast of the heater. He removed the letter from his pocket and looked at the title. From the little walking futon to his boss. Letters like little black flies crawled across her envelope. This was her handwriting. 'Mochizuki-san', it read in Romanji. He opened the dashboard glove compartment and stuffed the letter in roughly, then on second thoughts he searched the door pockets for the car manual and, with effort, he leant across to bury it beneath pages of redundant print. Having found an object for his anger he turned on the heater and, as it blew noisily, he allowed himself to calm down in its warmth.

Chapter 77

'The events of human life, whether public or private, are so inti-
mately linked to architecture that most observers can reconstruct
nations or individuals in all the truth of their habits from the
remains of their monuments or from their domestic relics.'
–Honoré de Balzac

With the champagne reception over, Kazuko and Mochizuki
had driven home discussing the sumo tournament where
they had been important guests. The man mountain ChiyonoFuji
had paced the chalk circle for his *dohyō-iri*, taken the *chikara-*
mizu and cleansed his body according to ritual. They were so
close to the ring, they could see the drops of water as the
wrestler flicked the vessel free of its contents. If it was to be
believed, courage was invested in the water that the wrestler
drank. Mochizuki knew Kazuko would need it. He would have
to tell her tonight. There was no ideal moment to broach the
subject. The confines of the car were too close. He would wait
to tell her. Reluctance led him several times to the very edge
of opportunity and then drew him back.

It was not until they were undressed, sitting in bed, that he
found the moment. She handed him his water. And he spoke
into the blue-edged handblown glass. It fell from his lips: 'The
girl will not end the pregnancy.' He left the words lying between
them for her to do with them as she would.

Slowly, quietly, she reacted, as he would have expected of
the woman with whom he had spent so many years.

'What?' she said quietly. And then she became for him someone that he did not recognize. '*Inafu*. She is nothing but a comfort woman,' she wailed. 'This is how we live, Mochizuki. I find you the toy to dally with, and you and I inhabit the rest of the world as one, together. When we met you had such unreliable prospects. No one would have taken you on. Your family lay behind you like a sea drogue, dragging you down. No respectable woman would have given you the time of day. Who but me would have taken the risk? I ran the chance of besmirching my own name.' Everything she had never dared voice threatened to wind her.

She got up quickly and put on her short, silk housecoat and tied the sash with the vehemence of an act of violence.

'You didn't just come from the wrong side of the tracks you came from the underclass.' It came in the strength of her rage. Circling him, she paced around the bed, where he sat, vulnerable to her attack.

'You said you didn't believe in any of that,' he queried, quietly shocked as if she had hit him between the shoulder blades, unawares.

'I didn't but it seems everyone else has agreed that you and your forebears will never wash their stained hands of dirty work. The only work they can get. Tending the carcasses of men with a stench that all the waters of soap land couldn't clean. The lingering smell of prostitution, like running sores. You think I don't know how much you rely on that yakuza you call Ukai?' She did not pause for breath. 'Sure, you were bright. You were talented but they weren't merely holding you back, they were going to sink you. I cut you loose and together we have built this existence.' She spat the last word.

He was left blinking in the strength of light that she had shed on her innermost thoughts. He could see that if she had been anyone else but Kazuko from the start she would have fallen in with the ingrained prejudice that would have him tied to a caste as old as Buddhism. They had lived together all these years and she had absolved him of this accident of birth that had once found him one of the dispossessed.

She walked to the en suite.

In the past she had told him she did not care. His mind screamed; he had lived, nourished by this premise, and he had now pushed her to the point when she had reneged upon it.

She emerged, with over-the-counter sleeping pills that she occasionally resorted to, and left their bedroom.

Were they not equal in one another's eyes, despite the fact that her forebears had held elevated positions in government? A cabinet minister had no bearing on who they were as a couple, as individuals, or as man and wife. He had sought to buoy them up. They held their heads high.

The last thought brought him choking for air like a man caught in the tidal wave that will inevitably drown him. This invective threatened to destroy everything they had built, leaving debris in its wake that could not be pieced together and reassembled. He saw the vision of his loss.

This was the same woman who had nursed his night sweats when fevered, the same woman who had reviewed his early submissions of work with good counsel, who had brought the burden of cultivating a network upon herself, on his behalf, when he had lacked the confidence and the connections. And now . . . and now she had written the unspoken secret between them across his eyes and he was blind. And she was blind. She had so washed away his ability to feel, that anything he might say to her would amount to no more than the mutterings of the air in a seashell.

He had broken the vow of which they had never spoken. He could not remind her of why it was that she had taken up with his crippling past. He owed her everything and she had given him all and he had betrayed her. He cast the first blow and could not retaliate. He could not raise another blow in the game of injuries. She had been accepting of him for so long.

The weedy rushes of his past were now pulling at him,

dragging him below, as if he never had been free – as though he had let go of her hand, the very hand that had reached down for him from the lifeboat. It was her face looking to find him, Kazuko's and no one else's; hers was the only hand to pull him up.

He could hear her crying in the other bedroom. He remained with the covers around him like a loincloth, immobilized like a man with hypothermia. Then she came to him, silhouetted against the doorframe.

'If I am to give up something so must she,' Kazuko said coldly, and went back to her sobbing.

Chapter 78

A dusting of snowflakes fell on the waxed fleece-lined hat. With the brim tucked into her collar and her trousers tucked into her boots Mrs Mochizuki was lost in a walking overcoat, beneath a hammer-grey sky. Unbalanced by a heavy bag, she stepped carefully over the dirty ruts that led from her car to the temple across the road. In the flat light the whitewashed walls were sullied beside the snow that lay curled like a great sleeping cat beneath the high walls. Reduced to going cautiously up the steps until she reached the gravel path towards the visitor's kiosk, where her pace quickened with a purpose. Though the wooden shutter was propped open, she found it empty. Nobody was around.

'Hi,' she called. Her breath clouded the glass and then vanished behind her reflection against the temple and the silence of the snow.

'Hi,' she called again with the knuckle of her gloved hand.

She could raise nobody and would have to look for the temple lodgings where she knew the girl was living.

Shifting the bag to the other shoulder, the absent young woman who usually manned the kiosk caught up with her. She was in red hakama robes, though it was a quiet day for visitors to the temple.

With a muffled clap of her hands at having found someone to ask or in a bid for warmth, Mrs Mochizuki asked the way, 'To the . . .' She debated: should she or should she not ask for the directions to the lodgings? Then she settled on, 'Classrooms?'

Regretting that her indecision might seem odd to the girl who studied her as if she found a lone woman odd today.

As if reading her mind, Kazuko said, 'A friend. I come to visit a friend.' The corners of Kazuko's mouth curled reassuringly.

Even so her enquiry elicited a degree of surprise. In the middle of the morning the children would be in their lessons.

Further reassurance was needed and so she placed her hand on the forearm of the girl with the intimacy of friendship. 'What I would really like to do first . . .' she demurred, and then said, 'Could I trouble you . . . I would like to take a look . . . at . . . I would like to buy an omamori.' Kazuko thought to buy a souvenir amulet and at this simple request they turned for the kiosk.

'And which prayer would you like?' the girl asked as she brought up a display board of silken amulets from under the counter.

Kazuko removed her heavy, heavy bag and rested it on the thin lip of the counter.

'Here?'

The girl proposed an amulet that was to safeguard students and their studies. She handed Kazuko a woven pouch of a frog.

'No.' Kazuko passed it back and began turning each amulet on the board as she made her choice.

Kazuko's cheeks, full-bloodied with the cold, prickled on reading the next, Anzan: a prayer for pregnancy and a healthy delivery. And beneath it, in vermillion and gold brocade, the tasselled prayer was labelled, 'Kanai Anzan', for the peace and prosperity of the household.

It could not be both. In this case she supposed it could not be both.

This choice was proving difficult. She regretted the diversion.

'What colour would you like?' the acolyte asked, trying to assist her.

'It doesn't matter.' She always chose the earth prayer. She would have the earth prayer. 'May peace prevail on earth.'

She clutched at the tasselled brocade and thrust it in her pocket. She complimented the girl on her hair ribbon and asked again for directions. The request was less strange when the lady carried a prayer in her pocket and with a wave of an arm she sent her in the right direction across the grounds.

Kazuko had secured enough promises from Mochizuki to believe she had him tethered but curiosity drew her to seek out the girl, and see her condition for herself. Under the umbrella of the funematsu pine she sheltered for a moment beside the snow-crusted fishpond where the cold-blooded carp lay unseen on the bottom. Across the expanse of ice a scantily clad novice came to the edge of the frozen water and rolling up his sleeves he caught up a large steaming bucket. As he poured the contents of scalding water over the frozen pond he momentarily disappeared behind a cloud of steam that enveloped him like a genii from the myth.

Beside him now she asked him engagingly what he was doing. He explained that he made an ice hole so that the fish could breathe. If he did not ensure the pond could breath they would lose the old whiskered carp in this unusually fierce weather, he told her.

She nodded sagely. 'Can you tell me the way to the lodgings?' she asked, cajoling him as if he were smart if he could do so.

Hakuin the monk pointed her in the direction of the bell tower and watched her disappear beneath the pine.

She headed towards the renovated teahouse. Moments after she had passed beneath it a large icing of snow reached critical mass and fell from the branch and met the ground with a dampened thud, covering her tracks.

She would not look at the teahouse. She skirted the eastern end of the lake and arrived to find the living quarters were deserted. In the lee of a mordant wind, she stopped beneath the eaves, drawing up her collar and wrapping her arms around her, a gloved hand resting on her bag. It weighed heavily. It was still there. She patted her load. And then questioned again her intentions with the girl. She should leave now and head home. But hearing distant murmurings across the compound she began to meander between the deserted buildings, scanning for lights. Looking in each window for bearings she found what she was sure was her room. Snow danced as she opened the unlocked door. She could make out a pile of English books in the shadows, on a stool beside the bed. From the bottom of her own bag she retrieved a hardback book and cast it like a skimming stone towards the thin pillow on the bed and then as quickly as she had entered, left.

Her trail of footprints to the living quarters described an elaborate kanji alphabet, arcing and doubling back on itself across the compound where she heard, from the low purpose-built block beneath her, faint children's voices. She sheltered under cover of the eaves and, as she drew closer, could make out they were the younger children at class. Off balance, her glove touched the crisp snow on the window ledge and she steadied herself to peer into the classroom at their young teacher. The class of kids were 5th grade and younger, a mixed group, in an optional language class perhaps. The girl wore a long soft cardigan of blue and paced confidently at the front of her class, her arms wrapped across her front. It was when she turned in the other direction that Kazuko saw her extended belly, flaunting her condition like a personal jibe. Seeing this swollen evidence, she made up her mind to go into the classroom.

But in a moment's hesitation she changed her mind. She too taught children. This audience of infants was too large, too young, and too innocent for what she wanted to say. She must come back and confront the girl. Leaving in a hurry, the cold air on the warmth of her throat had cauterized it. She could not scream. Gasping for air, the now-familiar thought played on her mind: if I am to give up something so must she.

But there was another way.

If the girl would not give up the pregnancy, she determined that she, Kazuko, should keep the child and bring it up.

If I am to give up something so must she, she thought again.

Chapter 79

Naomi's swollen legs began to feel tight; she stopped pacing back and forth across the front of the class, like a caged creature. She had been in danger of wearing a groove across the floorboards.

The classroom was too warm. Out across the snow-covered contours of the hill the bare trunks of the deciduous trees stuck out like the underbelly of a young animal where the flesh was visible beneath scant hair. Inside, the smaller children chanted and repeated the colours of an absent rainbow. But gradually she began to lose control and they began to misbehave. As one lost interest, the others caught the infection, and their attention was lost like melting snow, as each read her own distraction. Her mind wandered. Thoughts of Mochizuki surfaced with the repetitive pattern of her fabric stencil. She had not seen him in two weeks and he had made no attempt to be in touch but she reminded herself that this was natural. His lifestyle. The last refrain from the chanting class trailed off and petered out in an unenthusiastic end. They began to wriggle. Her focus returned when one wandered off to the back of the class. She dropped the paper sun in her hand and she called him. Bending, with the limited agility of an older woman, she retrieved the disc she had coloured. and as she pinned the clock hands like whiskers across its face, she thought she saw someone crossing the compound from the direction of her room.

At eleven she would usually return to her room while the children had their break. For fifteen minutes she could lie on her bed and rest the object, which she assumed was a head lying on her pelvis, and she would ease the weight from her watery, blown ankles. Never had the mindless contemplation of an unremarkable ceiling held such attraction. Without the trapping of her collected fabrics, her ikats and prints, the sparse room had no personality but even so it was a haven. She resorted to number chanting to calm her runaway mind in the hope that she could displace the skulking anxiety that threatened to consume her.

Inside her room she found wet footprints on the floor and then she saw her, sitting in a large overcoat beside a leather bag on the bedside stool. Kazuko threaded the brim of her hat through her fingers as if she were sifting the fabric pensively or was it nervously?.

This gave Naomi to understand her visitor was not a threat.

'You are not surprised to see me?' Kazuko made no attempt to move.

Naomi said nothing. What could she say?

Kazuko broke their silence. 'I have been meaning to come and see you for some time.'

And what could this woman tell her? Did she come to announce that she had her blessing? Naomi stayed by the door rather than venture in further.

Kazuko beckoned Naomi into her own room, indicating with a pat of the coverlet that she should come and sit beside her on the thin single bed.

A role reversal that had begun when Naomi had played at being Mochizuki's wife. Of course Kazuko would make herself at home now, in her room.

She could't take a single step towards her.

'Will you?' Kazuko tried patting the bed again.

'Why have you come?' Naomi could not look, waiting for an answer, but she closed the door.

Chapter 80

'I thought it was time we spoke,' Kazuko explained. Woman to woman, she thought about saying, but cut it short. It was too forgiving too soon, lacking in credibility. This girl no longer belonged to the sorority and would have to make her own way.

'I am not in a position—' Naomi began with a protest.

'The past,' Kazuko began, cutting her off. Kazuko did not need to be reminded of the position she was in, what Naomi would or would not deign to talk about. She could see better than the young girl herself and did not need to be told. Her hardened face relaxed in an act of extreme will.

'The past, memories of the past, are our *kasa*.' She used the Japanese word for umbrella. 'We think that our past unfolds and stands over us like some shelter from the elements.' Her voice now soft and conciliatory, Naomi finally came to sit on the bed, at the very furthest edge beside the door. 'And yet life can blow it inside out.' She paused. 'And we protect our memories for good reason. What would so-and-so do in just such a situation.' She went on.

'But we cannot cast aside the past when it's always attached to us. Who we are is integral to our past. Our past will always catch up with us.'

Naomi heard her out. Her own history before she came to Japan was so severed from the present that it seemed to belong to someone else.

'There are things you do not know about my husband, that you should know.'

Kazuko undid the top buttons of her coat and continued.

'He is, sadly, tainted by his past and his future is not his own. He has limited his options because the choices he makes do not wholly belong to him. He owes people.'

Naomi would have seen the cormorant tattoo on his left shoulder. Would he have said he owed Ukai or that he belonged to a band of brothers? Kazuko believed not.

Naomi looked away.

Kazuko's eyes narrowed. 'I do not mean a debt to me. He owes the yakuza and neither you nor I can shelter him from that and neither you nor I could ever get close. It is not as simple as you imagine; it goes way back. More than one generation. We are an old society and we have different values of loyalty. Once he became known, and his past was a hindrance, these men gave him an opportunity to lose it. He chose to live under their, shall we say, guidance.'

She is quiet enough now, Kazuko noted. It was going her way. She would win her confidence. Her trust.

'He can do nothing without their agreement. You are young. You know nothing of the way life really works here. You don't expect to live here? No one would support that. Your best option is to go home and start again. You should go home. Nobody knows what has happened to you here. You must leave and begin again without being saddled with a child. Start afresh, not as a single mother with a half-caste child. You will not have a life here.' Her voice softened. 'Leave now for England.' She paused. 'And you may leave the child with us.'

Naomi appeared dumbstruck by her suggestion. But must hear her out.

'Leave because he will leave you now, sooner or later.'

The older woman worked on her insecurities. He had been away. She had not seen him recently. It seemed ten days absence still could not detract from the fact that she trusted every word he had said to her. She looked defiant but still she pressed her

'You do not have to go through with this pregnancy. Give up the child.'

Chapter 81

She had heard enough. 'You must leave now, Kazuko.' And it was easier to get rid of her than she thought.

She rose without a word of objection. She must have said everything that she had come to say. They both knew of his past, though Kazuko obviously believed she was bringing her news. There was nothing she could tell her that she did not know already.

'I must not forget.' Kazuko lifted her heavy bag from the floor. 'I have come to give you something. '

They faced one another.

'I have a gift,' the older woman said. She stretched across the slim pillow to retrieve the faded, red, bound book. 'Here. This is for you. A gift.'

The Japanese always wrap gifts, Naomi thought.

The book was worn at the corners and a cascade of kanji fell across the top left cover. She did not know what it read.

'Open the cover,' Kazuko urged her, and it was as if she did not have the will to refuse.

'On the frontispiece is a handwritten dedication in Japanese,' she continued.

'These are haiku poems,' Kazuko told her. 'It is a book of haiku poems.'

Both women knew his love of haiku. Naomi was thrown back to the very first summer lunch with Mochizuki at the viewing platform, to his talk of Bashō.

Kazuko indicated the frontispiece of dark-blue washi paper.

'The inscription is from him. Shall I translate? Kite wheeling in the lifting sky—'

But Naomi shut the book quickly and flung it aside, stung that he had shared this very poem.

Kazuko retrieved and brandished the book.

'Let's open it. See the pages marked.'

She ran her hand along the head of the book and it fell open at the well-marked page.

'Here are two poems: butterfly and moon viewing.' Her voice was harsh; she intended to be cruel. 'See the next page. He marked his favourite poems for me,' Kazuko taunted.

Naomi lifted her hand in protest as if scorched. Kazuko let the haiku poetry book slip to the floor.

'We are not so very different, you and I. This man, my husband; we both admire him, and perhaps we both love him. He gave this to me when we first decided to live together. He wooed me with his love of poetry. You too?'

And with that salvo she left Naomi to contemplate his sincerity, his poetry and the truths he told.

Chapter 82

Drink had no part in her decision to stay and she was grateful for this. In his company Hana felt entirely relaxed now. She nursed a mug of coffee and she and Ed talked long into the night. They laughed about Peach Blossom Nikki. He was sympathetic to her Kafkaesque search for information on her father, buried somewhere deep in a bureaucratic language she didn't speak. He promised her answers and guaranteed that with the help of the Japanese lawyers in his office they would find out.

It was late and as he gathered cushions they argued politely over who would take the sofa. He was sort of quaint and she liked it.

He touched the bedside light panel and showed her his room. There was an irresistibly huge soft bed. He had personalized the space with worn trainers, and in the corner was a pile of dirty sportswear. She paused on the threshold of this inner sanctum.

'You might lose me in here,' she said, beginning to walk around the spacious room but tripping over an open grip bag at the end of the bed. 'Weekend case?'

He seemed keen to show what was inside as if she might mistake it as belonging to someone else.

He unpacked it. 'Water. Couple of tins of tuna.' She was amused to see him checking the sell-by date.

'Planning a camping trip? Or is it nightly cravings for tinned food?'

He held back from an answer playfully.

Warming to the game he drew out a helmet and sitting beside her on the bed put it on her head for size.

'Potholing passion?' She gave him a cheeky grin. 'A fetish?' and then lay back laughing till the plastic helmet fell off and rolled on the floor.

He picked it up and moved over to her gently. 'No regulation earthquake kit?

She shook her head.

'I guess travellers don't.' He fumbled in the bag. 'No problem,' he said. 'I have two.' And he brandished another hat.

She took it from him and placed it on her head, laughing at her own reflection in the darkened window before throwing it aside and falling back on the bed.

It was an awkward moment, then he broke it

'Bathroom.'

Pristine light across the marble floor revealed a navy towel, limp with overuse. It smelt of him and she wondered how this could already be familiar. It was the only towel. And then saw the lipstick on the marble sink top. Did a woman share his bathroom? It might have been left that night? She abandoned further thought.

The bedroom lights were low and he was dozing, fully clothed on top of the duvet. She flipped the light and stripped to her underwear, getting under the covers to lie beside him. Through his gentle breathing he stirred and his hand came to rest lightly on her arm.

'Stay,' he mumbled, barely awake. With a small thrill she realized she would like nothing better.

In the morning he was up first and ready for work. He kissed her goodbye.

'I'll see you tonight?' He was quite confident about it. 'Stay here today.' And he left her in the expanse of his apartment to sleep.

She turned over. It was as if all the time she had been in

Japan she had been waiting to reach this place of sanctuary. She drifted off – there could be no nicer place to be.

It was late morning; still no light penetrated the wall of the blackout curtains as she finally opened her eyes to the unfamiliar shapes across his room. Coming round hazily she identified the doorbell. She clung to the white duvet in modesty as if dragging an enormous kimono with her she shuffled sleepily to the door of the apartment and expected to see, perhaps, the daily cleaning lady? After a beat she recognized the piano teacher.

'Hello.'

'I let myself in. I have come to get my suit,' she said, walking past Hana, as if quite at home,

Hana trailed after her, duvet in tow until they reached the bedroom cupboards.

Pointing to the large walk-in wardrobe behind the headboard, the arrival said, 'Can I?'

'Yes, sure.'

The girl picked up the curtain remote and dawn broke as they opened.

Officiously she tossed the remote on the bed and headed for the walk-in wardrobe. She obviously had a lot to do and time was short. She emerged regally from the walk-in, holding a suit and a pair of shoes.

'I'm gonna get my lipstick.'

From the bathroom Hana heard the shriek of a woman possessed. Clearly all composure lost. A word emerged.

'Paizuri!' It was blood curdling.

This was the mild-mannered mouse she met last night? Hana had no idea what it meant. But it took her no time to calculate that she was very pissed off.

When the Japanese girl returned to the bedroom they stood at a face-off. Hana wanted no part in a confrontation she didn't understand and over someone she barely knew. She sounded ready to tear her hair out. Nothing. The piano teacher said nothing. But her look said it all. Slowly smoothing the suit over her arm she turned on her heel and brushed passed. In a slow, dignified manner, she made for the lift. A large silence followed her out of the room. Thank God. Hana could breath again with the closure of the lift doors. She hung about but they didn't reopen.

Alone on the king-sized bed she observed would easily have accommodated all three of them. Extremely dramatic though it was, it was nothing to snigger about and she must be in a mild state of shock. She rested her head against the headboard, as she would have done after a nasty fall.

Getting up she stumbled over the large bag at the end of the bed where the sunlight fell on the protective foil cape and the yellow helmet. She looked out the window at the refuse men down below, emptying the bins. Last night's promise now left her exposed and it was as if she had woken from a dream.

Chapter 83

Nuclear meltdown, Level 7, release of radioactive material

1989

Josh had hosted a delegation from China and the contract was ground-breaking; the animosity between the two countries was such, they rarely sought one another out as business partners. The Japanese economy had so far outstripped that of China that it was a delicate source of discontent and a great incentive for change. He had thrown himself into work of late and picked up on any lead, no matter how slim.

Miho had agreed to meet him at five when he would take a break from hosting the clients he had been seeing that day, before collecting them from their hotel and taking them to dinner. He consoled himself; this group were no worse than the garlic kimchee-riddled visitors from Seoul the previous week. He was usually the first in the firm to offer his services to corporate visitors; since Naomi had left him, he volunteered whenever he could.

Miho didn't often visit this plaza in the business district. Swept with huge tides of lunchtime traffic it was dead in the intervening hours between flashpoints. It was easy to find Josh in the atrium and she pretty quickly made out the crumpled man, chin in hands. He was sitting under a pot-bound tree, with his back to her when she approached. When he greeted her, his kiss was so light it was as if he had never left his chair. He looked exhausted. A bit of an apparition of his former self.

'She has left,' he told her redundantly.

'I know.'

'And is she happy?'

Miho was reluctant to admit to him she had not seen her for a while. She had nothing but old news.

He came quickly to the point. 'What I want you to do—' Miho tensed – it wasn't going to be easy '—is to go and tell her I will have her back.' He said it quickly as if it choked him to say so. His feelings embedded a long way inside him.

She found it valiant coming from Josh, whose brilliant mind left him a bit arrogant. It was unexpected. She had seen little advantage in trying to bring them back together but this gesture from him was large.

Finally she owned up, cutting clean. 'I can't do that, Josh, and in any case I haven't seen her for a fortnight.'

The light music from the plaza atrium cushioned his silence. She could only imagine what was going on inside him. After an interlude during which a virtual destruction might have occurred as his defenses blew; but then again he might have been low enough not to expect a thing. He said, 'Where is she?'

'The temple at Shimo.' Miho slid her arm round his shoulder. She registered his resistance. It might be that he was clinging on against an urge to get up and run, his deracination now complete. She held him until she felt him brace against the strength of his emotion. It took a while. Josh came back. He managed to wipe away his own concerns and he turned to her. It was less painful for him to debate her loss. Sam's departure. He missed him too.

'Sam'll miss you,' he said. 'Can you get out to him soon?'

'He'll let me know when's best. Maybe in the spring I'll go join him.'

It would be no comfort to him if they survived, Miho thought without pleasure. This outcome had not been in his game plan.

'We were all so . . .' he said, searching for the just description but gave in, unable to come close. 'So . . . together.'

'We were, Josh,' she said, stroking him on the back in consolation. An act of friendship without empty words that might revisit the scene of their mistakes. She couldn't give him comfort or protect him from the fallout but she could give him Naomi's address.

The temple where she was teaching was not far, but for days he could not bring himself to go. Josh neither knew what he would do when he got there nor what he would say. Finally this inconclusiveness held him to account and he needed confirmation. Bright snow and sharp air fought the rheumy sunlight, the temple grounds where she lived were vacant and chill. What was it now, about three or four months? She would show very pregnant and she would wear it like an insult. A yakuza child. He had prepared himself for that.

He came to the lodgings to find her in. She opened the door of the thatched outbuilding, lying somewhere way behind the twenty-first century towards the thirteenth, her heavy, wadded jacket was in keeping and beneath it her condition remained hidden so that when he first set eyes on her he couldn't tell. She looked like a woman from the fields.

'You look very tribal. Where's the yak?' he said in the most awkward moment of his life.

She didn't get it for a moment and then, hanging on the doorframe, she laughed and in the light her breath filled the air.

She smiled without embarrassment, confident and self-justified in a way he hadn't expected in front of him.

'Are you coming back?' he asked immediately. 'You don't belong here. You never will,' he threw out.

She smiled a wan smile that was maybe close to exhaustion.

Whether this was because of the life she had chosen or the very thought of explaining it to him was as closed as the affair had been to him.

Her response was immediate. 'No, Josh, no, I'm not.'

'What? You are crazy,' he shouted. He'd lost it when he had promised himself he would not. And irritated by the situation as much as this outburst of his he turned and marched furiously down the hill. He had raised his voice – as people would not often do round here. He had displaced a monk from the teahouse who he saw running in her direction as he left. He hoped he might be going to comfort her.

Chapter 84

Kazuko was often drawn to visit the temple where she watched the girl unobserved. Today, with widening eyes, she saw Naomi hurry barefoot from the classroom across the open courtyard to her room. Midway across, ankle deep in snow, she kicked it playfully, into the air. It was taunting exuberance. Without shoes, months pregnant and running in the snow. How careless could she be? The door slammed hard against the frame in defiance of the muffled blanket of sound that had fallen over the whole temple. Kazuko considered the lunacy of the scene and was, moments later, rewarded by the sight of Naomi re-emerging in a large coat, a hat and short snow boots. The girl bent awkwardly to collect a handful of snow and compacted it between her hands before she lifted her head to contemplate the bright steel sky.

Kazuko shrank back from being seen. Naomi gently nudged the ball of snow across the ground, stooping to coax it ahead of her. Her belly must be cumbersome Kazuko thought. Round and round Naomi circled until the ball she rolled was the size of one the larger meditational stones in the gravel garden. She began the process again.

Kazuko turned up the collar of her coat and shoved her hands, frozen at the thought of handling all that snow, down into her pockets, searching for a warmth that was unlikely to emanate from anywhere inside her. The girl eventually made a small snowman and was clearly delighted as she clapped her hands and took congratulatory steps back to look at it. In thanks the snowflakes grew larger and began to fall thick over the whole compound.

The funematsu pine began to lose its shape, like an aging woman, beneath uninterrupted snow. Delineation between the pond ice and the path grew faint. At the heavier snowfall Naomi gave in graciously and turned to go back inside. Kazuko, her curiosity, sated for this visit, turned for her car. She passed the small field of votives to Jizo. Many, many times before, she had come to pray to the god of unborn children for a deliverance from her barren hopes. Many times, according to custom, she had stooped to tie a small red bib around the dead weight of the cold stones, as a gift to Jizo. The army of ranked stones were becoming buried under indiscriminate white drifts. Piteous immutable and as hopeless her prayers. In places small pieces of crisp red were still visible, and the carpet of snow was spotted with gashes of frozen fabric. Jizo, the patron of travellers too. An unwelcome thought. Impulsively she tugged and ripped a bib from one of the taller stone cairns. As she left she took the long route back towards her car.

The following morning Naomi emerged to see that someone had tied a red bib around the small snowman she had made. They must have come before the last snowfall, because there were no tracks. The god of the underworld and guardian of small souls. Who had done this? If they had intended to unnerve her, they had succeeded.

Sunlight shot the frozen ground on Hakuin's way to the large meeting room; he shivered in his thin robes but wore a woollen hat, covering the head he would shortly bare for the weekly razor. He passed the English girl's rooms. He noted that the snowman he had seen her build now wore a garish red bib and he took sudden offence at the sight. Who had done this, he wondered, looking for tracks. He pulled at the sodden cloth, hoping he might remove it before it offended the girl. He stopped short of pushing over the amorphous mound but would return the bib to the Jizo stone piles and tie it to the largest sutra where he knew it belonged.

Chapter 85

At his home office, under the collected paper hauntings of invoices, half-approved plans and various scribbling's of seminal ideas, Mochizuki found the matches on his desk. He spotted a new Dharuma doll had been added to the clutter. Another of her meddlings, he supposed. Kazuko had encircled one eye on the papier-mâché doll and the other remained blank in the tradition where a wish is made to the god Dharuma and once it is fulfilled the face is completed. He would challenge her about this. He called to her.

'What are you doing here? You're not superstitious? When did we ever bother with this mumbo jumbo?'

Kazuko, having waited upon him at supper, was just finishing the washing-up.

Seeing that he was nearing the end of his first cigarette and about to light a second from the first, she stopped him. Waving a tea towel at him, she signalled that he should join her in drying the crockery from supper.

They stood side by side facing the fading light in the garden.

'So what are you doing with the doll?'

'I wish to have the child,' she said.

He found her simplicity chilling.

'The girl is not fit,' she continued, 'and I believe we must look after it. She should leave. She should go home to England and I should take on the child when she goes home.' Her voice was hardened with determination and he was, at first, stunned to silence.

He had made promises to Kazuko and now she had tied his

hands behind his back she was testing the limits in her powerful hold over him.

'But we . . .' He replaced the hard white crockery on the draining board. 'That is completely ridiculous,' he objected. A seeping horror that Kazuko, in holding a position of strength, had begun to believe she could abuse it, crept over him and with it a doubt in his own agency over those events. So often she had readily taken control. Everything they had built they had built together.

He found his shoes suddenly covered in water as the linen cloth in his hand had, as he relaxed hold, dropped a corner into the sink. And he was soaked by his own negligence.

'Argh,' he complained, and Kazuko took the wet towel from him and began mopping the trail of water. Immovably and quietly, he said, 'No, this will never be the case. Do you understand me?'

Kazuko continued mopping and she did not answer him.

Chapter 86

Ishinomaki, Miyagi, Summer 2011

Years had passed. Kazuko sat alone in front of a TV special report. A procession of men got off the bus, it was the same sort of vehicle that the school had hired last time they took the children from the Yochen on an outing to the Minkaen Park in Kawasaki to see the old farmhouses. The line of TEPCO employees, immortalized in seconds of National Television coverage, walked down the steps as if alighting for a countryside trip. The men in protection suits each carried a box, sized somewhere between a toolbox and a lunch pack.

The NHK commentator explained the latest TEPCO employees on the clean-up following the Tohoku nuclear plant disaster wore gas masks with 0.0001 per cent fallibility. They were there to stem the flow of toxic waste as it leeched into the Pacific. Kazuko shivered.

The report continued; where she wondered, where were the international friends when you needed them most? And who was it that would volunteer for this role? These men would be *Etahin*. She knew this. She began to flip channels on the remote, pressed mute and held it between her hands like a prayer. A distance had crept surreptitiously between her and her old campaigning zeal. At one of her conferences, it was in Canada, she had become close, maybe too friendly, with one of the other delegates. They'd had coffee during the recesses and he had slapped her on the back and called her 'comrade' and they had decided they were fighting guerrilla warfare. She still had the Che Guevara T-shirt he had given her. Of course she'd never worn it. So many missed opportunities: She didn't get to know him. She didn't get to Kyoto. She didn't get to Copenhagen and the list rang in her ears. She had given up so much. The ticker tape of world events ran on and because of the small dramas of her own life she had left the big issues unattended.

When Mochizuki had first come on to her, she was attracted to his broad sensibilities. She had to admit her personal life had interrupted any bigger achievements she'd once hoped for, easily caught up with more immediate issues. She had sidelined the bigger stuff and left the world to its own devices to focus on *mainichi no toso*, the daily struggle. She had held on to Mochizuki after the affair with the girl all those years ago and this had been for her an important victory. She took out her glasses and went back to her sudoku. It was like the siren from a passing ambulance; The noise distorted as it went and depending on where you stood, it became less shrill. Perspectives changed as events moved on.

Four days later, over their fish supper, Mochizuki had told her he would be volunteering to offer his architectural skills in the reconstruction operation in Fukushima. Years ago she had spent time struggling to keep a hold of her man with the cormorant tattoo and this time she had lost the fight for him. He was unleashed and she understood his need to go, no matter how unwelcome she found it. He was an outsider, *Etahin*; he had to go with his people.

Chapter 87

:)

After 11.03.11 comes 2012

Ed headed back to his flat expecting to find the arts and crafty girl waiting for him. He imagined her dark hair across his sofas, lying in wait for him, reading, perhaps. He was looking forward to sharing a meal. On arrival the flat was empty and the girl was gone. It was very tidy and felt unlived in again. The empties were in a bag at the door.

He guessed she hadn't taken him seriously. Why wouldn't he mean it. He should have skipped work for the day? He should but he knew it was unthinkable in his job. If he thought he knew who she was, how come he had no idea of where she might be now. What was she doing and was she with someone else? He would leave a message once he had checked with the doorman for his keys.

His keys had been returned to the desk, so he guessed she wasn't planning to come back. He ignored any reservations and decided to take the JR Yamanote line out from Shibuya go on to Shimo's Club. It was too early for a doorman and a few minutes were enough to establish that the girls weren't there. At the bar a woman in jeans wearing a traditional wig stopped him. She was such a walking carousel of dangling ornaments, he was tempted to look for price tags. Perhaps it was because he had an English accent – he didn't know- but she told him Hana no longer worked there but that he could try an address.

She scribbled the number and *chome* on a receipt and handed it to him saying it was minutes away

At the junction of the road and the track that led to Hana's lodgings he overshot, missing it completely. Unable to find the address, he double backed on himself and decided to try the track. By now, approaching nine in the evening, he guessed she could have left and be might be out for the night. A wasted journey. He looked a little desperate – even to himself – now the effort wasn't likely to amount to anything. He passed the cracked pots on the wall beneath a gate light and after some time he resolved to knock. Even before his hand left the door someone opened it and an older woman stared at him quizzically, a middle-aged man was behind her,.

Armed with Japanese picked up on the company language course he tried to explain to the woman that he was looking for Hana, a girl from England. And while he felt moderately confident that she would understand he couldn't fully get what was being said in response. If she wasn't there, where was she? He turned away, remembering in time to thank them. He was halfway down the path when it occurred to him that she might be in a serious relationship with someone else. They hadn't exactly covered that. Maybe she was spending the night somewhere else in Tokyo. But after the plane – talking last night, on balance, he guessed he knew. He went back to the door.

'Tomorrow,' he said. 'I will come tomorrow.'

Hana was alone in the room and from the window saw him by the gate lamp. As he opened the gate to leave she could see it was Ed. She hesitated. He shouldn't have asked her to stay. What was he doing? Had she left something at his flat? Like the last girl? She remembered with embarrassment. And how had he found the address? She opened the window and taking a full lung of night air was about to shout. Her voice might have reached across the city, but she let it go, deciding not to call after him, instead sinking onto the end of her bed. All she wanted was company. If only it was as easy as instant coffee; taking a spoonful, adding water, stirring. She was homesick and it was time to leave. Her ticket was open-ended and she would head home. She had, at least, found the teahouse and it had brought back memories of her mother. In the morning she would go and say goodbye to Miho.

Chapter 88

The following day Ed's newspaper carried editorial on the opening ceremony for the World Trade Centre, a sustainable design by Fumihiko Maki, the Pritzker Prize-winner. Limited carbon footprint, the usual copy with sustainability tick boxes . . .

Yoshi kicked Ed as he passed. 'Not working today, Ed? What can we bring you? I'll maybe read it after you? Couple of things to do. For clients it might possibly be in our interests to keep happy?'

Ed threw aside the newspaper. 'Okay, okay. What can I do for you? he said, warming to his company.

'In actual fact,' Yoshi said. 'I was doing something for you. The Municiple Registration question.'

Hana's Registration. Ed needn't bother now but wouldn't let on Yoshi had wasted his time.

'What have you got?'

Yoshi sat down. 'Well, it depends on what sort of parentage your friend has. Did he say?'

Ed thought about telling him but decided that, just now, as the source of the enquiry had disappeared from his life, he really didn't need to divulge who it was.

'No, he didn't. In what way do you mean?'

'So you are interested in registration of births right? So firstly the Koseki registration will cover births, deaths, and everything in between. Japanese lineage. It'll all be documented. I don't foresee much trouble finding out. Adoption, divorce. Life's intricacies. Legal paternity has to be listed here in the koseki. It should cover illegitimate children, unmarried mothers and *Etabin*. Well, I should say *Dowa*. Anyway, I'll look into this for you.

Ed had had his ear bent by Roddy on this topic not too many nights ago.

'They will have to sign our terms of engagement, of course.'

'Come on, Yoshi. Will that be necessary? Can we call in a favour?' Why he bothered to pursue the issue when the girl was as good as gone, he couldn't be sure. 'The point is, Yoshi, can we get to see a copy of the certificate with the parents names?'

'No, company guidelines – not unless they're a registered client.'

'I see. Right.'

This seemed to be Yoshi's last word on the subject and Ed was inclined to assume the cause was no longer his responsibility.

'Okay,' he gave up, threw down his paper gearing up to start the day .

At the end of the evening Ed walked the short distance from the Hiroo subway home. Hana was waiting for him on the verge outside the apartment block in the last of the sunshine. He didn't know how long she had been there but she was sitting down beside her cloth bag, reading a book.

'I left a basket,' Hana said.

Wasuremono, he thought. That is what she was to him. Lost property.

In a momentary stand-off, he finally gave in to a natural reaction.

'Well, come on up.'

He turned excitedly to punch the key code into the lobby entry system. How many times had he keyed in the number and now the process failed.

'You left the key?' he asked her

Hana smiled. 'No, I have a key and can let you in to your own apartment.'

But the porter had told him? He suddenly got it. The piano teacher had returned a key. He was off the hook. The right girl had kept his key.

'Did get you get to Tsukiji fish market.?'

She shook her head.

'How about tomorrow?' He called the lift.

'Why not?' she said brightly

Under the lights of the elevator he kissed her.

She took to the runway sofa as he poured her a drink.

'You find out any more about your father?'

Hana laughed as if the question was ludicrous.

'At the office . . .'

Ed wondered whether he should pass on that Yoshi told him her father might be from the Dowa, the Etahin. Perhaps he might not.

She had his full attention.

'It isn't easy,' he began as she interrupted him.

'I'm done with looking back.'

Chapter 89

'The first gesture of an architect is to draw a perimeter, in other words, to separate the microclimate from the macro space outside. This in itself is a sacred act. Architecture in itself conveys this idea of limiting space. It's a limit between the finite and the infinite. From this point of view all architecture is sacred.'
–Mario Botta

Kazuko had not been up to the temple grounds for many years. It was a long time since she had visited in that heavy winter when she had gone to spy on the girl carrying Mockhizuki's child. Today she walked purposefully around the familiar waters of the ornamental lake. She drew her light coat around her, fists in patch pockets. Stopping at the little field of Jizo, tied with red rag bibs, she surveyed the rows of small stone figures piled into cairns by many women. Quickly she bent down and began to fill her wide pockets with the smooth round stones from the larger statues. Her summer coat had ample room and the stone collection hit her knees as she took laboured paces towards the water. She stood for a moment on the side of the lake and then stepped closer towards the damp and reedy edge. She had not said goodbye but she knew anyway she would not see Mochizuki again. Calmly, as if she were about to take an analgesic to rid her of her insomnia, she stepped into the water and began to wade across the reeds to the depths the centre with the teahouse in her sights.

Chapter 90

From the window of the train, a temple torii stood on the hill. The kanji for heaven. He remembered the torii at Shakira's temple where he and the girl had played out their affair at the teahouse. Mochizuki had loved the girl and he was in no doubt about that. She often lay on his mind like a drowsy hangover from their wild enjoyment of one another, and it was twenty years or more since he had seen her.

He became old the morning he left her. Even now silent tears crossed the bridge of his nose. Naomi had waited patiently for him to explain why it was that every promise he had ever made to her was to be broken. Why it was that though he had agreed with her that they should keep the child, he urged her to leave for England. When he handed her money for the ticket she had not cried. Had she overlooked the rotten heap of more than shattered vows he had made to her? Over the years since she had left Japan the temptation to make contact her, which, at first he had to resist, had faded completely.

Travelling north-east, the morning sun was at his back and the carriage was warm and without distraction. The JR train line ran through agricultural land and across orchards. The bright arms of cherry trees waved at him. Hanafubuki, he had renamed her. The moment in spring when the wind catches the blossom and a snowstorm of petals falls, driving it to the ground in drifts.

Reaching the flood plain, the flotsam that was once a whaling town lay in stubborn desecration. Kazuko had remarked sardonically that the great tsunami had at least finally interrupted the

375

whaling. It had carried the boats inland to rest on a sea of broken shards of debris. The giant carcass of a huge ocean-going cargo vessel remained several kilometres inland beyond the highway, but without carrion for the scrap metal it lay at anchor with its navigational and fish-factory lights still laced across the upper deck like a festival. The conning tower could have housed the population of an outlying village but they had all been swept away on the riptide and, besides, as the port was now prone to flooding, efforts had been made to offer accommodation on the higher ground in container units. He would work on this.

Ukai's passing had released him. He had never been able to break loose since he'd given him his first commission and coaxed him into a line of schemes that were never wholly legitimate. An outsider from the same village, he'd threatened to destroy the reputation he had fought so hard to win. What did he expect of the yakuza? He could not say that he had fared entirely badly from the association. Kazuko, during all those years of complaints, understood how strongly he had shaped their lives. He had not attended his memorial and he now had no need to stay. He had remained deaf to Kazuko's pleas,

The train rocked on a signal change. As he travelled closer to the eye of the disaster, he felt the better for it. He was doing the right thing for the first time in a long time. It was common knowledge that the resilience of those housed in the temporary village was ebbing, and though he carried no evangelical hopes, he wanted to add his efforts to the process of rebuilding.

The long, slow, reconstruction process of Ishinomaki Genki Fukko (happy recovery) following Tōhoku 2011 would take decades. From the carriage window a fisherman cast his line over the sea wall and over his head a cormorant flew in a graceful free dive towards the Pacific Ocean.

Author's Note

Etahin or Dowa People

The *Etahin* are part of an old caste system that has survived in Japan until the twenty-first century. For generations they have been the subjects of sectarian discrimination and carried separate identity cards, and it is only in the last decade that they have had the right not to disclose their racial origins when applying for a job. In feudal times they were regarded as outcasts and deemed impure – finding work as tanners, butchers and undertakers. Today they remain ghettoized. Seventy per cent of the main criminal yakuza gangs are made up of these dispossessed people. They populate the subculture of Japan, working in the gambling and sex industries. In the nineteenth century one of the Etahin, 'village people', rose to become a regional politician. They originate from the regions of Kobe and Osaka.